Jane Austen in the Context of Abolition

Also by Gabrielle D.V. White

REGIONAL ACCESS TO LIBRARIES AND INFORMATION SOURCES: Report
(co-author, under former name G.D.V. Garthwaite, with A.M. James)

Jane Austen in the Context of Abolition

'a fling at the slave trade'

Gabrielle D.V. White

First published 2006 by
PALGRAVE MACMILLAN
Houndmills, Basingstoke, Hampshire RG21 6XS and
175 Fifth Avenue, New York, N.Y. 10010
Companies and representatives throughout the world

PALGRAVE MACMILLAN is the global academic imprint of the Palgrave Macmillan division of St. Martin's Press, LLC and of Palgrave Macmillan Ltd. Macmillan® is a registered trademark in the United States, United Kingdom and other countries. Palgrave is a registered trademark in the European Union and other countries.

ISBN 13: 978–1–4039–9121–8
ISBN 10: 1–4039–9121–9

This book is printed on paper suitable for recycling and made from fully managed and sustained forest sources.

A catalogue record for this book is available from the British Library.

Library of Congress Cataloging-in-Publication Data

White, Gabrielle D. V.
    Jane Austen in the context of abolition : "a fling at the slave trade" / Gabrielle D. V. White.
        p. cm.
    Includes bibliographical references and index.
    ISBN 1–4039–9121–9
        1. Austen, Jane, 1775–1817–Political and social views. 2. Literature and society–Great Britain–History–19th century. 3. Antislavery movements–Great Britain–History–19th century. 4. Political fiction, English–History and criticism. 5. Slave trade in literature. 6. Slavery in literature. I. Title.
    PR4038.P6W47 2005
    823′.7–dc22

2005047460

10   9   8   7   6   5   4   3   2   1
15   14   13   12   11   10   09   08   07   06

Printed and bound in Great Britain by
Antony Rowe Ltd, Chippenham and Eastbourne

In memory
of my mother-in-law
Sue White
1909–2004

'You quite shock me; if you mean
a fling at the slave-trade,
I assure you Mr Suckling was always
rather a friend to the abolition.'

Emma (Chapter 35)

Contents

Acknowledgements

I should like to take this opportunity to acknowledge a long-standing debt to friends, colleagues and former students, but above all to my own teachers and mentors especially Alan Montefiore, Michael Tanner, Ian Hacking, David Holdcroft and my husband Roger White. I am also glad of the encouragement of my step-daughter Tabitha.

For their encouragement, advice and comments on early drafts of Chapters 2, 3 and 4, I am grateful to Charmian Knight and Luke Spencer at the University of Leeds. On Chapter 5, Raymond Hargreaves discussed Kant's German with me, Mark Day discussed Hume as a historian and I am also grateful to Richard Francks, Ulrike Heuer, Chris Kenny, Matthew Kieran, Mark Nelson, Andrew McGonigal, Peter Millican, Seiriol Morgan and Adrian Wilson in the Leeds School of Philosophy.

I am particularly grateful to editors and the anonymous reader at Palgrave Macmillan for suggestions and encouragement, and also to Derval Small and to Alan Garthwaite.

I thank staff of the University of Leeds Library and Special Collections, the Information Systems Services, staff of the Yorkshire Archaeological Society, of the Museum and the Public Library at Lyme Regis, of the York Minster Library, and of the British Library.

Above all, I am glad of the help, comment and encouragement of my husband, Roger White.

GABRIELLE D.V. WHITE

Preface

I argue that amongst its other riches Jane Austen's later fiction not only presupposes the British outlawing of its transatlantic slave trade, but also undermines the status quo of chattel slavery, the most extreme form of slavery. Her last three novels were written in the first decade of the interim period after the 1807 Abolition of the Slave Trade. It would be over 16 years after her premature death in July 1817 that chattel slavery was abolished for British colonies in the 1830s.

In *Emma*, Mrs Elton's talk of 'a fling at the slave trade' is integrated into the novel as a whole. My focus is on that novel and my chapter on *Emma* is at the heart of this book. There is a twist described by the crime novelist P. D. James as the detective story element of this novel. The author gives the reader all the clues, but the reader misinterprets, just as Emma herself misinterprets.[1] Since we are not in Jane Austen's position or that of her contemporary audience, of being faced with an abolished slave trade and yet unfinished business over those remaining in slavery, the dynamics of the twist may be lost on ourselves. The twist alters the perceived circumstances in which Jane Fairfax speaks out against governess trade and the slave trade.

My keynote is William Cowper's question: 'We have no slaves at home – Then why abroad?' Since my emphasis is on the three later novels, my chosen background material has been left until the second section. Slavery, as is well-known, had been experienced world-wide in different cultures since time immemorial, but concern would have been natural for her, living when she did during the mobilization of massive popular support for the abolitionist campaign.[2]

There is subtlety in Jane Austen's allusions to people and thought-provoking references to writers, places and topics associated with the great abolitionist campaign of her time. To stimulate thought in this way, I believe, undermined the status quo of slavery.

GABRIELLE D.V. WHITE

ix

1
'We Have No Slaves at Home – Then Why Abroad?'

The state of slavery ... is so odious ... Whatever inconvenience, therefore, may follow from the decision, I cannot say this case is allowed or approved by the law of England; and therefore, the black must be discharged.

Lord Chief Justice Mansfield, 1772[1]

We have no Slaves at home – then why abroad?

William Cowper, *The Task*, 1785

Introduction

Jane Austen, born in 1775, grew up during the time of increasing popular support for the abolitionists. She died in 1817. The British slave trade was abolished in 1807, and British emancipation of slaves within the Empire was achieved in the 1830s. Historical controversy indeed continues as to how to explain the major change by 1833, its consolidation by 1838 and why emancipation occurred in a relatively short time.

The last three novels, the so-called Chawton novels, were written in the decade after the 1807 Abolition.[2] Amongst Jane Austen's favourite writers were people who were passionately anti-slavery, such as William Cowper, Doctor Johnson and Thomas Clarkson. One of her naval brothers was known to be abolitionist. I use the term 'abolition' in connection with both the slave trade and slavery. Cowper's tirade against slavery in lines 37–9 of Book Two of his epic length poem *The Task* is severe, and leads up to the question: 'We have no slaves at home – then why abroad?' Jane Austen would have been aware of the popular campaign for abolition.

It is clear that Cowper spoke of chattel slavery, the most extreme form of slavery in which a person is legally the property of another. It was this form of slavery that the abolitionists targeted, and that would be abolished in the 1830s for British territories.[3] Cowper's question was akin to the slogan: 'Am I not a Man and a Brother?' This inscription was on the medallion manufactured and distributed from the summer of 1787 by Josiah

Wedgwood. Jane Austen was 12 when 'the wearing of the medallions set as hatpins, bracelets, rings, and buckles became quite the fashion'.[4]

The decade after the 1807 Abolition saw a pause for reflection in abolitionist activity before campaigning resumed for the ending of chattel slavery in the colonies. Awareness of the plight of those brought by the slave trade into slavery may be the main focus of the reference to the slave trade in *Mansfield Park* and in *Emma*. This is not to deny that there are other debates 'which figure more explicitly in her books than does the abolitionist campaign'.[5]

Edward Said claimed that Jane Austen passes over the sufferings of slaves in the Caribbean. This view is not warranted by the Austen texts. In *Culture and Imperialism* he offered a provocative interpretation of two of the novels, in which he said *inter alia* that she is a writer:

> who in *Mansfield Park* sublimates the agonies of Caribbean existence to a mere half-dozen passing references to Antigua.

Edward Said did not mention *Emma*, but did offer the comment on *Persuasion* that:

> just because Austen referred ... to realms visited by the British navy in *Persuasion* without any thought of possible responses by the Caribbean or Indian natives resident there is no reason for us to do the same.[6]

This book is intended to offer an alternative reading, paying particular attention to *Emma*, where I believe the deficiencies of his approach become most apparent.

I. Summary of main chapters

Mansfield Park was published in 1814. The heroine Fanny Price asks her uncle a question about the slave trade after he returns from Antigua. Dates emphasized by reference to more than one source for Fanny's reading matter indicate the question to be after the 1807 abolition, and her question is set within a theme of absenteeism that is emphasized and amplified. Detrimental effects of more instances of absenteeism are seen to compound each other and to undermine supposition that all is well in the lifestyle of this English family.

I think that the text in relation to Fanny Price's question operates in three different ways. It challenged the pro-slavery lobby amongst readers in a context after slave trading had been made a felony; it gave succour to the anti-slavery campaigners; and it told the story of a young girl that could retain readers' interest once the hopes of abolition and emancipation would be achieved. It is only after change that the author is prepared to have done with everything else and restore all to 'tolerable comfort'. The narrator stipulates a change for the better 'for ever' in the eldest son and heir, Tom, who is reformed. The fictional world of Mansfield Park in the context of abolition warrants portraying the novel as a subversive view of English society and as undermining the status quo of slavery. The upshot of Mansfield Park is relative to the abolitionist climate in which it was written. That a tone is set and an agenda bruited by the references to Antigua and the West Indies becomes apparent as the plot unfolds.[7]

Emma, published in 1815–16, is very different from Mansfield Park. I think the logical form of the dialogue on the slave trade in Emma and its position within the complex structure of the novel as a whole lead to an abolitionist reading. I begin by suggesting an allusion to the Biblical phrase 'one flesh' for the phrase 'human flesh' that is used by Jane Fairfax.The obnoxious Mrs Elton interjects that the governess-to-be must mean by the sale of human flesh 'a fling at the slave trade'.

Within the context of the novel, and related to discourse about the nouveaux riches at Maple Grove, the setting of the dialogue on the slave trade suggests that just as Mrs Elton was not after all much of a friend to Jane Fairfax, so the owner of Maple Grove, Mr Suckling, may not have been much of 'a friend to the abolition'. Since the respect in which governesses are compared to slaves is in being traded, both may be regarded as commodities. Furthermore, since these objects of trading are said to be victims and to be caused misery, in the case of the slave trade its guilt also being affirmed implies its victims should be freed from their misery.

Persuasion is different yet again. Unlike the other two, it does not refer to the slave trade. However, the Royal Navy in the actual world would have to enforce the banning. One of her nephews in his 1870 Memoir declared Jane Austen's concerns to be with her family and not at all with politics, but goes on to say that she was conversant with naval matters because of the contact with her naval brothers.[8] Her contacts and knowledge, I suggest, encouraged her to celebrate the Royal Navy in Persuasion and, by implication, its impending work to enforce the change in law over slave trading.

Persuasion was published posthumously. The novel is permeated with references to the Royal Navy. Reference to the West Indies, emphasis on precise dates, and praise of the Royal Navy together bring to mind the 1807 Abolition. The date also of the summer of 1814 emphasized within the narrative coincides in the non-fictional world with intense lobbying of Parliament to negotiate an international ban on the transatlantic slave trade on the part of European nations, in the wake of the Napoleonic wars. Dates emphasized in Persuasion would mean that Captain Wentworth makes his fortune at sea after abolition of the British slave trade. I hope that indications I give about the plot of each of these novels will suffice as background to my own interpretations. I shall not, however, reveal the identity of the secret fiancée in Emma, in order that new readers will still be able to discover that for themselves.

II. A context of abolition

My concern with the context of abolition does not imply that there are not myriads of other ways of reading Jane Austen, nor that the issues I shall turn to were her first let alone her only concern.[9] In an article 'Jane Austen and Edward Said' Susan Fraiman suggests:

> Yet had Said placed Sir Thomas Bertram, for example, in line with the deficient fathers who run unrelentingly from *Northanger Abbey* through *Persuasion*, he might perhaps have paused before assuming that Austen legitimates the master of Mansfield Park. If truth be told, Said's attention even to his chosen text is cursory: Austen references to Antigua (and India) are mentioned without actually being read, though Said stresses elsewhere the importance of close, specific analysis. Maria Bertram is mistakenly referred to as 'Lydia' (CI, 87) – confused, presumably, with Lydia Bennet of *Pride and Prejudice*. And these are just a few of the signs that *Mansfield Park*'s particular complexity – including what I see as its moral complexity – has been sacrificed here, so ready is Said to offer Austen as 'Exhibit A' in the case for culture's endorsement of empire.

Susan Fraiman's criticisms here of Edward Said's treatment of *Mansfield Park* indicate that his sensitivity was not enough if he did not maintain careful attention to the text. However, although I agree that 'commodification' is at issue in *Emma*, I diverge from her reading of the passage in *Emma* on the slave trade:

> Jane Fairfax likens the commodification of British women by the 'governess-trade' to that of Africans by the 'slave-trade', hinting that the sale of 'human intellect' is no more tolerable than the sale of 'human flesh'.[10]

I think sale of human flesh is said by Jane Fairfax to be less tolerable than sale of human intellect.

Predating Edward Said is R.S. Neale's 1985 work.[11] It is remarkable in recognition of colonial references in *Mansfield Park* from a Marxist perspective without falling into over-simplification, for which Edward Said has been criticized by Rajeswari Sunder Rajan, who observes:

> Said's reading is not without problems, both as a matter of interpretation of Austen's style (he overlooks, for example, the operation and effects of irony), as well as in historical understanding (of her position on abolition, for instance).[12]

Such aspects as Jane Austen's position on abolition are amongst those I try to address. Both the influential involvement of those abolitionists some of whose work Jane Austen was drawn to, and her own treatment, as I see it, of the slave trade in the later novels, lead me to think that the opposite would have been more appropriate when Edward Said claimed:

It would be silly to expect Jane Austen to treat slavery with anything like the passion of an abolitionist or a newly liberated slave.[13]

Jane Austen grew up in the time of massive mobilization of popular support for abolition, when 'the passion of an abolitionist' became widespread.

In contemporary publicity on behalf of abolitionists there was a tendency to slip into sensationalism.[14] On a film version of *Mansfield Park*, one critic writes of its explicit anti-slavery sentiment that it 'condemns the text from which it derives'.[15] That may be unfair on both the film and the novel, because of the difference between representing an anti-slavery stance to a sympathetic audience now, living in a world where international law enshrines a ban on slavery, and, on the other hand, the position for any writer in Jane Austen's era of presenting an anti-slavery stance in such a way that it stood a chance of influencing readers towards anti-slavery.

I hope to have given, at least, a viable alternative reading consistent with the texts. I offer readings that I argue to be fully consistent with the texts, in my interpretation of the three last novels. This consistency is all that is important to me, minimally in order to offer a viable alternative to Edward Said's interpretation. Less minimally, I regard it as subversive on Jane Austen's part to be able to lead us such a dance that we are in effect forced to include within our focus in *Mansfield Park* one of the very large issues of her time, the abolished slave trade and continuance of slavery, and to keep the issue in focus in *Emma* and *Persuasion*.

III. The Mansfield decision

Before Jane Austen was born, Granville Sharp's pioneering work against slavery in collaboration with black people in London in the 1760s show consciences at work and with influence.[16] Injustices had already been brought to notice, helping to create a fertile ground for the 1780s popularization of the abolitionist cause. Her life coincided with heroism against formidable opposition from those with much to lose from disturbing the wealth-creation enabled by development of sugar plantations.[17] Even if, following Eric Williams, economic arguments against the slave trade and slavery are thought to have swung the balance, the efforts of many people, both black and white, bear witness to struggle.

The 'West India interest' must have been annoyed by the legal decision in 1772 of Lord Chief Justice Mansfield.[18] The decision, three years before Jane Austen was born, was that a black defendant James Somersett could not be taken against his will back out of England and returned to slavery in the colony of Virginia. Thomas Clarkson in his *History* makes much of Cowper's celebration of the Mansfield Decision. It has been suggested that the title of *Mansfield Park* may be an allusion to Lord Mansfield, whose name had become associated with liberty for slaves after the 1772 Somer-sett case.[19] That could mean saying that Jane Austen echoes the mythology of the time over the case, but that need not surprise. The Mansfield Decision had no time for non-English legal rights abroad to property in slaves. Its importance, according to one commentator, lay in part in, 'recognition of the right of the negro slave to be heard and judged as a free citizen', and according to Gretchen Gerzina:

> all over England, and sometimes in America, the 'nephews' of James Somerset left their masters and struck out on their own.[20]

It seems to me that Mansfield's interpretation of English law was seen at the time to be contrasted with developing colonial legislatures. As an important part of pre-popularization time, the Mansfield Decision would also have had repercussions for those in the American colonies contemplating independence from Britain.

Following the loss soon afterwards of the American colonies, the changed situation after 1776 was that Britain could risk further loss of colonies, if the British Parliament legislated to ban slavery in its territories abroad to bring colonies into line with the earlier recognition in the Mansfield Decision that the power claimed over James Somersett, as I quote at the head of this chapter, was not 'allowed or approved by the law of England'.

In the history of black people in Britain Lord Mansfield's own household is significant, and the following anecdote is reported about a Jamaican planter's view of him:

> While the Somerset case was pending, a Jamaican planter was asked what judg-ment Mansfield would give. 'No doubt,' he answered, 'he will be set free, for Lord Mansfield keeps a Black in his house which governs him and the whole family.'[21]

The planter would not have known that Dido was Lord Mansfield's mixed race grand-niece. There is a portrait of Dido with her cousin Lady Elizabeth Murray.[22] As stipulated in his will, a painting of him by Van Loo seems to be the one Lord Mansfield wanted Dido to have in her room:

> to put her in mind of one she knew from her infancy & always honoured with uninterrupted confidence & friendship.

In his will Lord Mansfield ensured an annuity for life for her and 'confirmed' her freedom.

Lord Mansfield had emphasized that he had to interpret the law, and that a change in the law would be for Parliament. The workings of Parliament are seen in *Mansfield Park*; Sir Thomas Bertram, owner both of the English estate named in the novel's title and of business interests in the

West Indies, muses when he is out in Antigua thinking of his prospective son-in-law as having 'the same interest' as he has. Later, Sir Thomas's English neighbour Mrs Grant and her guest, her half-sister Mary Crawford, speculate on his impending return from Antigua in helping to get this prospective son-in-law into Parliament. At the time of writing of Jane Austen's three last novels, it would have been unclear whether the British abolition of its slave trade would be followed by Parliament abolishing slavery. Whatever our interpretation now should be of the Mansfield Decision, what would be at issue would be the range of contemporary perceptions Jane Austen tuned into if her choice of title is taken to allude to the Mansfield Decision.

IV. Interaction with the reader

There was a need to avoid being counter-productive. Some of Jane Austen's contemporary audience would have been happy with the status quo of chattel slavery abroad, and she could not afford to trigger resistance to anti-slavery thought. Debate was vigorous:

> And, of course, the struggle may be charted in terms of arguments employed, often with extreme cunning, by the two sides. In this sense the conflict was far from mindless.[23]

Such emphasis on arguments accords with the subtlety in her own references to the slave trade. In her lifetime there was practical need for careful campaigning in order to avoid backlash. Such an example in 1789 concerns a Parliamentary debate when William Wilberforce offered illustration of cruel self-interest of the planters and profit-takers, but it was to no effect:

> But far from arousing general reproach, 'a cry of assent was heard in several parts of the House'. For the abolition movement ... it was necessary to demonstrate that Christian virtue could go hand in hand with economic advantage.[24]

Pious proclamations might fuel resistance.

On the abolition movement in Britain, the historian of slavery David Brion Davis asks why colonial slavery should have come to take centre-stage when there were competing problems:

> But why should so many Britons of different rank and background be concerned about Negro slavery ... ? When there were so many competing human rights and humanitarian causes, why should colonial slavery take center stage?

He later goes on to note: 'Mary Wollstonecraft's remark in her last novel, *Maria, or the Wrongs of Women* (1797) "Was not the world a vast prison, and women born slaves?"'. The method of hyperbole Wollstonecraft adopts may not have been to Jane Austen's taste. Contrasting the feminist movement in America and its relations with abolitionism during the nineteenth-century, David Brion Davis sees the linking together of radical issues in America as having 'seriously weakened the antislavery cause'. By contrast concerning Britain he reflects:

> I'm impressed by the fact that it was a united if diverse movement in Britain, including thousands of women, that achieved the abolition of colonial slavery and ... at remarkably early dates.[25]

Such single-mindedness may have been absorbed by Jane Austen.

In my reliance on historical context and the work of historians there is hazard as some historians for their part look to literary sources for help in interpreting events. It has been claimed of *Emma*:

> Jane Austen could assume enough of a consensus against the slave trade to use it to attract attention to the plight of governesses.

On the contrary, I should prefer to say that talking about governesses is used by Jane Austen to attract attention to the continuing plight of victims of the slave-trade. The same historian suggested of *Mansfield Park* that Jane Austen 'pointed to the responsible stewardship with which some of the absentee planters used their wealth'.[26] However, I see Jane Austen questioning what constituted 'responsible stewardship'. If interpretation of events by a historian has already been influenced by elusive literary allusions, there is risk of illicit circular argument, in looking to historians' views of events in attempting to interpret attitudes apparently shown in literary sources.

Bringing us from the eighteenth century to the twentieth century with an account of how 'the rights of man' came to be replaced by 'human rights', the political philosopher D.D. Raphael says:

> The change of name was due to Eleanor Roosevelt when acting as chairman of a United Nations Commission charged with reviving the rights of man and making them effective. A delegate from one benighted country said he trusted that the expression 'the rights of man' meant what it said, the rights of man, not of woman; and Mrs Roosevelt promptly knocked that idea on the head.[27]

In Jane Austen's time, 'the rights of man' were not extended to any slave. It is difficult to get back to what it was like within the earlier status quo, to gauge what could risk reinforcing attitudes opposed to the abolitionist cause. For a writer, interacting with readers might lead to their acting upon having the ear of those in Parliament or able to influence legislation, but a counter-productive result would be to risk hardening attitudes and entrenching the status quo.

V. The earlier novels

The earlier novels show interest in current affairs. Even some of Jane Austen's very early writing gives the lie to any notion that she might have been too closeted to know much about current affairs. Probably written at the age of sixteen, a 'minor work' *Catharine* has the following interchange:

'Well, I cannot conceive the hardship of going out in a very agreeable Manner with two or three sweet Girls for Companions, having a delightful Voyage to Bengal or Barbadoes or wherever it is, and being married soon after one's arrival to a very charming man immensely rich – . I see no hardship in all that.'

'Your representation of the Affair', said Kitty laughing, certainly gives a very different idea of it from Mine.'

Minor Works, p. 205

R.W. Chapman remarks in his editing notes: 'Mrs Musgrove in *Persuasion* is similarly ignorant of our possessions in the West Indies'.[28] By contrast, the author in her teens had already taken an interest.[29]

Northanger Abbey was 'finished in the year 1803' as Jane Austen tells us in her 'Advertisement by the authoress', which was written in 1816. Printed at the beginning of editions of the novel it makes for a touching reference to delay in publication.[30] She shows seriousness when she says 'places, manners, books, and opinions have undergone considerable changes' in the intervening time:

ADVERTISEMENT,
by the authoress, to NORTHANGER ABBEY

This little work was finished in the year 1803, and intended for immediate publication. It was disposed of to a bookseller, it was even advertised, and why the business proceeded no farther, the author has never been able to learn. That any bookseller should think it worth while to purchase what he did not think it worth while to publish seems extraordinary. But with this, neither the author nor the public have any other concern than as some observation is necessary upon those parts of the work which thirteen years have made comparatively obsolete. The public are entreated to bear in mind that thirteen years have passed since it was finished, many more since it was begun, and that during that period, places, manners, books, and opinions have undergone considerable changes.

Reference to 'parts of the work' being 'comparatively obsolete' has various interpretations.[31] It is unclear what revisions were made to this early novel, which was published posthumously. The heroine Catherine is introduced to us as a child who likes nothing better than to roll down the green slope at the back of the house. If the heroine was thought eventually to grasp the essentials, then one of the basics was that in her part of England 'servants were not slaves'. Catherine uses the term *'slave'* in the basic literal sense of *'mancipated'* that Doctor Johnson gives in his *Dictionary*.

The first publication was in 1811 with *Sense and Sensibility*, thought to have been started in 1797. The heroines lose their home when their father dies, and in chapter 21 some newcomers to the scene in a hothouse atmosphere of concern with money and property are described as stuffing the mouth of a small spoiled child with sugarplums to help stop her crying. The child is 'too wise' to stop crying being thus rewarded. This talk of 'her mouth stuffed with sugar plums' may allude to the boycott of West Indian sugar that was undertaken in the early 1790s. As far as I can see, the historian Hugh Thomas was mistaken to suppose any other reference to sugar in this novel.[32] In the case of the sugar plums episode, there is no sign of outward-looking sympathy on the part of the wife of the heroines' benefactor. Against a real-world backdrop of abolitionist pressure, the episode may be social comment that women's involvement could not necessarily be counted on.

There is a satirical cartoon of the Royal Family by James Gillray of 1792 that illustrates hypocrisy:

> Boycotting West Indian sugar was one way of showing support for abolition ... the Royal family is shown joining the boycott: King George III mutters 'Delicious' as he sips his tea.[33]

The full title is '*Anti-saccharrites, – or – John Bull and his family leaving off the use of sugar*'. The Queen's words are:

> O my dear creatures, do but taste it! You can't think how nice it is without sugar in. And then, consider how much Work you'll save the poor Blackamoors by leaving off the use of it! – and above All, remember how much expence it will save your poor papa! – O its charming cooling Drink.

Gillray satirized George III and his Queen for their avarice, and they are shown missing the point of the boycott of West Indian sugar.

The heroines of *Sense and Sensibility*, Elinor and Marianne Dashwood, face a marriage market, which is a forerunner of the 'sale of human flesh' in *Emma*. Elinor is attracted to Edward, but his widowed mother ruthlessly threatens to do all she can to stop him earning his own living, and attempts in chapter 43 to negotiate with him a price for marrying a rich heiress, offering to raise his annual income from £1,000 a year to £1,200 a year when Edward digs in his heels:

> offered even, when matters grew desperate, to make it twelve hundred

Edward is described by the heroines' half-brother Mr John Dashwood as 'so unfeeling' as to resist his mother's entreaties. Satire in the description of Edward as 'unfeeling' relates to another forerunner of themes in the later novels. False sensibility in the earlier novel could give the lie to any notion that in *Emma* Jane Fairfax has any truck with it.[34] In the penultimate chapter Mr John Dashwood tells Elinor and Marianne that his wife 'had suffered agonies of sensibility'. The satire of false sensibility is withering.

There is a frame for the action with a *tour de force* in the second chapter balanced by the penultimate chapter. The heir to the heroines' home, John Dashwood, in the second chapter had been talked out of financial help by the arguments of his wife, talking of an annuity as a nuisance:

> I have known a great deal of the trouble of annuities; for my mother was clogged with the payment of three to old superannuated servants by my father's will

The satire here was topical. Large sums of money could be involved in legal arrangements like marriage settlements and jointures to the point of over-heavily mortgaged estates. On the topic of annuities for relatives, the historian M.J. Daunton relates:

> The tenant for life was, complained Lord Winchilsea, made into 'the slave of the family' under pressure to meet the claims of portions and annuities created by his father, and with the prospect of creating more for his own children.[35]

This is a striking position of the time where an heir claims to be a 'slave of the family'. Metaphorical use of the term 'slave' in Daunton's example has something in common with the usage of the unsympathetic vicar Mr Elton in *Emma*, the bully Mrs Norris in *Mansfield Park* and Lady Catherine de Bourgh in *Pride and Prejudice*. In the hyperbole inherent in such metaphorical language, there is risk by these unattractive characters of downplaying the evils of chattel slavery.

Pride and Prejudice was published in 1813, though started in the 1790s. The heroine Elizabeth Bennet regards her sister Jane's eventual husband as 'a slave' to his friends' opinions in the crisis of initial separation, and here I think must be meant '*dependant*'. On definitions in Johnson's *Dictionary*, the literal term '*slave*' not only as '*mancipated*' but also as '*dependant*' is given, and both literal senses are characteristic of varying usage in *Pride and Prejudice*.[36] One critic suggests:

> In Austen's novels every word counts. By paying close attention to the nuances of her language, and the frequency with which key words recur within different novels, we can acquire a far greater insight into the implicit moral and social codes of her writing.[37]

In the usage of the not so attractive character, Lady Catherine de Bourgh, in chapter 29 the meaning '*dependant*' for '*slave*' is not present, but rather a hackneyed dead metaphor:

> No governess! How was that possible? Five daughters brought up at home without a governess! – I never heard of such a thing. Your mother must have been quite a slave to your education.

Humour emphasizes the impact of this passage. The effect in 'slave to your education' which would now be commonplace, is different in the context of the novel just because of the continuation then of the institution of chattel slavery, so that this way of talking by Lady Catherine de Bourgh offered a belittling effect on the enormity of the literal case of slavery. I think that must be why what we now take as a dead metaphor is to be found in the mouth of unsavoury characters, not used as Elizabeth Bennet or Fanny Price in *Mansfield Park* use it to mean 'dependant', but meaning 'working very hard'.

In the absence of a governess where the mother is said to be a 'slave to your education', Elizabeth is amused, but what also comes over is that the comparison of slave with person having to do the teaching is presented by an unattractive character. This could suggest that it would be inappropriate to see in *Emma* a likening between the rigours for slave and governess. The author worked out how the variables of slave and governess went together in her time.[38]

The topics of property and money had already been raised in laughter in the famous opening line of *Pride and Prejudice* in the suggestion that an unmarried man with money would be regarded as the property of some one or other of the girls of the neighbourhood. Before the 'slave to your education' passage, a different issue is broached of property left to a male heir cutting out the women:

> 'Your father's estate is entailed on Mr Collins, I think. For your sake,' turning to Charlotte, 'I am glad to hear of it; but otherwise I see no occasion for entailing estates from the female line. – It was not thought necessary in Sir Lewis de Bourgh's family.'

Daunton suggests:

> Mrs Bennet in *Pride and Prejudice* must have had many real counterparts when she complained 'bitterly against the cruelty of settling an estate away from a family of five daughters, in favour of a man whom nobody cared anything about'.[39]

The topic of property runs throughout all the novels, and is related to discussion of money and a love of domination. When Jane Austen integrates a reference to the slave trade in *Mansfield Park* and in *Emma*, it is interwoven with the topics of money, property and domination:

> Here, then, is the potentially radical message of *Mansfield Park*: the ownership of property is not in any sense a guide to the moral worth of the individual.[40]

Mary Evans here emphasizes the importance of property in Jane Austen's novels.

The topic of money in a marriage market runs throughout all the novels. It is complicated in *Pride and Prejudice*. There is a new element in the case of the homely Charlotte's decision to accept pompous Mr Collins as a husband. When Mr Bennet notes in a letter from Mr Collins that Charlotte is pregnant, this is a reminder that another factor to take into account in a marriage market is to do with children. A wish on Charlotte's part for the love and involvement of her own children could be as much an incentive for her decision as monetary ones. Since she makes it clear that she has never had much opinion of marital felicity there would be no incentive for her to look about for a 'love-match', but to secure an opportunity for supported children of her own before age complications set in.[41] The example of the well-known actress of the time, ducal mistress Mrs Jordan, able to mother children and work for her living on stage, could well be thought to be beyond the reach of a more average young woman.[42] Although I suggest concerning *Emma* that the marriage market is Jane Fairfax's initial comparison with 'governess trade' in the dialogue that leads on to discussion of the slave trade, it seems that the notion of a marriage market is not straightforward.[43]

VI. The slave trade

The slave trade was indeed a matter of trade. Trading with African chiefs and Africans in high places was part of what made possible the trans-atlantic slave trade. It has been argued that the 'control of slave supply remained firmly in the hands of African dealers and merchants'.[44] When it is said that the Industrial Revolution in England was aided by slave trading, this could refer to goods such as cloth from Yorkshire and guns from Birmingham being shipped to Africa to be exchanged for slaves. With the benefit to England of exporting goods to Africa, if supply ran dry of slaves it would be simple enough for African sellers to make war on neighbouring tribes to seize more prisoners of war to trade for goods.

Thus it was wise of Doctor Johnson to praise Adam Smith's *Wealth of Nations* as tackling the concept of trading. This is in opposition to Boswell's claim that Adam Smith could not know what he was talking about because he had not been in trade. Johnson instead picks up on the crucial nature of trading.[45] Later, William Wilberforce and Thomas Clarkson were keen to encourage legitimate trading with Africa so that artefacts could be bought rather than its people as commodities. Thomas Malthus inveighed against the trading of people. He dismissed attempts to hijack his own work on population:

> a consideration of the laws which govern the increase and decrease of the human species, tends to strengthen, in the most powerful manner, all the arguments in favour of the abolition.[46]

He insisted that the barbarity on both sides must be stopped:

> As long as the nations of Europe continue barbarous enough to purchase slaves in Africa, we may be quite sure that Africa will continue barbarous enough to supply them.

Malthus took this addition to a new edition round to his friend Wilberforce's house just in time for use in Parliament in connection with the Abolition of the Slave Trade.[47]

Where Jane Austen refers to the slave trade, the aspect of it specifically as trading, and treating human beings as commodities, may be what she was after. Whether it is slavery or the slave trade or both together that trigger her reference to the slave trade in *Mansfield Park* and *Emma* is unresolved by reference to background that included such well-known names as John Locke and Doctor Johnson. In relating Jane Austen to her society, both Locke and Johnson have been seen as influential:

> John Locke's political and moral philosophy had laid the foundations for the legitimation of gentry dominance, and it was left to more popular writers such as Johnson and the 3rd Earl of Shaftesbury to teach the gentry its morals and manners.[48]

There is the sobering thought that the seventeenth-century political philosopher John Locke saying that slaves are from war zones, and then noting the influence of money in furthering reserves of property, fails to comment on supply and demand.

In the second part of this book, background on some philosophers on race and slavery does not imply that Jane Austen was influenced by them. They helped to form the culture in which she grew up, and they expressed views on which Johnson and Clarkson commented. The fact that some favourite authors were abolitionist does not, of course, mean that she shared their views. I base my belief about her position on the later novels. Background on Cowper, Johnson and Clarkson shows views available to her to consider.

VII. Jane Austen and abolition

What I offer is not new, but has merely been overlooked in earlier times amongst the riches of her work. It could be conjectured amongst several reasons why Jane Austen's position alongside popular support of her time for abolition has earlier been overlooked. The early Victorian Age and onwards, I suggest, would not have wished to be reminded by anything in her novels that campaigning had been needed for the 1830s emancipation of slaves in the British Empire. Later still, there was a preference not to dwell on world affairs after each of the World Wars, as literary critics have noted.[49]

There is more than one reason why we have read past the references to abolition in the later novels without registering them. There is the obvious point that so much goes on in her texts. The richness of everything else in these novels can readily cause a reader no longer needing to be concerned with such issues to overlook considerations that interested Edward Said. It would be encouraging to think that the very subtlety in presentation that has caused us to pass over Jane Austen's references to the slave trade could be just the means to advance beyond earlier discord to better futures. If it is true that, as Edward Said suggested, early colonial practice is reflected in her novels, then the best antidote to being downcast by the past could be to adopt the very optimism for the future that is integral to her novels.

Turning to a relatively short time of 16 years after her death in 1817, legislation for emancipation of slaves in British territories would complete the 1807 success. The stage was set for a new set of values, and for those who had opposed such reform to be reconciled to abolitionist victory, for all and sundry to fall in with the new practice of the 1830s, slavery after 1833 finally being abolished by 1838. That being so, any earlier literary work purporting to persuade Britons would appear wildly out of date. Britons were now thought to be those who had seen the light, not those who needed converting to the cause of Emancipation.

It was just as well there was plenty else in the later novels to keep attention. If Jane Austen had concentrated on abolition, the texts might have risked becoming museum pieces, irritating those teetering on the brink of self-righteousness who would not have welcomed any reminder that some of them had needed to be coaxed and also those who had suffered as a result of the slave trade but who wanted to move forwards rather than focus on the past.

For Britons, the anti-slavery and anti-slave trade cause was, thereafter, one to be pursued even further afield.[50] Meanwhile:

> [explorers and missionaries] revealed that the ravages of the slave trade had criss-crossed the continent and that no indigenous people were either willing or powerful enough to stop it; this was something for the humanitarians to slowly mull over.[51]

There may have been continuing political reasons for literary critics not wanting to see these references. Neither in the editing of Jane Austen's novels by R.W. Chapman after the First World War nor in the literary New Criticism after the Second World War would there have been much heart for sombre issues involving values relevant to international affairs. The point here I think would be that in the former case, matters of empire were involved in hostilities leading to the First World War and these matters of empire would have been bound up with a British perception of having been doing the right thing with respect to being opposed to slavery and slave trading. This would have been part of the assumed moral justification for Victorian empire-building. There would not have been a welcome for reminders by such interpretation as mine of Jane Austen that she had recorded Britain needed coaxing into abolitionist legislation. In the later case of the Second World War it was enough to be on the victors' perceived side of right without being reminded that Britain had earlier needed guidance in other respects.

Part I
The Chawton Novels

2
Mansfield Park: Absenteeism, Autonomy and the Slave Trade

'I suppose I am graver than other people,' said Fanny. 'The evenings do not appear long to me. I love to hear my uncle talk of the West Indies. I could listen to him for an hour together. It entertains *me* more than many other things have done – but then I am unlike other people I dare say... Did not you hear me ask him about the slave trade last night?'

'I did – and was in hopes the question would be followed up by others. It would have pleased your uncle to be inquired of farther.'

'And I longed to do it – but there was such a dead silence! And while my cousins were sitting by without speaking a word, or seeming at all interested in the subject, I did not like – I thought it would appear as if I wanted to set myself off at their expense, by shewing a curiosity and pleasure in his information which he must wish his own daughters to feel.'

Mansfield Park, chapter 21

Introduction

The notion of pleasing her uncle Sir Thomas Bertram, who had returned after two years in the West Indies, when teenage Fanny Price questions and shows pleasure in his information on the issue of the slave trade has surprised a number of people. As one critic puts it, 'We may wonder what "pleasure" she could get from information about the slave trade.'[1] I think the author confronts us with a clear signal. Suppose that the word 'pleasure' was used pretty much as now, including the idea of a felon being detained 'at her majesty's pleasure', which would involve a concept of choice as in the fifth definition in Johnson's *Dictionary*. Ruled out would be the use of 'pleasure' as trivial enjoyment or delights pursued for their own sake.

There is also pleasure when something of immediate concern takes a turn for the better. Necessary to speaking in this way of pleasure is intensity of involvement. That is the sense I make of Fanny's and her cousin Edmund's way of talking, in the passage quoted at the head of this chapter. Such usage brings with it two implications. The position to be inferred is that

Fanny and Sir Thomas Bertram's younger son Edmund are concerned about that great issue of their times, the slave trade. A new situation facing contemporary readers was of the change in British law whereby slave-trading was illegal for Britons. Concern would seem to follow from the language the author introduced in this passage. Secondly, it looks as if Fanny and Edmund think Sir Thomas will be in sympathy with their attitude, because they see him as responding in like manner to their pleasure. A number of indicators suggest that Fanny and Edmund are abolitionist in their sympathies. However, if it is right to infer a rapport between them and Sir Thomas, in that they all take pleasure in the imparting of information on the topic, it would not be a straightforward issue of the owner of Mansfield Park speaking as a representative of the plantocracy that typically held out against the abolitionists.

By the time *Mansfield Park* was published in 1814, not only had Parliament abolished the British slave trade seven years previously but it had also passed follow-on legislation in 1811 making slave-trading a felony, 'punishable by 14 years imprisonment' for Britons.[2] The internal dating within the novel is relevant to the nature of the question asked about the slave trade. A striking point concerning Fanny's actual question about the slave trade is that we never learn what the question was. Jane Austen may use the 'dead silence' that meets the question to interact with her readers.

In her critique of Edward Said, Susan Fraiman has emphasized that there is a need to question what Mansfield Park stands for. She claims:

> Said's opinion that Austen is culpably indifferent to slavery in Antigua depends on a repeated but questionable assertion: that Mansfield Park epitomizes moral order and right human relations.[3]

I agree with her that it was missing the point to suppose Jane Austen is 'culpably indifferent to slavery in Antigua'. On my view literal slavery is her most solemn concern in this novel.

One of the main issues is absenteeism; Sir Thomas is an absentee planter, as critics emphasize. Jane Austen 'devastatingly exposes the contradictions inherent' in 'absentee landlordism'.[4] Criticism had been voiced in England of absentees, and amongst them prominent family names such as Lascelles had become well-known.[5] It may be significant that in chapter 40, Mary Crawford, whose principles are found wanting, is associated with the Lascelles name and so with its slavery connection that would have been well-known at the time. Mary Crawford writes to Fanny:

> [Maria] will open one of the best houses in Wimpole Street. I was in it two years ago, when it was Lady Lascelles', and prefer it to almost any I know in London.

Mary Crawford adds her brother Henry would not have been able to afford it, which emphasizes the wealth involved.[6]

Absenteeism as a theme runs throughout *Mansfield Park*, and the theme is associated with the gaming and extravagance of Tom, the eldest son and heir. It is introduced in half-comical fashion by Lady Bertram's leaving Sir Thomas to his own devices in London during his Parliamentary duties. The theme is furthered by Sir Thomas's departure for Antigua. Some of the repercussions of his absence from England, combining with the final case of absenteeism, this time on the part of the flirtatious Henry Crawford from his estate, surface in the denouement of the scandal of Maria Bertram and Henry to affect the social success of Sir Thomas's family, as Maria's adultery wrecks her new society marriage. The importance of absenteeism is further amplified in the case of Henry Crawford, because there is a focus on the wider topic of what might be said to be ordained in people's destinies. The term 'ordination' here takes up a different or extended sense from a narrower definition in terms of ordination to be a parish priest. It is now often thought that ordination in the narrower sense is not after all the topic of the novel.[7] Ordination in the sense connected with a person's destiny does loom large, however, in the case of Henry Crawford and, by implication, in a wider abolitionist context. In the context of a family with West Indian connections, Jane Austen invites thought.

The quotation twice by Fanny from William Cowper's work is suggestive of the topic of abolition because Cowper's abolitionist poetry had become well-known. Quotation stimulates association of ideas between the references to Cowper on the one hand and abolitionism on the other hand. Association of ideas could also be provoked by the name 'Mansfield' in the novel's title, following Lord Chief Justice Mansfield's 1772 decision, not least because of its celebration by Cowper in *The Task*.[8] On a whimsical note, the reference on the visit to Sotherton to 'sofas' in:

Sofas, and chit-chat, and *Quarterly Reviews*

could be an inter-textual allusion to Cowper's *The Task* from which Fanny later quotes, in which much is made of his initial task to carry out the wishes of a lady who had instructed him to rhyme on the topic of sofas.[9] From his spoof epic beginning:

I sing the sofa ...

Cowper will go on to graver questions including slavery and predestination. An initial keynote in chapter 2 is set for the novel by the sofa, which becomes a symbol of Lady Bertram:

To the education of her daughters, Lady Bertram paid not the smallest attention. She had not time for such cares. She was a woman who spent her days in sitting nicely dressed on a sofa, doing some long piece of needlework, of little use and no beauty ...

The novel *Mansfield Park* will also go on to graver questions including the slave trade and destiny.[10]

I. Absentees

Coinciding with the child Fanny first entering the family as a poor relation, in chapter 2 there is an introductory instance of absence. It is not Sir Thomas's initiative but is Lady Bertram's doing that the London house is given up; Lady Bertram:

> in consequence of a little ill-health, and a great deal of indolence, gave up the house in town, which she had been used to occupy every spring, and remained wholly in the country, leaving Sir Thomas to attend his duty in Parliament, with whatever increase or diminution of comfort might arise from her absence.

There is a sharp edge that Sir Thomas is not guaranteed a quality of life within his own home that he would have hoped for in marrying someone he found attractive. As a consequence of Lady Bertram's indolence, their daughters grow up in the country and there is novelty value when Maria, in chapter 4, in coming to the conclusion that it is her duty to marry Mr Rushworth, takes into account that it will give her a house in town. Lady Bertram by her indolence has made her own contribution to the later events. The indolence associated with her absence will compound the effects of Sir Thomas's absence, as we are prior warned in chapter 3, when Sir Thomas muses about his daughters:

> He could not think Lady Bertram quite equal to supplying his place with them, or rather to perform what should have been her own.

Lady Bertram although used to her husband's being away in London disliked Sir Thomas going to Antigua, but, in chapter 4, she is reconciled not only to her son Tom's absence but 'was soon astonished to find how very well they did even without his father'. Chapter 4 begins:

> Tom Bertram had of late spent so little of his time at home, that he could be only nominally missed.

Tom's own absence is noted, as it occurs in England and in his being taken to Antigua to separate him from the company he had been keeping. Meanwhile, comment on the progress of the absent is provided by the widowed aunt, Mrs Norris, who is thwarted in offering *schadenfreude* at the prospect of Sir Thomas coming to grief in his journey to Antigua, and who on his successful arrival has to lay aside her fears for the absent Sir Thomas. Humour underlines his going away.

Sir Thomas tries to redress his absenteeism from Antigua by his absence instead from England during Volume One, at what in chapter 3 is described as his daughters' 'most interesting time of life'. His absence extends to two years. In the next chapter, Maria's engagement:

> with a due reference to the absent Sir Thomas, was entered into ...

The usual case of the absentee planter is turned on its head so that the father is absent from his family. His absence contributes causal links with the developments at Mansfield Park while he is away, which contribute to Maria's botched seduction of Henry Crawford. There is what Edward Said draws attention to, a suggestiveness in the play-acting, 'in which something dangerously close to libertinage is about to be (but never is) enacted'.[11] Maria's later liaison with Henry Crawford may not be debauched, but loses her the house in town and trappings of the marriage, which constituted success for her and her family. We are left to work out some causal links with later events, since his absence is not cited by Sir Thomas as a contributory factor although he blames himself in so many other respects. Sir Thomas disregards his absence in Antigua, but, unlike the reader, he is not to know how free Henry Crawford had been in Sir Thomas's own house during the rehearsals for the play to lead Maria on with his flirting, so that she feels slighted when the longed for marriage proposal is made not for herself but for Fanny, provoking Maria's anger and Henry's temptation to overcome her coldness, which leads to the break-up of Maria's marriage.

Tom's own tendency to absenteeism is seen when his father sends him back from Antigua after one year, and he goes off to race a horse. On his return, Tom resists pressure from Edmund, and presses on with structural alterations for the provision of the play. Tom in his father's absence helps himself to the use of what on return Sir Thomas is to refer to as 'his own dear room', one of the first things he wants to see after greeting his family. In chapter 3 there had been Tom's reflections after a showdown with his father, when he had reflected 'with cheerful selfishness':

> ... 1st, that he had not been half so much in debt as some of his friends; ...

The seriousness of the matter was acknowledged by Tom in his supposition that the problem would be solved by the death of the new clergyman in a post that had been intended for his younger brother Edmund when ordained, but given to another instead to help pay Tom's debts.

Another instance of absenteeism arises, this time in connection with clergy residence, once Sir Thomas has returned. In chapter 25 Mary, Henry Crawford's sister, is dismayed by Sir Thomas's 'little harangue' that Edmund must be resident. In rejecting a wish from Henry Crawford to rent the house at Thornton Lacey where Edmund would go when ordained, Sir Thomas says:

a parish has wants and claims which can be known only by a clergyman constantly resident ... Edmund might, in the common phrase, do the duty of
Thornton, that is, he might read prayers and preach, without giving up Mansfield
Park; he might ride over, every Sunday, to a house nominally inhabited, and go
through divine service; he might be the clergyman of Thornton Lacey every
seventh day, for three or four hours, if that would content him. But it will not.
He knows that human nature needs more lessons than a weekly sermon can
convey, and that if he does not live among his parishioners and prove himself by
constant attention their well-wisher and friend, he does very little either for their
good or his own.

It is ironic that Sir Thomas sees no analogue with the duties of a father,
when he supposes that the job cannot be carried out unless a clergyman is
'constantly resident'; but the irony is intensified in that it would be possible for Edmund to carry out his work in the parish; it is clear that he is
accustomed to riding out and about and could therefore provide 'constant
attention'.[12] This 'little harangue' is odd, since from chapter 3 it could be
inferred that two livings, seven miles apart, should be held together by his
younger son, who responds that Sir Thomas:

undoubtedly understands the duty of a parish priest. – We must hope his son
may prove that *he* knows it too.

Edmund's reply sounds distanced. Whether two livings were intended for
Edmund is unclear.[13] There would be nothing to prevent Edmund from
serving all his parishioners in two parishes that are no farther apart than
areas of a single parish that is extensive on the ground. So the work
involved could be done without detriment. Their position becomes the
same as that of some modern-day clergy. The living at Thornton Lacey is a
modest one, in monetary terms, unlike some livings, and the need is felt for
a higher income when at the end of the novel Edmund and Fanny have
embarked on married life and there is a hint of need to finance having children. Sir Thomas exemplifies by the features that are at fault in his own
practice both in England and in Antigua, the sort of snags that would not be
a problem for Edmund as a clergyman resident eight miles away. A perceived problem of absenteeism of clergy in the Church of England contrasts
with and highlights absenteeism amongst planters.[14]

The irony in this difference would be borne out in legislation of 1838,
under which no more than two simultaneous livings were to be allowed
and those no more than 10 miles apart, addressing inequalities by alleviat-
ing on the one hand extreme poverty of some clergy, while on the other
hand curbing gross excesses in wealth of other clergy.[15] Edmund's practice
would be within these later guidelines and later twentieth-century practice.[16] A contemporary reader could hear a concern over the job of a clergyman as the same concern as that of the Evangelicals within the Church of
England to note the reforming zeal of dissenters and to offset the slackness

that had become obvious in the eighteenth century in the Church of England. Then on being confronted with an absentee plantation owner talking about non-residence of clergy, such a reader could go on to think of another concern of the Evangelicals, its most famous, that of abolitionism. It is possible that we are offered only an apparent reference to Evangelicalism here, when all the while Sir Thomas's own worries and experience arising from Tom's debts and his own absenteeism from England are undermining a reader's confidence in the credentials of the kind of people who are able to uphold the status quo. If this were so, it could suggest a serious endeavour to engage any contemporary pro-slavery reader on the issues of abolitionism. It would be a red herring for such a reader to try to combat Edmund and Fanny on Evangelical arguments for abolitionism, when all the while troubles with the status quo were being illustrated from within the family's way of life. That might seem a desperate ploy, but the text may be experimental in exploration of different possibilities for seeking to convince. It could be significant that Crabbe's *Tales* being read by Fanny illustrates the extreme difficulty of changing the beliefs of someone with a different ideology.[17]

Edmund is associated with Evangelicalism. In chapter 47, a taunt is flung at him by Mary Crawford in their last meeting:

> and when I hear of you next, it may be as a celebrated preacher in some great society of Methodists, or as a missionary into foreign parts.

In Britain, abolitionism having been associated with Evangelical Christianity found one of its voices in sermons.[18] Tension over reforming zeal in *Mansfield Park* is emphasized in the interchange between two characters that Jane Austen brings close to matching in marriage. Mary Crawford's taunt looks like allusion to Evangelical interests, and that would give rise to association of ideas with the Evangelical campaigning. Her taunt may be why she had to be parted from Edmund at the end of the novel. It may be this final taunt that causes Edmund to resist her smiling, interpreting it, as he says, as her intending to 'subdue' him. We had seen her planning to keep him away from his parish as much as possible in order to be in London. There may be the utmost realism in the portrayal of Mary Crawford, in that she is everything that is charming in society and that cannot be complained of without boorishness, save that, should it come to a showdown over loss of money in emancipation of slaves, she would most likely opt for maintenance of the status quo. Since emancipation of slaves, as I see it, is the most serious matter on Jane Austen's mind in this novel, I see it as no surprise that Mary has to go.[19]

The linking of abolitionism and Christianity at the time was making uncomfortable in Parliamentary circles people who were not pro-abolitionist. The overtones of Evangelicalism in Sir Thomas's defence of residence would be suggestive of abolitionism:

As with so much else attempted in the 1770s the new sensibility was not sufficient to bring about change. It needed the somewhat harder core of moral earnestness provided by the evangelicals to turn it into a weapon of real weight and effectiveness.[20]

This 'harder core of moral earnestness' swung support behind Evangelicals for their abolitionism even though on a wider front of other religious and social attitudes they would not be followed. The reader may be invited to remember Evangelical attitudes that would bring to mind campaigning for abolition and the intensity of the Evangelicals' position on abolition and emancipation.[21]

The last case of absenteeism figures in the denouement, and compounds the effects of that of Sir Thomas. Henry Crawford had looked set to progress in his courting of Fanny and parts from her at Portsmouth with a project of going back to his own estate to sort out a tenancy that otherwise will be mismanaged by his steward, who will arrange affairs to the advantage of one of his own relatives. This comes over as a worthwhile project, and Fanny wonders how it is progressing, surmising that she has to wait till she next sees him to learn further. It is the cancellation of this project – perhaps writing letters about it will do just as well thinks Crawford – in order to score a victory over Maria's anger at his proposal to Fanny, that sets in train the sequence of events which go further than he intended, causing him to lose a chance of winning Fanny, as he later accuses Maria, dashing her hopes of re-marriage after divorce, a servant's having made public to all and sundry their 'indiscretion'.[22] This final case of absenteeism warrants a startling list of counterfactuals on Crawford's destiny, in the last chapter, that emphasizes the serious tone of the novel. There is a list of subjunctive conditionals referring to his intention, before falling for her, of teasingly courting Fanny:

> Could he have been satisfied with the conquest of one amiable woman's affections, could he have found sufficient exultation in overcoming the reluctance, in working himself into the esteem and tenderness of Fanny Price, there would have been every probability of success and felicity for him ... Would he have deserved more, there can be no doubt that more would have been obtained; especially when that marriage had taken place, which would have given him the assistance of her conscience in subduing her first inclination, and brought them very often together. Would he have persevered, and uprightly, Fanny must have been his reward – and a reward very voluntarily bestowed – within a reasonable period from Edmund's marrying Mary. Had he done as he intended, and as he knew he ought, by going down to Everingham after his return from Portsmouth, he might have been deciding his own happy destiny.

The passage stuns, and the real sadness of the loss involved in the aborting of this alternative ending adds to the often remarked on more-than-sombreness of *Mansfield Park*.[23] Henry Crawford's absenteeism interacts with that of Sir Thomas from England in triggering destructive behaviour by Maria, absenteeism on the part of two men here having a cumulative effect.

Absenteeism on the part of Henry Crawford in turn involves a further consideration. In his case, absenteeism arises from what is represented as an autonomous decision. He could have done otherwise, even though we can see how his past experience led him to make the decision he did. So while all due force of causal connections is allowed for here by the author, there is still room for personal decision-making, presented as of the low-key sort that we take for granted in holding ourselves and others accountable: '...he might have been deciding his own happy destiny'. The consideration that some room for choice was left open for Henry Crawford would have relevance to reflections about slavery, because at the time it was not uncommon for it to be argued that slavery must be ordained by God or otherwise it would not occur. To cite the views of a wealthy Bristol absentee plantation owner:

'I was shocked at the first appearance of human flesh exposed for sale,' wrote John Pinney, an absentee Nevis planter in 1764. 'But surely God ordain'd 'em for the use and benefit of us: other his Divine Will would have been manifest by some sign or token.'[24]

Such a degree of determinism in the affairs of human beings in terms of what God 'ordain'd' is in effect brought into question in the deliberation on Henry Crawford involved in the list of counterfactuals.

In the theme of absenteeism in *Mansfield Park*, an implicit challenge on behalf of the continuing struggle for abolition has been taken up, because the theme of absenteeism would illustrate a weak link in any defence of slavery as practised by Britain. The practice of absenteeism, something that had been debated in Parliament as detrimental to the condition of those held in slavery, is illustrated in the novel as not being much good for the absentees themselves. By concentrating on absenteeism especially that of Sir Thomas in Antigua, which carries an obvious reference to slave-owning, the particular type of slave-owning practised by some British citizens has been pinpointed. Pro-slavery activists among planters and their supporters in Parliament might think of arguing that slavery was an institution that had always existed even in the Classical world.[25] Nevertheless absenteeism meant a system of slavery defined in a different way, involving in many cases vast geographical distances between those in chattel slavery and their owners.

II. Geographical and time coordinates

The geographical references are striking, having been initiated by early reference to Antigua and continued by our imaginative journey there, in chapter 4, when while Sir Thomas is in Antigua we listen into his thinking about Maria's engagement. There are frequent references to Antigua and the West Indies.[26] They range throughout the novel between the first chapter which mentions Sir Thomas's West Indian property and the final chapter where it is said of Sir Thomas that his opinion of Mrs Norris, whom he had relied on to guide his daughters, 'had been sinking from the day of his return from Antigua'. There are reminders of the plantation in Antigua in small details – throughout the novel, as in chapter 25 where, because Fanny's brother William has been ashore in the West Indies, Sir Thomas was keen to talk with him about dancing and 'the balls of Antigua'.[27] The geographical references are accentuated by William entering the Navy from a home town that is itself a gateway to the outer world, Portsmouth, and from Fanny's likewise hailing from Portsmouth.

Chronologically, the Portsmouth where we visit the naval Dockyard had become one where the Navy is no longer commissioned to protect a slave trade but now the reverse, being commissioned amongst other things to suppress that slave trade. There is no explicit reference to the new role of the Navy any more than there is any reference to the naval activity of that time in the environs where Fanny walks out with Henry overlooking the sea.[28] Knowledge of this background in the life of the nation could be assumed. After the publicity given to Portsmouth on the return to Spithead of the *Victory*, following the Battle of Trafalgar, with the body of Nelson prior to his State funeral, a quiet assumption that the reader does not need detail draws the contemporary reader in to shared experience.[29] There is a concentration on making the scene personal to Fanny in chapter 42:

> every thing looked so beautiful under the influence of such a sky, the effects of the shadows pursuing each other, on the ships at Spithead and the island beyond, with the ever-varying hues of the sea now at high water, dancing in its glee and dashing against the ramparts with so fine a sound...

I also think it likely that from her naval sources Jane Austen would have known of the surprising demonstration of power for change by the ordinary man that was involved in the 1797 mutiny at Spithead, which resulted in new legislation the men were holding out for:

> It was a famous victory for ordinary men who combined irresistibly to get their rights. Apart from the trouble in the *London* there was no bloodshed. No Spithead mutineer was court-martialled, imprisoned, flogged, sentenced to death or hanged.[30]

The mutiny may have resonance for this novel, as likely talk of it could be imagined etched into Fanny's early consciousness. Placing her origins in Portsmouth may offer a symbol of the mutiny as a prefiguring of power in the apparently weak to succeed in overcoming obstacles. Realism may also be implied on the conditions for the ordinary sailor, so that we are not given a disguised abolitionist tract. The historian Linda Colley compares discipline over slaves and discipline within the armed forces. She says 'the whip, the prime emblem of slavery, was deployed with sometimes lethal savagery' against British white soldiers. She points out that later:

> parallels between white soldiers and black slaves were laboured persistently, for their own purposes, by anti-Abolitionists. The polemic was already an established one when Edward Long compiled his unabashedly racialist *History of Jamaica* (1774). 'I need not *again* revive the comparison between them [plantation slaves], and the British sailors and soldiers', he wrote.[31]

Here, an anti-Abolitionist thrust seems to be that since sometimes lethal flogging could be used against white soldiers and sailors, there could be no special case against an institution of slavery involving the same treatment for black slaves.

> A further outlet to the outer world is provided by Sir Thomas's return from Antigua: he came directly from Liverpool, having had an opportunity of making his passage thither in a private vessel, instead of waiting for the packet.

This reference's effect makes for a stark reminder of the change of 1807, because Liverpool had been the preeminent port for the transatlantic slave trade. It is left vague as to what drew Sir Thomas to Antigua in the first place and what kept him longer. We may wonder about it therefore in chapter 4:

> Unfavourable circumstances had suddenly arisen at a moment when he was beginning to turn all his thoughts towards England, and the very great uncertainty in which every thing was then involved, determined him on sending home his son, and waiting the final arrangement by himself.

Chapter 5 gives us Tom speaking of having gone down to Ramsgate for a week with a friend 'last September – just after my return from the West Indies – ...', and, given the other dates assembled, this could have been in 1811. There is no indication, however, that the further legislation of 1811 making slave-trading a felony is part of 'the very great uncertainty in which every thing was then involved'. Nevertheless, the open-endedness is thought-provoking.

The significance of the geographical space coordinate is enhanced when combined with the coordinate of time. Published in May 1814, the opening words 'About thirty years ago' are followed within the opening paragraph by more detail, 'at the end of half a dozen years', apparently embracing the marriage of Fanny's mother. A time scale within the novel is given that is able to take the action to a time after the date of publication, and could take us to the end of the narrative to a time when Fanny apparently starts her own family. The narrator, not the author, gives the dates from within the story.[32]

In chapter 10, Fanny and the others 'lounge away the time as they could with sofas and chit-chat and *Quarterly Reviews*' during the visit to the Sotherton estate, while waiting for 'the Miss Bertrams and the two gentlemen' to return from their ramble. The *Quarterly Review* was begun in 1809. Later, in chapter 16, Edmund sees the books that Fanny has in the East Room, one of which is Crabbe's *Tales* published in 1812. This may suggest placing Sir Thomas's return a few days later at not until 1812. Given that he was away two years, his going to Antigua in the first place may have been no earlier than 1810. The reference to the *Quarterly Review* suggests Sir Thomas's return is after 1807. Modern editions of the novel, such as that edited by Claudia Johnson, point out in footnotes the dates given within the story. Previously, some critics after R.W. Chapman such as Avrom Fleishman and following him Warren Roberts, followed by Edward Said, had taken Sir Thomas's absence to be earlier.[33] Fleishman lost a year between his own suggested chronology and that of Chapman; the text is clear that the return of Sir Thomas and the ball he holds for Fanny are in the same calendar year. Chapman, having made a tentative suggestion for an earlier date for Sir Thomas's return, gives us part of an argument, while leaving it for us to draw conclusions against this date:

> The *Quarterly Review* was first published in 1809 (and therefore could not have been read at Sotherton in the summer of 1808; p. 104). Crabbe's *Tales* (1812) are mentioned (156).

Chapman concluded 'indications are slight' as to 'the "dramatic" date of the story'. Furthermore, Chapman pointed out that the ball after Sir Thomas's return is on Thursday 22 December, and we are later told the year following the ball had a 'particularly late Easter'. The ball could have been on that date in 1808, but could not have been followed by a late Easter in 1809. The same goes for 1814, the next occurrence of 22 December falling on a Thursday. In the following year Easter would not have been late. Having noted that 1812 could be the time of Sir Thomas's return, we are thwarted in giving this as a definite date by the fact that in 1812 the 22 December was not a Thursday, although there was a late Easter in 1813. A. Walton Litz suggested 1796–97 could give both the 22 December on Thursday and a late Easter the next year, but he goes on:

> too much emphasis should not be placed on these chronological considerations. They do not affect the dramatic date of the novel, which is vaguely indicated as 'the present' (there is a reference to Crabbe's *Tales* of 1812).

As far as I can see, there seems to be a deliberate puzzle about the internal dating. Fanny's question would have had a different response from Sir Thomas before the turn of the century from that which he would give at an indeterminate date after 1812. This could be part of author interaction with her audience, for whom she has in the first four chapters introduced the brooding backdrop of references to the West Indies and Antigua.[34] I conclude Jane Austen painted realism while avoiding being pinned down to any given year.[35]

Through the puzzle set by the dates Jane Austen may ensure that there is a timelessness whereby some of what is considered in the story does not become out of date.[36] Indeterminacy of dates looks deliberate, and could have the effect that issues remain topical and of fresh concern. Chapman concluded that she had consulted an almanac when giving dates. A letter of 1813 shows an interest in detail. Writing to her sister Cassandra, on 24 January, and commenting on what her mother had been reading, Jane Austen writes:

> I learn from Sir J. Carr that there is no Government House at Gibraltar. I must alter it to the Commissioner's.

Chapman says that is a reference to *Mansfield Park*. In Volume Two there is constant reference to the timing of events, which had begun with Sir Thomas's sudden return. It ends with Fanny's resolve not to be imposed on. In between we have Fanny's question about the slave trade and then the ball in her honour with Sir Thomas's advice as to when she should leave the ball and retire for the night, an 'advice' which the narrator describes as 'absolute power'. Some of the events in the story-line could take on extra significance, as in a parable. If it is right to think of a major concern in this novel as being with slavery, then indeterminacy in dating would underscore such a serious concern. This is achieved by implying that there is a topical issue that will not be out of date until it is seen to. When Fanny does not take any further in the face of dead silence her questioning Sir Thomas, the explanation to Edmund in chapter 21 that she did not want to push herself forward in front of her cousins is adequate reason for not continuing.[37] However, by the end of the book, there is nothing to stop Fanny's further questioning a by-now chastened Sir Thomas, whose object latterly had been to get Fanny back to Mansfield, Fanny being now in his eyes the daughter he wanted.

Contrasting terminology sets up ambiguity in Fanny's attitude over her question about the slave trade. The tone established by 'graver', as Fanny describes herself, could appear offset by the lightness of 'I love.... entertains *me*'. But 'entertains' is not necessarily light-hearted; to hold the attention or thoughts of someone could equally well be meant. This relative lightness in turn gives way to 'dead' in the description of the silence that meets the question Fanny has asked. Fanny's apprehension of enquiry does seem to be of setting herself off at her cousins' expense, as if query would be commended by her uncle. The juxtaposition of the earlier 'graver' with 'dead' a few paragraphs later within the same dialogue between Fanny and Edmund ensures a possible tone of the dialogue as sombre. There is opportunity for association of ideas, of 'dead' and 'grave' derived from 'graver'; additionally, time seems to slow down for Edmund though not for Fanny, while her other cousins the girls are grave-like in their 'sitting by without speaking a word'. Their not 'seeming at all interested in the subject' also smacks more of the non-activity of the grave than does Fanny's lively interest in the topic of her uncle's business. Their grave-like stillness and silence – the silence of the grave? – contrast with their frenetic activity in vying for the affections of Henry Crawford, before their father's return from his absence in the West Indies. The reference to the slave trade is subtle.

There is no sitting lightly to the practice of slavery in the tacit judgement shared with the reader on Mrs Norris as, after she accuses her own sister's daughter, Fanny, of ingratitude with the sharp words 'considering who and what she is' bringing tears to Fanny's eyes and making Edmund too angry to speak, Mrs Norris declares to Fanny on preparations for the play-acting:

> I have been slaving myself till I can hardly stand, to contrive Mr Rushworth's cloak without sending for any more satin.

With a light touch, a different meaning of 'slaving' is jerked back to life given Sir Thomas's immanent return from Antigua. It is inappropriate, as is underscored during the initial consternation at Sir Thomas's return when it is observed of Mrs Norris that:

> except by the instinctive caution with which she had whisked away Mr Rushworth's pink satin cloak as her brother-in-law entered, she could hardly be said to shew any sign of alarm.

The humour used here to relate back to Mrs Norris' talk of slaving, by the detail of the pink colour of the satin cloak, ushers us also into the area of the play where the costumes are kept, so that we can now dwell on the carelessness with which Tom has appropriated the use of his father's own room as a green room. There is an air of trespass in the use of the room behind his father's back that may be underlined by dint of showing how even Fanny has the use of the East Room as hers even if only because no one else wants it. In that case Mrs Norris had been meticulous about the status of the room being acknowledged by stipulating that there should be no fire. It becomes doubly significant that Sir Thomas when he discovers this organizes a fire for Fanny, showing a kindness but also a due attention to what is conventional practice in the use of a person's own room.

The topic of slavery may remain in Fanny's mind when, in chapter 36, Fanny thinks 'Miss Crawford was not the slave of opportunity'. Was Miss Crawford, in William Cowper's phrase in *A Negro's Complaint*, one of the 'slaves of gold'? One view claims:

> the West Indies figures as little more than a remote place of business, for the 'arrangement of affairs'. Yet it is clear that the Mansfield Park estate is sustained by Sir Thomas' sugar plantation in Antigua – an island where slavery was practised until the 1830s.[38]

A similar view claims:

> Having acknowledged the existence of slaves, Jane Austen drops the subject without examining the links it has with the baronet's affluence in England or its morality.[39]

In my view, on the contrary, this novel's concern is with that set-up. By the time Fanny asks her question about the slave trade we have learnt that her interests are by no means only at the local level. Fanny's enthusiastic reading in the East Room includes work on China. She is no longer the 10-year-old, laughed at by Sir Thomas's daughters because she 'cannot put the map of Europe together', perhaps an allusion here to a map like Spilsbury's 1766 jigsaw map of Europe.[40] That had looked like a joke at Maria's own expense, given the upheavals of boundaries during the Napoleonic Wars. 'The map had been totally changed.'[41]

A sharp contrast is drawn; there is no mechanical piecing together of geographical information. Fanny is involved. Edmund stresses her 'trip into China', and this acts as a precursor to her question on the slave trade in that we can see her as interested in other countries. In the view of Meenakshi Mukherjee, 'Jane Austen herself was neither unaware of nor indifferent to the larger world outside England'.[42] Since she had been keen to read about China, and had to wile away time at Sotherton in the company of *Quarterly Reviews*, a possible allusion is available for contemporary readers to the first year's volume in 1809 of a review of another book on China with observations on the nature of slavery there.[43] What Fanny asked about the slave trade is less important than the effect that any such query would have in triggering possible questions about the prohibited slave trade. An obvious train of thought for a reader, raised by Fanny's questioning, or so it seems to me, is that if slavery is to continue now that the slave trade is prohibited, there needs to be adequate reproduction:

> An embargo on a further transportation of Africans to the West Indies could occur without serious economic consequences only if the slaves' birth rate increased.[44]

In another *Quarterly Review* amongst those possibly available to Fanny at Sotherton, she would have been able to read in the 1811 volume of conditions for childbirth amongst slaves in Jamaica, which could in turn have led to questions from Fanny very difficult for Sir Thomas to handle on his return.

After the recent Abolition of 1807, there was understood to be unresolved issues over the management of slave-worked estates in the West Indies. The first volume of the *Quarterly Review* in 1809 did not sound sympathetic to the new legislation. It had an article on the history of Barbados, which ended with reflections on the abolished slave trade ending with a claim that abolition:

> is, with respect to Africa, an act of self-denial and of benevolence; but towards our colonists it is merely restrictive...[45]

This is suggestive, I think, of the *Quarterly Review*'s political position at the time. It had been meant to counter what were thought to be the radical views of *The Edinburgh Review*. Walter Scott and the publisher John Murray were at the centre of launching this periodical. John Barrow at the Admiralty had an intimate knowledge as one of its core contributors from the beginning, and his 'Historical sketch of the *Quarterly Review*', describing its start in 1809, indicates the central concern with politics.[46] Since the owner of Sotherton and his mother are ridiculed, their choice of reading matter may have been thought to have been queried. That could be sufficient reason in itself for Scott and the publisher Murray not to draw attention to *Mansfield Park*.

There is a possible allusion in *Mansfield Park* to the *Quarterly Review* that could be thought critical of the *Review* in a different way. In one of the earliest editions for Fanny to have looked at while waiting at Sotherton, there is a long review of a French novel *Amelie Mansfield*. The female author Madame Cottin had been so racy that the anonymous reviewer says he cannot possibly recommend the novel for polite reading. Supposing Fanny left with the less up to date numbers, she could have settled down to the exploits of Amelie Mansfield.[47] However, later, at the Mansfield Park amateur theatricals, by an association of ideas with the names involved, Amelie of the French novel could be associated with Amelia of *The Lovers' Vows*, played by Mary Crawford. In the review it says that after elopement, Amelie's married surname becomes Mansfield, which could suggest to Fanny's imagination not only that Mary Crawford would like to marry into the family at Mansfield, but that as Amelia in *The Lovers' Vows* she is being helped to pursue that aim by having to woo Edmund, who acts as Anhalt in the play. Since the sexual exploits of Amelie Mansfield are described in some detail by the *Quarterly Review*, it may not be surprising that Fanny becomes unsettled about the progress of the amateur theatricals, especially between characters Anhalt and Amelia, in chapters 17 and 18. The review ends:

We lament...that there should be a wish in Britain for importing, from the schools of France and Germany, those novels and dramas which tend at once to corrupt the taste and deprave the national character.[48]

If Fanny is to be understood as picking up on this review, disquiet would have been augmented by these closing remarks. For a reader conversant with this 1809 edition, the occurrence of the name 'Mansfield' could offset an association with the Mansfield decision on slavery that might otherwise appear blatant. Meanwhile, association with *Amelie Mansfield* would accentuate the falling apart, during Sir Thomas's absence, of family life and a failure in propriety that is symbolized by the free use made of the play rehearsals for *The Lovers' Vows*.

Points relevant to the subsequent reception of all the later novels have been made in connection with Walter Scott's review of *Emma*; Margaret Kirkham suggests that Scott may have been influenced, in agreeing to write a review, by the dedication to the Prince Regent that had been invited by the Prince Regent himself, and that the talk of Cupid in the review obscures the theme of cupidity in the novels.[49] Scott's review of *Emma* in the *Quarterly Review* may have influenced Victorian readers to overlook social challenges in the novels.

The first edition of *Mansfield Park* had been published by Egerton in 1814, but that publisher had declined to handle a second edition. Arrangements were made with John Murray, to whom on 11 December 1815 Jane Austen sent a letter saying:

I return also *Mansfield Park*, as ready for a 2d edit: I believe [sic], as I can make it.[50]

Sales of *Emma* would be set against sales of the second edition of *Mansfield Park*. As documented by Samuel Smiles, Murray invited the review of *Emma* in a letter of 25 December 1815, and Scott sent his review to Murray on 19 January 1816. Printed as for October 1815, the review came out six months later in March 1816.[51] Scott ignored *Mansfield Park* when he reviewed *Emma*, although he included *Sense and Sensibility* and *Pride and Prejudice*.[52] Scott may not have known of *Mansfield Park*, although he does add '&c.' to the citation of publications.

Jane Austen was disappointed by 'the total omission of *Mansfield Park*'. A copy sent from John Murray of the anonymous review draws from her the reply of 1 April 1816:

I return you the Quarterly Review with many Thanks. The Authoress of *Emma* has no reason I think to complain of her treatment in it – except in the total omission of *Mansfield Park*. – I cannot but be sorry that so clever a Man as the Reviewer of *Emma* should consider it as unworthy of being noticed.

A review would have helped sales. Losses on the second edition of *Mansfield Park* may already have been felt by her after its publication in February

1816. Another letter, of 1 April 1816, this time to the librarian James Clarke, after she had been writing *Persuasion* for nearly eight months, has the remark 'though I may never succeed again'. Jan Fergus suggests that this clause:

> though properly modest – may hint at a fear that [*Persuasion*] might fail to earn money, as her second edition of *Mansfield Park* was failing.[53]

In the event, losses were incurred on the second edition of *Mansfield Park*, which were duly set against profits from *Emma*.[54] Could a fictional tale showing deleterious absenteeism arising from a two-year visit to a plantation in Antigua have been regarded as subversive? Was there sophisticated censorship of the second edition?[55]

III. Critique of slavery

There were pitfalls to avoid, such as risk of 'objectification' in any comparison between relative feminine weakness and the predicament of a victim of the slave trade.[56] Chapter 23 of *Mansfield Park* may suggest a scenario modelled on the Antigua plantation. Not submissive, but organizing herself to 'appear properly submissive' is the girl who appears at the beck and call of an imperious Lady Bertram, who denies freedom to Fanny and appears to manipulate a Sir Thomas busy as overseer of his plantation:

> On his way from his plantation to his dressing-room, she called him back again ...with 'Sir Thomas, stop a moment – I have something to say to you'. ... Fanny immediately slipped out of the room; for...she might not be able to appear properly submissive ...

This is part of a complex presentation leading up to the end of Volume Two that will see Fanny determined not to be imposed on. Her holding to her resolve is one cause of Henry Crawford's going astray leading to the dismantling of Maria's marriage, which in turn leads to the disruption of Edmund's wooing Mary Crawford, of Henry's hopes of winning Fanny, and of the peace of mind of Sir Thomas. At the last, a possible ironical analogue of Fanny's timidity with the dependant status of a slave is shown to be just that – pure irony. Fanny has what the slave does not have, and she makes use of it. She is legally free to refuse the marriage with Henry, and she does so, exercising her autonomy.

Fanny's quiet determination against all the odds may parallel the determination of abolitionists to oppose the might of the plantocracy, and to argue for and to pressure for the right of autonomy for slaves, harnessing appropriate power. Fanny's love of horsemanship, once she has overcome her childhood fears of the novelty of riding, may be a symbol of potential power. Her sheer 'delight' becomes apparent in chapter 4, when the narrator emphasizes Fanny's 'pleasure' in riding:

She had not supposed before, that any thing could ever suit her like the old grey poney; but her delight in Edmund's mare was far beyond any former pleasure of the sort; and the addition it was ever receiving in the consideration of that kindness from which her pleasure sprung, was beyond all her words to express.

By contrast, Mary Crawford loaded with confidence has no fears when she is taught to ride by Edmund. Fanny had had to overcome diffidence in order to reach her pleasure in riding.[57] The word 'pleasure' is used here with respect to what Fanny feels with the horse. By the beginning of chapter 8 it is established that Fanny rides both for 'health and pleasure'. It is her later 'pleasure' in her uncle's 'information' about the slave trade that constitutes another source of pleasure. It could be implied that to have such pleasure Fanny had to overcome fears, prior to asking her uncle about the slave trade.

The heavy 'stillness' that has been seen in the novel may be related to the heaviness of the power of the plantocracy and the brooding presence in England of an abolitionist campaign that still awaited a final resolution.[58] Fanny's vulnerability emphasized time and again contrasts with her resolve, in chapter 31, not to be presumed on in the matter of others wanting her to accept Henry's marriage proposal, and makes for a climax at the end of Volume Two. Showing all the signs of not being wayward, carrying out her resolve of 'not being imposed on' has impact.

In *Mansfield Park* there is no endorsement of Sir Thomas's previous handling of his overseas affairs; there is no sign of unwitting testimony of approval of the plantation involvement. This is unlike the case of Maria Edgeworth in *Belinda* published in 1801, where at the end in the improbable 'Denouement' an additional hero was plucked from nowhere and had his credentials presented as in part those of one who had helped an adventurer from the metropolis, who had become a wealthy West Indian planter, to stave off what is described as a Negro revolt on his plantation. Jane Austen could, however, be seen as borrowing and adapting another part of Maria Edgeworth's *Belinda*. In that novel, the wealthy West Indian plantation owner, Mr Vincent, feted in England for his wealth, courted disaster in that he has a mania acquired in the West Indies for gambling. He was given a second chance after having gambled away the whole of his fortune including all his property. Jane Austen may have borrowed this scenario for *Mansfield Park*, with the West Indian-born man of property changed to an English-born heir.

The heir apparent, Tom, is a potential drain on the whole of his inheritance, not only the Antiguan connections but the English estate itself, which could be forfeit to 'debts of honour', as in *Belinda* when Mr Vincent is brought to the state of being penniless. Tom's gaming was a real hazard, more ruinous than his racing a horse or the heavy drinking which, combined with a neglected fall, leads to fever and his illness.[59] As with his father's extra year in Antigua, details are lacking about Tom's illness. He is a changed man 'for ever' on recovery. Since he is the heir, this change is fundamental to the story of *Mansfield Park*, having gained urgency by his profligacy leading to the initial loss of one of the two possible livings for Edmund and additional urgency on our seeing how Tom has erred in the guardianship of his absent father's property.

Sotherton does not seem to enjoy the same approval as Mansfield itself. It does not sound right when Edward Said says of the country house that:

> in Jane Austen's *Mansfield Park* it is the very embodiment of all that is benign and actively good in England.[60]

In practice the estate at Sotherton is seen to work because the people staffing it are competent. Thus Mrs Norris knows where to go when, as Maria calls it, she is 'spunging'; Mrs Norris gets plants from the gardener and cheese from the housekeeper, whom we have seen as the guide for the owner's mother in getting to know about the family portraits in the picture gallery. Mrs Rushworth 'was now almost equally well qualified to shew the house'. This lack of know-how is not redolent of the landed interest, but it does underline that it is well-established residents who can ensure things prosper. Chapman in Notes to his edition of *Mansfield Park* sees the suggestive language and says:

> Probably Mr Rushworth did not succeed his father, and 'the late Mr Rushworth' was not this Mrs Rushworth's husband.[61]

This possibility is left open in chapter 4 at:

> The introduction of a young man who had recently succeeded to one of the largest estates and finest places in the country.

The gloom of the showing of the house at Sotherton seems accentuated by Mrs Rushworth's mode of presentation. After her first description of the chapel, her 'lesson' is to be repeated: 'Mrs Rushworth was gone to repeat her lesson to Mr Crawford'. It looks as if the owner's mother blunders in her guided tour, in the matter of 'profusion of mahogany' in the chapel that 'was fitted up as you see it in James the Second's time'. Mrs Rushworth adds 'Before that period, as I understand, the pews were only wainscot'. As Chapman illustrates in his Notes, the introduction of mahogany to England was an eighteenth-century innovation. He speaks of an anachronism. The conversations here look crafted so as to suggest this is no anachronism on the author's part, but an illustration of people coming into possession of property that they do not appreciate other than for its status and monetary value.

There is no endorsement of the owner of Sotherton. There is satire in the account of the visit to the house and grounds of the Sotherton estate in chapter 9, as in an authorial aside when Maria's fiancée had expressed doubt about timing:

'For if', said he, with the sort of self-evident proposition which many a clearer head does not always avoid – 'we are *too* long going over the house, we shall not have time for what is to be done out of doors'.

Mr Rushworth's 'self-evident proposition' does not augur well for his contribution to the nation once in Parliament. This wealthy fiancée, thought to be so desirable a match by Sir Thomas for his daughter, had in chapter 4 come in for criticism by Edmund, who had thought: 'If this man had not twelve thousand a year, he would be a very stupid fellow'. This is the man for whom a place in Parliament will be sought with the help of Sir Thomas.

Sir Thomas was seen in chapter 2 to be a Member of Parliament as well as absentee: 'the lobby of the extremely wealthy West Indian planters, the British owners of the slave plantations ... exerted an enormous influence on British politics'.[62] An absentee planter as Member of Parliament is seen as we tune into Sir Thomas's thought processes alone in Antigua, when he has been thinking of Mr Rushworth as a prospective son-in-law:

> It was a connection exactly of the right sort; in the same county, and the same interest.

In his edition of the novel, Tony Tanner says:

> As Chapman suggests, this probably means the landed interest as opposed to the moneyed interest, or new commercial merchant class.

However, it could be the planter interest. Notwithstanding later rapport with Fanny over her question on the slave trade, Sir Thomas may have amelioration of conditions in mind not the autonomy of emancipation. In any case, apparently 'the distinction between old and new wealth is not always easy to make in this period';[63] the owners of many country houses had derived income from West Indian plantations.[64] Perhaps Mansfield Park 'is an estate without land'.[65] This view seems feasible. The signs seem to point either way. When Edmund speaks of 'our farmers' to Miss Crawford in chapter 4, he may only be speaking of himself as a countryman as against her as a Londoner. This view is relevant to the economic set-up at the Park. If Jane Austen leaves open various scenarios, I think that supports my view of her as subversive, because the text provokes questions about the status quo.

At Sotherton, Mr Rushworth's assets command power. In chapter 17, Mary Crawford says to her half-sister, Mrs Grant, 'A man might represent the county with such an estate'. Mrs Grant replies:

> I dare say he *will* be in Parliament soon. When Sir Thomas comes, I dare say he will be in for some borough, but there has been nobody to put him in the way of doing any thing yet.

The notion of 'some borough' is reminiscent of accusations of corruption in the parliamentary process prior to its reform. He seems to be so reliant on Sir Thomas for a seat in Parliament and that may be a reference back to the point about their having 'the same interest'. That money was needed for a seat in Parliament is noted by Edmund; in chapter 22 Edmund replies to Mary Crawford's criticism that instead of planning to be a clergyman he should have gone into the army or into Parliament:

> as to my being in parliament, I believe I must wait till there is an especial assembly for the representation of younger sons who have little to live on.

With such references to Parliament we have a combination of absentee planter interest and power in Parliament where the outcome of further abolitionism would be decided. Additional details of Sotherton are forthcoming in Sir Thomas's prospective son-in-law being enthusiastic about improvements to his own estate in landscaping, perhaps by Humphrey Repton, the 'subject next his heart'. Such a description of a man engaged to be married comes as a surprise, and is suggestive of a love of power at the prospect of man's control over nature.

It was on the matter of cutting down the avenue of oaks at Sotherton that Fanny had been critical prior to the visit, in saying to Edmund 'Does it not make you think of Cowper?' and then quoting from lines 338–40 of Book I of *The Task*: 'Ye fallen avenues, once more I mourn your fate unmerited'. While at Sotherton, Fanny's view of proposed improvements to the grounds is upheld in the narrator's telling us of already existing 'sweets':

> the young people, meeting with an outward door, temptingly open on a flight of steps which led immediately to turf and shrubs, and all the sweets of pleasure-grounds, as by one impulse, one wish for air and liberty, all walked out.

There could be an inter-textual allusion in 'one wish for air and liberty' on the part of the younger generation in *Mansfield Park* to lines 40–1 of Book II of *The Task* concerning the Mansfield decision: 'Slaves cannot breathe in England; if their lungs Receive our air, that moment they are free'. The Sotherton garden context itself could prompt a link between Fanny's quotation beforehand from Book I, talk of improvements as in William Cowper's Book III entitled *The Garden* and possible allusion in the phrase 'air and liberty' to a linking passage from Cowper's Book II.[66] In *The Task* Book II there had been Cowper's celebrated rejoicing in what he takes to be freedom from slavery for anyone arriving on English soil, a reference to Lord Chief Justice Mansfield's decision of 1772 that has been variously interpreted.[67] The words spoken in the defence about arrival in England 'that moment they are free' are repeated verbatim by Cowper at line 41 of

Book II. Crucial would be Jane Austen's own perception of the significance of the Mansfield decision, if the same name is not mere coincidence. Thomas Clarkson in his 1808 *History* had described the upshot of the Mansfield decision as follows:

> The great and glorious result of the trial was, that as soon as ever any slave set his foot upon English territory, he became free ... The eloquence displayed on the side of liberty, was perhaps never exceeded on any occasion.

Clarkson says thereafter there was not the same confidence in advertising for return of runaway slaves who had been brought into the country.[68] Fanny's quoting from Cowper, in talking about the avenue of trees at Sotherton, is suggestive of Fanny's sympathies in the lead up to Sir Thomas's return and her questioning him about the slave trade. Cowper was so well-known for support of abolition that there would be ready association of ideas between Cowper and abolition on the part of contemporary readers.

The beauty of the Mansfield house and parkland being acknowledged by Fanny and loved by her does not endorse a continuance of the practice which has contributed to the family's overall income. The end need not justify the means. Whereas there is no denying the desirability of the wealth involved and the excellence of the architecture, arts and landscaping funded by it, there is nevertheless no automatic vindication of the means by which such well-being may have been brought about. As we see Fanny's love for the place, acknowledging the product but condemning the means would be relevant to financial questions implied in this novel. There is a redeeming of Mansfield Park itself by Fanny's love of it, as we see in chapter 37, when preparing to leave for Portsmouth:

> though going, as she did, willingly and eagerly, the last evening at Mansfield Park must still be wretchedness. Her heart was completely sad at parting. She had tears for every room in the house[69]

Ultimately it would be a subdued Sir Thomas who needs Fanny, before he can again enjoy Mansfield Park. By the time that the final outcome for Fanny and Edmund of living at the parsonage is brought about by Sir Thomas, influences have shifted. There is a reversal of values; not maintenance or restoring of values only but change in values that is brought about by the final chapter. It had been seen as a danger that the poor cousin might be romantically attached to one of his sons; now that is a necessity for Sir Thomas's well-being. Sir Thomas is not the only one to have been mistaken. The worldly-wise Mary Crawford, recommending a solution to Maria's problems in a remarriage but not taking into account her brother's refusal to marry Maria, had earlier in chapter 5 seen Tom as eligible:

with the advantage of being tied up from much gaming at present, by a promise
to his father, and of being Sir Thomas hereafter.

But she later overplays her hand, having transferred her sights from an
absent Tom to an impressionable Edmund, in expressing in a letter to
Fanny the hope that Tom's illness may result in his death leaving Edmund
as the heir, a calculatedness that is more chilling than anything her brother
comes out with. The black humour of the book emerges again here, in that
Mary's hopes for Tom's death echo Tom's earlier hopes for the clergyman
Dr Grant's death so that Edmund may be given the Mansfield Parsonage
living. Chapter 45 ends uncompromisingly, after Fanny receives the letter,
with Fanny's judgement about Mary: 'She had only learnt to think nothing
of consequence but money'.

In the final chapter we are told Sir Thomas is almost glad of the evil that
brought about the departure of Mrs Norris from Mansfield. He had resisted
Mrs Norris's wishing Maria to be reinstated at Mansfield, and there is
almost a touch of comedy in Mrs Norris's blaming the fact that Fanny is
again resident as the reason Sir Thomas will not agree to it. This detail can
bring out the realism of the novel that one of the basic things for any
person is residence somewhere. Where a home might be found is a recurring theme throughout all the novels, from the opening chapters of *Sense
and Sensibility* to the changing fortunes of the Elliot family in *Persuasion*. It
looks significant that the novel should end with emphasis on Mansfield
Park itself.[70] While in Portsmouth, once the news has got through to her of
Tom's illness, Fanny thinks of Cowper, this time quoting from his poem on
education *Tirocinium*, which was published along with *The Task*, and she
repeats to herself the same yearning of the schoolboy to go home. Back in
chapter 2, 'just ten years old' she had been 'longing for the home she had
left'. She now realizes that whereas she had thought of Portsmouth as
home, she is regarding Mansfield Park as home:

> the word had been very dear to her; and so it still was, but it must be applied to
> Mansfield. *That* was now the home. Portsmouth was Portsmouth; Mansfield was
> home.

What is interesting to me in exploration of possible abolitionist sentiment
in this novel is that Fanny's reference to Mansfield as home might bring to
mind Cowper's line in Book II that introduces his reference to Lord
Mansfield's decision, in which Cowper asks: 'We have no slaves at home –
Then why abroad?'. Could one regard Mansfield Park itself as being associated with what is acceptable so that it is standing in for an England where
slavery is not legally recognized? Chapter 45 has Fanny thinking:

> to have confinement, bad air, bad smells, substituted for liberty, freshness, fra-
> grance, and verdure... Could she have been at home

For Fanny, 'liberty' is at Mansfield not in Portsmouth. If that is so, much will depend on the outcome of the question-mark hanging over how the heir to Mansfield will conduct its affairs. There is realism over relative poverty in Fanny's environs in Portsmouth. There could here in the reference to air and liberty also be allusion to the sentiments expressed by the defence for Somersett: 'it has been asserted, and is now repeated by me, this air is too pure for a slave to breathe in: I trust, I shall not quit this court without certain conviction of the truth of that assertion'.[71] These are the words of Serjeant Davy on behalf of Somersett. When Lord Mansfield gives his Decision, the defence has the decision it wanted. The family of the Bertrams meanwhile undermines supposition that absenteeism is unproblematic, absenteeism being characteristic of English slave-owning families.

The text may work in three ways simultaneously, as a subversive indicator of inadequacy in an absentee planter family that confronts a pro-slavery audience, undermining confidence in their competence to rule; references to the poetry of Cowper through Fanny's quoting him that appeal to an anti-slavery audience by association of ideas with his abolitionism; and an ongoing story that can maintain interest long after Emancipation, a story of a young girl's inner struggles.[72] In the ongoing story, Fanny as teenager not only has to contend with the feelings held by Edmund for another woman. Before the news of Henry and Maria breaks, Fanny finds that report of her suitor Henry's flirting with the newly married Maria is mortifying to herself: 'She was mortified. She had thought better of him'. Then, after more news from Mary Crawford but before she knows about the adultery, in chapter 46 we read:

> She had begun to think he really loved her, and to fancy his affection for her something more than common – and his sister still said that he cared for nobody else.

After she learns of the adultery through the newspaper her father reads to her:

> Fanny seemed to herself never to have been shocked before... a man professing himself devoted, even *engaged*, to another

This follows the stress of her father having said:

> 'But by G – if she belonged to me, I'd give her the rope's end as long as I could stand over her. A little flogging for man and woman too, would be the best way of preventing such things.'

An echo of Mrs Norris's earlier 'I've been slaving myself till I can hardly stand' may be heard with the repetition of imagery of not being able to stand. The language of Fanny's father is less figurative, but both echo possible Antiguan plantation conditions, thought of which may have been brought to mind by Fanny's question about the slave trade.

If property in slaves remained buoyant, conditions in the real world could tally in the novel with a strain on the Antiguan resources deriving as much from Tom's financial demands as on anything else. Robin Blackburn finds that actual returns were still high notwithstanding problems:

> The problems of the Jamaican planters in the 1770s and 1780s led to a rising incidence of bankruptcy – figures that did much to persuade Lowell Ragatz and Eric Williams that the onset of West Indian decline should be traced to these years ... it paid the merchants to let the planters stand in the front line and bear the initial impact of risk. If they fell into ruin then the merchants took over, sometimes sharing ownership of a particular estate with other merchants or with the planter on a *contrat de liason* basis.

He goes on to say: 'as J.R. Ward and Seymour Drescher have shown, the British West Indian planters enjoyed great prosperity for nearly thirty years after 1790'.[73] Taking up this idea that prosperity was still to be had from the sugar plantations in the Caribbean, I think the novel may anticipate the so-called 'mighty experiment' upon the occasion of 1830s Emancipation, in which Adam Smith's 'prediction' that even outside Europe the servant could be more economical than the slave would be contemplated. It should be noted that even if this idea were in the wind, it would not follow that the author captured or wished to capture such an idea in her work. Nevertheless, sense would be made of the journey to Antigua, if Sir Thomas wanted to cover possibility of forthcoming emancipation and consequent need to adapt to a wage economy from a slave economy, necessitating an adequate cash-flow. The more the income to support Mansfield Park is thought to depend on Antigua, the more important forward planning would be for Sir Thomas.

The mechanics of hiring and firing servants in England is a topic considered by Fanny, as she converses with her mother in Portsmouth about difficulty in hanging on to servants at all, unlike the situation at Mansfield where, as Fanny recalls, an unsuitable servant may not have a contract renewed. Because Fanny muses about such contracts in England, the reader has a cue to compare and contrast with the set-up in Antigua. Entrepreneurs would be happy, in Robin Blackburn's terms, to relieve the likes of Sir Thomas of his investments if his cash flow should prove inadequate to meet a contingency of emancipation of slaves and a need to find minimal wages. The relevance of Tom's drain on cash is important in this context. Those with vested interests could be thinking through various scenarios. New conditions were encountered after abolition of the slave trade.

The insight of R.S. Neale writing on property and alienation in *Mansfield Park* has received acclaim.[74] Neale's is a Marxist critique and to my mind convincingly has Jane Austen taking a close look at property relations under

English law and the alienation brought about in England by property-related issues. He also queries whether, in the light of the numerous West Indian and Antigua references before Sir Thomas's return, the author would have known that, after the 1807 Abolition, Antigua exported slaves to other parts of the West Indies.[75] Neale concludes with a riveting challenge:

> Antigua *was* the occasion that triggered the fall from propriety of all the main characters in the novel ... unless one supposes that Jane Austen thought Antigua could be comprehended within a moral order different from the one with which she informs the rest of the novel, then it is not Jane Austen who is 'naked in the cold wind of casuistry', merely those of her critics who believe that while her head is in heaven her feet are not upon the ground, and whose placing of and judgement upon cultural productions leaves out the mode of production, and the codes and signals in which domination is expressed ... So I leave you with a question. Is it Jane Austen or Fanny Price who speaks in the last paragraph?

Neale relates property at home in England in *Mansfield Park* to other property in Antigua. Appropriate interpretation of the final paragraph of the novel may well reside with Neale to distinguish between the author and Fanny. What indeed could it mean in the final paragraph of *Mansfield Park* that the parsonage became:

> as dear to her heart, and as thoroughly perfect in her eyes, as everything else, within the view and patronage of Mansfield Park, had long been.

If it is Fanny's view, not Jane Austen's, in the last paragraph, there is the thought that whereas Jane Austen may find fault with the system, the over-simplicity of Fanny that has worried many critics, although forgiven by Jane Austen because of Fanny's inexperience, could not be condoned on the part of the more knowledgeable about property, on the part of those who should know better.

However, if it is the author's long view rather than Fanny's, it could be said that the notion of 'as thoroughly perfect in her eyes' is reminiscent of the ending of *The Task* in so far as there is the unusual notion of something's becoming 'perfect'. In Book VI, Cowper talks of predestination and gives it as his belief that the ultimate state of things will be a restoration for all to being perfect:

> Thus Heavenward all things tend. For all were once
> Perfect, and all must at length be restored.[76]

Support for this Universalism can be seen in the New Testament.[77] Jane Austen also speaks of restoring, beginning the final chapter by declaring an impatience to restore and to have done with all the rest. Rather like *A Midsummer Night's Dream*, in this text there is restoration but only after change. In upshot, a possibility here is that a theological Universalism expressed by Cowper is used as a model by Jane Austen for a secular counterpart, in which a future political set-up might be redeemed from condoning slavery to become a society that banishes chattel slavery. The very name *Mansfield Park* could suggest a park that symbolizes a paradise prepared to bear witness to the popular idea of the Mansfield Decision.[78] This would suggest a redeeming that is not, to use Tony Harrison's phrase in his poem *v.*,'an accident of meaning'. It could be said that this novel 'is named after its theme'.[79]

In the ending of the novel, there may also be a final link by the mention of 'patronage' with emphasis on the work of a resident priest and the theme of absenteeism. The point here could be to emphasize the need for residence for the proper ordering of affairs, with implied criticism of an absentee planter as a corollary of such concern. The term 'patronage' shows up in Johnson's *Dictionary* as concerned with protection and also as concerned with the provision of a benefice.[80] In the ending, the phrase 'within the view...of' looks ambiguous between looking at or looking from Mansfield Park. Either way, the overtones of 'view' with respect to what is within sight may subliminally suggest vindication of the existence of such an English estate but only as one that is cut down to size without reliance on plantation slavery for unlimited pleasures. This could be at once reassuring and reforming. Fanny's seal of approval for Mansfield Park may reassure that reform would not mean that all would be lost; such pragmatic reassurance had to be felt if Parliament were to be influenced to go further with the abolitionism that had already borne fruit in the 1807 legislation.

Significant terminology of 'judgement words' in this novel has been emphasized by literary critics.[81] Earlier, in chapter 3, depriving Edmund of the Mansfield living had been seen as a matter of Sir Thomas's conscience and is explained: 'he could not but feel it to be an act of injustice'. The serious tone of the language used is striking. In the previous chapter we had learnt: 'His eldest son was careless and extravagant, and had already given him much uneasiness'. In chapter 3, Sir Thomas had spoken to his son referring to the years ahead when his extravagance might result in real drawbacks for the younger son. The notions there of 'conscience' and 'injustice' are solemn in connection with these financial problems, and may also carry over in a reader's mind to all that Sir Thomas is coming to terms with in Antigua, which is money-related. The link with depriving Edmund is pivotal. The eldest son's extravagance had put at risk the younger son's inheritance. So, it could be inferred that profits from Antigua must also have gone to fund Tom's spending. It is possible that the running of Mansfield Park itself would be regarded as being funded from within its own resources, in a standard, traditional way, even though there could be a question arising from the description of it as newly built.[82] Sir Thomas's return saw him at work:

He had to reinstate himself in all the wonted concerns of his Mansfield life, to see his steward and his bailiff – to examine and compute.

Contemporary accounts books present the coupling of estate improvements to estate rentals, even where the owners enjoyed huge fortunes derived from West Indian property.[83] Nevertheless, additional expenditure on extravagance would be funded from the profits of the sugar plantation. Tom's extravagance and his gaming throw the family's lifestyle into disrepute and threaten the whole estate.

Is Tom's change of heart merely to be conducive to more prudence in looking after his own inheritance? It could be interpreted as such, which is hardly an abolitionist message. On the other hand, there is something destabilizing about the ease with which the propertied and their heirs can go off the rails, emphasizing that there is no absolute right to property. The last lines of the novel may cut down what can be approved for the future to a local set-up only. There would then be 'patronage' referring to the clerical living made available at Thornton Lacey and, secondly, the English domain 'within the view' of Mansfield Park. Money derived from property rights in Antigua has already by implication been squandered left, right and centre by Tom and also at Mansfield itself in a manner adding insult to injury when he disregards property rights at home.

The occurrence of men on their own being reported without female presence is striking. There is not only the example of Sir Thomas while in Antigua being reported as thinking alone about Maria's engagement and of Mr Rushworth as having 'the same interest' as himself, but earlier still there was conversation between men, Sir Thomas and his eldest son, with no female present to filter the male views. There is the further example on Sir Thomas's return. The detrimental nature of Tom's behaviour is brought out in a scene of comedy when Tom, having admitted to himself that there had been a breach of his father's rights in the use made of his own personal room during the playacting, arrives in the billiard room just in time to see the meeting on stage of a declaiming Mr Yates still practising his part and Sir Thomas stepping out of 'his own dear room' through the door that had been opened up by the play-actors' removal of a bookcase.

The great good humour of the absurdity of these proceedings could illustrate a fundamental point. Here, Tom stands condemned of having sat too lightly with respect to his father's personal property. That the heir to the Antigua estate should not respect property rights at home at a personal level is disturbing. It may make for an undermining of any claims that might be forthcoming amongst readers, from a pro-slavery lobby in the non-fictional world, that property rights in slaves in the colonies must be respected. It has been noted how in this scene, 'the head of the house' 'is confronted at the heart of his own terrain'.[84] Tom's mismanagement here touches Mansfield Park itself and not superficially; it touches on property.

In the final chapter although the details are brief they are specific about Tom:

> He was the better for ever for his illness. He had suffered, and he had learned to think ... He became what he ought to be, useful to his father, steady and quiet, and not living merely for himself. Here was comfort indeed!

The reader of the phrase 'not living merely for himself' is free to wonder whether the eldest son and heir might be more favourably disposed to future moves to overcome the guilt and misery that Clarkson had referred to in his *History* regarding the slave trade. Be that as it may, the 'comfort' Jane Austen exclaims over augments the earlier opening lines of the final chapter:

> Let other pens dwell on guilt and misery. I quit such odious subjects as soon as I can, impatient to restore every body, not greatly in fault themselves, to tolerable comfort, and to have done with all the rest.

There is parody of these opening sentences of the last chapter of *Mansfield Park* by Virginia Woolf.[85] Having said 'Orlando was a man till the age of thirty; when he became a woman and has remained so ever since', Virginia Woolf follows immediately with inter-textual reference to *Mansfield Park*: 'But let other pens treat of sex and sexuality; we quit such odious subjects as soon as we can'.

However, an heir who would have been in the future a selfish spend-thrift, careless of whether or not he is hypocritical about property rights, is banished by virtue of the quiet transformation of Tom that happens in the background, while the focus has been on the drama of Maria. The phrase 'useful to his father' is left indeterminate in that we do not know in what respect. I think that realism has been achieved by placing the change in Tom in the background, as happening while our attention is elsewhere with Maria. The force for the future is already subject to change within the narrative just because the eldest son's previous mode of living is changed 'for ever' by illness. As with Fanny's earlier question about the slave trade, the open-endedness of the possibilities invites thought.

There remains the earlier serious language of 'conscience' and 'injustice' as Sir Thomas thought about Tom's extravagance especially his gaming and debts and the potential loss to the younger son for a lifetime of more than half his intended income. That would bring into disrepute the power over the property that Tom can wield by one means or another. Not for nothing, as a recent publication has observed, that during the discussion between the young people over what play to put on, *The Heir at Law* is favoured by Tom with himself playing the lead role.[86] Terminology in the opening lines of the final chapter is suggestive. The terms 'guilt' and 'misery' will reappear in *Emma* as part of the dialogue on the slave trade, and a possible inter-textual reference to Clarkson on the slave trade is possible. The word 'odious' is interesting too as used by Jane Austen to characterise subjects dwelling on guilt and misery.

The word 'odious' is used by Lord Mansfield at the end of the Somersett case as he is about to deliver his Decision, as I quoted at the head of my own first chapter. The proceedings of the Somersett case make for such high drama that although knowing the outcome it is still possible to hold one's breath in the final summing up by Lord Mansfield as he moves to the last words revealing his decision for freedom. On the Somersett case, in the previous argumentation it had been mulled over under what circumstances James Somersett was first as a child sold in Africa and then via Virginia found himself eventually in England. What is described by Mansfield as odious is the state of slavery.[87] That is the final note, although earlier condemnation had been made in the course of the defence for Somersett, of the barbarity of the slave trade. Both slavery and the slave trade are referred to in the proceedings, which illustrates how abolition of the slave trade by the time of *Mansfield Park* would still leave an associated issue of slavery abroad as unresolved and as highlighted by the Mansfield Decision.

One critic puts it that the Mansfield Judgment of 1772 has 'become commonly accepted as the reason Austen titled this novel *Mansfield Park*'.[88] If this is a right and proper acceptance of the significance of the title, it would be appropriate to have echoes of Mansfield's summing up at the end of the court case echoed here as Jane Austen begins her own summing up in the last chapter. If terminology from the trial had been picked up by Jane Austen in her general reading, the term 'odious' at the beginning of her final chapter may signal that she had engaged in a critique of a slave-owning family, which is now seen to be going on to better things aided by principle. Their slave-owning status is noted again in the reference in the last chapter of the novel, in connection with the departure of Mrs Norris, to Sir Thomas's earlier 'return from Antigua'. A question left for the contemporary reader to ponder may be what action in Parliament Sir Thomas and his heir would take.

IV. The novel as subversive

To sum up, significant disadvantage, not profit only, accrues from one instance of absenteeism being compounded by another. Absenteeism has been shown to result in disastrous consequences for the Bertram family. Absenteeism was entailed by the continuance of slavery in the Colonies with owners preferring to live in England, whereas slavery was not an institution in Britain itself. It is likely that for contemporary readers there would be association of ideas between the 1772 Mansfield Decision and the title of the novel. Pointing in the direction of questions is the broaching of the issue of the slave trade by Fanny. This is done against a backdrop of coordinates of geographical space and of date time, the geographical background being given by the numerous references to Antigua and the West Indies. By the time Fanny reads copies of the *Quarterly Review*, prior to Sir Thomas's return from the West Indies, the British slave trade has been outlawed.

In the period after this first round of abolition, rather than being preached at in a strident voice, there is opportunity in this novel for a contemporary reader to think about what could be the best way forward in the real world, inspired by the change in the novel on Sir Thomas and his heir. The sombre ending of the novel may acknowledge that decisions had to be made in the real world, now that the slave trade had been banned, over whether amelioration of conditions for slaves was to be the way forward or whether emancipation should be envisaged. Sir Thomas may be a changed man after the vicissitudes falling on his family and young Tom may be changed 'for ever', but that would still leave the issue of future decision-making and links with Parliament, as matched in the real world, with an outcome hanging in the balance.

At this juncture, Jane Austen does not know what we know and, in the event, what her readers after 1833 would know. With her choice of plot and its geographical and date coordinates, she had written herself into one of the most distressing issues of the day. Having to end *Mansfield Park* with no knowledge of the future outcome could leave her and a concerned reader in a sober frame of mind. What may seem fleeting references to us now that could go unnoticed because our attention is more caught by all that is in the immediate foreground, could for the contemporary reader have been almost insistently obvious. In looking beyond the foreground of Mansfield Park, the more far-reaching view shows Antiguan and West Indian connections on a horizon. Until recently the more far-reaching view had dropped out of focus for her readers, but I think that until the Emancipation of the 1830s resolved the matter, the West Indian references in this novel would have been clear. We owe to Edward Said the insistent reminder that Jane Austen integrated geographical references.

However, Edward Said had supposed an earlier date for the absence of Sir Thomas. This has provoked others to reconsider her references to dates, and we hesitate now before accusing Jane Austen of anachronism in Fanny having Crabbe's *Tales* of 1812 to read.[89] That a reference to the 1812 *Tales* interferes with a critic's favoured time scale is more likely now to make us query that critic's theory. Even if reference to the *Tales* were to be discounted as a printer's error for earlier Crabbe publications, there is still the reference to *Quarterly Reviews*, which would bring the return of Sir Thomas up to at least 1809. Fanny would be in tune with the readership over the outlawing of the slave trade. The contemporary readership itself was well-primed by the laws of their land that slave trading as since 1811 was a felony. As far as I can see, there remains a genuine puzzle about the internal chronology, as Chapman explained, that options are cut down by authorial or narrator's stipulation of the day of the ball being on Thursday 22 December and the following Easter being late. My own view is that the puzzle flags attention, which is to be associated with ongoing topicality of the slavery issue.

In addition to such detail in the novel, there is Jane Austen's remark in an 1813 letter to Cassandra, when she says that a 'said he' or a 'said she' would sometimes make the by now published *Pride and Prejudice* dialogue clearer. She remarks in the context of clarity in writing in what Chapman calls a parody of the ending of Scott's *Marmion*:

> I do not write for such dull elves as have not a great deal of ingenuity themselves.

I think this could in addition indicate that she would expect her friends and relatives to keep their wits about them. Leaving something for posterity to read may also be envisaged.

A contemporary reader not already won over to what would be the second stage of abolition could well have felt challenged by destabilizing ideas when confronted by absenteeism. For such contemporary readership, such questioning on a topic related to a status quo would carry with it the possibility of that questioning having a subversive effect. I conclude that *Mansfield Park* is subversive, because through its complex theme of absenteeism it places the then status quo of chattel slavery under a spotlight.

3
Emma: Autonomy and Abolition

'Excuse me, ma'am, but this is by no means my intention; I make no enquiry myself, and should be sorry to have any made by my friends. When I am quite determined as to the time, I am not at all afraid of being long unemployed. There are places in town, offices, where inquiry would soon produce something – Offices for the sale – not quite of human flesh – but of human intellect.'

'Oh! my dear, human flesh! You quite shock me; if you mean a fling at the slave-trade, I assure you Mr Suckling was always rather a friend to the abolition.'

'I did not mean, I was not thinking of the slave-trade', replied Jane; 'governess–trade, I assure you, was all that I had in view; widely different certainly as to the guilt of those who carry it on; but as to the greater misery of the victims, I do not know where it lies. But I only mean to say that there are advertising offices, and that by applying to them I should have no doubt of very soon meeting with something that would do.'

'Something that would do!' repeated Mrs Elton.

Emma, chapter 35

Introduction

This novel uses satire to such effect that by the end Mrs Elton and Mr Suckling's estate Maple Grove can feature in the last paragraph as comic backdrop. The sombre issue of the slave trade and its outcome is integrated in the narrative because the dialogue raising the issue is linked with Mrs Elton and Maple Grove. Both Mrs Elton and Maple Grove are ridiculed and their being targets of satire belittles their status as worthy models to follow in society. The link with the slave trade is via Mr Suckling as the owner of Maple Grove and brother-in law of Mrs Elton. Mr Suckling 'was always rather a friend to the abolition'. In addition to their being discredited, there is the opportunity to consider that just as Mrs Elton is not much of a friend to Jane Fairfax so Mr Suckling may not be much of a friend to the abolition. The highlights of comedy make for seeing Mrs Elton and Maple Grove as not only uncaring but also incompetent. This satire is at the heart of both content and structure, with scenes such as Mrs Elton's strawberry-picking establishing her as a comic figure. Structurally, Maple Grove is emphasized again in the concluding paragraph of the novel. The values of Maple Grove have lost credibility and are by the end presented as not worthy of imitation.

Linking the narrative with contemporary life, we could contemplate the situation confronting true friends of abolition, that prohibition of the British Slave Trade in 1807 does not necessarily ensure that support for the abolition of the institution of slavery itself will be forthcoming. Howard Temperley quotes Thomas Clarkson as having said in his 1808 *History* that aiming at the abolition of the slave trade 'they were laying the axe at the very root' and notes that:

> the arguments being used to discredit the one could also be used (as they later were) to discredit the other. To this extent the position from which the second stage of the assault would be launched was already being prepared. Nevertheless, the fact remains that so long as the struggle over the trade continued, little thought was given to the practical problems of coping with slavery itself.[1]

Looking at the dialogue one can initially be struck by the solemnity of the terms 'guilt', 'misery', 'victims'. But it is the import of the individual statements in which these three terms occur and the cumulative argument produced that is of more significance. The argument could be said to proceed as follows with three initial premises:

- If these are the only choices and a choice is to be made, then the sale of human intellect is to be preferred to the sale of whatever may be meant by human flesh. (This is the force of 'not quite'.)
- The slave trade is a guilty one, whereas governess-trade is not, or not particularly, however otherwise undesirable. (One has had to work this out as a consequence of the two trades being 'widely different certainly as to the guilt of those who carry it on'.)
- Where the greater misery for the victims lies between the two trades, Jane Fairfax does not know.
- Therefore, from the second and third premise the first conclusion is that even if governess-trade makes as much misery for its victims there is less guilt on the part of those who carry it on than there is on the part of those who carry on the slave trade.
- The second conclusion, drawn from the third premise, is that the slave trade is a misery-producing one for its victims.
- Therefore, finally, following from both the first and second conclusions, the final conclusion is that there is guilt on the part of those who carry on the slave trade and it is a trade which is misery-producing for its victims.

I. Marriage and sexuality

Supposing there to be an initial comparison in the dialogue, it could be seen in the following light. Jane Fairfax at first compares actual alternatives facing her: on the one hand 'the sale – not quite of human flesh', and on the other hand the sale of 'human intellect'. A celebration of a marriage is the occasion, with the vicar Mr Elton and his new bride the guests of honour, at Emma's invitation. Marriage has been an issue in the last year for all four women present during the dialogue: two of the women, Mrs Elton and Emma's former governess now Mrs Weston, have married; the other two have attended a marriage ceremony, Emma her governess's and Jane Fairfax her childhood friend's. All four will then be familiar with the terminology of 'one flesh', which derives of course from the Genesis Creation story of Eve as a companion for Adam. Importantly, it is a phrase used by St Paul in the Letter to the Ephesians; the passage is printed in the *Book of Common Prayer* to be read at the Marriage Ceremony if there is no sermon.

Matrimony and related sexual matters could be freely spoken of by the four women alone together in the drawing room while the men are still in the dining room. Marriage and becoming a governess will be contrasted in the final dénouement of the overall plot which is precipitated in part by Jane Fairfax electing to become a governess rather than to risk a dubious marriage of apparently equivocal affection, or to return as she could to her home in London with the Campbells, on their return from Ireland, where as a reader knows by this stage her sheer beauty, elegance and accomplishments could only attract attention which would make marrying for money a strong possibility for her. My first suggestion then is of an association of ideas between 'human flesh' and 'one flesh', an association entirely bypassed by Mrs Elton in her response.

But there may be no such formal comparison. Having said 'There are places in town', Jane Fairfax continues with what could be seen as a correction in the word 'offices', and the phrase 'not quite of human flesh' could then be understood as specifying what is available for sale at the 'places in town'. Reading the sentence in this way would explain why she subsequently says 'governess-trade, I assure you, was all that I had in view'. If we take her word for it and the 'I assure you' seems like an endorsement, she only had one thing in mind, and was not setting out to make any comparison. The overtones of a phrase like 'places in town' might be viewed as having been seen by her as soon as she had uttered it, and, possibly riled by the amusement just expressed at her lack of experience, she might rather wittily qualify the notion of 'the sale' of 'human intellect'. In addition on Jane Fairfax's part to marrying for money there can be another reading of her gaining resources for the period after Mr and Mrs Campbell die when she would be without a home and upkeep, their assets intended to be inherited by their now married daughter with whom she as an orphan has been brought up, a related idea of becoming the mistress of a wealthy admirer.

Emma had already in chapter 27 put into our minds the risk of irregular goings-on, with her fanciful speculations which she has even voiced to Frank Churchill after the costly gift of the piano arrives for Jane Fairfax, a point on which, not too surprisingly:

> [Emma] was not quite easy. She doubted whether she had not transgressed the duty of woman by woman, in betraying her suspicions of Jane Fairfax's feelings to Frank Churchill. It was hardly right; but it had been so strong an idea, that it would escape her, and his submission to all that she told, was a compliment to her penetration which made it difficult for her to be quite certain that she ought to have held her tongue.

Once the conundrum of the gift of a piano has been cleared up, we realize that Frank would probably have told Jane Fairfax the next morning on his visit to the Bates about Emma's speculations. This, in addition to being irritated by Mrs Elton's saying 'Your inexperience really amuses me!' just prior to the dialogue on the slave trade, might trigger the voicing of such an option. The sort of valuable jewellery given to Jane Fairfax on her marriage might instead have been acquired as assets by encouraging an admirer in London or in the highly fashionable resort in Dorset, frequented by George III for his health, which she has visited, a cosmopolitan experience that is emphasized by the reference twice to the dramatic turn of events in Weymouth of her being saved from being swept from a boating party into the sea. Of course, 'places in town' where 'human flesh' is sold could involve her with more than one admirer. This is presumably the thought of those who have seen a possible reference here to prostitution.[2]

There is an even more straightforward use of association of ideas with the phrase 'one flesh', whereby Jane Fairfax may have indicated that she would have to be on her guard once in a post against being approached by a rake. Earlier novels by women writers had involved such unwelcome attentions.[3] The remark that follows, about preferring not to be in a rich family but merely in that of a gentleman, would enforce the notion of her being aware of potential nuisance in rich households.[4]

If Jane Fairfax plays with the phrase 'one flesh' as associated with marriage, she can also be seen as chiding Mrs Elton for, at no stage, ever regarding her as having any marital prospects. This would suggest an unwitting testimony on the new bride's part that her money has played a key part in her marriage as indeed we have already gathered is certainly the case. So there is a good reason why Mrs Elton could not easily take up any possible reference to marrying for money. We have learned in chapter 22 of Mr Elton that:

the lady had been so easily impressed – so sweetly disposed – had in short, to use a most intelligible phrase, been so very ready to have him, that vanity and prudence were equally contented.

It is one thing for Mr Elton to be able now three months later to have a carriage, like the sheepskin–lined one he had hankered after on the previous Christmas Eve when he had proposed to Emma, but not the sort of thing to be alluded to by the bride who has made it possible, in any conversation with Jane Fairfax about the respective merits of earning one's living or marrying for money.

Mrs Elton's response interpreting 'human flesh' as a reference to the slave trade is to ascribe to Jane Fairfax a 'fling' against the slave trade. Douglas Jefferson sums this up succinctly by observing that Mrs Elton's language at this stage indicates that all is not well with her family connection on this matter.[5] And this is consistent with what we have already been told in chapter 22 about her being:

> the youngest of the two daughters of a Bristol – merchant, of course, he must be called ... Bristol was her home, the very heart of Bristol ...

Bristol had been a major port for the slave trade.[6] In her rejoinder Mrs Elton risks raising questions in the listener's mind as to where her brother-in-law's money has come from for funding the aptly-named Maple Grove, an estate near Bristol which, in the chapter following the dialogue, she is to observe, in conversation with Mr Weston, has: 'Such an immense plantation all round it! You seem shut out from everything'.[7] This is suggestive of an unwitting testimony on Mrs Elton's part to an acquisition costing too high a price in some other way.

There is much comic effect, all at her own expense, created by Mrs Elton's conversations during the rest of that evening, including her inept claim that being from 'the old established families' the brother-in-law is someone:

> who has been eleven years a resident at Maple Grove and whose father had it before him – I believe, at least – I am almost sure that old Mr. Suckling had completed the purchase before his death

Of newcomers from Birmingham, Mrs Elton declares 'how they got their fortune nobody knows', adding:

> One has not great hopes from Birmingham. I always say there is something direful in the sound.[8]

But a reader of Thomas Clarkson, as Jane Austen apparently was, would be in a position to know that Birmingham had been one of the towns visited by him on his journeys throughout Britain, engaged in to work for opposition in Parliamentary circles to the slave trade, and that he had spoken of how those he met in Birmingham threw full support behind the campaign for abolition. Doubtless an opposing view could also have been heard, from gun manufacturers, whose products were used in exchange for slaves on the West African coast.[9] Following the 1807 prohibition of the British Slave Trade, Clarkson's *History* would be a major source on the issue of slavery and the slave trade for contemporaries. It may be the 1808 *History* that Jane Austen had in mind in the letter to her sister which mentions Clarkson.

The impact of the dialogue within the narrative is amplified by satire continuing throughout at Maple Grove's and Mrs Elton's expense on issues of money, marriage and property. In the history of the abolition of the British institution of slavery, money and property were of central importance.[10] The later Abolition of Slavery in 1833 was made possible in part by an accompanying scheme for a Compensation Fund of £20 million to pay out, for example, about £11,000 to the likes of the Bishop of Exeter for the loss of property in the form of slaves in the West Indies.[11] At the time, abolitionists were dismayed at this compensation since they regarded it as unjustified for slave-owners to be paid to stop something that they ought not to have done in the first place.[12] Clearly the whole of the Church of England was not behind the Evangelicals in their continued campaign on behalf of slaves after 1807, and it is probably significant that Mrs Elton as the vicar's wife and her husband of presumed like-mindedness are the targets of sharp ridicule, that they are the ones who do not learn from their blindness and blunders in the course of the novel, unlike Emma, who by chapter 54 can reply to Mr Knightley's saying 'You are materially changed' to acknowledge: 'I hope so – for at that time I was a fool'.

The impact of the dialogue is further amplified by the continuously occurring notion of a friend. In the dialogue itself, interference is heralded by what friends would 'require', Jane Fairfax preferring no inquiry to be made by her friends. The notion of a 'friend' is to recur throughout and the vagaries of friendship be explored as an essential part of Emma's progress as well as of Mrs Elton's befriending of Jane Fairfax, so that at the end we can consider that just as Mrs Elton was not much of a friend to Jane Fairfax, so might Mr Suckling not have been much of 'a friend to the abolition'.

Meanwhile 'Jane Fairfax had yet her bread to earn' as we learn in chapter 20. On this Adam Smith-sounding note, it would appear she is not in the market for a monied husband regardless of affection. Her view would appear to be more that of Jane Austen's own as expressed in a letter of advice to her niece Fanny during the same year as the writing of the novel: 'Anything is to be preferred or endured rather than marrying without Affection'.[13] In chapter 48, after Mrs Weston relates that Jane Fairfax has been in a 'state of perpetual suffering' since entering on a secret engagement, Emma concludes 'it must have been from attachment only, that she could be led to form the engagement'. In chapter 49, Mr Knightley has no doubts on the point. On the secret engagement now made public, he speaks of 'disinterested love, for Jane Fairfax's character vouches for her disinterestedness' and of:

> equality in every point but one – and that one, since the purity of her heart is not to be doubted, such as must increase his felicity, for it will be his to bestow the only advantages she wants. – A man would always wish to give a woman a better home than the one he takes her from; and he who can do it, where there is no doubt of *her* regard, must, I think, be the happiest of mortals.

That the impoverished Jane Fairfax had agreed to a governess post, after breaking her secret engagement, which she concludes after a lovers' quarrel is no longer viable, puts into effect the force of 'not quite' if we think in terms of the phrase 'one flesh' when interpreting her reference to 'human flesh'. The sale of human intellect would be 'not quite' as bad as the sale of human flesh. To marry for money ('the wickedest thing in existence' as Catherine Morland puts it in *Northanger Abbey* in chapter 15) is therefore not a course of action Jane Fairfax is prepared to countenance.

Surprise that there should apparently be protest at doing the job of a governess when it was one of the few professions open to women has been expressed, but if the initial comparison was with marrying for money it need not have included the comparison introduced by Mrs Elton in her outburst about the slave trade and so need not have sounded so anguished a protest.[14] In any case, being a victim of 'governess-trade' does not so much describe carrying out the duties of a governess as applying at the 'Offices for the sale...advertising offices' and so being a victim of those who trade in posts. In terms which bear out Emma having surmised in the chapter before the dinner party that Mrs Elton would be 'continually insulting [Jane] ... with praise, encouragement and offers of service', this trading is immediately parodied during the continuation of the dialogue by Mrs Elton's:

> Your musical knowledge alone would entitle you to name your own terms, have as many rooms as you like, and mix in the family as much as you chose; – that is – I do not know – if you knew the harp, you might do all that, I am very sure; but you sing as well as play; – yes, I really believe you might, even without the harp, stipulate for what you chose.

The commerce ridiculed is of a different nature from that conducted by all and sundry at Ford's shop.[15]

Although the dialogue can be taken to be protest about governessing, it is not confirmed as such, independently of Emma's assumptions and Jane Fairfax's teenage horror at the thought. This has been described earlier in chapter 20, but in its extreme it is gently mocked as a vision of her resolve:

at one-and-twenty to complete the sacrifice, and retire from all the pleasures of life, of rational intercourse, equal society, peace and hope, to penance and mortification for ever.

The mention here of 'sacrifice' prefigures the term 'victim' in the dialogue, leading us to hear the dialogue with the same ambivalent attitude as Emma to being a governess. By contrast, however, there is a career for Emma's former governess, followed, as the novel opens, by her marrying, settling in her own home, and within the year we see her happiness with her baby. Teaching as a job in Highbury does not seem to be such a bad deal either, and in the third chapter there is the idyllic description of Mrs Goddard's school:

she had an ample house and garden, gave the children plenty of wholesome food, let them run about a great deal in the summer, and in winter dressed their chilblains with her own hands.

Protest expressed could as well be at Mrs Elton's insistence on doing what Jane Fairfax has planned to arrange when the time is right at the 'advertising offices', and so be a protest at Mrs Elton's presumption in trying to take matters out of Jane Fairfax's hands. She had said: 'When I am quite determined as to the time, I am not at all afraid of being long unemployed'. Here it is not just that she knows more about 'governess-trade' than Mrs Elton, it turning out on her later accepting a post, in chapter 44, that it has to be taken up 'Within a fortnight'. Jane Fairfax treasures her autonomy.[16]

As the writing of the novel is completed seven years have elapsed, seeing the long war with France coming to an end, since abolition by Britain of its slave trade.[17] The novel was written during 1814, a year that saw considerable petitioning of Parliament to pressure other European Powers to end their slave trades.[18] This 1814 flurry of anti-slave trade activity could be the contemporary background to the sequence 'if you mean a fling at the slave trade'. There is levity in the terminology of a 'fling'.[19] Mrs Elton appears to assume the appropriateness of a bland use of the terminology of slavery to make comparison with a post as a governess. Mr Elton's usage had been similarly bland in chapter 13 ushering in the climax on Christmas Eve of Volume One. In reply to John Knightley saying 'I know nothing of the large parties of London, sir – I never dine with any body', Mr Elton had replied:

'Indeed!' (in a tone of wonder and pity), 'I had no idea that the law had been so great a slavery.'

Once the riddle of Jane Fairfax's behaviour is explained and it is realized that at the time of the dialogue she did not need after all to speak of herself as a victim of governess-trade, a contemporary reader before 1833 might be prompted to consider in a more serious frame of mind a link between the prohibited slave trade and the continuing institution of slavery, prompted by the considerations raised in the dialogue where Jane Fairfax has broken through hackneyed use of slave imagery to literal, direct comparisons with unexpected implications.

II. Analysing the dialogue on the slave trade

So far I have suggested that the 'sale' of 'human flesh' is a reference to marrying for money and related sexual matters. This means that the sale of human intellect is not initially compared by Jane Fairfax with the slave trade in her reference to:

Offices for the sale – not quite of human flesh – but of human intellect ...

Turning now towards the response to Mrs Elton's outburst on the slave trade, Jane Fairfax distances herself from Mrs Elton; her response seems temperate, in tune with the use of 'ma'am' earlier and contrasts in this respect with Mrs Elton's own language with the two exclamation marks and the 'You quite shock me'. Initially Jane Fairfax tries to fend off Mrs Elton's looking for a 'situation' for her as had been very clearly shown by the earlier 'Excuse me' which challenged Mrs Elton's previous statement: 'we must begin enquiring directly'. It makes for a confrontational dialogue with Jane Fairfax exercising her own autonomy. Jane Fairfax's coolness also has the effect of warding off sentimentality and sensationalism on the issue of the slave trade.

When Mrs Elton claims 'Mr Suckling was always rather a friend to the abolition', quite what did she mean? The word 'always' indicates she suggests her brother-in law was in favour of abolition before the change in the law. Jane Fairfax could well think Mrs Elton has climbed on a moral bandwagon after it is the socially acceptable thing to do. Mrs Elton's phrase with a definite article suggests that 'the abolition' is a one-off event, and the simple past tense 'was' rather than saying 'has been' implies that he is not necessarily now any sort of a friend to abolition of the continuing institution of slavery.[20] It may be significant that Mr Suckling was spoken of as a friend 'to' rather than 'of' the abolition, the preposition actually used being suggestive of conferring a favour, and for the notion of 'rather' we could substitute 'in some degree' as the most appropriate of dictionary entries for 'rather'.

Jane Fairfax emphasizes that it was not the slave trade but 'governess-trade' that she had in mind in first observing that offices were in town for the sale of 'human intellect'. 'I did not mean, I was not thinking of the slave trade' makes the denial twice, and could also indicate a 'neither ...

nor' assertion in which if one had posited a difference between what she was thinking about and what her words meant, then in both cases 'replied Jane; "governess-trade, I assure you, was all that I had in view"'. Her repetition of Mrs Elton's words 'I assure you' indicate her staking a claim to be believed as Mrs Elton had. After Mrs Elton's introduction of the slave trade, Jane Fairfax refers to 'governess-trade' indicating trading in governess posts. She does not use a definite article before the phrase here which she would have needed to if she had referred to doing the job of governess. The authorial focus of the dialogue shifts to the slave trade by the discussion being in terms of trading, a reference which had already been introduced by the reference to offices where inquiry could be made.

Having emphatically denied that reference to the slave trade was her own original meaning, Jane Fairfax confronts what Mrs Elton has said, and in her own comments uses terminology that is reminiscent of Clarkson's *History*:

> Are [our feelings] not more or less elevated as the evil under our contemplation has been more or less productive of misery, or more or less productive of guilt?.[21]

Jane Fairfax continues:

> widely different certainly as to the guilt of those who carry it on...

She can say 'certainly' with confidence in observing that the guilt is 'widely different'. The inference is that there is guilt on the part of those who carry on the slave trade. The word 'certainly', however, may not owe solely to its being a factual matter of what is now against the law. Jane Fairfax qualifies 'guilt' not just as 'different', which might have yielded only that unlike 'governess-trade' the slave trade is against the law. The slave trade is described as 'widely different'.[22] This suggests the guilt to be of the sort that can be measured on a continuum which would mean that it is not a matter of whether a practice is or is not against the law, but rather of its being morally wrong or indeed rightly against the law. Mrs Elton had left it quite open whether there had been such guilt on the part of the slave trade.

We could, notwithstanding, try to take 'widely different' as indicating instead that the slave trade is very different merely in now being against the law, and so as a precursor to nevertheless protesting on behalf of the plight of governesses. But such a plight would have to be understood as residing in being traded, not in doing the job. That is because of the reference to 'those who carry it on' which could not refer to the victims of the guilt, and in the case of governesses would have to refer to those who offer posts at 'places in town, offices'. This is apart from her having referred to 'governess-trade' as all that she had in view, which I read as also a reference to trading in jobs not to doing the job of governess. To try to take Jane

Fairfax's comparison as pleading the cause of the governess would not yield protest about carrying *out* a job of a governess, but protest over becoming a victim of those carrying *on* the trading of governess posts, a protest about being treated as a trading article of commerce.

There is also suggestiveness about 'those who carry it on'. In referring to the perpetrators in the case of the slave trade it could mean carrying on now as before in the case of those flouting the 1807 prohibition. There could then be a possible allusion to the 1811 legislation introducing stiffer penalties for evaders of the prohibition.[23] But there is the possible overtone of 'going further' in the case of those who look forward to continuing the enslavement of the victims and carrying that on through natural reproduction and selling on. Jane Fairfax continues:

> but as to the greater misery of the victims, I do not know where it lies...

This reinforces that she had not originally been speaking about the slave trade, as she is not prepared to be drawn into grading in the context of the slave trade. She could not at first have been speaking of the slave trade because what she says now does not bear out the earlier readiness to grade implicit in 'not quite of human flesh'. That Jane Fairfax is indeed willing to measure when she thinks it appropriate is demonstrated moments later. Mrs Elton declares she is determined to find her a post where she will be 'delightfully, honourably and comfortably settled'. Jane Fairfax dryly replies that Mrs Elton may well class the delight, the honour and the comfort together as 'they are pretty sure to be equal'.

There is an essential link made by the conjunction 'but' which is in this case logically equivalent to 'and', so that what comes before and what comes after the word 'but' are understood as standing together as two true statements making up one complex true statement in Jane Fairfax's judgement. This ensures that the big difference in terms of guilt is affirmed by her because it is not superseded. Syntactic structure is suggestive too, with the 'as to' in the first sequence being echoed in the sequence that follows by a further 'as to' so that we read '...as to ...but as to...' as a composite statement. Each of the two sequences gains its full force only from the comparison with the other contrasting sequence. The word 'but' is also used simultaneously in the sense of 'even though' to mark a contrast to the considerable difference in guilt of the trading, indicating that one could nevertheless draw a likeness between the victims. One way in which they could be directly compared is in their wishing not to be treated as a commodity. Such an identifying would presuppose their common humanity.

Jane Fairfax does not need to grade whose misery is greater in order to condemn the continuing practice of chattel slavery, because the condemnation has been achieved by the combination of propositions that the slave trade is a guilty trade and that its victims are in misery. Just in so far as there remain victims from the slave trade in misery, so is guilt still accruing to the slave trade through maintenance of the status quo of chattel slavery.

The term 'misery' is an evocative term and carries its own evaluative message. Jane Fairfax had been described as having 'the fortitude of a devoted noviciate' in chapter 20 and so of someone entering a nunnery for life unwillingly. Such a scenario is understandably a nullification of all that she would wish for. There is a reminder of this in her looking upset on the same evening as the dialogue, just before dinner, after an old friend, John Knightley from London, apparently not associating her with the job of a governess, expresses his hope of seeing her in due course, like himself, happily married with a family. Perhaps the main feature to note is that there is, as far as I can see, an inescapable presupposition on Jane Fairfax's part that there is misery on the part of victims of the slave trade. Jane Fairfax presupposes that there is misery when she uses the phrase 'as to the greater misery'. Concerning victims of the slave trade there had been arguments that those taken into slavery were better off than those who remained in Africa, than an English peasant, or than a soldier in the Army being disciplined, and these arguments would be urged yet again against abolition of the institution of slavery. These comparisons had been meticulously addressed and opposed by Clarkson in his earlier 1786 *Essay* on the subject of slavery when he stressed the slaves' lack of autonomy.

Jane Fairfax also presupposes that there is a fact of the matter, that there is something to know when she says '... I do not know'. Where the greater misery of the victims lies is a matter for judgement not merely for feeling and imagination, let alone for individual prejudices. Johnson in his anti-slavery views had been accused of prejudice by Boswell in his *Life of Johnson*. Talk of a fling against the slave trade sounds as if Mrs Elton could think it a matter of opinion only where the greater misery lies.

Jane Fairfax speaks of 'victims' – an evocative term which would also have intended evaluative overtones. With respect to the slave trade, it seems to reinforce the term 'guilt'. Nor is it a first-person report, for citing 'the victims' in the third-person plural introduces a note not only of distancing but also of objectivity, also emphasized by the vocabulary of 'I do not know' with its implicit reliance on standards of verification in the use of the word 'know', an objectivity lacking in Mrs Elton's contrasting subjective vocabulary of 'a fling'. The claim 'I do not know' could also be seen as a way of closing ranks, of solidarity between victims, challenging whether Mrs Elton is well able to judge.

If Mrs Elton is herself not in favour of abolition of slavery, what sort of possibility might be ruled out for her in Jane Fairfax's refusal to grade? Mrs Elton could otherwise have agreed to greater misery being claimed for slaves and graciously hasten to speak of ameliorating their condition, just as she is trying to with Jane Fairfax's situation. Amelioration of conditions was a strategy to be used by both abolitionists and non-abolitionists: 'The amelioration of conditions would, in the long run, benefit the owner as much as the slave' is Howard Temperley's rendering of Hansard for 15 May 1823.[24] This was suggested by an abolitionist. The year 1815 was to see talk in Parliament of how conditions could be improved for slaves, and the Colonies be recommended to promote the comfort and happiness of the slaves.[25] But to try to lessen misery by amelioration of conditions for slaves would leave untouched a major source of misery, the victims' lack of freedom. William Law Mathieson cites Hansard in 1816 in saying:

> Wilberforce complained that people wished only to be assured that the slaves were well treated, a question equally appropriate to cattle, and were too often blind or indifferent to their social condition.[26]

Acknowledging greater suffering on the part of slaves could have invited a response in terms of amelioration, risking deflecting the concern of abolitionists who stressed a need for human autonomy.

Mrs Elton could alternatively have agreed if Jane Fairfax had claimed greater misery on the grounds of a well-educated sensibility. But there is no place in Jane Fairfax's direct comparison with the victims of the slave trade for the sort of analogy tacit in other work of the period. No analogy is implicit in what Jane Fairfax declares, as by contrast it is in chapter 45 by Mr Woodhouse when on learning that she had engaged to go to Mrs Smallridge's as governess, he assures Emma that 'she is going to be to this new lady what Miss Taylor was to us'. That might have been well-meaning on Mr Woodhouse's part, but it begged a question as to the nature of the second term of the analogy, the circumstances at Mrs Smallridge's. Jeremy Bentham's sensitive exploration of attempts to weigh up degrees of happiness or misery for his utilitarianism had tried to take into account the varying sensibility of different individuals to comparable situations.[27] But a danger for an abolitionist of placing reliance on Bentham's attention to differing sensibilities could be that non-abolitionists might misuse it in being dismissive of posited greater suffering on the part of slaves on grounds of presumed diminished sensibility. Because she has refused to grade, such dismissiveness is not invited by Jane Fairfax. Refusing to grade, on the one hand, avoids the potentially diversionary tactic of amelioration, and, on the other hand, avoids potentially belittling analogy derived from demands of sensibility.

Jane Fairfax's answer 'as to...but as to' responds to Mrs Elton for a second time in terms which Mrs Elton cannot easily follow up without compromising her own position. The first time she may not have wanted to talk about the utility of money in matrimonial prospects; this time, if Mrs Elton is indeed regarded as pro-slavery, Jane Fairfax's reply in terms of not grading, with its implication of a parity, most likely with respect to targeting human autonomy, certainly with respect to their being fellow human beings, would leave Mrs Elton without a ready rejoinder.

It is tempting to see any implied plea for autonomy for victims of the slave trade as unconnected with a second implied plea about the moral status of the money involved in households such as Maple Grove, which may be seen as in contrast to Donwell Abbey where it seems to me a remark of Adam Smith's is illustrated. For Adam Smith, in contrast to a slave, a freeman has 'attachment to his master's interest'.[28] This is very near the description of William Larkin and Mrs Hodges in chapter 27.

The second implied point takes up the threads in the novel of money and property, and the fact that no hint is made of the origins of the Woodhouse wealth could be taken as suggestive that the hints about Mrs Elton's background and Maple Grove are indeed intended to be assessed by the reader.[29] However, these two points though separable are intimately related. A concern over autonomy could well be why it matters that Mr Suckling at Maple Grove may think of the abolition issue as in the past. So, since Maple Grove and Mrs Elton do not come over as very attractive, what they stand for, with respect to not necessarily supporting abolition of slavery, is degraded. Maple Grove on the one hand is shown as irrelevant to the real concerns of the people of Highbury. By chapter 42 we learn that:

> After being long fed with hopes of a speedy visit from Mr and Mrs Suckling, the Highbury world were obliged to endure the mortification of hearing that they could not possibly come till the autumn.

On the other hand, there is sufficient reference to Maple Grove to ensure we do not forget it, to the extent of its providing the sharp edge to the sunlit ending of the novel, the values of Mrs Elton and Maple Grove making the background contrast in all three sentences of the concluding paragraph.

III. The twist in the plot and the riddle of Jane Fairfax

That Jane Austen endorses Jane Fairfax's attitude as over against Mrs Elton's is evidenced abundantly in the text. The dialogue is flanked by indicators. Initially, 'If Jane repressed her for a little time, she soon began again...' and finally, 'In this style she ran on; never thoroughly stopped by any thing till Mr Woodhouse came into the room; her vanity had then a change of object'. The new bride, the proper hub of attention, goes on to alienate fellow guests and 'was wanting notice, which nobody had inclination to pay' during that evening, ending with the observation: 'Mr Knightley seemed to be trying not to smile; and succeeded without difficulty, upon Mrs. Elton's beginning to talk to him'. This may be seen not as gratuitous ridicule of Mrs Elton but as seriously backing up the issues raised in the dialogue. Thus ends the Second Volume, not to Mrs Elton's credit, the dialogue placed in a pivotal position in the middle of the three concluding chapters devoted to the evening of this dinner party. Indeed the high spirits of the end of the book in the final lines of Volume Three owe much of their delight and humour to the inability of Mrs Elton and her sister Selina at Maple Grove to see events in the same light as do the 'small band of true friends'.

The final Third Volume goes on to see Mrs Elton exposed as herself not a true friend of Jane Fairfax. There is cause to wonder at the start of the ball at the Crown, in chapter 38, at her 'What a pleasure it is to send one's carriage for a friend!', after she had overlooked her own arrangement to bring Jane and Miss Bates in the first place, suggesting a double meaning – it is a pleasure for Mrs Elton to help a friend but also to be seen to do so. It is at the same ball that the most obvious example of real ill-will to someone on her part occurs. There 'while smiles of high glee passed between him and his wife', Mr Elton, but for Mr Knightley's rescue, would have humiliated Harriet. Emma though 'did not think he was quite so hardened as his wife, though growing very like her'.

It is no surprise when Mrs Elton later resents the cancellation of her arrangements for Jane Fairfax to take up a post as governess. To Mr Knightley Emma says, in chapter 51, 'by the bye, I wonder how Mrs. Elton bears the disappointment'. On her next visit, in the following chapter, Emma observes Miss Bates: 'And from her great, her more than commonly thankful delight towards Mrs Elton for being there, Emma guessed that there had been a little show of resentment towards Jane, from the vicarage quarter, which was now graciously overcome'. Before Miss Bates had entered, Mrs Elton had just said to Jane Fairfax:

> I only wanted to prove to you that Mrs S. admits our apology and is not offended ...You remember those lines – I forget the poem at this moment:
>   'For when a lady's in the case,
>   You know all other things give place.'
> Now I say, my dear, in *our* case, for *lady*, read – mum! a word to the wise. – I am in a fine flow of spirits, an't I? But I want to set your heart at ease as to Mrs S. – *My* representation, you see, has quite appeased her.

At the point of the 'disappointment' being confirmed, Mrs Elton quotes from a poem inappropriately. It is from John Gay's Fables of 1727: Fable L – *The Hare and many Friends*.[30] The couplet actually runs:

> Love calls me hence; a fav'rite cow
> Expects me near yon barley mow:
> And when a lady's in the case,
> You know, all other things give place.

Replacing what a 'stately bull' pleads as excuse with the word 'For' could intend a mean jibe by Mrs Elton at the secret engagement; though perhaps it is all just a muddling through. That in itself, however, is hardly the frame of mind one looks for in someone giving assurances and purporting to lead society's attitudes. Significantly, this short poem is a Fable of having 'many friends' who profess to want to help but then find some reason why they cannot, whereas a single good friend could rescue a hapless hare from being hunted down by pursuing dogs.[31] By extension now we can backtrack to the claim that her brother-in-law 'was always rather a friend to the abolition' to question again what being such a friend meant. In the case of both Emma and Mrs Elton we have seen that being a friend can involve making blunders and injuring the interests of the person purportedly being helped. By contrast with this Fable, the 'small band of true friends' at the ending of the novel gains further resonance.

Degrees of friendship have been illustrated by Emma's own earlier personal taking stock. From her own use of Harriet in chapter 4 in being 'quite convinced of Harriet Smith's being exactly the young friend she wanted – exactly the *something* which her home required' (my italics), and so as something of a commodity, Emma moves to the realisation in chapter 16 'I have been but half a friend to her', the preposition 'to' being used here as well, and then on to her acknowledgment in chapter 47 that 'Mr Knightley had spoken prophetically, when he once said "Emma, you have been no friend to Harriet Smith." – She was afraid she had done her nothing but disservice'. While Emma changes, Mrs Elton does not.

There is no parallel progress on Mrs Elton's part. We see for ourselves that Miss Bates had been over-optimistic at the time of her niece's agreeing to the governess post, in chapter 44, in describing Mrs Elton as 'The most indefatigable, true friend'. Contrary to the prognostication of Mrs Elton in chapter 33 in saying that Jane: 'is now...so thrown away. – Whatever advantages she may have enjoyed with the Campbells are so palpably at an end! And I think she feels it. I am sure she does', Jane Fairfax returns to Colonel Campbell the 'real friend' of chapter 20 as, prior to her marriage, in the last chapter she is 'restored to the comforts of her beloved home with the Campbells' in London. Although Mrs Elton had thought that Jane Fairfax suffered at the thought of becoming a governess, there was no enthusiasm from Mrs Elton for Jane Fairfax not after all having this fate. The world shrinks in an unexpected way in *Emma* because someone with difficulties in England, who knows she has difficulties, aligns herself with people far away, and declares the guilt of the slave trade.

Light amusement seamlessly takes us by virtue of the terminology of confession to the sombre tone of the dialogue in which Jane Fairfax would speak of the guilt of the slave trade and the misery of its victims. Before the dinner at which the dialogue takes place, in chapter 33 Mrs Elton continues her prognostication to Emma that '[Jane] is now...so thrown away':

I am a great advocate for timidity – and I am sure one does not often meet with it. – But in those who are at all inferior, it is extremely prepossessing.

Shortly afterwards, Mr Knightley speaking to Mrs Weston and Emma suggests: 'you may be sure that Miss Fairfax awes Mrs. Elton by her superiority both of mind and manner'. But Emma demurs:

I have no faith in Mrs Elton's acknowledging herself the inferior in thought, word, or deed.

Emma here ends the discussion using phrasing from *The Book of Common Prayer*.[32]

Mr Knightley uses an image of Cowper seeing shapes of things in the fire, to express the idea of looking at events in such a way as to make the interpretation of them entirely fanciful.[33] He had feared in chapter 41 that he was:

like Cowper and his fire at twilight, '*Myself creating what I saw*.'

This becomes a superb symbol, accentuating the mystery surrounding Jane Fairfax. Specifically Mr Knightley was coming to realize that there might be need of some explanation about Jane Fairfax. The fact that he is right could be seen as a clever device for getting the contemporary reader to reconsider the terms of the dialogue, once the puzzle about Jane Fairfax's behaviour has been explained and it is seen that indeed she did not at the time of the dialogue have the expectation of spending the rest of her life as a governess. For the contemporary reader there would have been a real point in considering again what was being claimed about victims of the slave trade in the dialogue.

Before the dialogue we receive a warning in chapter 33 not to jump to conclusions about Jane Fairfax's views and behaviour when Emma muses about her:

'She is a riddle, quite a riddle!' said she. – 'To chuse to remain here month after month, under privations of every sort! And now to chuse the mortification of Mrs Elton's notice and the penury of her conversation, rather than return to the superior companions who have always loved her with such real, generous affection.'

Solving this riddle tends to be done by the reader adopting Emma's point of view, until Emma herself is disabused of it.

In the dialogue Mrs Elton cuts the other two women present out of the conversation. However, it is more than likely that Jane Fairfax in the presence of Emma's former governess would not have initiated a comparison with the slave trade nor taken up Mrs Elton's introduction of the issue by describing doing the job in such terms. The delicacy escapes Mrs Elton, but as Mr Knightley is to say in chapter 51: 'There is no saying much for the delicacy of our good friends, the Eltons'. Mrs Elton had previously exasperated Emma by expressing surprise at having found Mrs Weston to be a lady; Emma had been quick to think that she had after all been brought up by her former governess following her mother's death about 15 years previously. These reflections support a reading of the dialogue available straightaway even before we learn that Jane Fairfax had been secretly engaged, a reading in terms of protest at people being treated as saleable commodities. This reading is that out of consideration to Emma and to her former governess there could be no question of Jane Fairfax herself making a comparison between the slave trade and being a governess, but because Mrs Elton has made the comparison Jane Fairfax neatly turns the reference into a criticism of anyone's regarding people as commodities.

Emma is much readier to associate Jane Fairfax with becoming a governess than are others, as had been illustrated in chapter 24 when Emma had said to Frank Churchill: 'You know Miss Fairfax's situation in life, I conclude; what she is destined to be'. Mrs Weston who is present comments:

> 'You get upon delicate subjects, Emma', said Mrs Weston, smiling; 'remember that I am here. – Mr. Frank Churchill hardly knows what to say when you speak of Miss Fairfax's situation in life. I will move a little farther off.'

Emma says immediately to Frank Churchill:

> 'I certainly do forget to think of *her*,' said Emma, 'as having ever been anything but my friend and my dearest friend.'

By contrast with Emma, in chapter 12 Emma's sister residing in London spoke of seeing Jane Fairfax 'now and then for a moment accidentally in town!' and surmised with a similar attitude to her husband, 'now their daughter is married, I suppose Colonel and Mrs Campbell will not be able to part with her at all'.

Crucially one is hearing the dialogue with Emma's ears, and may easily interpret what is assessed in the dialogue as being about the status of the governess only. Mrs Elton and Emma clearly think in terms of carrying out the job as the problem. Neither of them is up to seeing the distress caused by being treated as a commodity, though Emma will come to see how potentially disastrous it was to treat Harriet in that way, and so be less susceptible to what is described in the opening chapter as her having 'the power of having rather too much her own way'. With such power, Emma is at the opposite end of the spectrum from those whose autonomy is denied.

Abolition of slavery may not have looked inevitable from the standpoint of 1814. Even if Eric Williams' Marxist analysis were to stand, it would leave unaffected that people at the time not able to rely on any such inevitability needed to consider their own strategies, regardless of whether their strategies however implemented would have any effect on events. For all that Jane Austen regards entertaining her reader as a necessary aim, it does not follow that it was her sole aim, and part of the pay-off in succeeding in entertaining is her interactive dialogue with readers.

There are two different attitudes attributable to Jane Fairfax, and the one we learn of later has to be taken as her actual attitude at the time of the dialogue. The reference to marriage, as I take it, using an association of ideas between 'human flesh' and the biblical phrase 'one flesh', prefigures the later announcement by her fiancée of their engagement, which had been secretly agreed nine months previously, before she began her long visit to her aunt and grandmother in Highbury. When we learn of this we can infer that at the time of the dialogue she had not expected to become a governess and that her views about finding a governess post expressed not only a fear of becoming a governess, but also a second viewpoint as one who is not a participator.

Expressed from a fellow victim's point of view, which we at first take hers to be, the refusal to grade whose is the greater misery can sound like a plea for governesses. Expressed from an external observer's point of view which is later revealed as hers, that same refusal still sounds like an expression of commonly-held humanity but with an objectivity derived from not after all being so situated as to speak subjectively. The fellow-feeling is retained but any aura of self-pity has gone. Mrs Elton undermines her own position; in expressing shock that a comparison might be made, she had induced Jane Fairfax to make a comparison presupposing the common humanity of both sorts of victim. The second viewpoint is even more effective and more influential in provoking thought because it has been emphasized as a result of discovery, following clarification about Jane Fairfax's actual rather than apparent destiny.

To sum up, at the time of the dialogue Jane Fairfax did not have the investment in such a job to warrant a protest about the lot of a governess, though faced with Mrs Elton she could express extreme distaste for any-one's playing at trading in such jobs. This topic of trading in governess jobs, the reference for the phrase 'governess-trade', makes possible a com-paring and contrasting with trading in the case of the slave trade, an issue which has burst into the dialogue as if Mrs Elton can no longer hold back acknowledging involvement within her own family, when she speaks as if the issue of the slave trade is in the past with no repercussions.

Jane Austen takes for granted the guilt of the slave trade. The impression can be given that because she takes for granted agreement on the slave trade she focuses on governesses. But authorial focus is not so likely to be on the job of a governess if it was not after all the focus for her character Jane Fairfax. The author does not herself in the narrative seem to focus on protest at the job of a governess. In any case, where governesses are concerned the description targets not doing the job but the experience at the hands of governess-trade at 'advertising offices'. To be traded is to be treated as a commodity. To change that in the case of victims of the slave trade would be to cease having slaves as property.

IV. The novel as subversive

I draw the conclusion that in comparing the victims of the slave trade to those of governess-trade the author's concern is for the victims of the prohibited slave trade who remain enslaved. The need later in the narrative to reassess one's ideas about the secretly engaged Jane Fairfax provides a way of emphasizing this issue of the slave trade, by inviting a second look at what has been said and done earlier, including what was actually said in the dialogue. The need to reassess indicates there could be a need to change one's mind about what may at first have been taken to be the case in the dialogue.

Jane Fairfax's influence in the wider world is represented as something to be relied on. In chapter 51, speaking of her and her fiancée, Mr Knightley says:

> I am very ready to believe his character will improve, and acquire from her's the steadiness and delicacy of principle that it wants.

For a contemporary reader in Britain, prior to Emancipation, he or just as importantly she is part of a reader audience for whom the need to reassess what has been said and done earlier in the novel could mean being prompted to think further about the continuing slavery of the victims of the slave trade.

The concern about abolition raised in the dialogue is carried through the entire narrative because of the link with Maple Grove. Another effect of seeing so much in the narrative through Emma's consciousness is that we are grounded with her in Highbury so that what is kept distant, keeps itself distant or is excluded, becomes alien and its ideas not those we wish to identify with. Looking back, this is effective from the first chapter, when the topic is raised of a marriage for Mr Elton, who will use casual imagery of slavery in his Charade and again at the end of Volume One, through Volume Two from the introduction of Mrs Elton, whose first topic of conversation when returning Emma's call is Maple Grove and its promise to visit in the spring or summer at the latest, to the climax of Volume Two incorporating the dialogue referring to the slave trade, and is then consolidated in the final Third Volume by the discrediting of Mrs Elton as not welcoming a happy outcome of Jane Fairfax's secret engagement, calling into question thereby Mrs Elton's credentials for judging friendship in her earlier description that 'Mr Suckling was always rather a friend to the abolition', the narrative culminating in the resolution of all difficulties at the finish, bar those perceived by the excluded and rejected, satirized world of Maple Grove. The world of Maple Grove has effectively been marginalized.

This is subversive of the status quo, in presenting a world that readers would not want to identify with but from which they would prefer to disassociate themselves. Maple Grove has broken its promise to visit the newly married Eltons, and Mrs Elton, in trying to cling on to the wealthy connection, involves herself in hypocrisy for the comedy of the concluding paragraph. Having earlier expressed a horror of finery shortly after her outburst on the slave trade, she now declares that, from the particulars given her by Mr Elton, the lack of finery at Emma's wedding makes for so shabby an affair that when she heard of it Selina would stare. Such a light touch can nevertheless succeed in planting the idea that, over against Mr Knightley's stewardship of resources and the relative modesty of expenditure in Highbury, excessive consumption at Maple Grove is unwarranted. In viewing Maple Grove from this perspective there would be no succour out in the external world for any idea of supporters of the status quo that emancipation would wrongly injure vested interests. To be so suggestive, of there being no good future for Maple Grove values, is in itself subversive.

Thus I conclude Jane Austen sought to undermine the views of those still supporting the status quo of chattel slavery. This would be a quiet revolution in the sense that opposition is not forced upon the reader but clearly suggested. Earlier, before 1807, abolitionist emphasis had been on abolition of the slave trade itself. To work now for abolition of slavery in the face of offers of amelioration of conditions for an institution that, it could always be said, went back to time immemorial would be tougher going. The subtlety of Jane Austen's approach was particularly called for in order that what she said in speaking of the guilt of the slave trade and the misery of its victims could not be used counter-productively.

4
Persuasion: Radical Change and the Royal Navy

the dread of a future war, all that could dim her sunshine. She gloried in being a sailor's wife, but she must pay the tax of quick alarm, for belonging to that profession which is, if possible, more distinguished in its domestic virtues than in its national importance.

Persuasion, closing lines of final chapter

Introduction

In this novel, after the loss of hopes in their early relationship, the triumph of Anne and Captain Wentworth is a cause for celebration. In the world external to the novel, as radical a turnabout as that reached for this pair of lovers by the end of the novel had been brought about in 1807 for the role of the Royal Navy by the abolition of the British slave trade. The absence of explicit reference to abolition does not mean that *Persuasion* escaped the attention of Edward Said, as I indicated in my first chapter. But his view does not take into account the change in the duties after 1807 of the Royal Navy. The Royal Navy now had a task to enforce the 1807 abolition. James Walvin speaks of this as 'such a transformation in British behaviour'.

The magnitude of Britain's previous involvement with the slave trade began to be matched after 1807 by the extent of effort to make British abolition effective. Barry Gough says:

> the navy was guardian of seaborne commerce and was servant of official policy. Thus after the British slave-trade was abolished in 1807, it fell to the navy to try to eradicate the trade where diplomacy failed. The historiography of the navy and the slave trade is a branch of Imperial history, for in order to promote and secure legitimate trade the navy assisted in imperial expansion.

Of course, Jane Austen could not know of the rest of the nineteenth-century's patrols of the seas and the controversial role in empire that it took.[1]

The love story can be seen as a celebration in honour of the Royal Navy. The celebration is not self-congratulatory and is accompanied by a gentle teasing of the protagonists. The teasing is spaced out through the narrative, and may be taken into account in the concluding lines of the novel, quoted at the head of this chapter, where the words '...if possible...' draw attention to the Royal Navy's 'national importance'. The function of the phrase 'if possible' is not straightforward to elucidate, and it is not mere embellishment of a straightforward comparison.[2]

Accumulation of abolition-relevant dates and places in the novel seems to have structural significance within the narrative. There is an integrated topic of property in the West Indies that Jane Austen insists on. References in the novel to dates and places coinciding in the external world with dates and places of significance in the chronicle of abolition could also be seen as preparation for the topics of West Indian property, of money and of sources of happiness at the end. I put forward a different interpretation from that of a commentator who says about *Persuasion*: 'Traces of a concern with slavery disappear in Austen's most questioning novel about gender and class power'.[3] The emphasized dates of 1806–7 in the novel echo public affairs of the same dates, and it is a story that begins its main action between June and August of 1814, another significant date for abolitionism. During that summer period of 1814 there had been petitions to Parliament to campaign for an international ban on the slave trade.

I. The Royal Navy

Events kept both the Royal Navy and issues over slavery in the news. There was a slave rebellion in Barbados, in April of 1816,[4] and it was also possible for white men at the time still to fall into slavery.[5] Another sea-faring nation at risk from piracy, the Dutch, had much earlier illustrated the risk. A Dutch engraving of 1684, 'A slave market in Algiers' had shown the display and sale of white slaves.[6] Such European experience may have coloured the reactions to slavery of earlier writers like John Locke. One of the naval engagements called for in 1816 by press and public opinion was the liberation of white Europeans held by Muslim captors in the Mediterranean. John Winton says:

> The war might be over, but piracy continued. In the Mediterranean, the Turks in Algiers, Tunis and Tripoli made a profitable business from piracy and from ransoming their European captives. In 1816 press and public opinion forced the admiralty to take action. Lord Exmouth, the Commander-in-Chief... was ordered to show the flag.

The action took place in August 1816. As a result '1,600 European slaves' were released 'none of whom were British'.[7] The action taken on 27 August

1816 succeeded in liberation of white slaves held in Algiers, but not without 'a 16 per cent casualty rate which made this as bloody a battle as any in the age of sail'.[8]

Paradoxically, the Battle of Algiers emphasized the 'circumscribed power' of the Royal Navy, as Linda Colley points out in commenting on the act of aggression by Britain in the rescue:

> In 1816 the Royal Navy bombarded the city of Algiers from the sea in an attempt to put an end to corsairing and white slavery ... but corsairs soon returned to work, while Britain's naval casualties in this action – as a proportion of the men involved – were heavier than at the battle of Trafalgar fighting the French and the Spanish.[9]

The August 1816 naval action to rescue white slaves took place at the time that *Persuasion* was undergoing final revision. Public calls for that naval action coincided with initial completion of *Persuasion* and with subsequent alteration of its final chapters from burlesque to the near sublime. It may have been external pressure of events on the reserves of the Royal Navy that in part inspired the rewriting.

Concerning the completion of *Persuasion,* details on the manuscript of the cancelled chapters show a completion date: 'Finis July 16, 1816', which is scrawled out, and then one manuscript page later another attempt at completion: 'Finis July 18, 1816'.[10] But this was to be superseded. '*Persuasion* was not finished before the middle of August', writes a nephew.[11] Jane Austen's letters to her niece Fanny Knight of 13 March and of 23 March 1817 indicate the readiness for publication of what would be published posthumously as *Persuasion*.

D.W. Harding complains that in the final rewritten work we are kept waiting for the passing on of Mrs Smith's revelations.[12] However, it is by no means a flaw for the author to flag attention to this delay by Anne's thinking about Scheherazade. Anne muses:

> and Mr Elliot's character, like the Sultaness Scheherazade's head, must live another day.

What is signalled by keeping us waiting materializes in the concluding paragraphs of the novel in Mrs Smith's property. There may be allusion to slavery probably involved in her West Indian property. When the allusion to *The Arabian Nights* is made, a contemporary reader could have been prompted to think of slaves by being reminded of white slaves 'under Barbary'. At this relatively early stage of empire, perception of such risk to whites might also have triggered fellow feeling for anyone held as a slave in British colonies. Not only may there be allusion to white slavery and Anne's 'dread of a future war', but implied may be invitation to think of the plight of black slaves in the West Indies.

The allusion to *The Arabian Nights* is multifaceted. It was popular, so that Jane Austen may express cosmopolitan attitudes at the time of the Battle of Algiers, to remind readers of what have been described as 'basic human predicaments' exemplified in *The Arabian Nights*.[13] Scheherazade voluntarily undertakes marriage to the Sultan with her own plan to stop his revenge killings. Slavery at that time was, of course, practised in common both by Islamic countries and by European countries in their colonies.[14] Scheherazade sets out on her mission to restore all to well-being, armed only with her learning and ability to tell good stories, and brings about the redemption of the Sultan. Eighteenth-century translations to some extent had a 'universalizing emphasis'.[15] I think the reference in *Persuasion* implies a universal purpose for entertainment sometimes as an instrument for reform.

Jane Austen had a special interest in the Royal Navy, as a result of two brothers serving in it. She was in an even better position than her heroine to track events. In chapter 4 on Captain Wentworth's progress, it is observed of Anne:

> She had only navy lists and newspapers for her authority, but she could not doubt his being rich.

An easy familiarity is seen with naval matters in Jane Austen's letters; writing to Cassandra on 21 January 1801, she speculates about prospects for their relatives:

> Eliza talks of having read in a Newspaper that all the 1st Lieuts of the Frigates whose Captains were to be sent into Line-of-Battle ships, were to be promoted to the rank of Commanders...

She would not need to say what had happened in 1807; any reader of the time would know. With two brothers in the Navy, one of them voicing anti-slavery views, there is every reason to suppose that the potential work of enforcing the abolition of 1807 would have been known to her.[16] Independently of the measure of her agreement with her brothers, they were a source of points of view and information.

Edward Said is right to note the emphasis on the Navy, but he misses the significance. There is a contrast with the villainous admiral of an earlier generation in *Mansfield Park*, who had corrupted the young Crawfords. The presence of the Navy permeates *Persuasion*, and throughout it is seen as a profession of humane men and of fearless prize-winning feats at sea making for honourably won wealth. 'This peace will be turning all our rich Navy Officers ashore' says Mr Shepherd, cautious lawyer, visiting Kellynch Hall and, having just 'laid down the newspaper', addressing himself in chapter 3 to the financial embarrassment of Sir Walter. The reference to peace could draw attention to the external world, including the need for radical changes in deployment of the Royal Navy.

As exemplified in the 'foolish, spendthrift baronet', Anne's father, the traditional landed element is by no means more impressive, but rather the reverse.[17] The Royal Navy is seen as a force for freedom and progress. Anne escapes into it 'belonging to that profession'. John Winton in connection with the Navy policing the abolition of the slave trade quotes William Cowper:

> 'Slaves cannot breathe in England; if their lungs receive our air, that moment they are free; They touch our country, and their shackles fall'. So wrote William Cowper in *The Task* in 1785 ...The carriage of slaves in British vessels was abolished in 1807. In 1811, slave-trading was made a felony, punishable by 14 years imprisonment.[18]

The outlawing of the slave trade had been shown to be in earnest by this punishment of 14 years imprisonment.

The whole plot turns on Navy references. It is Admiral and Mrs Croft's taking over Kellynch Hall, which Sir Walter can no longer afford, that brings in Anne's way again Mrs Croft's brother, Captain Wentworth. It was his former kindness on the *Laconia* to young Dick Musgrove that makes him so welcome in the Musgrove household, throwing him into the company of their daughter Louisa and also Anne staying nearby who has been invited to aid her sister, the Musgroves' daughter-in-law. It is another Navy connection that takes them all to Lyme Regis and Louisa's fall from the Cobb.[19] In reading this novel we note the feat of the difficult actually being achieved in the re-union of Anne and Captain Wentworth. The potentially momentous change of the 1807 Abolition of the British Slave Trade to the British Caribbean way of life could be thought of as having a fictional analogue in the momentous change of the eventual re-uniting of Captain Wentworth and Anne.

The triumph of the lovers is ensured by the fine reworking of the ending of the novel, in the replacement for the original penultimate chapter by two new chapters with a much enhanced presentation, which are then followed by substantially the same concluding chapter.[20] It is not only the fine achievement of the lovers' personal development which is present in the revised ending. Although the revision has changed mere burlesque to a moving climax, there is nevertheless something that remains the same and that is the occurrence of naval references in securing the denouement. In the rejected chapter all was resolved in the London residence of Admiral and Mrs Croft making for the necessary discretion, enabling the lovers' reunion. In the revision, this London residence disappears and the denouement turns on Anne's conversation with Captain Harville, the naval connection from Lyme Regis, concerning constancy in love, a topic raised by Captain Benwick's engagement to Louisa and overheard by Captain Wentworth.[21]

Given the fact that Jane Austen made important changes to the ending of the novel, the emphasis on Captain Wentworth's naval link with the West Indies in the last two paragraphs of the book looks the more significant as definitely intended. In fact this matter is further accentuated because Jane Austen made some changes to the concluding chapter itself. Specifically, she changes what had been a long concluding paragraph, which began with reference to Lady Russell, to make instead, using the same words throughout, three smaller paragraphs. The effect is the highlighting of the material on Mrs Smith and her West Indian property.[22]

This link with the West Indies is a striking feature of the novel; there appears to be an authorial intention to keep issues that could be associated with abolition before a reader's eye. There is certainly an emphasis on the impoverished widow's property. This would be sorted out by Captain Wentworth for Mrs Smith, as we learn in the penultimate paragraph of the novel. If this placing in the penultimate paragraph were not sufficient highlighting in itself, the same matter is further discussed in the first half of the final closing paragraph of the novel. As Susan Morgan says in connection with Mrs Smith's property:

> The relations of slavery to British West Indian agricultural profits were a matter of visible public debate in the first decade of the nineteenth century. Austen's references to West Indian properties simply do not mean an acceptance of slave labour there.

She continues this by going on to say that 'In fact, it is more plausible that Austen's references imply the opposite'.[23] Nevertheless, Tim Fulford claims:

> The gentry, Austen suggests, has been renewed by the careers that its less wealthy sons have taken up. It has been revitalised by opportunities that empire gives for character-building employment. That it has also been renewed by the income stemming from the ownership of slave colonies is a point that Mrs Smith's case raises but that Austen chooses not to pursue.[24]

However, Jane Austen prefers instead to invite the contemporary reader to pursue the case, having structurally highlighted the matter by the alterations making three smaller paragraphs for the end of the novel.[25] John Wiltshire notes the increasing significance of Mrs Smith:

> Anne Elliot, then is initially the only reflective consciousness of the novel. (The late-introduced invalid Mrs Smith is perhaps a second.)[26]

Mrs Smith's wish had been to influence Mr Elliot to retrieve property, described in chapter 21:

> She had good reason to believe that some property of her husband in the West Indies, which had been for many years under a sort of sequestration for the payment of its own incumbrances, might be recoverable by proper measures; and this property, though not large, would be enough to make her comparatively rich.

By the reference to 'a sort of sequestration' we gather that she is indeed the owner, but that there are legal constraints on benefit from its income or sale.[27]

Geographical references introduced through the naval detail point us to the West Indies, dates show that the time is now post-1807 Abolition, and the property itself is in the West Indies. The last paragraph of the novel begins:

> Mrs Smith's enjoyments were not spoiled by this improvement of income, with some improvement of health, and the acquisition of such friends to be often with, for her cheerfulness and mental alacrity did not fail her; and while these prime supplies of good remained, she might have bid defiance even to greater accessions of worldly prosperity. She might have been absolutely rich and perfectly healthy, and yet be happy. Her spring of felicity was in the glow of her spirits, as her friend Anne's was in the warmth of her heart.

The bridge thus made to Anne, the last few lines of the novel can ensue, but the emphatic last impressions of the novel suggest we are intended not to miss the reference to Mrs Smith and her West Indian property. There has to be a point in this, unless we are to conclude as does John Davie that 'the introduction of Mrs Smith is *Persuasion*'s only serious flaw'. Yasmine Gooneratne also sees Mrs Smith as irksome.[28] I suggest that the point could be to involve a contemporary reader in abolition-specific thinking. Topical questions would abound amongst some of the readers and their acquaintance.

This naval experience in the West Indies in the penultimate paragraph, when Captain Wentworth is able to act for Mrs Smith, is the topic that had earlier triggered the revealing by Mrs Smith of Mr Elliot's treachery, giving a further emphasis to how wrong Lady Russell, Anne's substitute mother who had persuaded her to break her engagement to Captain Wentworth, had been to admire Sir Walter's male heir Mr Elliot so unreservedly as a suitor for Anne. Anne's caution that Mr Elliot had not seemed to weigh up is thus vindicated. Her kindness to Mrs Smith has enabled this revelation. This is 'domestic virtue' on Anne's part! The domestic setting for this West Indian reference is perhaps foreshadowed by a joke of Captain Wentworth in chapter 8 that since the *Asp* was only suitable for 'home service' he was sent off to the West Indies in it, a nice joke considering the considerable distance involved. The joke could get an edge by referring to an area of some British territory, as opposed to accompanying a voyage to, for example, China, about which Fanny was avidly reading in *Mansfield Park*, an account of the diplomatic visit by Lord Macartney written up by his interpreter, John Barrow at the Admiralty.[29]

On foreign exploration by the Navy, it seems to me that John Barrow's geographical interests at the Admiralty were in competition for funding with the enforcing of the banned slave trade.[30] 'During all this period of tranquillity there was but little demand on the services of the royal navy', he says blithely in his *Autobiography* of the peace following the ending of war with France and of hostilities with America.[31] Christopher Lloyd, on the task of policing the seas, points out:

> To these activities must be added the achievements of the surveyor and the hydrographer ... The preventive cruises off the coasts of Africa and in the Pacific were often engaged in all three activities.[32]

It seems operations were combined.

Emphasized amongst the naval detail are the places visited, geographically: not only the West Indies but also the Cape and the East Indies. It is in the Cape that Captain Benwick had had his picture painted by a German artist, as we learn towards the end. In chapter 8 the topic of the West Indies is emphasized by the conversation between Admiral Croft's wife and Mrs Musgrove. Mrs Croft says that for all her seafaring, accompanying her husband, she 'never was in the West Indies', only in the Bahamas and Bermuda and that though at Gibralter she 'never went beyond the Streights'.[33] This dialogue is emphasized by Mrs Musgrove being comically out of her depth in conversation with Mrs Croft:

> 'We do not call Bermuda or Bahama, you know, the West Indies'.
>   Mrs Musgrove had not a word to say in dissent; she could not accuse herself of having ever called them anything in the whole course of her life.

Captain Wentworth had done well after his broken engagement to Anne and come back to England the following year. The point made earlier in the novel that he then had charge of the *Laconia* is taken up again in the penultimate chapter where he asks Anne whether she would have accepted in '08, before he had the *Laconia*, if he had proposed to her again. Anne eloquently answers 'Would I!' If Captain Wentworth had come to terms by then with his pride he would have found as great a personal transformation in Anne by 1808, as had potentially come about in the West Indies during his voyage there with the *Asp*.

As well as places geographically, dates are decidedly emphasized, and the dates link up in significance for the progress of abolition and its knock-on effect for the enforcing work of the Royal Navy. In her first chapter it is noticeable that Jane Austen points out the dates on which the action of the novel takes place. As Tony Tanner says:

> There is of course much emphasis on the past and the pastness of the past: '*That was in the year six*'...[34]

Having been given Anne's date of birth as 9 August 1787 and also her sister's, we could deduce Anne's age and that it is now at least June of 1814, since we are also told her sister's age. In any case, the date is reinforced because we then read 'at this time (the summer of 1814)'. We learn in chapter 4 that it is seven or eight years since Captain Wentworth had first come on the scene 'in the summer of 1806' as, though promoted, he was 'not immediately employed' after 'the action off San Domingo'. This was a British victory over the French of February 1806 at which Jane Austen's brother Frank had been present. Captain Wentworth stayed half a year, and then went to sea again after the whirlwind romance leading to the engagement which 'principally for *his* advantage' Anne breaks.

Following the broken engagement, his next year's experience at sea being in 1807, at first going to the West Indies, would be during the time of the abolition of the slave trade. Charles Arnold-Baker gives the dates of the legalities:

> The Slave Trade Abolition Act, 1806, came into effect in 1807... British naval supremacy was now used to suppress it.[35]

In chapter 5, after the decision has been made to rent out Kellynch Hall to the Admiral and his wife, Anne has to plan where to live, 'though dreading the possible heats of September in all the white glare of Bath'. It is, consequently, from some time between June and the end of August of 1814 that the narrative begins its running.

Mr Shepherd in looking at the newspaper at Kellynch Hall and then commenting on the peace that is bringing rich navy officers ashore, could have been reading something along the lines described by Joseph Lew:

> In the summer of 1814, popular opinion in England about the international slave trade rose to a fevered pitch. In June, the Houses of Parliament were deluged by ... petitions ... demanding international abolition. On August 1, 1814, Castlereagh, foreign minister and British plenipotentiary at the Congress of Vienna, wrote to the Duke of Wellington: 'The nation is bent upon this object ... and the ministers must make it the basis of their policy'.[36]

The historian Linda Colley says:

> In 1814, the anti-slavery pressure groups mobilised 800 petitions urging the British government to persuade the restored French monarchy to abandon its slave trade. Three-quarters of a million men and women signed.[37]

Eric Williams speaks of the abolitionists in 1814 sending to Parliament: '772 petitions with a million signatures', adding: 'the pressure on the government was terrific'.[38] The peace that Mr Shepherd refers to is the spur both to Kellynch Hall being found a tenant, and in the external world, to which we are actually directed by reference to the newspaper, the spur to the nations that had been at war with Napoleon meeting to arrange provision for the future and Britain having international banning of the slave trade much in mind.

References seem to be so integrated as to be functional. There appears to be a deliberate widening of horizons, beyond the experience of the women that is land-based with the exception, of course, of that of the sea-going wife of Admiral Croft. If there is deliberate focusing on the Royal Navy in its work, then it would be relevant to remember that there had been the radical change in the duties of that Navy with respect to now upholding the ban on slave trading. The view, that there is now an enhanced 'raison d'être' for the Royal Navy, is certainly consistent with the concluding lines of the novel. After 1807 there is a new way of thinking about it after two hundred and fifty years of English slave trading. Its duty was transformed in 1807 from the earlier protecting of the British transatlantic slave trade to being at least in principle the practical agent for enforcing its abolition, although with the country then still at war with France, ships had not readily been available. One can appreciate the transformation by trying to imagine what Admiral Nelson, who had fiercely defended the slave trade, would have made of the complete reversal constituted by the new policy two years after his death at the Battle of Trafalgar.[39] Raymond Howell also indicates not only the delays in progress but also the vital role of the Royal Navy as 'the key instrument'.[40]

II. Analysing '...if possible...'

In the last line of the novel where the Navy is said to be 'that profession which is, if possible, more distinguished in its domestic virtues than in its national importance', the inclusion, as Jane Austen has it, of '...if possible...' marks out a targeting of superlative merits. A possible interpretation of this part of the conclusion might be as a play on words, given that a possible reading of the concluding sentence is that the Royal Navy's work is lauded more highly at the domestic level than at the national level. Its domestic virtues might then be contrasted with its national importance seen when protecting the nation at war. The term 'domestic' could mean 'not foreign' as in Johnson's *Dictionary*.[41] Jon Mee stresses the involvement of women in the war effort as part explanation for these concluding lines of the novel,[42] but I think it is important to take into account as well that the 'domestic virtues' are predicated apparently of the Navy as a whole not just of those who have married into it.

It is possible to focus on the domestic virtues in the sense in which the sailors of *Persuasion* look good husband material.[43] Furthermore, part of their charm is their humanity, unlike Anne's own immediate family in the sight of whom Anne 'was nobody'. Humanity being seen as a virtue, the phrase 'domestic virtues' would be solidly based in light-hearted reference but could nevertheless carry over as a complex phrase to another use, as in phrases like 'domestic policy' or 'gross domestic product'. Humour of a good-about-the-house interpretation would then nicely offset any risk of sounding sanctimonious about the role that the Royal Navy could, and in due course did, play in effectively policing the ban on the slave trade.

Christopher Lloyd warns against 'the dangers of complacency':

> Throughout the whole movement Britain led the van. The dangers of complacency in the study of such an aspect of national history are obvious. While we may justifiably congratulate ourselves on the magnitude and persistence of the effort made, it is well to remember that in the past Britain's record was as black as that of any other nation ...
>
> The Europeans did not inaugurate the Slave Trade, since the Portuguese learned it from the Moors, and the Arabs carried it on for a longer period than any other people, with the hearty co-operation of the more warlike African tribes. But by the suppression of the Slave Trade, and by the subsequent, if belated, improvements in colonial administration, Europe has gone some way to repaying its debt to Africa.[44]

There are a number of respects in which Navy action could be termed 'domestic' in connection with the 1807 Abolition: it would be a matter of carrying out the domestic policy of British legislation; other countries are not to anything like the same extent joining in the patrolling of the seas even if they have endorsed abolition for their own countries; British colonies affected in the West Indies could possibly be regarded as 'home', rather than as exotic destinations like those brought to our attention by puzzling over the pronunciation of Byron's *The Giaour* on the part of Captain Benwick, earnestly conversing with Anne in Lyme Regis on this 'Turkish fragment' poem of the fate of a slave girl and its repercussions, exotic destinations that were to continue to captivate the Romantic imagination and that approved a slave trade.[45] This reference is made again immediately before Louisa's fall from the Cobb, when Captain Benwick and Anne are about to resume their discussion of Byron. Finally on a domestic note the policing can only be of ships in British ownership, because the right to search other nations' ships came about much later.[46]

However, there is a contrasting non-domestic setting. The realism of: 'The dread of a future war all that could dim her sunshine', concludes in the penultimate sentence a possible celebration of the Royal Navy and of humanity, portrayed in the drama of the novel that has been played out in the scene-setting between 1806–14 and in depth between 1814–15. The thought of a future war reinforces the relevance of the term 'national', which has earlier been pointed up. Captain Wentworth in chapter 8 had related falling in with the very French frigate he wanted, and again referred to France, speaking of 'our touch with the Great Nation' not having much improved the condition of his sloop. Captain Wentworth is obviously showing off his prowess here, much to everybody's satisfaction, playing off capturing a French frigate with his less powerful sloop. Anne, too, in chapter 3 is immediately able to place Admiral Croft, her father's prospective tenant for the ancestral home: 'He is rear admiral of the white. He was in the Trafalgar action'.

Following the ending of war, especially war at sea, the use of the Royal Navy turning from national defence could now be more in accord with the domestic policy of the nation. Talk of the West Indies could bring to a contemporary reader's mind the part of the world so much affected both by the change in the Navy's role following the 1807 Abolition and the work begun by the Navy in the years up to 1814–15, the two years when the novel is primarily set, just prior to the novel being finished in 1816. On the other hand, it does perhaps counter an emphasis on the domestic aspect, that the work of the Navy was also felt on the West Coast of Africa in intercepting the capturing of people as slaves. One could, however, think domestically in terms of the colony of Sierra Leone because it had been taken over by the Crown following the 1807 Abolition as 'the centre of suppression activities' in 1808.[47]

Sierra Leone is described by Christopher Lloyd as: 'Founded by the Abolitionists in 1787 to afford a refuge for liberated negroes and an encouragement for the development of legitimate commerce'. On the other hand, Lloyd also tells us that there was indeed no international force forthcoming to police the abolished slave-trading. Lloyd discusses the 1815 Congress of Vienna following the end of the Napoleonic Wars, saying that Castlereagh:

> Spurred on by Wilberforce...proposed a convention between Britain, Russia, Prussia, Austria and France to suppress the trade by means of an armed international police force. This was an idea far in advance of the times.

An international force did not materialise. He notes that only 'a vague General Declaration' was obtained.[48] A national force was left to fill the gap; Lloyd continues:

> It was left to the British ... to provide the necessary police force and thereby to establish what, perforce, became the *Pax Britannica*.

Lloyd's interpretation concludes that the heaviest burden for the next 75 years 'fell upon the junior officers and men of the Royal Navy'.[49] Since the international force was not forthcoming, it could be said that a national force on the part of Britain is to be seen in action.[50]

The concluding lines would then have to be read differently from supposing there to be a pun on the word 'domestic'. It may not after all look a viable interpretation of the conclusion of the novel to think of such a play on words. The references throughout the novel to the West Indies probably do not allude to policing since that critically took place off the West Coast of Africa. As T.C. McCaskie says, 'After 1808 the Royal Navy patrolled West Africa in order to intercept slave ships'.[51] He says that after Court hearings in Freetown it was there that the freed slaves were settled. This policing takes a while to become established.[52] Peter Burroughs cites later years:

'Between 1815–1846 ... naval squadrons suppressed ... African slave trading'.[53] As an alternative to thinking in terms of a pun on 'domestic', the last lines of the novel might instead be seen as acknowledging the new policing by virtue of allusion in the words 'national importance'.

The 'domestic virtues', in the last paragraph of the novel, echo a reference to domestic affairs that occurs in the first paragraph of the novel. There, it is Sir Walter's domestic affairs being unsettling that causes him to seek comfort in perusal of the tome giving the history of his family. The link of the domestic at the end of the novel with sorting out Mrs Smith's income may take up the link at the beginning of the novel of domestic affairs with Sir Walter's local domestic economy, all of which may set a keynote for us to interpret reference to the domestic in this novel as very much to do with the handling of money and property. In relation to the property in the West Indies that is under 'a sort of sequestration', issues in the external world were emerging that were relevant to progress in following up the abolition of the slave trade with moves towards emancipation. Understanding the concluding sentence should possibly be in terms of the precedence of the 'national importance' over the 'domestic virtues' of the Navy. It would be of interest, I think, to note that in Jane Austen's revision can be seen the change in the manuscript to 'importance' from possibly 'renown' that she had written before. R.W. Chapman in his Notes to his facsimile of the manuscript says that he reads the word crossed out and replaced by 'importance' as 'renown'. I cannot myself decipher the word.[54]

Whether labelled 'national' or 'domestic', the new task of policing the abolished slave trade, just because it is now part of the Navy's duties, could be part of what is lauded and that would be best served by not omitting the vital phrase 'if possible' in the novel's concluding sentence, which I quote at the head of this chapter. This phrase establishes as a superlative rating what would otherwise have been a comparative. My reading is different from that of Brian Southam, who speaks of:

> the playful irony of the closing lines. This is a Navy held in the embrace of romantic comedy, a service now 'more distinguished in its domestic virtues than in its national importance'.

His reading depends on his not including Jane Austen's phrase 'if possible'.[55] But omitting this phrase radically alters the clause in which it is actually embedded. The whole clause targets superlative merit. Indeed, without her phrase 'if possible', the concluding lines would be consistent with the Navy not being particularly distinguished in either respect. That outcome would certainly not be consistent with Anne's endorsement of the worth of the Navy, when, in chapter 3, on finding a tenant for Kellynch Hall, Anne says:

The navy, I think who have done so much for us, have at least an equal claim with any other set of men, for all the comforts and all the privileges which any home can give.

Southam had earlier set out one of the purposes of his book in saying:

The Navy closest to Jane Austen's heart is that described with a sly diminuendo in the final words of *Persuasion*, a 'profession' 'more distinguished in its domestic virtues than in its national importance'; and it is one of the purposes of this book to determine, as well as we can, why Jane Austen should choose to confront the reader, as she does, in presenting this amusing and surprising reversal of values: the 'domestic' above the 'national' and 'virtues' above 'importance'.

However, contrary to his view, with the retaining of the 'if possible' phrase it is open to infer that it would not be possible to get better than the Navy's national importance.

It looks as if there could be three different readings of the final clause with its 'if possible' phrase: firstly, that domestic virtues are preeminent. Alternatively, it is not possible for domestic virtues to take the prize, and that would be because there is equality between the rating of domestic virtues and national importance, or thirdly because national importance takes precedence. If the whole clause is indeed not a mere comparative, which would not necessarily issue in praise on either count, but is instead a targeting of the superlative, then that the national importance might take precedence over the domestic virtues has to be a possibility. Otherwise an attempt to target the domestic virtues as superlative would collapse. It is only if the domestic virtues might be outmatched by the national importance that they are seen to be highly praised. But that entails that it at least makes sense to read the whole 'if possible' clause as meaning that the Navy is after all most distinguished with respect to its national importance.

Depending on a reader's own preference in rating, one possibility is asserting the even greater superiority of national importance. Doubtless someone such as Francis, Jane Austen's naval brother who as an abolitionist would be impressed by the new naval work following 1807, would accord greater importance to the national importance than to the domestic virtues, and take up the opening left by the author for a reader to introduce a judgement '... but it is not possible ...', so affirming a higher rating of the national importance.

The author's intentions with respect to the rating of the domestic virtues of the Royal Navy will be judged in part by any element of humour that has become attached earlier to its display of domestic virtues. At the time of the fall on the Cobb, Captain Wentworth appears slightly ridiculous:

'Is there no one to help me?' were the first words which burst from Captain Wentworth, in a tone of despair, and as if all his own strength were gone.

Captain Wentworth's own coming back down to earth, after his having been basking in the admiration of the girls, is noted by his dashing away as soon as Anne says 'A surgeon!' and Anne having to recall him saying that it would be better if someone went who knew where to find a surgeon. Anne too, once we have been given confidence that she looks set to succeed, can be teased by the author:

> Prettier musings of high-wrought love and eternal constancy, could never have passed along the streets of Bath, than Anne was sporting with from Camden-place to Westgate-buildings. It was almost enough to spread purification and perfume all the way.

Then later, in the concluding lines of the novel, at one and the same time the domestic virtues of the Navy are both genuinely lauded but known to have been earlier teased. The high rating of them at the later stage could derive not only from our being impressed by the love story but from an earlier teasing of the domestic virtues, so that they can then later be placed literally alongside the national importance with no absurdity. We would already have had the fun at the expense of the domestic virtues. An option would remain to take the later comparison with a pinch of salt because of the element of indulgent humour that has accompanied the ups and downs of the lovers' relationship, but nevertheless the very teasing could clear the way for targeting of the superlative for the domestic virtues, as a possible reading.

The Navy has been lauded to the skies, in my view, which is different from Brian Southam's interpretation. This is secured by the careful phrasing of 'if possible' included within the closing sentence, so that a superb compliment has been made. His alternative view sees more credit potentially being accorded to the Army. Interestingly his view runs counter to Edward Said's view. On Brian Southam's view the Navy is seen much more modestly, especially relative to the Army, than would be suggested by the view of Edward Said. Alternatively to both of them, the Navy could be lauded while one would need to take into account that by this time enforcing the abolition of the slave trade is part of the Navy's work, even if it is only in the early stages. Lauding the national importance could be deprived of a crudely patriotic note by the nice juxtaposition of the highly rated domestic virtues. The way could be cleared for targeting of the superlative for the national importance, as a different or preferred reading.

III. West Indian property

Important dates within the text coincide with significant dates in the change in policy of 1807 of eradicating Britain's own slave trade and the seven subsequent years have already involved naval help which Jane

Austen would probably have learned of through her Navy brothers. This naval support of abolition should not be overlooked as part of the chronological external context of the carefully placed dates within the fictional narrative of *Persuasion*. At the very least, Captain Wentworth becomes rich essentially after the abolition of the slave trade. Jane Austen makes absolutely clear the dates of his progress.

It could, however, be countered that many of the apparent allusions are just that, merely apparent. Specifically, could not the starting point in the Battle of San Domingo of 1806 be nothing other than a compliment to her brother who had fought in it?[56] The novel's back references over more than seven years would then be seen as merely accommodating time for Captain Wentworth to make his fortune and to trigger the drama of the main story. This might in any case be a safe conclusion, given historical controversy surrounding the causes of the 1807 Abolition and its aftermath. The reference to San Domingo gives rise to differing reactions. There is Christopher Lloyd's dismay at the earlier massacre in Haiti where successful slave revolt was at issue.[57] By contrast there is C.L.R. James's analysis of this same phenomenon from a different perspective.[58] Jane Austen's probable intense interest was complex. Selma James notes the significance to the Austens of San Domingo, the island of the Haitian revolution:

> The Haitian Revolution? Her sister Cassandra, the person to whom she was always closest, was to have married a man who died on San Domingo, the island of the revolution. Napoleon's troops were there to put down the slaves and were dying like flies of fever. He dies at that time; he may even have died of the same fever. He may have been involved – for or against is now irrelevant. What is more to the point is that having the future husband of her beloved sister there would have made all the Haitian happenings of intense personal concern.[59]

However, it would not be easy to divest contemporary readers of associations of thought on encountering the Navy in this text with such a background of precise dates and references to the West Indies.

Readers would not be thinking with hindsight of the author's family connections but would be going by what they read, and some of them could be expected to read with knowledge of current affairs, particularly of the 1807 Abolition, if not in detail of the crucial role of the Navy. Furthermore, it looks as if a contemporary reader who did see allusions to the 1807 Abolition would also see the placing, within the concluding two paragraphs at the end of the book, of the business of Mrs Smith's West Indian property as topical. Captain Wentworth's acting on her behalf, the difference it makes to her income and the implied upshot that if the income had been greater it would not have corrupted her outlook on life, all go to make a contrast with the attitudes of Sir Walter and Anne's sister Elizabeth, whose monetary affairs are discussed but not followed through. The discussion of their finances is superseded in the text by the subsequent details about Mrs Smith's finances. Just as we look set to concentrate on a happy outcome for a hero and heroine, we are plunged in the final two paragraphs into fine detail about the handling of the West Indian property.

I infer, therefore, that there is a surprise sting in the conclusion of this novel. That Jane Austen directs our attention to such matters is to rock the boat. Specifically, there is one element in common between this abolition relevant issue in *Persuasion* and the integration in the two earlier novels of reference to the slave trade. The common element is the critique of the role of money and property. In *Persuasion* as the final paragraph opens, part of the surprise is the terms in which money is discussed. Whereas money and good health would standardly be offered as desirable prerequisites for happiness so that one expects the author to be noting this very improvement to be coming about, in her actual remarks the author presents the matter as of Mrs Smith being able to retain her happiness despite the improvement in fortune and health. She then goes on to praise Mrs Smith as one who would even have been able to be happy had she attained greater wealth and health. To take us by surprise, in this reversal of some renderings of conventional wisdom about money, interacts with readers to invite reflection on issues of money in the aftermath of the 1807 Abolition.

Questions would have been necessary for some contemporary readers to consider at the time as to what to do now that there will be no further supply of slaves from a slave trade. There would have been an additional question for someone in Mrs Smith's relatively modest circumstances that if the earlier campaigning is continued and results in emancipation, there could be a cash flow problem with no money to pay wages however small, so that it might be prudent to sell up in good time. Even for someone without such a personal interest, thinking about another's problem puts the issue on an agenda for debate. It would bring attention to the sort of queries that supporters of the status quo might rather not see raised for a public debate that could be unsettling.

Historically, the new role for the Navy in policing abolition made for a radical change. Jane Austen's interest in the Navy put her in a position to be very well-aware of this radical change, and it looks suggestive that her story should itself involve radical change in personal lives against a naval backdrop. Sufficient detail is given, of the future for Sir Walter and Elizabeth, before turning to Mrs Smith's West Indian affairs, to indicate that the financial future, particularly for Elizabeth, looks uncertain. This illustrates that there is nothing written in stone about the apportioning of money and property, a point taken up again in the resolution of Mrs Smith's sequestered property in the West Indies. To raise the topic of rights over property is to raise the topic that is top of the agenda for debate following the abolition of the slave trade, when the continuing supply and future status of slaves as property was an issue that would not be going away.

From the time of Mrs Smith's revelations about Mr Elliot's character, with the attendant detail about her sequestered property that Mr Elliot could have helped her to recover it, the issues involved are kept in mind by Anne's wanting to tell Lady Russell of Mr Elliot's ruined character and having to put that off continually. In the allusion to the *Arabian Nights*, delay is ironically compared to the Sultaness's success in putting off being beheaded. By means of the emphasized delay, the reader can then, I suggested, focus on the resolution of Captain's Wentworth's dealing with Mrs Smith's problem in the penultimate paragraph, just because it is a topic that has not been dropped but that has skilfully been kept for development until its highlighting in the conclusion.

It remains conjectural whether a possible reference to the new policing following the 1807 Abolition is intended. It also looks conjectural whether there is provocation to think further about conditions still obtaining in the West Indies, through Mrs Smith's affairs being highlighted at the end. What does seem inescapable is that the contemporary reader's attention is drawn to abolition relevant dates and places and also property issues, and that such attention serves better the interests of reform than of those looking to gain from a continuation of the status quo of slavery. Subtlety would pay off again in the care needed not to be counterproductive.

Mr Elliot provides a domestic link between the opening and closing paragraphs. He is involved as male heir in the future of Sir Walter's domestic affairs as they relate to Kellynch Hall. At the end of the book it is he who has held up the retrieval of property in the West Indies triggering some of the display of domestic virtues on Captain Wentworth's part in taking over the matter. There is a nice irony here that it might have been better for Mr Elliot to have gained such legal experience himself, since he looks potentially set to follow in Mrs Smith's footsteps with sequestered property where Kellynch Hall is concerned. Although Sir Walter decided not to sell the property, we learn in chapter 1 that he had mortgaged Kellynch Hall as much as he was able. The beginning of chapter 2 had implied that the lawyer, Mr Shepherd, is deeply involved in the management of the estate. Mr Shepherd's influence may be further felt now that his daughter has become the mistress of Mr Elliot with a view to marrying him, an aim on Mrs Clay's part that Jane Austen indicates. One can even wonder whether Mr Elliot had more than one motive in courting Mrs Clay; in addition to stopping the possibility of her marrying Sir Walter himself, Mr Elliot may regard Mrs Clay as an insurance policy when it comes to inheriting and having legal dealings with her father, Mr Shepherd.

The closing lines of the final chapter of *Persuasion* could have the effect of inviting a reader to map the fictional story line onto a narrative of events in the external world. Then if one situation is modelled on another situation, analogies could be drawn between the two situations, those of the novel and of the external world, to enable viewing alternatives involved in resolution of the 'if possible' proviso. Dates and places already given within the novel would be key parts of the data. So, too, is the wide-ranging term 'domestic' looking to money management in the affairs of Sir Walter and of Mr Elliot the heir-apparent to Kellynch Hall and, on the other hand, to perceived humane qualities on the part of the Royal Navy whether in the fictional story or in the external world.

At the time of the setting of the action, beginning with 'in the year six' and with emphasis on the summer of 1814, an external factor to take into account along with the Abolition of 1807 would be the continuing public interest in international action to abolish the slave trade. In the light of the intense public interest during the summer of 1814 in campaigning for the slave trade to be abolished internationally, it might be that the focus of the author would be more likely to be on that international consideration rather than on the less peaceful implications of naval enforcement of the British ban on slave trading.

On the enforcing aspect, the Navy's work was in the early stages and in any case gave rise to fresh considerations. Eric Williams makes a striking point: that abolitionists became concerned about the level of force needed to work a slave squadron and the possibility of causing suffering by the policy of forcible suppression of the slave trade.[60] This makes, therefore, for a more tentative conclusion about what was going on and what attitudes would have been.

IV. Policing the British abolition of the slave trade

Jane Austen had certainly taken notice of international events in London during the summer of 1814. A letter to Cassandra, who was staying in London at the time, for 14 June 1814, shows interest in the visit of the Emperor of Russia to London, when she refers to Tsar Alexander of Russia, feted in London as hugely popular following Russia's contribution to the defeat of Napoleon:

> Take care of yourself & do not be trampled to death in running after the Emperor.

It was in the same summer of 1814 that popular opinion about the international slave trade had been intense in England and in June the Houses of Parliament had received such a considerable number of petitions demanding international abolition of the slave trade that the Government had to take that into account in foreign policy in the shaping of the new Europe at the end of the Napoleonic Wars.

In conclusion, in *Persuasion* it is open to think in terms of celebration of the Royal Navy and to remember its new role following the 1807 abolition of the slave trade. The occasion may be seen as paralleled by a story of triumph over difficulties of the lovers that can be offered as a tribute to the Royal Navy. Brian Simpson highlights the part the Navy would play:

The Royal Navy served as a highly efficient police force ... freedom from slavery as a fundamental human right was not, however, formally recognised in any international instrument before the adoption of the Universal Declaration in 1948 ...Back in the nineteenth century when it all began the Foreign Office and Royal Navy provided an alternative to any international institution. At a national level in states committed to its abolition individuals could effectively protect their liberty through domestic law.[61]

If there is concern about abolition issues in this novel, then it could also be said that focus swivels between anti-slave trading and anti-slavery. Issues raised by sequestered property in the West Indies are related to slavery rather than to the slave trade. Where emphasis is on the work of the Royal Navy, it is the banned slave trade that is relevant. Indeed, policing the abolition of the slave trade could affect the work of Jane Austen's own naval brothers. The 1807 Abolition had a more practical effect on the Royal Navy than on any other segment of English society because it affected the work its people were required to do.[62]

Celebration could be seen as in honour of the gains made by abolitionism, just as Thomas Clarkson rejoiced in 1808 in the conclusion of his *History*. As Anne and Captain Wentworth were able to make a new beginning, so was the Royal Navy.[63] In the case of the lovers, the mistake of eight years ago is superseded; *Persuasion* is very much a novel of moving on after radical change of mind, with a keynote set in chapter 4: 'Anne, at seven and twenty, thought very differently from what she had been made to think at nineteen'. In the case of the Navy, eight years previously had ushered in the phenomenal change in their role from protecting the slave trade to stopping slave trading by British ships, a momentous change after two hundred and fifty years.

Part II

The Context in which Jane Austen Wrote the Chawton Novels

5
Some Philosophers on Race and Slavery: Opposing Viewpoints

in the central part of England ... Murder was not tolerated, servants were not slaves, and neither poison nor sleeping potions to be procured, like rhubarb, from every druggist.

Northanger Abbey, chapter 25

I am fond of history – and am very well contented to take the false with the true. In the principal facts they have sources of intelligence in former histories and records, which may be as much depended on, I conclude, as any thing that does not actually pass under one's own observation, and as for the little embellishments you speak of, they are embellishments, and I like them as such. If a speech be well drawn up, I read it with pleasure, by whomsoever it may be made – and probably with much greater, if the production of Mr. Hume or Mr. Robertson, than if the genuine words ...

Northanger Abbey, chapter 14

Introduction

For a long time, received opinion held that the Enlightenment marked a decisive advance in human thought and understanding. Latterly, however, a more nuanced approach has emerged, in which, alongside the undoubted strengths of Enlightenment thought, darker sides have also been recognized. In particular, it is possible to detect that some of the most important thinkers of the Enlightenment had fallen into racism. Richard Popkin had noted:

Historians of philosophy are just beginning to become aware that many of the philosophical heroes of the Enlightenment ... expressed views that sound shockingly racist today. When I have quoted the following note which Hume added to his essay 'Of National Characters', philosophers ... have been shocked and dismayed ...

The note which Hume added to his essay *Of National Characters* referred to by Popkin is one I shall consider. Popkin also cites the British empiricist philosopher George Berkeley and the German philosopher Immanuel Kant, and for these two he may have had in mind passages I look at. However, I think that a distinction should be made between these two philosophers on the one hand and Hume. There is a view ascribed by Popkin to earlier thinkers of:

> Biblical humanism and with it the conviction that everyone, no matter what he looked like, was an image of God.[1]

I think Berkeley and possibly Kant would hold such a view of mankind in common with Jane Austen.

Diametrically opposed views on race and slavery were characteristic of the time in which Jane Austen wrote. As illustration of part of the intellectual world into which she was born, I consider some eighteenth-century Western philosophers. In the 1759 *Theory of Moral Sentiments*, Adam Smith speaks of the magnanimity of enslaved Negroes, ascribing to them a degree of magnanimity of which their 'sordid' masters were scarcely capable of conceiving. His pointing out that slave masters were justly held in contempt by the vanquished, and his praise of those taken from the coast of Africa as coming from nations of heroes, set him apart from many of his contemporaries. Jane Austen may have come across Adam Smith's work, perhaps through Thomas Clarkson's *History*.

I. Immanuel Kant

The work of the German philosopher Immanuel Kant was translated in her time, and translation was available of some of Kant's writings that Jane Austen might have had an opportunity to see.[2] Kantian ethics may be alluded to in *Sense and Sensibility*.[3] Opposed by Elinor, Marianne declares that she would know whether she did the right thing. Marianne had allowed Willoughby to take her around his aunt's home, and Marianne is very sure about the position she takes. It has been suggested to me that this could be a Kantian position, where in the context of his belief that: 'ought implies can', he thinks a person is typically aware of what ought to be done. Kant's is an egalitarian position, and teenage girls would not be excluded from knowing what was right.[4] Given that it is not obvious that Marianne is in the right but nevertheless claims knowledge, this could be a look at the snags thought to arise with Kant's famous 'ought implies can' ethical stance.

Moreover, towards the close of Volume 1 in chapter 21, Marianne refuses to carry out the social niceties; it is left to Elinor to smooth the waters in trivial matters by telling the 'lies':

> 'What a sweet woman Lady Middleton is!' said Lucy Steele. Marianne was silent; it was impossible for her to say what she did not feel, however trivial the occasion; and upon Elinor therefore the whole task of telling lies when politeness required it, always fell.

This contrast between the sisters does seem to be stressed in the novel, as if the author is interested in how people should proceed with regard to truthfulness. However, Kant 'insists that truthfulness is an unconditional duty'.[5] Nevertheless, there is a strong current throughout the novels of an ethical position akin to Kant's, in so far as a key Kantian concern was that people should be treated as ends in themselves not as means to others' ends.[6]

More recent translations bear out Kant's internationalism. In his *Physical Geography* there is a terse dismissal of any attempt to denigrate on grounds of skin colour.[7] Kant challenges:

> Some people imagine that Ham is the father of the Moors and that God made him black as a punishment which now all his descendants have inherited. However, one can provide no proof as to why the colour black should be the mark of a curse in a more fitting fashion than the colour white.

This robust defence of black men by Kant is heralded by an aesthetic remark:

> In Africa one calls Moors those brown people who are descendents of the Mauren. The actual black people are the Negroes. The above-mentioned Moors stretch along the coast of Barbary to Senegal. In comparison, from there to Gambia are the blackest Moors, but also the most beautiful in the world, above all the Wolofs.[8]

Wolof peoples had been enslaved in the sixteenth century, according to Philip Curtin who notes the 'uncertainty of eighteenth-century nomenclature'.[9] Kant here singles out Wolofs in celebrating the beauty of a black skin.

II. John Locke

Echoes in Jane Austen of the British Empiricist philosopher John Locke have been suggested by the literary critic Jocelyn Harris, and she comments on *Northanger Abbey* that Catherine:

> deals in verifiable fact when she asserts that 'murder was not tolerated, servants were not slaves, and neither poison nor sleeping potions to be procured, like rhubarb, from every druggist', a sequence that echoes Locke's '*Rhubarb* will purge, *Hemlock* kill, and *Opium* make a man sleepy'.

Jocelyn Harris had said that 'Catherine ... traces her error back to romances, allowing like Henry, like Locke, that the morality of the romances she has been reading may be local and relative'.[10] While it may be coincidence that there is an echo of Locke in *Northanger Abbey*, his views had been influential in discussion of how knowledge is acquired.

In an earlier book Jocelyn Harris raises the question of slavery with respect to Locke and quotes the beginning of his *Two Treatises of Government*.[11]

However, the historian Robin Blackburn comments on this same Lockean passage:

> he had no intention of challenging the appropriateness of slavery for commoner Africans.[12]

Some argue that there is inconsistency between Locke's theory of liberty and his practice, as in his buying shares in the monopoly English slave trading company.

There were already stark contrasts in attitudes in the time of Locke, whose *Essay Concerning Human Understanding* had come out in 1690. His *Two Treatises of Government* came out at about the same time. The historian Simon Schama quotes Richard Baxter in 1673:

> How cursed a crime is it to equal men to beasts. Is not this your practice? Do you not buy them and use them merely as you do horses to labour for your commodity? ... Do you not see how you reproach and condemn yourselves while you vilify them all as savages?[13]

Richard Baxter is praised by Clarkson in his 1808 *History* as one of the earliest people to speak out against the slave trade, when more became known of it by 1670–80.[14]

At that time, Lord Chief Justice Holt also spoke up for freedom from slavery where a Negro coming to England was concerned. This is later noted by W.J. Gardner in his 1873 *History of Jamaica*, lauding Chief Justice Holt:

> The legal question of man's right to property in his fellow-man was first judicially raised in England in the days of William and Mary. Chief Justice Holt then decided that a negro coming to England was free: for 'one may be a villeyn in England, but not a slave' (Salkeld's 'Reports', vol. ii. p. 666.) Unhappily this decision was suffered to fall into abeyance. Men did not then think sufficiently of rights other than his own, still less could they see the logical deduction that might be drawn from such a decision. It was nearly a century before men said: 'We have no slaves at home: then why abroad?'[15]

Gardner here, two hundred years later, indicates some conflicting views from the last years of the 1600s with nearly a century to go before Cowper's question is put and heard as a compelling challenge.

Documented experience then available of Europeans enslaved may have entrenched a view of slavery as an established fact of life, in Locke's thought.[16] Locke when he was in Holland may have seen Dutch engravings showing white slaves in slave markets in North Africa. Although it is thought that his *Two Treatises of Government* were written between 1680–83, they were not published until 1689, and there was time for his ideas to settle during his exile in Holland between 1683–89, mainly in Amsterdam until early 1687, and then in Rotterdam.

The possible allusion in *Northanger Abbey* would be to Locke's *Essay Concerning Human Understanding*, where he talks of the properties of rhubarb for purging, of poison and of sleeping potions. Locke says in the chapter 'The Extent of Human Knowledge' that such properties, unlike supposed *a priori* knowledge, have to be learned from experience.[17] However, in *Northanger Abbey* what is referred to by the narrator is not experience of sensory perception, but instead reference to how these things are procured in the social system, as shown in the comedy of inexperienced Catherine as so cautious that she speaks for central England only, being prepared in ignorance to concede different practice for the northern and western extremities of England.

The additional observation that 'servants were not slaves' is also a part of Catherine's daily life experience of the social system. The reference to slaves may be related to issues raised in the political philosophy of Locke's *Second Treatise*. However, as Mark Goldie says: 'There is a deep puzzle about Locke's commitment to natural law in the *Two Treatises*' as over against the *Essay* which 'declares the mind at birth to be a *tabula rasa*, a blank slate; Knowledge comes only from experience'.[18] It remains unclear whether there is inconsistency on Locke's part, an inconsistency between the empiricism of the *Essay* and the readiness in the *Two Treatises* to posit natural rights.

Locke on liberty had been quoted at the 1772 Somersett Trial.[19] Jane Austen's saying 'servants were not slaves' could be an affirmation of the Mansfield Decision. Since 'servants were not slaves' is in the same sentence as the apparent allusion to Locke, it may be indication that she knew Locke's work had contributed to the 1772 case by his views on liberty in England being quoted in support of the person on trial. Jane Austen could be running together allusion to Locke's *Essay* and a further allusion to the use made of him in the Somersett case, clustering articles of trading together, as an experiment. In this respect there is an echo of *Emma* where seeing people as commodities is satirized. If the passage in *Northanger Abbey* was part of revision, it may have been written at about the same time. In the proceedings leading up to the 1772 Mansfield decision, Locke was drawn on as an authority in the 'Argument of Mr Hargrave for the Negro':

> Mr Locke has framed another kind of argument against slavery by contract... and the substance of it is, that a right of preserving life is unalienable; that freedom from arbitrary power is essential to the exercise of that right; and, therefore, that no man can by compact enslave himself.[20]

Locke's view is made relevant amongst the arguments on opposing sides by Mr Hargrave, who wished to eliminate any claim that James Somersett was obliged by contract to carry out his master's instructions to leave the country to return to slavery in Virginia. The fact that in the hearings leading up to the Mansfield Decision it is asserted that on Locke's view one cannot enter a contract to enslave oneself, may give particular pertinence to the point in *Northanger Abbey* that 'servants were not slaves'.

What, however, is to be said of Locke's contact with slavery in the American Colonies?[21] He was not only involved in providing in the 1670s for absolute dominion over slaves in the Constitution for Carolina. He had also been involved in the English slave trade after that trade was entrusted in 1672 to the Royal African Company. He bought shares in the company. These are two factors in Locke's practice, which seem to be inconsistent with his political theory.[22]

Another literary critic Donna Landry refers to the work of Jocelyn Harris utilizing Locke's abhorrence of slavery:

> Jocelyn Harris...continues, 'slavery' is the first word of Locke's first treatise of government.[23]

In referring to Locke on slavery, Jocelyn Harris appears to have thought in terms of abhorrence at an English gentleman suffering slavery under an overbearing monarch. Although Robin Blackburn rounds out a wider context, his rendering is misleading. Locke distinguishes different sorts of rights, not all to be lumped together. Blackburn says:

> When Locke declared that the principal aim of government was the 'defence of property', he meant this in a larger sense; land, buildings, cattle, offices of profit, privileges and exemptions, the liberties of the subject and the latter's rights over other persons, including wives, indentured servants and slaves, all counted as 'property'.[24]

I think Jocelyn Harris underestimated how far Locke had already included women as protected from slavery, in an England without an absolute monarch. Where it suits Locke to emphasize the accompanying power of the mother over a minor, the mother's power as well as the father's is made much of.[25]

The opening sentence on slavery of the *First Treatise* refers to Sir Robert Filmer, as Locke tells us on the title page. The writer he was opposing had wanted more power for the sovereign over his subjects. By the end of the *Second Treatise*, it looks as if, in the event of the ruler forfeiting his power through misuse, the people of the community are sovereign. This offsets an impression given by Robin Blackburn that it is the case of the English gentleman only that concerns Locke.

Is there, however, tension on Locke's part between political theory and actual practice over the literal engaging in chattel slavery? He had had significant involvement and influence in the system of slave holding in the Colonies. Robin Blackburn notes that 'In 1672 the English slave trade was entrusted to a new monopoly, the Royal African Company'. He adds that John Locke who 'was for a time the secretary of the Committee on Plantations' was a shareholder.[26] Wayne Glausser discusses in more detail Locke's support for the slave trading company and also his involvement with the group of people who had been granted proprietorship of Carolina. For Glausser, 'Apparently Locke could endorse the Carolina slavery clause without qualms even if he did not himself compose it'. Glausser goes on to discuss others' different interpretations of Locke's attitude to the provision that 'every freeman of Carolina shall have absolute power and authority over his negro slave of what opinion or religion soever'.[27]

It is unclear to me what significance if any should be accorded to Locke's work on Carolina being 20 years earlier than the eventual publication of the *Two Treatises*. Robin Blackburn is right that reference to conquest and the state of war would appear to lead to a justification, such as it is, for slavery. Blackburn, however, on a further point misrepresents Locke:

> John Locke ... famously declared: 'Slavery is so vile and miserable an estate of man, and so directly opposite to the generous temper and Courage of our nation; that 'tis hardly to be conceived, that an *Englishman*, much less a *Gentleman*, should plead for it' ... He wrote of primitive man that 'to turn loose to an unrestrain'd Liberty, before he has Reason to guide him, is the not allowing him the privilege of his nature, to be free'.[28]

Blackburn misrepresents Locke here; in the *Second Treatise of Government*, section 63, which Blackburn quotes concerning: '...Reason to guide him...', Locke says:

> This is that which puts the authority into the parents' hands to govern the minority of their children.

Locke here speaks about children, not about so-called 'primitive man'.

Chattel slaves were regarded as property. Locke had been cited in Johnson's *Dictionary* for '*property*' as yielding an entry 'right of possession'. Robin Blackburn discusses the concept of property in the philosophy of Locke, and writes:

> Locke's famous definition of property could easily be extended to plantations and their products: 'Thus the grass my Horse has bit, the Turfs my servant has cut: and the Ore I have digg'd in any place where I have a right to them in common with others, become my *Property*.'[29]

However, Blackburn leaves out the crucial introduction by Locke of the fact that money changed the picture of what was captured by his 'famous definition'. That was in terms of 'I...my...my...I...I', suggesting a small scale enterprise.[30]

Suspect provenance of property in a slave found to be captured in peace-time against his will, would not meet Locke's criteria for legitimate property. Glausser points out that 'Locke denies to conquerors any claims on the children of captives'.[31] Locke says that the condition of slavery is not a hereditary one, in the *Second Treatise*, in chapter 16 'Of conquest'. It is possible he may have thought this irrelevant to chattel slavery in the plantations if he reckoned on slaves being imported to work and planters not being interested in slave breeding. As Robin Blackburn says:

> Locke's summary defence of slavery was that it represented 'the state of war continued, between a lawful Conqueror, and a Captive'.[32]

Locke says it is part of what is meant by slavery that the master acquires absolute power. Otherwise a contract would have been entered into, and to enter into a contract would have been inconsistent with his view of slavery as a continuation of a state of war.

What looks crucial in his view of slavery in the *Second Treatise* is the emphasis on war, and its significance for forfeiture. In chapter 7, section 85 he says:

> slaves, who being captives taken in a just war, are by the right of nature subjected to the absolute dominion and arbitrary power of their masters. These men having, as I say, forfeited their lives ... cannot in that state be considered as any part of civil society.

Such a state of war is revisited in chapter 15, section 172:

> captives, taken in a just and lawful war, and such only, are subject to a despotical power...

In Locke's view, slaves could have been procured through war between Africans, giving rise to trading.

There is a passage in the *Second Treatise* chapter 4, section 23 to add to the respect in which in relation to God, people are 'His property, whose Workmanship they are', as he puts it in section 6. Locke says:

> Nobody can give more power than he has himself; and he that cannot take away his own life, cannot give another power over it.

For this reason, he thinks no-one can sell himself into slavery. However, his views on slavery are chilling when extended from the English Constitution to the American colonies. He says in section 23 that if someone has been made a slave but no longer wants life then that person can:

> draw on himself the death he desires

by resisting the will of his master. He seems to envisage the primary case of slaves as of people reprieved from a justifiable death, because they were conquered in a just war. A later challenge to this view would be over the original trading of the slave: '... by whatever fraud or violence he might have been originally brought into the merchant's power', as Doctor Johnson would later put it.

There was not racism in Locke's views on chattel slavery. Robin Blackburn says Locke is to be interpreted as accepting 'that negroes are indeed men'. Regarding him as 'one of the founders of English colonial slavery', he says:

> Yet he regarded any attempt to exclude Negroes from the human race as a childish delusion.[33]

Locke treats this matter in the chapter called *Maxims* in his *Essay*.[34] I agree with Robin Blackburn in his interpretation of this obscure passage. However, Locke does not consider whether in any case colour could be a minor factor compared with speech and action.

I think that Locke's practice and his theory on slavery can be rendered consistent, but at the cost of his having disregarded chattel slaves' interests.[35] A major concern for Locke, after so much earlier religious-political unrest, was the issue of toleration.[36] But leeway for people in England did not curb excesses abroad.[37] In the *Two Treatises* his real concern is with the people as a community in England; he sees people as free in a state of nature, but with natural rights that are fragile. On his view, as a result of some version of a social contract being acknowledged by a community, its citizens are regarded as having their liberty. Although liberty for citizens would be underpinned by reference to natural rights, it would be the laws of their own community and their Constitution that could guarantee those rights. Otherwise, as has been said in the context of American settlers, 'such rights went without safeguard'.[38] There would be no moral obligation on citizens to ensure natural rights outside their own citizenship body. Slaves brought in from outside would live without the protection accorded to citizens. Locke had made clear that by definition a slave is not in any form of contract with his master. He stressed that as soon as any form of contract is entered into, as with a servant, the life of the slave ceased to be forfeit to the master. His position accorded crucial status to the social contract that he saw as binding together a discrete community.

James Farr is convincing in arguing that Locke writes of war and slavery 'with more local objectives in mind'.[39] It appears Locke was well-informed on the practice of the slave trade. James Farr puts it:

> when Locke died in 1704, precious few Englishmen could have boasted of equalling his intimate knowledge of colonial life, foreign peoples, or slavery and the slave trade.[40]

Wayne Glausser thinks there is 'a fairly settled consensus' about the 'facts of Locke's involvement in slavery' amongst scholars, 'if not about how to evaluate them'.[41]

In connection with Locke's involvement in framing the constitution of Carolina, Lawrence James points out the effect of giving 'absolute authority' over slaves:

> According to the constitution of Carolina that was framed by the philosopher John Locke in 1669 'every free man' was 'to have absolute authority over his negro slaves', a principle which, in different forms, obtained throughout much of North America and the West Indies. Its everyday application gave plantation life a peculiar and often grotesque brutality.[42]

This crucial factor in New World slavery of 'grotesque brutality' would be compounded by increasing efficiency in slave-holdings during the course of the eighteenth century.

Locke uses the term 'slave' literally in such discussion. He had also used the term metaphorically in discussing the Englishman under an absolute monarch. Locke at one point seemed to think that absence of condemnation of slavery must be equated with an acceptance of it in a more fundamental sense. This is apparent in his *First Tract on Government* and in the slightly later *Second Tract on Government*.[43] However, absence of condemnation of slavery in the Gospels has to do with realistic appraisal of political conditions under the Roman Empire, rather than with condoning the practice. In the case of the New Testament and also of Locke, metaphorical and symbolic use of the term 'slave' rests upon a basis of undesirability of literal slavery, as in chattel slavery.

III. George Berkeley

Looking at a fellow British Empiricist philosopher George Berkeley gives us a different picture of attitudes to the colonies from those of Locke. There is no reason, so far as I know, to think that Berkeley's *Proposal for a College in Bermuda* of 1725 would have been known to the Austen family, although Bermuda was a place known to members of Jane Austen's family, and was, of course, referred to in *Persuasion* as one of the places visited by Mrs Croft.

In his *Proposal* Berkeley urges a college for training Native North American Indians as local clergy for missionary purposes. He thought that having Native American ministers of religion would be desirable because compatriots would be apt to trust them more, regarding foreigners as having:

> designs on the liberty or property of their converts.[44]

That was a shrewd pragmatic insight. Berkeley singled out Bermuda for a number of reasons, and it was from another clergyman that he derived a reason to suggest Bermuda as suitable for a seminary to train American

Indians to become clergymen. Berkeley sees the colonists in Bermuda as showing humanity. Of the colonists there he says that they:

> shew much more humanity to their slaves, and charity to one another, than is observed among the English in the other Plantations. One reason of this may be that condemned criminals, being employed in the manufactures of sugar and tobacco, were never transported thither. But, whatever be the cause, the facts are attested by a clergyman of good credit, who lived among them.

His reference to 'condemned criminals' as employed in other plantations helps to explain the barbarity that could occur in New World slavery, and is contemporary evidence of conditions at the time.

In the Preamble to the *Proposal*, Berkeley castigates the lack of Christian teaching and prevention of opportunity for baptism to slaves being brought in to the Colonies. He challenges the morality of the masters of slaves:

> the negroes of our Plantations, who to the infamy of England and scandal of the world, continue heathen under Christian masters, and in Christian countries.[45]

The strong language here of 'infamy' and 'scandal' would not have endeared him to slave owners, suspicious of the unsettling effects Christianity could have. This was to be an ongoing dispute, on the one hand the spread of Christianity being seen by some as the vocation of its present adherents, and on the other hand, the propagation of its core beliefs and invitation to reflect on them seen as inculcating social unrest.

James McKusick does not take as rosy a view of Berkeley's Bermuda enterprise as I do.[46] He may not, however, have taken on board in suggesting that the project is to produce better-behaved slaves that Berkeley does not claim such as a main aim. Berkeley points out that such an outcome would be a by-product, encouraging the reluctant to vote in Parliament for the setting up of the college and for money for it. He is practical about effects of the enterprise, just as at a later date some abolitionists were to appeal to self-interest on their opponents' part in order to bring about Parliamentary votes to their advantage. James McKusick also thinks in terms of Native Indians being brainwashed at this college to train them for ordination, so it is worth pointing out that Berkeley waxes enthusiastic about a wide curriculum including mathematics and rhetoric, subjects providing a training in independent thinking that would encourage questioning. Against anticipated objections to training native Indians for ordination as clergymen as a waste of time, Berkeley says:

> They shew as much natural sense as other uncultivated nations: that the empires of Mexico and Peru were evident proofs of their capacity, in which there appeared a relish of politics and a degree of art and politeness, which no European people were ever known to have arrived at without the use of letters or of iron, and which some perhaps have fallen short of with both those advantages.[47]

Locke, too, in the *Two Treatises* had noted the power of these empires. The wry conclusion, while typical Berkeley humour, would not have been what early empire builders intent on subordinating would have wanted to hear.

As a bishop, Berkeley had personal influence in Parliamentary circles at the time of his attempts to gain support for the college in Bermuda, which is described by G.J. Warnock. Although it failed to materialize, his project had obtained Parliamentary approval and promises of money; the money was never made available. Locke had earlier expressed concern for the spiritual well-being of Negro slaves.[48] But it is Berkeley who insists on this as a priority. There were attempts in Bermuda in the nineteenth century after Emancipation to set up non-segregated education in a college bearing Berkeley's name and commemorating that earlier *Proposal*. Kenneth Robinson has outlined the origins and early history of the Berkeley Educational Society in Bermuda.[49]

Robin Blackburn suggests that Berkeley takes slavery as a given in the world as it then was, referring to *The Querist* written between 1735–37 and citing *query 384* on the possibility of:

> making 'sturdy beggars...slaves of the public for a term of years', echoing Protector Somerset and John Locke's proposal of 1696–97.

Robin Blackburn had earlier said that Locke proposed 'three years compulsory labour' for English 'able-bodied beggars'.[50] Berkeley's whole book, *The Querist*, comprising a series of questions, concerns grinding poverty in Ireland where he was an Anglican bishop.[51] He asks whether able-bodied beggars should be made public slaves for a set period of time. *Query 384* is:

> Whether all sturdy beggars should not be seized and made slaves to the public for a certain term of years?

It is important to note that a 'certain term of years' ends this query, which would distinguish such from the life-sentence of the victim of the slave trade. George Fredrickson has rammed home the 'lifetime servitude' that characterized chattel slavery.[52]

Another important difference is that 'the public' would not have absolute rights of life and death, as was typical for chattel slaves. Robin Blackburn himself underwrites this point, because he shows how the New World developed a different system of chattel slavery. He says:

> New World slavery developed a novel ferocity, scale and focus ...The New World did not simply reproduce the prior features of slavery in Europe, the Mediterranean or Africa. It brought about what might be termed a *degradation of slavery*, violating on a massive scale even traditional notions of what slavery meant.[53]

Robin Blackburn here pinpoints a factor of vital importance that may have influenced the later abolitionists, appalled at the wrong-doing.

Berkeley's attitude to slavery may be that it was a misfortune for the slave rather than an appropriate condition for any human being. I think *Query 384* looks forward. It reads in accord with a view put forward by Bernard Williams, who argued that what prevailed in Ancient Greece was not Aristotle's attitude but an attitude that slavery was not so much a natural state as bad luck. Enslavement would occur as a result of a misfortune in being captured in war. Bernard Williams showed that the famous suggestion of Aristotle, that some people are suited to the condition of slavery, is out of line with the views of a number of his fellow intellectuals writing in Ancient Greece.[54] In the Berkeley *Query*, it is likewise not a matter of being suited to such treatment by nature, but of wondering whether such punishment might focus someone on avoiding punishment again at the finish of the 'certain term of years', and meanwhile of avoiding starvation, already a problem over a hundred years before the terrible Irish potato famine.

In Berkeley's *The Querist*, his *Query 384* is juxtaposed with another query whether he should be looking again at the use in the Greek New Testament of '*doulos*'. This would be translated as either 'servant' or 'slave', as in Classical Greek. Christianity began under the Roman Empire, which held slaves. In the earliest writing of the New Testament 1,700 years earlier, slavery was a fact of life to be endured, and was accompanied by symbolism based on that experience to indicate that slavery of sin, or of '*hamartia*', as in Classical Greek the missing of a rightly desired target, was a condition from which Christianity offered release.

The historian James Walvin suggests that in due course the hope inspired in black converts and also the fellow feeling in congregations in England was influential in the later process of abolition. Berkeley had proclaimed a duty to extend the Gospel and set his face against what he saw as 'irrational contempt of the blacks' who supposedly 'had no right to be instructed or admitted to the sacraments' in the words of his nineteenth-century biographer, A.C. Fraser.[55] Setting his face against such a view, Berkeley in the *Proposal* had thought it 'to the infamy of England and scandal of the world' that people should be excluded. Berkeley's biographer Fraser takes a Victorian self-righteous attitude to anyone who had had the ownership of slaves. Fraser is unable to put himself in the position of Berkeley a hundred and fifty years earlier, who in going to America to further his *Proposal* apparently took on slaves who were in due course baptised. Of course, as far as New World slaves were concerned, their slave songs, the later spirituals and the development of black Gospel music testified to messages slaves had derived from the teachings of both the Old and the New Testaments on release from bondage.

IV. Jane Austen on David Hume

Echoes in Jane Austen of another British Empiricist philosopher, David Hume, have been considered, suggesting Hume's ethics to be relevant to

Sense and Sensibility.[56] Running on different lines from this, I think, but on the topic of Hume and scepticism, it has also been suggested:

> Hume does not seem to have any sceptical doubts about our ability to grasp the motives of others.[57]

This would also be relevant for *Sense and Sensibility*, given that a recurrent experience for Elinor is her feeling that she is misrepresented and that her motives are misinterpreted. Turning away from Hume's philosophy, in the passage I quote at the head of this chapter, Jane Austen has her own comment on Hume's writing of history.

In *Northanger Abbey*, in chapter 14, the reference to David Hume when Miss Tilney expressed interest seems to be to his *History of England*. His Volume 1, chapter 1 has Caractacus and Agricola whom Miss Tilney cites and Hume's chapter 2 has Alfred the Great. Miss Tilney states her preference in chapter 14 for 'the production of Mr Hume or Mr Robertson' over 'the genuine words of Caractacus, Agricola, or Alfred the Great'. Reference had been to popular historical works by Scots historians Hume and William Robertson.[58]

Much of the reading public for history was female, and Hume was keen that history should be read by female readers.[59] Views on history in *Northanger Abbey* may echo Dr Johnson, who had said in 1769:

> We may know historical facts to be true, as we may know facts in common life to be true. Motives are generally unknown. We cannot trust to the characters we find in history, unless when they are drawn by those who knew the persons, as those, for instance, by Sallust and by Lord Clarendon.

Some literary critics have been more interested in finding Hume the philosopher rather than the historian in her novels. It is as well not to confuse the two. Paul Giles mistakes a remark by Johnson on Hume's history to be about Hume's philosophy, and compounds his mistake by misquoting the remark on Hume's history.[60] Johnson preferred Hume to Robertson as a historian. A few years after the 1769 remark about history and its writing by Lord Clarendon, Johnson says:

> I have not read Hume ... You must look upon Robertson's work as romance.

Two years later he had done his reading of Hume's history. He is noted as quipping and comparing the writing of history by Scotsmen unfavourably with that of the Englishman, Clarendon:

> Robertson, he said, used pretty words, but he liked Hume better, and neither of them would he allow to be more to Clarendon, than a rat to a cat.

The admiration had not been for Clarendon's style but for his 'matter':

> he is supported by his matter. It is, indeed, owing to a plethora of matter that his style is so faulty.

As in the earlier 1769 reference, Johnson seems to favour the Englishman Clarendon as a historian for being circumspect in his description of people.[61]

The apparent praise of Hume by Jane Austen turns out to look ironical.[62] The first impression of what Miss Tilney has to say can be of praise for the accounts by Hume, and since he does write in a very interesting way this would be no surprise. But it looks as if there is more to it than that, since the talk is also in terms of the false and the true. If the true could be said to be the 'genuine words' of these characters then Miss Tilney in saying she prefers instead the 'production of Mr Hume' may imply that what Hume gives us is in part false. Concerning a historian such a description must always sound like a criticism.

Now it would seem innocent enough that Hume should interest us with details of Alfred's burning the cakes. As Hume puts it in chapter 2:

> The good woman, on her return, finding her cakes all burnt, rated the king very severely, and upbraided him, that he always seemed very well pleased to eat her warm cakes, though he was thus negligent in toasting them.

And yet an apparent criticism remains in what Miss Tilney has said. Why could it matter that David Hume fleshes out the human interest with a likely rendering? That was a matter of Hume's liveliness in putting words into the mouth of historical characters whose career he described.

The implied criticism in *Northanger Abbey* may be that it could matter in those circumstances where what is expressed in the 'little embellishments' misleads. Since people's 'genuine words' were not often recorded there was a strong case for such invention, but the novel's sharp comment does point up risks of misrepresentation.[63] It has been suggested that:

> Hume forgot his own doctrines, over causation for example, the moment he turned to writing about past events.[64]

Jane Austen's reference to Hume as a historian is barbed and appears to show uneasiness over Hume's embellishments to 'the principal facts'.

V. David Hume

Hume shows interest in the affairs of his time in his *Essays: Moral, Political, and Literary*, and a good general knowledge. Modern economists speak highly of the stature of his essay, *Of the Balance of Trade*.[65] However, in a recent article in *Hume Studies*, Aaron Garrett has noted Hume's by now much publicized footnote in *Of National Characters* and asked 'Why should we care about one footnote?'[66] What is the footnote?[67] Robin Blackburn comments:

> The Enlightenment was not so antagonistic to slavery as was once thought. ...even such distinguished intellects as David Hume, Immanuel Kant and Georg Hegel casually employed racial stereotypes derogatory to Africans.[68]

As an addition by Hume to his 1748 essay *Of National Characters*, a footnote was added in 1754 and revised with a posthumous version appearing in 1777. The 1754 footnote began:

> I am apt to suspect the negroes, and in general all the other species of men (for there are four or five different kinds) to be naturally inferior to the whites. There never was a civilised nation of any other complexion than white. ...[69]

The 'I am apt to suspect' phrasing is used elsewhere by Hume, in his *Essay concerning the Principles of Morals*, for endorsing views that he reckons are 'solid and satisfactory'.[70] The first version of the footnote was commented on by contemporaries and by modern writers including Richard Popkin; Clive Ponting highlighted the first two sentences.[71] The passage continues with the wording retained in the revised version.[72]

Hume had referred in the footnote to a scholar Francis Williams, a free black man from Jamaica, who had been extensively educated in England. Hume is quoted in *The History of Jamaica* of 1774 by Edward Long:

> Mr Hume, who had heard of Williams, says of him, 'In Jamaica indeed they talk of one Negroe as a man of parts and learning; but 'tis likely he is admired for very slender accomplishments, like a parrot who speaks a few words plainly'.[73]

However, on Hume's influence, the historian Seymour Drescher says that it waned after the 1780s:

> The pre-abolitionist hypothesizing of racial inferiority, in the manner of David Hume, had little scientific standing in the generation after 1800.

Hume revised the footnote. The word 'species' was left out of the opening sentence in revision. He changed the second sentence to: 'There scarcely ever was...' and deleted 'very' from before 'slender accomplishments' in the last sentence. The final form of Hume's footnote published posthumously is:

> I am apt to suspect the Negroes to be naturally inferior to the Whites. There scarcely ever was a civilised nation of that complexion, nor even any individual, eminent either in action or speculation. No ingenious manufactures amongst them, no arts, no sciences. On the other hand, the most rude and barbarous of the Whites, such as the ancient Germans, the present Tartars, have still some-

thing eminent about them, in their valour, form of government, or some other particular. Such a uniform and constant difference could not happen, in so many countries and ages, if nature had not made an original distinction between these breeds of men. Not to mention our colonies, there are Negro slaves dispersed all over Europe, of whom none ever discovered any symptoms of ingenuity, though low people, without education, will start up amongst us, and distinguish themselves in every profession. In Jamaica, indeed, they talk of one Negro as a man of parts and learning; but it is likely he is admired for slender accomplishments, like a parrot who speaks a few words plainly.[74]

Garrett answers his question why we should care by saying that the footnote is bigoted. This answer could imply that Hume had not given the matter much thought, but changes in the revision make it implausible to say the footnote is a casual remark.

The revised version is regarded by Kenan Malik as 'but in footnote', and Malik supports his defence of Hume by suggesting the footnote 'is out of sympathy with his usual line of reasoning'. However, the passage Malik cites as illustration, from the end of the essay *Of Commerce*, is on people affected by climate in the tropics and its domain of discourse is of all such peoples world-wide, whereas the target of the revised footnote is specifically of a subset of such peoples, the Negroes. Marina Frasca-Spada in *Philosophical Books* says that Hume's 'views of race and class were not ahead of his times'.[75] Of course, what Marina Frasca-Spada says does not mean that his views were distinctive of his times. Opposed outlooks were to be found, not least amongst Hume's fellow Scotsmen of the Scottish Enlightenment, principally Adam Smith, whose different view of Negroes expressed shortly after Hume first added the footnote, did not lead to Hume modifying his view on Negroes in the revisions over the next 15 years.

Although Glasgow had a commercial interest in slave-trading, Thomas Clarkson's praise in his 1808 *History* is noteworthy in defence of its university:

> It is a great honour to the university of Glasgow, that it should have produced, before any public agitation of this question, three professors,* all of whom bore their public testimony against the continuance of the cruel trade.
> *The other was professor Hutcheson, before mentioned in p. 49.

Clarkson had also cited Adam Smith and John Millar, as precursors to change. Murray Pittock points out that John Millar, a Professor of Law at Glasgow, was proud of the 1778 Scottish judgement against slavery as he shows in the later 1779 *The Origin of the Distinction of Ranks*:

> Millar ends the book with a discussion of the 1778 Scottish judgement against slavery, the first to state that 'the dominion assumed over this negro' was itself ipso facto 'unjust', as against previous judgements which had centred on the extent of master's rights. Millar is proud of the decision, which in itself points forwards to a new state of society in a world beyond that in which he writes.

However, Chris Jones suggests that 'Millar's enthusiasm for the liberty of slaves' was an anachronism in 'an opulent commercial society', while Philip Flynn suggests that Millar 'made powerful enemies'.[76]

In addition to Clarkson's praise of Francis Hutcheson, Adam Smith and John Millar 'all of whom bore their public testimony against the continuance of the cruel trade', Clarkson notes criticism of Hume's footnote by Scottish poet and philosopher James Beattie.[77] Clarkson speaks of 'the aspersions of Hume':

> Dr. Beattie took an opportunity ... of vindicating the intellectual powers of the Africans from the aspersions of Hume, and of condemning their slavery as a barbarous piece of policy, and as inconsistent with the free and generous spirit of the British nation.[78]

Edward Long in the 1774 *History of Jamaica*, however, had rejected Beattie in favour of Hume:

> Mr Hume presumes, from his observations upon the native Africans, to conclude, that they are inferior to the rest of the species, and utterly incapable of all the higher attainments of the human mind. Mr Beattie, upon the principle of philanthropy, combats this opinion; but he is unfortunate in producing no demonstration to prove, that it is either lightly taken up, or inconsistent with experience.[79]

Clarkson seems to have shared with Beattie a perception that denigration of Negroes could be used in attempts to justify the status quo of plantation slavery.

Clarkson's concern over slavery is expressed in his earlier 1786 prize-winning *Essay on the Slavery and Commerce of the Human Species*, in which he argues against slavery. Jane Austen may have come across this work. In that earlier work as well, Clarkson comments on Hume's assertions:

> As to Mr. Hume's assertions with respect to African capacity, we have passed them over in silence, as they have been so admirably refuted by the learned Dr. Beattie, in his Essay on Truth to which we refer the reader. The whole of this admirable refutation extends from p. 458 to 464.[80]

Clarkson here comments at the end of his discussion of African poetry including quotation from Phyllis Wheatley, who had published in 1773, and reference to Ignatius Sancho.[81]

Aristotle's view on slavery had been run through by James Beattie before he tackled Hume's footnote, and Beattie said that Aristotle:

> wanted, perhaps, to devise some excuse for servitude; a practice which, to their eternal reproach, both Greeks and Romans tolerated even in the days of their glory.

Beattie concluded his discussion of Hume's footnote:

> It is easy to see, with what views some modern authors throw out these hints to prove the natural inferiority on negroes. But let every friend to humanity pray, that they may be disappointed ...Let it never be said, that slavery is countenanced by a people ... who are animated with that heroic passion, the love of liberty

Beattie was tactical here in concluding his comments on Hume's footnote with appeal to the 'love of liberty'. In a later work in 1793 Beattie argued that procuring servants rather than slaves need not be a problem were conditions to be improved on the plantations in the West Indies.[82] Richard Popkin suggests that racism figured in the eighteenth century because 'there was an economic need to justify African slavery'.[83] A need to justify an economic basis for slavery could be thought to arise once stress was laid on liberty. Another Scotsman speaking out for the contribution that Negroes could make to 'learning' and the 'arts' was George Wallace in 1760, and I return to this later.

Outside Scotland, another commentator on Hume's original footnote was Kant. His position in an early, 'pre-critical' work *Observations on the Feeling of the Beautiful and Sublime* can be read as a parody of Hume. Isaac Kramnick has a similar attitude to Robin Blackburn on Kant, but they may have fallen into the same blunder. As a young man in 1764 Kant tackles Hume with what looks like effective satire. It is wrong to read Kant's phrase 'the lowest rabble' as a description of black men as Isaac Kramnick does, because Kant was paraphrasing Hume's description of 'low' white men. Whereas Kramnick sees Kant as citing 'approvingly Hume's verdict on the races', Kant was pointing out Hume's challenge:

> Mr Hume challenges anyone to cite a single example in which a Negro has shown talents, and asserts ...[84]

There is a comment from Kant that is heart-rending in the light of reflections by Melvyn Bragg, who points out the linguistic skills needed in the Diaspora for slaves to find a common language in the face of efforts to deprive them of linguistic communication.[85] Kant says:

> the blacks ...are so talkative that they must be driven apart from each other with thrashings.[86]

The term 'black' used here means 'in most C18th contexts indigenous peoples of Africa and their descendants'.[87] Kant continued to monitor from Königsberg such servitude with considerable concern, later speaking of the 'cruellest and most calculated slavery'.[88]

Kant's German is in a light-hearted style, which the translation of 1798–99 did not capture. The 1960 English translation 'preferred to err on the side of heaviness or colourlessness', because the translator John Goldthwait saw the message as elevated views on the dignity of human nature.[89] In his comment on Hume's footnote, Kant's prime purpose is to uphold 'the dignity of human nature'. Disputes about which race, if any, is superior are by the bye compared with the issue of the intrinsic worth of human nature.

Kant narrates a story in which he could endorse what is said by a black carpenter about women. Kant relates Father Labat's story of how he had reproached a black carpenter for haughty treatment toward his wives, whereupon the black man's rejoinder was that whites were indeed fools, 'for first you make great concessions to your wives, and afterward you complain when they drive you mad' or off your head (*Kopf*). Kant comments that the black man could be said to have a good point, were it not that this man was quite black 'from head to foot, a clear proof that what he said was stupid'.[90] An inevitable reaction is to think that anyone who believes this final conclusion would believe anything. I think Kant intends us to conclude exactly that.

By satire Kant undermined the challenge of Hume's footnote without giving it status. Kant avoids being diverted, but at the same time is subversive just because he is light-hearted and witty. What is established is a database, so that nations discussed and both sexes are subsumed under the umbrella of human nature. It is to the concept of human nature that Kant directs his attention, as Michael Freeman puts it, to: 'the dignity of other persons as rational and autonomous moral agents'.[91]

The passage that Kramnick annotated from Kant turns out to be one of irony. In the German the black man's reply is in enlarged letters drawing attention to what is said. There is wordplay on '*Kopf*', the black man's reply calling whites fools being in terms of a white man's head, so that an impression is given of Kant playing the fool in knock-about fashion, taking up reference to the head in his repartee on the carpenter's reply to the priest. In the German, the word order, the enlarged print for what the black man says, and the punctuation with liberal use of commas that invite pauses, point up the satire:

> allein kurzum, dieser Kerl war vom Kopfe bis auf die Füsse ganz Schwarz; ein deutlicher Beweis, dass das, was er sagte, dumm war.

In a review of the translation, W. Mays says Kant emerges as 'a man of warmth, feeling and humour'.[92] The Kant scholar Manfred Kuehn notes 'To be sure, there is irony in some of these passages', when he comments in passing on Kant's *Observations*.[93]

Kant's comment can be misinterpreted if taken out of context. In establishing a context, there is an introductory footnote that expands on the title of section 4, not only pointing out the contingency of climates and modes of government, but also speaking of 'the great multitude of those who lay claim to a finer feeling'. Of this finer feeling, he says that 'no nation lacks dispositions that combine the most excellent qualities of this sort'. He adds:

> On that account the blame that might occasionally fall upon a people can offend no one, for it is of such nature that each can hit it like a ball to his neighbour.[94]

There is light-heartedness here that each can hit the ball on to his neighbour and that what he will say 'can offend no one'.

There might be a clever feature of Kant's approach. He entitles section 4: *'Of National Characteristics, so far as They Depend upon the Distinct Feeling of the Beautiful and Sublime'*. The phrase 'Distinct Feeling' in this sub-title echoes the title of the work as a whole, which offers observations on the '...Feeling...'. As Yu Liu puts it:

> Since it only manifests itself empirically through the feeling of pleasure and pain, the Kantian sublime obviously also has something to do with the emotional responses of a reader or spectator.[95]

Because his prime source is the feeling of the sublime and the beautiful that people have, the human beings he characterizes are seen as able to put in their own claim 'to a finer feeling'.

There is an inclusive context of people speaking for themselves in laying claim to feeling. Within that context there is recurrent teasing of the Dutch, who have 'little feeling for what in the finer understanding is beautiful or sublime'.[96] Near the beginning of section 4 he said that 'Holland can be considered as that land where the finer taste becomes largely unnoticeable'. In introducing Hume's views he says: 'The Negroes of Africa have by nature no feeling that rises above the trifling'. David Theo Goldberg conflates this remark about the 'trifling' with the remark three pages later about the black carpenter being 'stupid'.[97] But all these remarks by Kant are in that inclusive context of people speaking for themselves.

There is a different, excluding context when Kant says two pages before the story of the black carpenter that: 'So fundamental is the difference between these two races of man, and it appears to be as great in regard to mental capacities as in color'. The context here is that this is structurally a continuation of his paraphrase of Hume. What Hume had offered us is described as what 'appears' to be so, and Kant sounds sarcastic.

Kant paraphrased Hume as saying that 'among the whites some continually rise aloft from the lowest rabble'. This seems to me to be one of the weakest attempts at argument by Hume, since, as James Beattie observed, there is no reason to deliver an accolade to what Hume calls the 'low' sort

of whites because they are racially related to those who, in Kant's paraphrase, 'through superior gifts earn respect in the world'.

Kant himself looks askance at those who fall short of Enlightenment
ideals over the use of reason. Elsewhere, the newly discovered people of
Tahiti come in for criticism when Kant disapproves that 'the human being
should let his talents rust'.[98] Kant held to a view of the unity of mankind,
which would have been weakened had he chosen to use Hume's 1754 terminology of 'species'. Kant speaks of races rather than of species.[99] As
Werner Sollors says, for Kant:

> the proof for the existence of a single human species lay in the fact that people of
> all races could procreate with each other, producing fertile offspring.[100]

By contrast, Henry Louis Gates, who refers to Hume's calling black people
'a different species of men' does not note that the terminology of 'species'
is not endorsed by Kant. Gates does not see that there is an alternative
reading constituting a sardonic send-up of Hume. Gates instead claims:

> *Observations on the Feeling of the Beautiful and Sublime* functions to deconstruct, for
> the black reader, Kant's *Foundations [of the Metaphysics of Morals]* revealing it to be
> just one more example of the remarkable capacity of European philosophers to
> conceive of 'humanity' in ideal terms (white, male), yet despise, abhor, colonise,
> or exploit human beings who are not ideal.[101]

But on the contrary, no such deconstruction is possible. Confronted by
Hume's talk of 'different species' Kant maintained a view of the unity of
the human species.

For Kant differences are not permanent inequalities. Robert Louden
describes Kant as a firm believer:

> in the unity of the human species, at least in the sense that he rejects all accounts
> of race which hold that the human races originate from a plurality of different,
> independent sources.

Louden discusses Kant in relation to Georg Forster on conceptual considerations in empirical investigations.[102] I think such 'unity' is shown also in
Kant's *Anthropology from a Pragmatic Point of View*. Human beings received
an ostensive definition in his lectures on anthropology throughout his
teaching career.

However, Mary Gregor asks what the point of it is, but misses that the
Anthropology can be viewed as an empirical move to gather together the raw
data on which Kant builds his ethical and political philosophy.[103] This task
is also missed by Meg Armstrong, when she compares the *Observations* with
the *Critique of Judgement*, having noted the lack of reference to national
characteristics in the third *Critique*: 'Perhaps Kant himself grew tired of

"counting" national types'.[104] But a mere 'counting' had not been the point; Kant quantifies over the domain of all and only human beings in the *Observations*.

Kant's conclusion does not laud the white-man's achievements, but hopes that, in the European Enlightenment, progress has been made. He criticizes African religion and the use of fetishes, but earlier Kant had found 'grotesqueries' in the practices of other civilizations in India and China. He goes on to express disgust at the practices of Western Mediaeval Christendom, in which he finds religion, science and morals distorted by 'miserable grotesqueries' abounding and 'a thousand scholarly grotesqueries'.[105] His conclusion proclaims that a major task is to draw into progress by education 'every young world citizen'.

Kant's *Observations* eschew cases of unusual merit, going instead for those experiences of which 'more ordinary souls are capable'. At the beginning of the whole work, on the second page in section 1, Kant had made clear the scope of his 'present sketch'. He precedes the following passage by saying; 'to that kind of feeling, which can take place without any thought whatever, I shall here pay no attention', instead speaking of a delicate feeling:

> There is still another feeling of a more delicate sort … It is this feeling of which I consider one aspect. I shall moreover exclude from it that inclination that is fixed upon high intellectual insights, and the thrill that was possible to a Kepler, who as Bayle reports, would not have sold one of his discoveries for a princedom. The latter sensation is quite too delicate to belong in the present sketch, which will concern only the sensuous feeling of which also more ordinary souls are capable.[106]

Here, to get at representative characteristics of human beings, Kant proposed to bypass 'high intellectual insights', and his 'present sketch' constitutes ostensive definition of 'more ordinary' human beings.[107]

I conclude Kant's treatment of Hume's footnote with the view of his translator John Goldthwait who said that this early work shows Kant's:

> charity toward the many human imperfections that strike the observer on all sides, and his noble respect for the underlying dignity of all humanity.[108]

When the last sentence of the *Observations* stressed a cosmopolitan aspect with his hopes for the education of 'every young world citizen', Kant uses the word *Erziehung* for education, for the upbringing of children. He had earlier used the same word in connection with the upbringing of a Canadian Indian, who:

> feels the whole worth of freedom, and even in his education [*Erziehung*] suffers no encounter that would let him feel a low subservience.[109]

He notes how the women among them are involved in decision-making about war. He suggests Indian superiority in this respect to 'civilized' nations, though notes that the women have the disadvantage of still being responsible for the domestic affairs as well. In the *Observations* those creatures that are to count as human are those inhabitants of different nations and the two sexes that have been paraded with their mixture of achievements and foibles. People's intrinsic worth and dignity is the presupposed context of Kant's response to Hume's footnote.[110]

A nineteenth-century comment on Hume's footnote comes from W.J. Gardner in his 1873 *History of Jamaica*. On Long's 1774 history of Jamaica, Gardner comments:

> It is to be deplored that Mr Long's history is almost the only source of information relative to the career of Williams, for his prejudices arouse the suspicion that a black man would not receive impartial justice at his hands...[111]

Gardner questions Edward Long's own claim that 'With the impartiality that becomes me, I shall endeavour to do him all possible justice...'[112] Gardner describes the career as a schoolmaster in Jamaica after studying in England of Francis Williams, and quotes a new translation of Williams's Latin poem honouring one of the dignitaries of Jamaica.[113] Long had provided a translation.[114] Gardner adds to his interpretation of Francis Williams's career a brief comment on Hume, referring to Hume as a historian:

> Hume the historian wrote disparagingly of his attainments, but he was not personally acquainted with him, or he would hardly have said, 'It is likely he is admired for very slender accomplishments, like a parrot who speaks a few words plainly'.

The comment on Hume is gentle but damaging, as he implies that Hume like Long had not accorded 'impartial justice'.

I turn now to Hume's essay *Of the Populousness of Ancient Nations*, relevant to his views on slavery and published in the same year as the added footnote. This long essay demonstrates knowledge of slavery in antiquity, and has references to contemporary experience by planters of slaveholding. On an issue of population and later catching the attention of Thomas Malthus, Hume's argument was that ancient nations had not been more populated than modern nations. Malthus was to criticise the essay's argument structure. David Wootton considers Hume's professionalism as a historian, and Moses Finley appreciates the sophistication while not being tempted, as have some, to see the essay as yielding any ethical opposition to the use of Negro slavery in the sugar plantations.[115]

Malthus argued Hume was mistaken in thinking he could form a judgement about the actual population of ancient nations and that if any inference could be drawn, perhaps the reverse inference should be drawn. Malthus concludes that the considerations Hume assembled in great detail enabled us to reckon whether population was increasing, decreasing or remaining stable, but could not provide a criterion by which to determine the actual size of the population. Malthus had first made these criticisms in chapter 4 of his *Essay on the Principle of Population* in 1798. In his much extended later editions he returns to the same matter, in criticism of Hume's inferences.

On the background of such work on population as Hume's, Eugene Miller is helpful, as is Seymour Drescher:

> A long discussion unfolded between those ... who believed that Europe's population had been greater in the past and those, like David Hume, who believed that modern European society contained a larger and growing number of inhabitants. New World slavery was occasionally invoked in this discussion ... [116]

Hume took the view that Europe's population had increased in modern times, a growth he associated with the withering away of domestic slavery, which he argued had not been conducive to population growth.

Hume expressed sympathy for slaves in the ancient world speaking of 'humanity' and 'compassion'.[117] He says that from considering 'the ancients' he infers:

> that slavery is in general disadvantageous both to the happiness and populousness of mankind, and that its place is much better supplied by the practice of hired servants.[118]

There was general agreement that free labour had become the preferred option in Europe.[119] However, as an alternative to population growth, numbers on the plantations could be maintained efficiently by the slave trade, and that seemed the preferred option amongst planters. Hume refers to modern planters in contrast to his discussion of those domestic slaves in the ancient world who had been born and bred within a household, and comments on the latter having been granted 'privileges and indulgences':

> a sufficient reason why the masters would not be fond of rearing many of that kind. Whoever is acquainted with the maxims of our planters, will acknowledge the justness of this observation.[120]

Seymour Drescher observes that Malthus agreed 'with David Hume ... that the slave trade indicated the disinterest of masters in the alternative of breeding'.[121]

Hume reflects on the economics of servants or slaves from the masters' point of view in a footnote:

> A man is obliged to cloath and feed his slave; and he does no more for his servant: The price of the first purchase is, therefore, so much loss to him: not to mention, that the fear of punishment will never draw so much labour from a slave, as the dread of being turned off and not getting another service, will from a freeman.[122]

The argument seems to be that minimal ongoing provision would have to be made either for a servant or a slave, so that purchasing a slave in the first place is wasted money up front.

This was not useful for later abolitionist arguments for emancipation, since Adam Smith had thought in terms of higher wages for employees making for more spending power, which would in turn stimulate economic growth.[123] Nevertheless, for Hume it had seemed a good argument for procuring servants instead of slaves, so why did he not say so outright?

It looks as if he may take into account that there are situations where forced labour is sought. Hume said in the same footnote:

> from the experience of our planters, slavery is as little advantageous to the master as to the slave, wherever hired servants can be procured.

Here, there is the proviso 'wherever hired servants can be procured', which implies that hiring cannot always be arranged. There appears to be allusion to coercion when he goes on to say that there is a need for 'a rigorous military government over the negroes':

> The treatment of slaves by the ATHENIANS is said ... to have been extremely gentle and indulgent: Which could never have been the case, had the disproportion been twenty to one. The disproportion is not so great in any of our colonies; yet are we obliged to exercise a rigorous military government over the negroes.[124]

Hume does not comment, however, that their servitude was life-long when he says that we are 'obliged to exercise a rigorous military government over the negroes'.

Relative advantages to domestic slaves in ancient slavery have been pointed out by some modern writers. Henry and Owen Chadwick note conditions under the Roman Empire during the first few centuries of Christianity:

> free wage labourers were worse off, so that one was better fed, clothed and housed as a domestic slave.[125]

Henry and Owen Chadwick here write concerning domestic slaves. Hume also assesses the position of domestic slaves. His preliminary remark may have been made with feeling, because in 'ancient times' Britons could be slaves under the Romans, during four hundred years of Roman occupation:

human nature, in general, really enjoys more liberty at present, in the most arbitrary government of EUROPE, than it ever did during the most flourishing period of ancient times.

Continuing this passage Hume points out two disadvantages of domestic slavery. Firstly, he says there are disadvantages to the domestic slave because of the master's nearness to hand, which would be felt as more oppressive than any civil subjection however arbitrary:

> As much as submission to a petty prince, ... is more grievous than obedience to a great monarch; so much is domestic slavery more cruel and oppressive than any civil subjection whatsoever ...
>
> The remains which are found of domestic slavery, in the AMERICAN colonies, and among some EUROPEAN nations, would never surely create a desire of rendering it more universal ...[126]

There is a rhetorical flourish here in the word 'surely', as if he relies on the reader's agreement that where there is an option of not being a domestic slave, non-slavery is preferable in spite of the utmost tyranny possible under some civil subjection.

In contrast, a Negro slave was not in a position to choose in favour of some such form of civil subjection. But is Hume implying there should be such choice for Negroes who are enslaved? If he is, any such implication is not clear. As it stands, it appears the scope of the argument is restricted to 'the most arbitrary government of Europe', with which he began his comparison. Hume has said that, judging from the remaining cases of domestic slavery in the American Colonies and some European nations, experience would 'never surely create a desire of rendering it more universal'. What relevance does this reference to the American colonies have? I think the reference is related to what he immediately goes on to say about deleterious effects on 'the man of rank'. As far as I can see, this makes for the only case in which Negro slavery would by implication be objected to by Hume, on the grounds that it would be deleterious for the master in a domestic context, as in the second disadvantage.

The second disadvantage of domestic slavery is for the 'man of rank'. Hume continues:

> of ancient times ... every man of rank was rendered a petty tyrant, and educated amidst the flattery, submission, and low debasement of his slaves.

The education from infancy of the 'man of rank' spoken of here is detrimental because domestic slaves present in the household show submission and flattery. The man of rank became a petty tyrant in the close confines of the household in 'ancient times'. Hume does not comment on his own remark concerning the 'dread of being turned off and not getting another service' that a modern servant showed.

Hume was in tune with his own times in Britain in his objections to slavery. By this time Britons were lustily singing that 'Britons never will be slaves', *Rule Britannia* having become popular in the early 1740s. Freedom from slavery for the Englishman, and indeed for the American colonist, was one of the most prominent themes of the eighteenth century. Unfortunately that was held in tandem with maintaining the status of Negroes bought through the slave trade.

Nevertheless, Eugene Miller recommends that we link the 1754 essay *Of Populousness* to the 1754 footnote added to the earlier essay of 1748. In annotating the added footnote to *Of National Characters*, Eugene Miller provides a cross-reference from one essay to the other. He may echo an earlier assumption about Hume on slavery by C. Duncan Rice, who compared these two essays describing the footnote as Hume's 'paternalistic comments on Negro inferiority'.[127] Miller says:

> Despite his views on the inferiority of the Negro, Hume strongly opposed the institution of slavery (see note 7 to Hume's essay *Of the Populousness of Ancient Nations*).[128]

Turning back to *Of Populousness* to take up Miller's cross-reference, we see that 'Note 7' by Miller says:

> This paragraph and the ones that follow are notable for their strong condemnation of domestic slavery as a condition far worse than submission to even the most arbitrary civil government. In this and in his insistence that slavery debases even the slave masters by turning them into petty tyrants, Hume anticipates the arguments of many in Britain and America who agreed with him in opposing slavery.[129]

This is not a very promising submission. Indeed, an absentee planter in Britain with an income from plantation slavery could have agreed with what Hume says.[130]

Hume is not doing any anticipating; the argument against slavery that he has in mind here was already very popular. In the eighteenth century, writers retained clarity about the domain of argument over slavery typically by using the term slavery in condemnation of the state for whites, while speaking of enslaved Africans as 'negroes'. Hume's first argument did not appear to include Negroes within its scope. On the second argument by Hume that Miller paraphrases, he slides from Hume's phrase 'every man of rank' to his own term 'slave master', to describe those turned into petty tyrants. Miller's term 'slave master' could cover overseers of either domestic or plantation slavery, but the term 'every man of rank' had been used by Hume with respect to the case of domestic slavery only, so that plantation slavery was not covered by Hume's second argument.

There is a further remark of some interest in the main text of the earlier essay *Of National Characters*. Hume made the following claim:

> You may obtain any thing of the NEGROES by offering them strong drink; and may easily prevail with them to sell, not only their children, but their wives and mistresses, for a cask of brandy.[131]

This is part of a description of nationalities' drinking habits. Alternative interpretations have been given of accounts of procurement of slaves from dealers in Africa.[132] Hume's remark here in the main text is relevant to the transatlantic slave trade, because the word 'sell' relates to trading. There is nothing to counter that such selling would be unjust for those being sold. A generalization is proffered only about those Negroes who had the power to sell human beings, rather than about those who were sold. The footnote offering an opinion more widely about Negroes that was added later to *Of National Characters* was inserted for an earlier section in the main text.[133]

In contrast to Hume a contemporary, George Wallace, seems to have stood Hume on his head. Aaron Garrett points out George Wallace's 1760 work on Scottish law, in which Wallace cites Hume. Wallace handles with subtlety any suggestion that the Negro does not contribute to civilization. Wallace was passionately opposed to Negro slavery in the American colonies, and with what looks like a comic dig at Hume's footnote, he declares that abolishing slavery in the Colonies would result in a flowering of civilization as the freed Negroes reproduce themselves. He alludes to Hume on race and slavery by way of citation of the author of a work on population as having assured us elsewhere in the influential essay *Of the Balance of Trade* that loss of trade need not be detrimental to the nation. I find this impressive on the part of Wallace to use Hume's own polemic against him in such a way that it effectively counters Hume's aspersions in the footnote.

Whether Hume attempted to justify the transatlantic slave trade and the chattel slavery of the plantations in the American colonies by his views on Negroes in the added footnote is an interpretative matter, on which assessment remains inconclusive. If he did, fortunately there were others who were eventually to make it understood, as I noted Richard Baxter in the time of Locke had said back in 1673, 'Do you not see how you reproach and condemn yourselves while you vilify them all as savages?'

VI. Adam Smith

Adam Smith's attitude was very different. On the Enlightenment and Adam Smith, Charles Griswold says:

> The words and deeds of a number of Enlightenment thinkers with respect to the moral status and enslavement of Africans in particular leave much to be desired. By contrast Smith is unimpeachable on that score.[134]

According to Adam Smith there was a reason for slavery that was not economic. Smith thinks that slaves might be preferred by some, and he suggests a love to domineer:

> The pride of man makes him love to domineer, and nothing mortifies him so much as to be obliged to condescend to persuade his inferiors. Wherever the law allows it, and the nature of the work can afford it, therefore, he will generally prefer the service of slaves to that of freemen. The planting of sugar and tobacco can afford the expense of slave cultivation.[135]

Henry and Owen Chadwick make a similar point: 'Slavery originated in lust for domination'.[136]

Adam Smith transforms the earlier ethics of Hume so that, instead of analysis of accepted ethical views, major moral reform could be broached.[137] In Hume's ethics, a recent suggestion is that distinction between the scope and degree of benevolence should be made:

> according to Hume the *scope* of benevolent motivation is very broad, such that it includes any creature that is conscious and capable of thought, but that the *degree* of benevolent motivation is limited such that a person is naturally inclined to feel benevolence more strongly for one with whom he or she has a 'connexion' (e.g., a family member or a friend).[138]

Hume had described 'a very simple method', wishing to: 'reject every system of ethics, however, subtle or ingenious, which is not founded on fact and observation'.[139] Hume wrote:

> we shall consider every attribute of the mind, which renders a man an object either of esteem and affection, or of hatred and contempt ... a philosopher ... needs only enter into his own breast for a moment, and consider whether or not he should desire to have this or that quality ascribed to him ...[140]

Hume looked to find in his 'own breast' accepted ethical views. However, Adam Smith is more far-reaching, and J.L. Mackie's discussion of the notion of 'the impartial spectator' is highly relevant to Adam Smith's wider concerns.[141]

It has been claimed that 'Jane Austen is likely to have read' some of Hume's *Essays Moral, Political, and Literary*, 'owing to the general popularity' of them.[142] Relating some of Hume's *Essays* and Hume's *Enquiry concerning the Principles of Morals* to Jane Austen's novels, another critic suggests:

> Austen's novels, which translate Hume's philosophical project into a literary project and in the process become powerfully descriptive of the new social-discursive rules – descriptive, in short, of the essential constraints of 'gentleman-like behaviour'.[143]

I do not see conclusive grounds for thinking that Jane Austen knew of these essays. Nevertheless, there is an interesting passage from *Mansfield Park* pointed out by Nancy Struever, which she contrasts with Hume's *Enquiry*. It occurs when Fanny Price makes a reply:

> We have all a better guide in ourselves, if we would attend to it, than any other person can be.

Nancy Struever is right to say that Hume is not followed in the making of this judgement. However, the passage from *Mansfield Park* could reflect Adam Smith's ethics. The passage is in reply to Henry Crawford, who considers visiting his estate manager and says:

> When you give me your opinion, I always know what is right. Your judgment is my rule of right.

In the event, Crawford does not visit his estate manager, allowing himself to be seduced into adultery with Maria. Adam Smith's view of conscience amongst others' may be echoed by Fanny Price in her reply.

Changes to Humean ethics by Adam Smith in his *Theory of Moral Sentiments* of 1759 were substantial. He was stimulated to disagreement with Hume, in the view of Raphael and MacFie:

> Among contemporary thinkers Hume had the greatest influence on the formation of Smith's ethical theory. Smith rejects or transforms Hume's ideas far more often than he follows them, but his own views would have been markedly different if he had not been stimulated to disagreement with Hume.[144]

Adam Smith emphasized the place of conscience.[145] He wrote:

> When we are always so much more deeply affected by whatever concerns ourselves, than by whatever concerns other men; what is it which prompts the generous, upon all occasions, and the mean upon many, to sacrifice their own interests to the greater interests of others? ... It is reason, principle, conscience, the inhabitant of the breast, the man within, the great judge and arbiter of our conduct.[146]

This is sufficient reminder not to equate the self-interest of the later work of *The Wealth of Nations* with selfishness. Knud Haakonssen warned against unwarranted conflation of self-interest with selfishness.[147]

There is an inspirational passage in his *Theory of Moral Sentiments*, where Adam Smith speaks of the 'magnanimity' of Africans who have been enslaved. He does not mention Hume, but describes their 'valour', something that Hume apparently missed when he wrote his footnote. The passage is preceded by an evocative description of extreme bravery among 'all other savage nations', typified by Native American Indians, who show contempt of death and torture. The passage is reminiscent of Berkeley's reference to white 'condemned criminals being employed in the manufactures of sugar and tobacco'. Adam Smith describes white 'refuse of the jails of Europe' as 'sordid' masters, referring to their criminality:

> There is not a negro from the coast of Africa who does not, in this respect, possess a degree of magnanimity which the soul of his sordid master is too often scarce capable of conceiving. Fortune never exerted more cruelly her empire over mankind, than when she subjected those nations of heroes to the refuse of the jails of Europe, to wretches who possess the virtues neither of the countries which they come from, nor of those which they go to, and whose levity, brutality, and baseness, so justly expose them to the contempt of the vanquished.[148]

Adam Smith here points out that the 'refuse of the jails of Europe' are held in contempt by the vanquished, and he regards those taken from the coast of Africa as heroes. Thomas Clarkson emphasizes the whole passage in his praise of Adam Smith.

The word 'magnanimity' that is used in this passage is defined in Johnson's *Dictionary* as 'greatness, of mind; bravery; elevation of soul', and the French equivalent is given as '*magnanimite*'. However, a 1764 French translation of *The Theory of Moral Sentiments* gives '*courage*' for 'magnanimity'.[149] His own term had expressed more than the French translation captures. The translation rendered the preposition 'from' by the French preposition '*sur*', which again changes the meaning. In the French it becomes Negroes remaining in Africa on the coast who show '*courage*'. In the original it is Negroes who are no longer in Africa who show magnanimity. The French version is a generalization about a country's people, whereas what he had actually said in *The Theory of Moral Sentiments* constituted a scathing appraisal of the transatlantic slave trade.

The later 1776 work, *The Wealth of Nations*, is also referred to by Clarkson. Adam Smith acknowledged that there were such enormous profits to be made by planters that an expensive form of labour could be afforded by those who preferred slaves to servants.[150] When Clarkson in the 1808 *History* quotes from and celebrates *The Theory of Moral Sentiments* of 1759, he does so by describing Adam Smith in that work as having held Negroes taken from the coast of Africa 'up in an honourable, and their tyrants in a degrading light'.

Adam Smith's work is celebrated as influential in both stages of abolition, by Clarkson in his *History* after the 1807 Abolition of the Slave Trade, and by Seymour Drescher concerning the Emancipation of the 1830s.[151] Drescher thinks in terms of a prophecy that was understood by abolitionists in the legislation of the 1830s, with a theory of moral sentiments lying behind it, of Adam Smith's saying 'I believe that the work done by freemen comes cheaper in the end than that performed by slaves'. Drescher points out Adam Smith's beginning 'I believe' in saying this. There is the impression for Drescher that Adam Smith's belief and the carrying through of Emancipation by Parliament was of the nature of 'a mighty experiment'.

Clarkson has both *The Theory of Moral Sentiments* and *The Wealth of Nations* in mind as he thinks of Adam Smith as a 'coadjutor' in working towards abolition.[152] Clarkson's 1808 *History* was a possible influence on Jane Austen. I turn now, from figures who helped to form the climate of her time and who had impact on those in a position to have influenced Jane Austen, to some favourite writers who were a source of ideas and attitudes on abolition.

The influence of such famous men as Adam Smith and Dr Johnson on behalf of enslaved Africans may have worried slave traders and, after the 1807 Act, absentee slave owners in places like Glasgow. Since such vast sums of money were at stake there may even have been attempts to break up the appearance of amicable relations between the two men that could have been suggested by Adam Smith's having wished to join 'the Club of which Johnson was the leader', as J.W. Croker puts it. An anecdote from Walter Scott was included in Croker's 1831 edition of Boswell's *Life of Johnson*, which has the two men meeting in Glasgow and at dramatic loggerheads over Adam Smith's letter in praise of David Hume following Hume's death. However, the Glasgow visit by Johnson had taken place three years before Hume's death, as Croker subsequently points out in his 1848 edition, commenting on the anecdote that 'this story is *certainly* erroneous in the important particulars of the *time, place,* and *subject* of the alleged quarrel', and adding the details of Adam Smith's application for Club membership 'to which he was admitted 1st December 1775'. It is interesting that the anecdote should have been aired in Croker's earlier edition of 1831, two years before Parliament passed the 1833 Emancipation Act.[153] By 1848 when Croker repudiates the anecdote, Britain has aligned itself with the anti-enslavement sentiments of Dr Johnson and Adam Smith.

6
Abolitionist Influences On Jane Austen: Some Possibilities

Our Garden is putting in order...I could not do without a Syringa, for the sake of Cowper's Line ...

But like my dear Dr. Johnson I beleive [sic] I have dealt more in Notions than Facts.
Letter to her sister Cassandra, 8 February 1807

I am as much in love with the author as ever I was with Clarkson ...
Letter to Cassandra, 24 January 1813

Introduction

Jane Austen's favourite writers include Doctor Johnson and William Cowper, as well as Thomas Clarkson.[1] One literary critic notes Fanny Price appearing to favour 'writers famous for abolitionist sympathies, such as Johnson and Cowper'.[2] Quotation when contemporary readers would associate references with abolitionist views is suggestive of agreement.[3] The historian Niall Ferguson suggests as inspirational to abolitionists the biblical injunction: 'Do unto others as you would have others do unto you',[4] and Samuel Johnson also quotes this in a passage that Fanny Price had available in the East Room.[5] Roy Porter says that it was not the figures of the Enlightenment but 'the Evangelical Christians and Quakers' who worked for the British abolition of slavery.[6] Cowper's religious beliefs look complex, with links to the Evangelicals, whilst Johnson was an orthodox Anglican, as was Clarkson. Although not sharing William Wilberforce's Evangelical Christian position, Clarkson was close to the Quakers.[7] As well as these authors I shall take into consideration other possible influences such as her brother Francis known for his abolitionist, anti-slavery views.

1. The loss of the American colonies

Jane Austen made a present to her niece Anna of *Mentoria* by Ann Murry, as Irene Collins points out;[8] this was after her father's retirement when the family moved and books were relinquished.[9] It was the second edition of

1780, and slavery is targeted in some abolitionist passages. If there is a tendency to move in the early days of abolition from emphasis on anti-slavery sentiment to a strategy of anti-slave trade campaigning, *Mentoria* between its second and sixth edition appears to reflect such a tactic. *Mentoria* was for use in homes without a governess. Mentoria, as governess, proclaims:

> The slaves, who are licensed in those countries ...whose freedom is bartered for gain ... the true use of riches consists in supplying our own wants, which should ever be confined within the rules of temperance and frugality, that we may be enabled to provide for thenecessities of others.

In the second edition the passage against slavery is embedded within Dialogue V: *On the derivation of words & Geography*.[10] The sixth edition of 1791 retains the above passage and tackles the slave trade on behalf of 'every class of rational creatures'. Reference for 'rational creatures' is unclear.[11] *Mentoria* in the sixth edition has additional dialogue on the slave trade in the section *On Elocution and Geography*:

> Lady Louisa
> Are not poor negroes sold in Africa?
> Mentoria
> Yes; the slave trade, as it is usually called, is transacted in Negroland, chiefly on the coast of Guinea; a kind of commerce which is repugnant to human nature, and an unjustifiable infringement on the privileges granted by Providence to every class of rational creatures ...

Analysis in the sixth edition of *Mentoria* of causes for the American Declaration of Independence also tunes into contemporary interests, analysing economic factors.

The loss of the American colonies in 1776 may have particular relevance for abolition. Zeal for abolition is characterized by the historian Linda Colley as in part arising from a perceived need for moral purpose following this loss.[12] She further suggests that after abolition and emancipation were achieved there was an underpinning of claims to British superiority abroad during the subsequent Victorian age, derived from abolitionist success. That, of course, was to come after Jane Austen's time. Linda Colley notes considerable ramifications, saying British experience in abolitionist campaigning becomes a precursor at home to the Reform Act of 1832 for a wider franchise. This would underline how effective in mobilising popular support the abolitionist campaign was.

Jane Austen's own opinion of America is shown at a time when further war with America might occur.[13] England's 1812 war-scare with America was apparently alluded to in *Mansfield Park* by Tom shortly before Sir Thomas's return: 'A strange business this in America, Dr. Grant!'. Jane Austen's view is expressed in a letter to Martha Lloyd of 2 September 1814:

Henry's...veiw...is not cheerful – with regard to an American war...as what is to ruin us. The [?Americans]cannot be conquered, & we shall only be teaching them the skill in War which they may now want. We are to make them good Sailors & Soldiers, and g[?gain] nothing ourselves. – If we *are* to be ruined, it cannot be helped – but I place my hope of better things on a claim to the protection of heaven, as a Religious Nation, a Nation in spite of much Evil improving in Religion, which I cannot beleive the Americans to possess. [14]

The previous month of August 1814 had seen the British entering Washington, setting light to public buildings and naval yards.[15] Reference to religion in the letter of 1814 could be in connection with unwillingness by America to have ships checked by the British for illegal slave trading.

The terminology of 'ruin' in war with America is similar to the views of Charles Pasley, an author she had read 18 months previously. Pasley discussed America in the context of needing to be careful about repercussions of subsidizing another nation to help in the time of war:

If it would be impolitic ... to go to the Americans, and furnish them with as much money as would enable them to build, equip, man, and maintain eighty sail of the line, and two hundred frigates and smaller vessels of war, on condition that they would join us against the French; it must be equally impolitic for us to persevere in the same system by land ... no doubt the Americans would join us in a moment ... but how long could we make sure that they would not turn that navy against us. If such a system, by sea, would evidently lead to our ruin ... it follows, that the same system, by land ... must...be equally ruinous.[16]

In a letter to her sister Cassandra of 24 January 1813, Jane Austen had spoken of Pasley's *Essay on the Military Policy and Institutions of the British Empire*, and it was in that letter that she mentioned the abolitionist Thomas Clarkson, writing: 'I am as much in love with the author as ever I was with Clarkson'.

II. Samuel Johnson

An earlier source than Charles Pasley for Jane Austen's opinion of America could have been Doctor Johnson's opposition to slavery in the American colonies. For Johnson 'the loudest yelps for liberty' came from Americans who were not according like considerations to slaves:

Towards the conclusion of his *Taxation No Tyranny*, he says, 'how is it that we hear the loudest *yelps* for liberty among the drivers of negroes?'

This entry for 1777 is preceded in the *Life of Johnson* by what his biographer James Boswell claims to be Johnson's 'violent prejudice against our West Indian and American settlers'. Boswell reports Johnson:

when in company with some very grave men at Oxford, his toast was 'Here's to the next insurrection of the negroes in the West Indies.' His violent prejudice against our West Indian and American settlers appeared whenever there was an opportunity.[17]

In his 1775 *Taxation no Tyranny* Johnson 'memorably demonstrates the relative nature of the right to secede' and shows his 'distaste for economic self-interest and the hypocrisy accompanying it [in American attitudes to slavery]' as Donald Greene discusses.[18] There was awareness in America itself by 1776 of a fundamental inconsistency to the point of hypocrisy of wanting freedom but not being prepared to accord freedom to those held in slavery.

Johnson complains about non-literal uses of the term 'slave' towards the end of *Taxation No Tyranny* in a passage partly against a contemporary woman writer but mainly against American settlers calling themselves slaves of British rulers:

> It has been of late a very general practice to talk of slavery…it will be vain to prohibit the use of the word 'slavery'; but I could wish it more discreetly uttered.

P.J. Marshall observes that 'West Indian whites found no difficulty in using the language of liberty in slave societies'.[19]

In a letter to her sister of 8 February 1807 Jane Austen refers to 'my dear Dr Johnson'. It is on an urbane note in *Mansfield Park* that Fanny quotes Johnson's *Rasselas* on matrimony, when in chapter 39 after returning to Portsmouth she sees what advantages Mansfield has as a home:

> In a review of the two houses, as they appeared to her before the end of a week, Fanny was tempted to apply to them Dr Johnson's celebrated judgment, as to matrimony and celibacy, and say, that though Mansfield Park might have some pains, Portsmouth could have no pleasures.

Fanny at the time is in Portsmouth as a result of having refused the marriage proposal from a man she thinks she cannot love.

It may be significant that Edmund observes Fanny has Johnson's *Idler* in her room. Unlike the *Rasselas* reference, the *Idler* had entries relevant to slavery and imperialism. The *Idler* for 3 November 1759 condemned imperialism. Written as from a North American Indian's point of view, Johnson resists the kind of enthusiasm Locke had shown for colonization:

> And when the sword and the mines have destroyed the natives, they supply their place by human beings of another colour, brought from some distant country to perish here under toil and torture.[20]

It also refers to Negro slavery in its reference here to 'human beings… under toil and torture.' I include this striking work as Appendix 1 in full.

It was five years after the first appearance of Hume's added footnote to *Of National Characters* that Johnson spoke of 'black men' 'now repining under English cruelty'. In *The Idler* for 15 December 1759, Johnson is sceptical:

> We seldom consider that human knowledge is very narrow, that national manners are formed by chance, that uncommon conjunctures of causes produce rare effects, or that what is impossible at one time or place may yet happen in another. It is always easier to deny than to enquire. To refuse credit confers for a moment an appearance of superiority, which every little mind is tempted to assume when it may be gained so cheaply as by withdrawing attention from evidence, and declining the fatigue of comparing probabilities.

Terminology of 'cause', 'effect' and 'probabilities' is reminiscent of Hume and talk of 'national manners' echoes the essay *Of National Characters*. When Johnson says that 'It is always easier to deny than to enquire', there is an Enlightenment ring akin to Kant's challenge to dare to question. Johnson is elsewhere recorded as saying:

> there is no permanent national character; it varies according to circumstances. Alexander the Great swept India; now the Turks sweep Greece.[21]

In an entry for 1763, Boswell relates an overheard conversation, which refers to skin colour.[22]

Boswell, himself a Scot, records for the year 1772 Johnson talking about Lord Mansfield and downplaying Scotland:

> He would not allow Scotland to derive any credit from Lord Mansfield; for he was educated in England. 'Much (said he) may be made of a Scotchman, if he be *caught* young.'[23]

Mansfield's judgment in the Somersett case was still forthcoming at the beginning of 1772. Johnson's concern about slavery court cases is discussed by Margaret Kirkham, who, in connection with Jane Austen, says:

> at the house of her brother Edward she met Lord Mansfield's niece on a number of occasions, and that Boswell reported Johnson's view on another slavery case, *Knight v. Wedderburn*.[24]

On Johnson's support for this later court case, Gretchen Gerzina quotes Johnson in more detail:

> No man is by nature the property of another: The defendant is, therefore, by nature free: The rights of nature must be some way forfeited before they can be justly taken away: that the defendant has by any act forfeited the rights of nature we require to be proved; and if no proof of such forfeiture can be given, we doubt not but the justice of the court will declare him free.[25]

The case being heard in Scotland, that of *Knight* v. *Wedderburn*, was 'Whether a perpetual obligation of service...' was to be understood of a Negro slave Joseph Knight.

In 1777 Boswell had requested Johnson to dictate to him 'an argument in favour of the negro who was then claiming his liberty, in an action in the Court of Session in Scotland'. Johnson was categorical in seeing no justification for slavery.[26] Boswell noted the difference of outlook between them, and recorded communicating the decision in the Joseph Knight case. In telling his readers that he had written to Johnson about the 'Negro cause', Boswell notes the support attending it, adding 'of which number I do not hesitate to declare that I am none'.

Johnson's dictated argument to Boswell was one that the anti-abolition Boswell admitted to be cogent, although he conceded only on the Scottish case being addressed. Boswell's objection to Johnson's argument is a striking example of conflicting attitudes within Jane Austen's own times and in the second half of the eighteenth century. The response by Boswell, which he gives in asterisked pages added to the second edition, speaks of 'immense properties' 'involved in that trade'.[27]

While Boswell's objection was added at the time of attempts to abolish the slave trade, Johnson had argued against slavery itself. Boswell's opposition to abolition is maintained into the 1790s in the face of a widespread abolitionist campaign. Boswell was perhaps schizophrenic in his attitude, since his courtesy to the manservant Francis Barber was called for when he sought Barber's help over Johnson's papers. Boswell accepted 'with earnest politeness', as Gretchen Gerzina points out, the position of Johnson's Negro servant Francis Barber, whom Johnson made his heir.[28]

On the Scottish case, Johnson said that no man was by nature the property of another, so that the defendant was, therefore, by nature free. He had claimed that the rights of nature must be some way forfeited before they can be justly taken away, that we require to be proved that the defendant has by any act forfeited the rights of nature, and that if no proof of such forfeiture can be given, the justice of the court will declare him free. The term 'forfeit' sounds like Locke's terminology. Locke can be revisited in the company of Johnson, who appears to use Locke's views on slavery including that it is not a hereditary condition.

Johnson's demand for 'proof' challenges what traders in Africa were doing in selling slaves. There had been emphasis in Locke on what belonged to man by 'nature'. Johnson's move is bold, to bring the discussion of slavery to bear not on the constitutional position of the Englishman, but on the position of those captured outside England in slavery. There is a point of legal terminology, also used in the Mansfield Decision, to note:

> It is said that according to the constitutions of Jamaica he was legally enslaved; these constitutions are merely positive.

A modern definition of the legal term 'positive law' appears to give what Johnson meant.[29]

Emphasis in Locke's *Second Treatise*, chapter 4: *Of Slavery*, on the inappropriateness of having so powerful a monarch that subjects would lack liberty like slaves, had been stressed in section 23. It is this section that Bernard Bailyn cites in looking at an American point of view at the time of Independence:

> The contrast between what political leaders in the colonies sought for themselves and what they imposed on, or at least tolerated in, others became too glaring to be ignored and could not be lightened by appeals to the Lockean justification of slavery as the favourable fate of people who 'by some act that deserves death' had forfeited their lives and had been spared by the generosity of their captors. The reality of plantation life was too harsh for such fictions.[30]

In section 24, Locke had linked slavery with continuation of a state of war. The later chapter 7, section 85 reiterated his position on slavery that it arises as a result of a just war, slaves having forfeited their lives and liberty 'to the absolute dominion and arbitrary power of their masters'.

When Johnson, however, says no man was by nature the property of another, his argument meets Locke's on its own terms over slaves as property. On property there is an odd footnote by Stephen Munzer in a section on *'Body rights as limited property rights'*. Munzer had asked 'Does each person own, or at least have limited property rights in, his or her own body?'[31] He says:

> St Paul and Hobbes apparently thought not but Locke...may have thought so. St Paul writes: 'You are not your own property; you have been bought and paid for'...As for Locke, he says that 'every Man has a *Property* in his own *Person*'... Earlier, though, Locke writes: 'All the Servants of one sovereign Master, sent into the world by His order and about His business, they are His Property, whose Workmanship they are'. Perhaps the lawyer's notion of relativity of title can harmonize the Lockean passages. Relative to all other human persons, each person has title to himself or herself. But relative to God, no person has title to himself or herself; rather, God has title to each.

Munzer makes his conclusion relevant to Locke, but not to St Paul. The Pauline New Testament passage that Munzer cites is not about human beings unrelated to God, and the imagery that appears to be presupposed by St Paul utilizing experience of bondage was that which was familiar both from the Old Testament and from the Roman Empire, of which he was a citizen. Illustration concerning being rescued by the price paid in the Crucifixion from a state of loss of freedom that had arisen from having gone astray and, to personify, having fallen into the clutches of the Devil, fits in with the annotation in legal terms that Munzer makes on Locke. There would, therefore, seem to be nothing in what St Paul said to rule out claims that 'No man is by nature the property of another. The defendant is therefore by nature free', as Johnson was to argue. Johnson would have wished to see his own anti-slavery stance as consistent with the New Testament.

Johnson's dictated argument was omitted in the first edition. In a foot-note Boswell said:

> This being laid up, somewhere amidst my multiplicity of papers at Auchinleck, has escaped my search for this work; but, when found, I shall take care that my readers have it.[32]

At the time of printing of the second edition in 1793, Boswell had still mislaid what had been dictated to him.[33] He must have been aware in preparing the second edition of the *Life* that references to slavery and the slave trade would be highly topical. There is a letter to him of 1791 from John Maclaurin who had defended Joseph Knight in the Scottish case. Maclaurin wrote to correct something in the first edition of the *Life*, but adds concerning his own paper in the defence:

> In the preamble it foretold in 1775 the abolition of the slave trade which now in 1791 is I think, thank God, nearly accomplished.[34]

In time for the binding to take place, the material Boswell had asked Johnson to dictate in 1777 had to be inserted in asterisked pages.

After Johnson's anti-slavery argument Boswell followed with a disassoci-ation from Johnson's views. However, because Boswell was commenting in 1793, his remarks make better sense as responses to the abolitionist activity of the 1790s, 16 years after Johnson's dictation. Later editions were to lose sight of the 16-year gap. Johnson's argument against slavery in the 1770s and Boswell's reply in terms of response to the 1790s anti-slave trade pres-sure are inserted as for 23 September 1777.

It is thought to be the second edition of the *Life* that Jane Austen referred to in a letter to Cassandra of 25 November 1798, that they:

> have got Boswell's *Tour to the Hebrides* and are to have his *Life of Johnson*.[35]

Johnson's dictated argument against slavery stands out at the beginning of the second edition. A separate publication giving additional material came out at the same time as the second edition, for those who had bought the first edition. Either in the separate form or asterisked at the beginning of the second edition, the format drew attention to the discourse on slavery and the slave trade.

Another entry not occurring in the first edition of the *Life* but present in the second edition concerns Johnson's close friend, the son of a planter. For the year 1780 Johnson is quoted:

My dear friend Dr. Bathurst, (said he with a warmth of approbation,) declared he was glad that his father, who was a West-Indian planter, had left his affairs in total ruin, because having no estate, he was not under the temptation of having slaves.

Jamaica was the island in question here. By then, Jamaica was well-known for the Maroons, the black population who had defied British military force and established their freedom.[36] Elsewhere Johnson describes Jamaica as:

A place of great wealth and dreadful wickedness, a den of tyrants and a dungeon of slaves.[37]

Johnson's argument against slavery presented in the second edition was also printed by the *Gentleman's Magazine* at the end of the first part of volume lxiii for 1793, entitled 'Dr Johnson's Argument on the cause of Joseph Knight, a Negro, who claimed and obtained his freedom in Scotland 1777'. This inclusion in the *Gentleman's Magazine* probably ensured even greater publicity for Johnson's anti-slavery views. I give Johnson's argument as Appendix 2 in full.

III. William Cowper

One historian has asked, 'And what role did poetry (as opposed to other literary forms) play in shaping attitudes about slavery?'.[38] The poetry of William Cowper was read aloud within Jane Austen's family,[39] and as I cited at the head of this chapter, a letter to Cassandra included talk of a garden saying: 'I could not do without a syringa for the sake of Cowper's line ... – We talk also of a Laburnam'. This is a refererence to *The Task* vi, 150 where Cowper had written: 'Laburnum, rich In streaming gold; syringa, iv'ry pure'. People also associated Cowper with the abolitionist cause, so that reference in the novels to him could be associated by readers at the time with his passionate abolitionist views.

Cowper had embarked, in *The Task* of 1785 at the beginning of Book Two, on his condemnation of slavery and praise of the Mansfield Decision, by declaring:

He finds his fellow guilty of a skin
  Not colour'd like his own.

In America, these words were incorporated in protest to the American president Thomas Jefferson. In a scathing letter of 24 February 1806, the senator Timothy Pickering protested:

are the hapless, the wretched Haytians ('Guilty', indeed, 'of a skin not coloured like our own' but) ... Free ... to be deprived of those necessary supplies ... to reduce them to submission by starving them!...[40]

The occasion of this was that Jefferson had prohibited commerce with the St Domingue slaves, who had freed themselves. The senator quoted as if *The Task* was common property among English speakers.

The Task was commented on by Eric Williams, and Gretchen Gerzina notes of the case of *Knight* v. *Wedderburn* in 1778, 'the one that Samuel Johnson so anxiously followed', that the Scottish case cited Somersett from the earlier Mansfield Decision. She says:

> In the end it didn't really matter what Mansfield had said, or what actually happened to James Somerset ... As long as everyone believed that slaves were free, it served as *de facto* freedom ... In only three weeks the Somerset case had passed from the legal to the apocryphal.[41]

This makes apt comment on Eric Williams's dismissal of the significance given to the Mansfield Decision in Cowper's poem. Clarkson in his *History* had quoted Cowper on Mansfield, as I illustrate in Appendix 3. The interest in Mansfield shown in *The Task* concerned the legal decision of 1772. Cowper wrote two short poems following the burning down of Lord Mansfield's house by a mob during the Gordon Riots in 1780 and the loss of many of his notes on cases. The two poems may have been triggered by his admiration for him as a lawyer, law having been Cowper's original training. Mansfield would have been well known to Cowper, but he did not want much fuss made of the two poems. Over ten years later he refers in correspondence to Mansfield's undoubted abilities.[42] Eric Williams's interpretation was scathing:

> 'Slaves cannot breathe in England,' wrote the poet Cowper. This was license of the poet...[43]

Cowper may have been a poet, but trained as a lawyer he may have focused in *The Task* on the judge's task to interpret the law. When Gretchen Gerzina said that 'the case became legend and to this day is still erroneously referred to as ending slavery in England', she added that for practical purposes the popular view at the time was in terms of liberation in England having been achieved.

In the abolitionist campaign there was determination of people like Cowper to press for change. He does that through his poetry, some of which had wide circulation. *Boadicea, An Ode* of 1782 compares enslavement of Britons under the Roman occupation with a better regime for others under the British Empire.[44] This is at the time that Britons needed to take stock over the loss of the American colonies.

The Morning Dream was published in November 1788 in *The Gentleman's Magazine*.[45] Extolling 'Liberty', Cowper ends the interpretation of his dream in the last verse:

> That Britannia, renown'd o'er the waves
>> For the hatred she ever has shown
>> To the black-sceptred rulers of slaves,
>> Resolves to have none of her own.

This seems to be an allusion to *Rule Britannia* from the early 1740s in which there is the famous line about Britons never being slaves:

> Popular bellicosity was intense during the early 1740s. It is notable that ...Thomas Arne's *'Rule Britannia'* and Henry Carey's *'God Save the King'* date from this period.[46]

The passion in Cowper's poem is captured by Kate Davies, in connection with fraught involvement of women in the popularization of *The Morning Dream*:

> the 'goddess like' woman of Cowper's 'Morning Dream' ...forcing slavers to drop their scourges in shame.[47]

A long poem called *Charity* on the topic of love or 'charity' interweaves an abolitionist theme. To my mind, linkage of topics is awkward in this poem, which may be experimental and in the nature of improvisation. While trying out ideas, it rhymes and scans, achieving structural integrity through its form rather than through its content. In his *Amazing Grace* anthology of poems about slavery, James Basker finds abolitionist sentiment in *Charity* condescending.[48] Overall as an impression of the whole, it appears to me that a seemly presentation of a lofty theme is achieved, but only as a function of incomplete thought processes of work still in progress.

The Negro's Complaint was widely used in abolitionist campaigning.[49] It was written in March 1788, and, after appearing elsewhere, was published under the title *Complaint* in 1793 in *The Gentleman's Magazine*, a magazine showing abolitionist sympathies, as in 1792 in noting marriage of the African Olaudah Equiano to a girl from Ely. Himself familiar with slave-owning inhabitants of West Africa from his childhood, he had been kidnapped for sale and trafficking to North America, and after gaining his freedom was active in campaigning in England for abolition of the trans-atlantic slave trade. In *The Interesting Narrative of the Life of Olaudah Equiano* of 1789, at the beginning of chapter 2, Equiano tells us of his fathers' slaves: 'My father, besides many slaves, had a numerous family'. Earlier, he said:

> Those prisoners which were not sold or redeemed we kept as slaves; but how different was their condition from that of slaves in the West Indies.[50]

There is an inscription on the tomb in Cambridgeshire of an infant daughter of Olaudah Equiano that writes of a child 'hap'ly not of your colour'. The inscription 'hap'ly' means 'perhaps', an acknowledgement that an

English visitor may not be of the same colour as Equiano's mixed race daughter. Such magazine entries as the one for Equiano's English marriage may illustrate the popularization of the abolition movement. The process of publishing in *The Gentleman's Magazine* has been described in a context of women's writing:

> The obstacles to women's writing make their success in publishing all the more remarkable ... anyone could submit short pieces of fiction or poetry to dozens of magazines – such as the *Lady's Magazine* or *The Gentleman's* – that printed selected readers' submission without payment.[51]

Roy Porter on media influence and the periodicals boom comments on the same magazine:

> only a quarter of the articles in *The Gentleman's Magazine* supported the traditional idea of women as the weaker sex to be kept from study and public activities...

Porter indicates that *The Gentleman's Magazine* founded in 1731... 'built a circulation of over 10,000 copies and, of course, a far larger readership'.[52]

As readers of Cowper, the Austen family may have been familiar with the change made to *The Negro's Complaint*. The word '*theirs*' was changed after the 1790s publication to '*slave*' in a version that appeared posthumously in 1808.[53] Originally Cowper had written:

> But though theirs they have enroll'd me,
> Minds are never to be sold.

The revised version of *The Negro's Complaint*, citing 'slave' in line 7 runs:

> Forc'd from home, and all its pleasures,
>   Afric's coast I left forlorn;
> To increase a stranger's treasures,
>   O'er the raging billows borne.
> Men from England bought and sold me,
>   Paid my price in paltry gold;
> But, though slave they have enroll'd me,
>   Minds are never to be sold.   8
>
> Still in thought as free as ever,
>   What are England's rights, I ask,
> Me from my delights to sever,
>   Me to torture, me to task?
> Fleecy locks, and black complexion
>   Cannot forfeit nature's claim;
> Skins may differ, but affection
>   Dwells in white and black the same.   16

...
Deem our nation brutes no longer   49
   Till some reason ye shall find
Worthier of regard and stronger
   Than the colour of our kind.
Slaves of gold, whose sordid dealings
   Tarnish all your boasted pow'rs,
Prove that you have human feelings,
   Ere you proudly question ours!   56

What provoked Cowper to change the word 'theirs' to the word 'slave' in line 7? It cannot be a shift from slave-trade to slavery concern, because Cowper died before there was certainty that the slave trade would be abolished. Abolition of the slave trade itself would therefore have remained a major concern for Cowper.

Alistair Duckworth suggests the influence of this poem in *Emma*.[54] He says Jane Fairfax's terminology of intellect being sold may acknowledge Cowper's point at the end of the first verse in line 8 that the mind may not be sold. However, on interpretation of abolitionist concerns, Donna Landry surmises:

> Even abolitionist discourse of the period, at the same time as it argues for the emancipation of slaves, is traversed by doubts and hesitations about the slaves' status as 'human', and hence discursive, subjects.[55]

But for Cowper, however, freedom of thought that is retained under enslavement enables the slave to question. Line 9 underlines the point that minds are never to be sold in saying 'Still in thought as free as ever'. The 'human feelings' of line 55 underlines human beings as the focus.

Ironically, in *Emma* Mrs Elton's interpretation of what may be a reference to marriage ('one flesh') as a reference to the slave trade would suggest selling oneself into marriage as a kind of slavery and becoming, in William Cowper's words in line 53, one of the 'slaves of gold'. Cowper's phrase in line 54 'boasted powers' is curiously echoed in the words 'boasted power' in the banal *Charade* with which Mr Elton had earlier courted Emma. Since this was an enterprise which, as Mr Knightley had observed, would be carried out with an eye to a good income, it could be seen in chapter 9 as unwitting portrayal of his own courtship as that of a slave of gold when Mr Elton pens:

> Man's boasted power and freedom, all are flown;
> Lord of the earth and sea, he bends a slave,
> And woman, lovely woman, reigns alone

Such a critical view of marrying for money would be consistent with all that goes on in the novel. It may be possible to see Mr Elton's *Charade* as a bowdlerized version of the *Complaint*, illustrating that Mr Elton has not responded to Cowper's abolitionist message but has merely absorbed some of the terminology in this well known poem. Contemporary readers could have seen allusion here to Cowper's poem. In the riddle presented by Mr Elton, Emma detects firstly 'court', then 'ship' and finally 'courtship'. In verse 4 of the Cowper there is also a court scene in Cowper's reference to one reigning on high and his throne; and in verse 6 the narrator 'crosses in your barks the main'. In the 7th-last verse of Cowper, lines 53 and 54 yield an interpretation of Mr Elton's actual position that he unwittingly suggests by following Cowper's terminology so closely.

The second verse of *The Negro's Complaint* could be read as critical of Locke when in line 14 the terminology of forfeiture is introduced, and of Hume when in line 13 'complexion' is introduced followed by lines 15 and 16. Lines 49–52 in the last verse are critical of such views as Hume expressed in *Of National Characters*. The poem ends in lines 55–56 utilizing reference to people's own feelings, and is like Kant in this respect.

Cowper is satirical notwithstanding caution expressed in *Charity* over the nature of satire. *Pity for Poor Africans* was published in the *Northampton Mercury* on 9 August 1788 and in *Poems* of 1800. It points out inconsistency in holding back from support for the abolitionist campaign:

> I own I am shock'd at the purchase of slaves,
> ...
> I pity them greatly, but I must be mum,
> For how could we do without sugar and rum ?
> Especially sugar, so needful we see ?
> What ? give up our desserts, our coffee, and tea !

The first line followed by this second verse is quoted by Dresser and Giles as being published: 'Anon, in the *Bristol Gazette*, 12 June 1788'. That was before the known Cowper publication.[56]

Cowper, although known as a supporter of abolition, or perhaps because of that, was accused of deserting the cause. He responded in his 1792 *Sonnet to William Wilberforce, Esq.*, sent for newspaper publication in the *Northampton Mercury* on 21 April 1792. H.S. Milford says:

> In his accompanying letter, dated 16 April, which is also printed in the *Northampton Mercury* Cowper says that the lines were 'written no longer since than this very morning' and that he wished to refute slanderous rumours that he was 'no longer an enemy but a friend' to the slave trade.[57]

Baird and Ryskamp point out circumstances of the 'second round' of replying to those who claimed Cowper no longer supported the abolitionist cause and give sad details of calumnies heaped on him.

Attempt to spread reports that Cowper had changed his mind from opposing the slave trade illustrates fierceness of opposing views at the time. Published in the *Northampton Mercury* for 12 May 1792, a short poem the *Epigram* makes its impact to shock and to challenge:

> To purify their wine some people bleed
> A *lamb* into the barrel, and succeed;
> No nostrum, planters say, is half so good
> To make fine sugar, as a *negro's* blood.
> Now *lambs and negroes* both are harmless things,
> And thence perhaps this wond'rous virtue springs,
> 'Tis in the blood of innocence alone –
> Good cause why planters never try *their own.*

There is allusion to the wine of the Last Supper, using the symbols of a lamb and of blood. It seems a challenge to planters on behalf of Christianity.[58] Baird and Ryskamp give technical detail about wine production and 'fining' 'on which the epigram depends'.[59] Talk of innocence may be meant in a technical sense that Negroes held in slavery had not forfeited freedom through any misdemeanour. The argument of the piece is highly compressed, so that it is difficult to interpret. The basic message is clear enough, but I am not certain if planters are to be regarded as acting in ways tantamount to crucifixion of their slaves.

In *The Task* of 1785 there is 'a retreat to the domestic, the small-scale', according to John Barrell, who argues for such retreat on the part of a number of authors writing after the loss of the American colonies.[60] Censure of Sotherton in *Mansfield Park* is in accord with retreating to the 'domestic, the small-scale' that Barrell sees in Cowper. Regret at felling oaks quoted from Cowper by Fanny could symbolise wanting to conserve the very old and traditional in England, while rejecting slave trading in the colonies as relatively new, mistaken so-called improvement. Getting rid of the 250-year-old transatlantic slave trade would have been getting rid of something not so established in England as oak trees that if old enough could have dated back to the mediaeval age or certainly to pre-Hawkins. Literary critics point out complexities in the idea of improvements.[61] On Cowper:

> After the American War, the loss of moral confidence in the integrative function of the empire became a georgic topic in its own right ... central to William Cowper's The Task ... with reflections on the moral failings of the British empire.[62]

This looks right about Cowper, and there may be a comparable attitude on the part of Jane Austen quoting from *The Task* in both *Mansfield Park* and *Emma*. On the concept of improvement, Elizabeth Bohls refers back to

Raymond Williams and his separation of potentially contradictory mean-
ings for this concept:

> 'the improvement of soil, stock, yields, in a working agriculture' and that 'of
> houses, parks, artificial landscapes ...' The contradiction to which Williams refers
> is, in part, a moral one: the taste displayed by the 'improved' house and grounds
> ...is not very compatible with the practices of engrossing, rack-renting, and
> enclosure ... nor, in the colonial case, with slavery, in the opinion of growing
> numbers of Britons.[63]

The topic of improvement is explicit in *Emma*, for it is noticeable that in
chapter 12 Mr Knightly tells his brother he intends to consult with the villagers about moving a path, and will not go ahead if the villagers do not
like the proposal.

On eighteenth-century ideas of improvements in relation to modern
economic policy, David Willetts quotes in admiration from Hume's
Of Refinement in the Arts:

> Hume was much wiser than some of today's fashionable critics when he wrote:
> 'The same age which produces great philosophers and politicians, renowned gen-
> erals and poets, usually abounds with skilful weavers and ships-carpenters. We
> cannot reasonably expect that a piece of woollen cloth will be wrought to perfec-
> tion in a nation which is ignorant of astronomy or where ethics are neglected.
> The spirit of the age affects all the arts, and the minds of men being once roused
> from their lethargy, and put into a fermentation, turn themselves on all sides,
> and carry improvements into every art and science'.[64]

However, there may here be a move on Hume's part to manipulate the
concept of 'improvements'. Remembering Hume's supposition over 'civil-
ised' nations in the footnote to *Of National Characters* and inferring such a
context for talk of 'improvements', it would be no wonder that talk of
'improvements' came to be regarded as double-edged.

Cowper's satirical rendering of a slave trader's attitudes at the prospect of
'trading is like to be o'er' in *Sweet Meat Has Sour Sauce* was not used, which
suggests careful selection of material on the part of the campaigners in
seeking to shape public opinion. John Baird and Charles Ryskamp as
editors say:

> The Committee for the Abolition of the Slave Trade made no use of this ballad. Its
> jocular tone probably did not appeal to them, and as moulders of public opinion
> they likely thought it unwise to appropriate the attitudes of their opponents.[65]

It is a sharp-cutting poem, not flinching from the violence involved in the
slave trade. As Baird and Ryskamp point out, what Cowper says corre-
sponds closely with description of the slave ship *Brookes* and details of

slavers' 'instruments'. It was not published until after the emancipation of slaves, so this is one poem that Jane Austen could not have known.

Jane Austen may have known of the slanders spread about Cowper and that he resorted to the *Northampton Mercury* to publish the sonnet on Wilberforce and then the *Epigram* condemning planters. If Jane Austen did know of the calumnies heaped on Cowper and his poetic ripostes in the *Northampton Mercury*, there may be allusion to this, as comment on Sir Thomas's position. The 1792 date of Cowper's defence in the newspaper coincides with the beginning of the time scale in *Mansfield Park* that sees Sir Thomas established in Northamptonshire. The town Northampton is referred to and visited a number of times during the course of the novel. Cowper's experience and his writing to the *Northampton Mercury* may have been thought of as part of the topical background for those at Mansfield Park.

IV. Thomas Clarkson and others

Thomas Clarkson in his *Essay* of 1786, a work that Jane Austen may have seen, says slaves having being converted would need to be accountable for their actions. He argues that slavery must be wrong in placing people in a position that Christianity could not condone. Clarkson writes:

> This strikes at the very root of slavery. For how can any man be justly called to an account for his actions, whose actions are not at his disposal? This is the case with the proper slave.[66]

Clarkson makes a distinction in a footnote: a 'proper slave', unlike 'the slave who is condemned to ... public works, is in a different predicament. His liberty is not *appropriated*'. By implication, since God would not unjustly call a slave to account for actions 'not at his disposal', a condition of slavery must be unchristian because in conflict with God's purpose for man's life on earth. For Clarkson this indicates that implicit in the Gospels from the start, and waiting only for implementation, there was such an understanding to be realized.

This argument from accountability should be distinguished from another version with different truth conditions, in which freedom is imagined to have been needed in the first place for conversion. Only freedom of thought as distinct from civil freedom would be needful, and as Cowper said in lines 8 and 9 of *The Negro's Complaint* that is retained: 'Minds are never to be sold. / Still in thought as free as ever'. A counter suggestion could contend that conversion would make no sense if converts are slaves, because we could never verify that they had freely accepted Christianity. But it would not be the onlooker who would need to be in a position to verify, since free acceptance would be a spiritual matter between the convert and his Creator. Clarkson's own argument from accountability for emancipation of slaves may have been shared by Jane Austen. In a prayer attributed to her, she writes:

> Another day is now gone, and added to those, for which we were before accountable.

At the least they shared an awareness of the importance of accountability.

Clarkson went on to collect material for the attention of Parliament. Working in tandem with William Wilberforce, he laboured to collect much of the information that was put before Parliament.[67] The detailed research documented in his 1808 *History* described not only interviews with many seamen involved on slaving runs, but also included engravings of instruments for punishment on the Middle Passage of the triangular trade. The engraving of a typical slaver like the *Brookes* showed the distribution of the human cargo in the hold, assembling a factual account of conditions. The detail of layout took up a four-page foldout spread, which was then multi-folded. The format draws attention to it, so no reader would miss the shocking engraving of what now is the definitive image of a ship laden with slaves for the transatlantic slave trade.[68]

Abolition of the slave trade was for Clarkson a move towards the abolition of slavery. In his 1808 *History* he wrote that in aiming at abolition: 'they were laying the axe at the very root'.[69] A London periodical of about 1817 *Axe laid to the Root* called for emancipation, and the title probably alludes to Clarkson's phrase, testifying to his influence.[70]

There is possible allusion to Clarkson's work when Jane Austen writes: 'I am as much in love with the author as I ever was with Clarkson or Buchanan, or even the two Mr Smiths of the city'.[71] The reference to Clarkson in a letter to her sister runs as follows relating activities of her mother and herself:

> I am reading ... an Essay on the Military Police & Institutions of the British Empire by Capt Pasley of the Engineers, a book which I protested against at first, but which upon trial I find delightfully written & highly entertaining. I am as much in love with the author as I ever was with Clarkson or Buchanan, or even the two Mr Smiths of the city – the first soldier I ever sighed for – but he does write with extraordinary force & spirit. ...

R.W. Chapman's editorial note to this letter of 24 January 1813 is odd given its date. Her letter would seem to be too early, being only three weeks into 1813, to allow that her reference is:

> perhaps *Abolition of the slave-trade* (1808), or more probably *Life of William Penn* (1813), reviewed by Jeffrey in the July *Edinburgh Review*.

On the contrary, just because of the dates, the reference looks 'more probably' to the *Abolition*. Indeed, Isobel Grundy considers it 'immeasurably more likely'.[72]

Something of the impact of the man in his time can be gleaned from Eric Williams, who while concerned with economic forces shaping events and the part played by black slaves in moving towards autonomy nevertheless praises Clarkson's work:

> One can appreciate even today his feelings when, in ruminating upon the subject of his prize-winning essay, he first awoke to the realisation of the enormous injustice of slavery. Clarkson was an indefatigable worker, who conducted endless and dangerous researches into the conditions and consequences of the slave trade, a prolific pamphleteer whose history of the abolition movement is still a classic.[73]

The 1786 *Essay* had been wide-ranging including reference to the black writers Ignatius Sancho and Phyllis Wheatley along with quotations from her poetry.[74] Jane Austen's reference to Clarkson may be to this work rather than to the *History*, though there is no particular reason to rule out that she may have seen both. 'Clarkson personifies all the best in the humanitarianism of the age', sums up Eric Williams. He describes him as 'Too impetuous and enthusiastic for some of his colleagues':

> His labors in the cause of justice to Africa were accomplished only at the cost of much personal discomfort, and imposed a severe strain on his scanty resources. In 1793 he wrote a letter to Josiah Wedgwood which contains some of the finest sentiments that motivated the humanitarians.

Given that Eric Williams had been concerned to draw out the sheer influence of economic factors in the success of abolitionism, he makes a telling tribute: 'Clarkson was one of those friends of whom the Negro race has had unfortunately only too few'.

The immediate context of the Austen reference to Clarkson is one of enthusiasm, as she writes in her letter of reading Pasley's *Essay*. Pasley is an interesting writer across the board. In his work on methods for teaching geometry to soldiers going into engineering, he avers that men beforehand have been impeded in learning by poverty not want of ability. Even this earlier book on the topic of teaching geometry to would-be engineers in the army makes for riveting reading.[75] Jane Austen's letter cites 'police' not 'policy' but, as Chapman explains, the *Oxford English Dictionary* gives both as synonyms for that time. Pasley himself normally uses the word 'policy', and defines 'martial policy' at the beginning of chapter 4, in a footnote: 'By martial policy, I mean the spirit and views with which war may be conducted'.[76] It may not be surprising that she was attracted to Pasley's book.[77] He seems to help in what was described as unsettling crisis at the time.[78]

Pasley looks for cooperation with the people of countries colonised, because gratitude on their part would make for an easier life on the part of the conquering country. Otherwise, he surmises, we should be asking for them to try to take from us.

Jane Austen's remark about Gibraltar in the same letter as the mention of Clarkson concerns a detail in *Mansfield Park*, her attention shown to be focused on standards in her own writing. In her comparison of Clarkson with Pasley, Claudius Buchanan and the authors of the *Rejected Addresses*, the main focus is on Pasley. Issues involved include abolition. This is significant in the context of emancipation, the fourth edition of his *Essay on the Military Policy and Institutions of the British Empire* having come out in 1812. Pasley comments that the West Indies would be more useful to Britain as an ally if its inhabitants were free men.[79]

Concerns are also with excellence in writing, money, issues of empire and championing the position of women in society. It is tempting to wonder whether enthusiasm for Clarkson could be for his sympathy with this last issue, his own writing on the Quakers having praised the organizational involvement of women. Nothing specific is cited by Jane Austen in connection with Buchanan. However, in Buchanan's *Sermons*, he too shows an abolitionist spirit. He expresses thankfulness that the 1807 Abolition of the Slave Trade has been achieved. He worries about suttee in India and about accidents that were interpreted at that time to be suicide associated with the Juggernaut in India, comparing their horror to that of the abolished slave trade. This was before reform of sati (anglicized as suttee) was achieved by pressure from a combination of Christian missionaries and Hindu moral reform notably from Ram Mohan Roy, suttee becoming legally homicide in 1829.[80]

It is impossible to guess what led Jane Austen to enthuse about them all. Much of the content of what they say might have been conducive to her approval. She may also have been excited by their outstanding qualities as writers of English prose and as a professional writer keen to appraise them. It seems she has enjoyed them all with Cassandra, and the humour of the *Rejected Addresses* must have given them moments of light-heartedness. Here as well, the success of the *Rejected Addresses* owed much to the skill of its authors 'the Mr Smiths'. *Rejected Addresses* had run to a number of editions with a ninth edition in 1813. The basic scenario was of addresses having been invited for theatre re-opening in Drury Lane after necessary repairs, and some entries having had to be rejected. The scene is nicely set for irreverence in the make-believe of presenting the rejected addresses. There is knock-about humour with Boswell being obsequious to Johnson.[81] *Rejected Addresses* are involved with pure fun and satire. There is a fascinating reconstruction by Ruth Perry of what some of these people are doing together in Jane Austen's esteem in the letter of January 1813, although I query whether the European Enlightenment rightly takes a place here.[82]

Whether it is right to lay the emphasis Ruth Perry does on enthusiasm for an imperialistic adventure is difficult to gauge. She left out of account in what she terms 'Austen's casual reference grouping them together' that the authors of the *Rejected Addresses* are included, which throws everyone's writing into a different and less solemn light.

The phrase 'or even' that occurs in her saying: '...I am as much in love with the Author as I ever was with Clarkson or Buchanan, or even the two Mr Smiths of the city... ', does, I conclude, show a delight in all these authors that is combined with a light-hearted self-mockery. Abolitionism appears with Pasley, Buchanan and Clarkson, but taking the *Rejected Addresses* into account skill in writing is one factor common to all the writers in the accolade of the letter of 24 January 1813. What comes over to me is that Jane Austen is expressing a genuine affection for all these writers. I admire her taste in men. However, which of Clarkson's books she had seen remains unclear.[83]

V. Francis Austen and the evangelicals

Jane Austen's brother, Francis, was in the Royal Navy, and was a fervent abolitionist as the historian Warren Roberts has documented using the work of J.H. Hubback, a grandson of this brother.[84] With the help of his own daughter and co-writer, Hubback used notebooks and other records relating to naval experience, that of her other naval brother Charles as well as of Francis Austen. The Hubbacks cite a report 'in the notebook of Francis Austen' after sailing to the Cape of Good Hope in 1807, and accompanying a convoy to St Helena the following year. They point out that:

> The following account of the island is interesting when it is remembered that at that time it was an unimportant spot, not yet associated with memories of Napoleon.[85]

It appears that, as distinct from the slave trade abolition of that same year, slavery is Francis's concern. The Hubbacks quote from his note on St Helena:

> slavery being tolerated here. It does not appear that the slaves are or can be treated with that harshness and despotism which has been so justly attributed to the conduct of the land-holders or their managers in the West India Islands, the laws of the Colony not giving any other power to the master than a right to the labour of his slave. He must, to enforce that right, in case a slave prove refractory, apply to the civil power, he having no right to inflict chastisement at his own discretion.[86]

This is a contrast with the provisions in the Constitution of Carolina for absolute power; here no power is given to the master other than a right to the labour of the slave. Francis Austen continues with condemnation of slavery:

This is a wholesome regulation as far as it goes, but slavery however it may be modified is still slavery, and it is much to be regretted that any trace of it should be found to exist in countries dependent on England, or colonised by her subjects.

This is the abolitionist note quoted by a number of critics. It opposes slavery in a situation where amelioration of conditions had already been achieved.

The Hubbacks suggest possible influence from both brothers; Charles Austen was also in the Royal Navy.[87] An addition to a notebook from Francis Austen amongst the Hubback source material is pointed out by Brian Southam:

Chaced a ship which proved to be a Portuguese bound for Rio Janeiro. She had on board 714 slaves of both sexes, and all ages. She appeared to be about 300 tons!! And in those days the *St Albans* was compelled to let the craft proceed on her course.[88]

This indicates difference between such an early encounter soon after the 1807 Abolition and later Royal Navy work when there were agreements giving power to engage with ships from other countries. Although no date is given by Southam for the chase of the slaver by the *St Albans*, the date can be worked out from details the Hubbacks provide. Francis Austen had command of the *St Albans* between April 1807 and September 1810:

In April 1807, Captain Austen took command of the *St. Albans*, then moored in Sheerness Harbour.

Later the Hubbacks say:

Francis Austen was superseded in the *St. Albans* in September 1810 by his own wish.[89]

They go on to say that from December in the same year till May 1811 he was Flag-Captain in the *Caledonia*, and that after a further holiday of about two months, he took command on 18 July 1811 of the *Elephant*, and became involved again in the Napoleonic wars. The chase of the Portuguese slaver appears to be an early experience after the 1807 Abolition of the Slave Trade and before September 1810.

Description of policing the abolition of the slave trade could have been available through her brother's news to Jane Austen. As Peter van der Veer says, 'The antislavery campaigns had made the British public aware of Britain's role in a larger world'.[90] Ruth Perry suggests that Jane Austen was attracted by the patriotism sometimes expressed in letters from her brother Francis in the Royal Navy.[91] The issue is complex, but Francis Austen after 1806–07 would have shown enthusiasm at Britain taking a lead in this Evangelical cause. It was inescapably the Royal Navy that had to do the enforcing of the new legislation of 1807 banning the transatlantic slave trade and enforcing the 1811 legislation making slave-trading a felony.

On issues of empire, in *Mansfield Park* Fanny's reading would have been sobering. Whereas Susan Morgan rues disgraceful anti-Chinese activity of the British in opium trading in the later part of the nineteenth century, Fanny's 'trip' to China, as Edmund calls it, would have been sobering in so far as the chronicling of Macartney's visit showed up the failure to make any dent in the Chinese Emperor's view of the British as unworthy of his attention.[92] From the Admiralty, John Barrow had accompanied as translator, and the same letter that sees her enthusiasm for Clarkson and for Pasley by comparison sounds rather slighting later of 'Barrows' and 'Macartneys ...'.

It might be objected that Jane Austen had mixed feelings about the Evangelicals. Francis Austen is thought of as a Christian Evangelical. In a letter to her sister of 24 January 1809, in the context of being unwilling to read Hannah More's *Coelebs in Search of a Wife* Jane Austen says:

> I do not like the Evangelicals.

However, as a number of critics have pointed out, five or six years later she expressed a different view.[93] In the context of marriage prospects for her niece Fanny Knight, Jane Austen says to her in a letter of 18 November 1814:

> I am by no means convinced that we ought not all to be Evangelicals, & am at least persuaded that they who are so from Reason and Feeling, must be happiest & safest.

A fortnight later, another letter to Fanny Knight of 30 November 1814 seems to affirm a positive image of the Evangelicals and ends:

> I cannot suppose we differ in our ideas of the Christian Religion. You have given an excellent description of it. We only affix a different meaning to the Word *Evangelical*.

The taking stock after the 1807 Abolition may have given rise to further reflections that were not obvious at the time of her 1809 remark. My own interpretation is that she demurred from a number of Evangelical views as in 1809, but that she wished to acknowledge and stand by their abolitionist stance. I agree that Jane Austen was not in favour of a total Evangelical package.[94] However, the Evangelicals' most famous and influential work was the abolitionist campaign.

Emphasis on moral principles may not derive from Evangelicalism alone. In *Mansfield Park* the interest that Fanny Price takes in nature can sound like a European Enlightenment theme as when, in chapter II, she looks out at the night sky with Edmund, and speaks in Kantian terms of the 'sublim-ity,' of Nature'. In the chapter following Fanny Price's question about the slave trade, her eloquence on the mystery of memory may be allusion to Locke's philosophy, whose views on slavery had been quoted in the Somersett case. However, although there may be other influences, the fore-grounding at the end of *Mansfield Park* of moral principles as indispensable echoes Evangelical force. Interest not only in ending the slave trade but also in campaign for anti-slavery legislation may explain the view in Jane Austen's letter of 18 November 1814 that she was by no means convinced that they ought not all to be Evangelicals. Harnessing both 'Reason & Feeling' behind Evangelical abolitionist zeal might be what is at stake.

Finally, with respect to all those discussed in this chapter, my focus is, indeed, not on whether or not the author was influenced by them but, rather, on the nature of the possible sources of information, views and influence. Eric Williams wishes to have importance of the humanitarians put in perspective:

> This study has deliberately subordinated the inhumanity of the slave system and the humanitarianism which destroyed that system. To disregard it completely, however, would be to commit a grave historical error and to ignore one of the greatest propaganda movements of all time. The humanitarians were the spear-head of the onslaught which destroyed the West Indian system and freed the Negro.[95]

This is a powerful acknowledgment of the humanitarians as the 'spearhead of the onslaught' in what Eric Williams calls 'one of the greatest propaganda movements of all time'.

7
Conclusion

> She was about seventeen, half mulatto, chilly & tender, had a maid of her own, was to have the best room in the Lodgings, & was always of the first consequence in every plan of Mrs Griffiths.
>
> *Sanditon*, an unfinished novel, chapter 11

> Our part of London is so very superior to most others! ... The neighbourhood of Brunswick Square is very different from almost all the rest ... Mr Wingfield thinks the vicinity of Brunswick Square decidedly the most favourable as to air.
>
> *Emma*, chapter 12

In the first decade of a transition period

I have taken as keynote Cowper's question: 'We have no slaves at home – then why abroad?' Jane Austen recorded awareness and formed awareness that would act as a future force. Each of the later novels displays an interest in the aftermath of the British slave trade in a different way. Seeing the most sombre of her novels set in the context of abolition helps to make sense of the solemn Evangelical tone of *Mansfield Park*. This sombreness was not repeated in *Emma,* and in *Persuasion* the tone is different yet again.

Further work at the end of her life in the fragment of a novel set in an imaginary developing seaside resort named Sanditon has a further reference to the West Indies. Jane Austen introduces, in the first passage quoted at the head of this chapter, Miss Lambe, who is 17, wealthy and a 'precious' addition to local society for that reason, an heiress who is described as 'half mulatto':

> Of these three, and indeed of all, Miss Lambe was beyond comparison, the most important, and precious, as she paid in proportion to her fortune.

The newcomer from the West Indies, accompanied by her maid and well-chaperoned, makes her appearance not long before Jane Austen had to put aside this unfinished novel a few months before she died. The manuscript named *Sanditon*, breaking off in 1817, is dated as what looks like March 18.[1] The passage in chapter 11 of the manuscript is clear and written without alterations.

I agree with Mary Waldron that: 'It is futile to try to guess how the story would have developed.' Nevertheless, I sympathise with guessing how things might turn out.[2] I disagree, however, with Kuldip Kaur Kuwahara's view that Jane Austen should be read in the imperialistic context of novelists discussed by Gayatri Spivak. It would be anachronistic to include Jane Austen. An appropriate later Victorian context for her subjects was given by Gayatri Spivak. The earlier Jane Austen could not know whether Emancipation would be carried by Parliament, whereas Victorian novelists were writing after that legislation of the 1830s. I think it is a crucial part of Jane Austen's context that she writes during a transition period between the two great events of legislation for abolition.

I. Poverty

Themes that are common to all the novels are linked with abolition – specific issues in the later novels. Jane Austen's treatment of the significance of money is wide-ranging, and includes direct reference and allusions to poverty. In the quotation from *Emma* at the head of this chapter, there is, in my view, allusion to Coram's Foundling Hospital in London. Frequent reference to Brunswick Square, nearby, by Jane Austen suggests introduction of the topic of poverty to be integrated with issues of seeking work as a governess and abolition of the slave trade. Samuel Johnson had referred to this Hospital:

> As I wandered wrapped up in thought, my eyes were struck with the hospital for the reception of deserted infants, which I surveyed with pleasure, till by a natural train of sentiment, I began to reflect on the fate of the mothers.[3]

The Foundling Hospital in the mid eighteenth-century arose from Thomas Coram's desire to rescue unwanted babies abandoned in the gutters and middens of the poorer part of London.[4] John Fowles shocked at slave-trading from ports including Lyme Regis notes the work of Coram, born in Lyme:

> They were not all greedy-blind merchants or naively simple mariners; indeed one of those last, Captain Thomas Coram of Lyme, was by means of the Foundling Hospital to provoke England in the 1730s and 1740s into a long-needed crisis of social conscience.

When Jane Austen stayed in Lyme in 1804, Coram, a former sea-captain, may have been talked of as a famous son. He had received the Freedom of Lyme.[5]

The campaign for abolition was accused of hypocrisy in ignoring conditions at home. William Wilberforce in particular was so accused. Grinding poverty and hardship at home were part of the cost of being the first nation to industrialize. A striking pictorial image included in some mid-twentieth-century English school textbooks on history was of English women crawling on their hands and knees in mines pulling coal trucks.[6] Not until the 1840s were women and children protected by legislation from such work. Concerning abolition:

> Cobbett considered this to be misplaced altruism, arguing that the government ought first to be concerned with the condition of the poor in Britain.[7]

In the wake of each mass-abolitionist mobilization, 'metaphors of enslavement' escalated in Britain,'by West Indians and among political radicals'.[8] I think the orphan Jane Fairfax looking for a post as governess should be seen against a national background of poverty for some males as well as females, if the poverty acknowledged by allusion to the Foundling Hospital is taken into account.[9]

Brunswick Square as a residential development would have been known as flanking Coram's Fields. The Foundling Hospital had appeared in Maria Edgeworth's 1801 *Belinda* as part of that story's resolution presupposing readers would recognize the reference. Funding for the Foundling Hospital was much helped by the big names of Handel and Hogarth. Then in the 1790s and early 1800s Brunswick Square, along with matching Mecklenburg Square on the East of the Hospital, were developed to fund it from rental returns, the land developed belonging to the Foundling Hospital.[10] Roy Porter picks up the reference: '... Jane Austen has ... Isabella, very full of it'.[11]

Brunswick Square as the London home of Mr and Mrs John Knightley provides a key part of the closure of *Emma*; there seems to be a link with the setting to order of affairs in *Emma*. Then as now, albeit in different circumstances, there would be the sounds and sights of children in Coram's Fields, filtering through plane trees first planted when Brunswick Square was developed. Harriet exchanges the sounds and sights of children at Mrs Goddard's school for staying as a guest with Emma's sister Isobella. It could concentrate Harriet's mind, so that she manages well the chance Mr Knightley provides in organizing for her former suitor, who is his tenant, to go to London on business and to call on Mr John Knightley at work. This leads to a social invitation, which leads to the renewed marriage proposal. The idyllic farmstead of the Martin family becomes Harriet's home.

But for the difference that Harriet's own illegitimate birth had been accompanied by her father having money to place her in Mrs Goddard's School, Harriet too would have been looking at the hard-working life of domestic service that the girls at Coram's Fields were being prepared for.

This is emphasized by the outrageous dictum of Emma herself, in the final chapter, on Harriet's illegitimacy that is no problem for Emma so long as a gentleman as father is posited but then breathtakingly is perceived by Emma as a stain indeed if 'unbleached by nobility or wealth'. This looks high comedy at Emma's own expense. There is no mention of Harriet's mother, and that is perhaps a reminder of the plight that had presented itself to Thomas Coram over half a century earlier.

Integrated in this novel are a number of references to contemporary provision for relief from poverty. It has been pointed out that, 'It is significant that caring for the really poor is the one social duty Jane Austen does not allow Emma to neglect'.[12] If ethical issues are raised by references in the novel to poverty it would not be without warning. There may be a humorous critique of Utilitarianism with Mr Knightley throwing the children up to the ceiling. The children show a delight that Mr Woodhouse cannot understand.[13] Different sorts of pleasures and a point recognized by welfare economists over Bentham's Utilitarianism that in the slogan 'the greatest happiness of the greatest number' there is scope ambiguity allowing more than one way of resource-allocation, are both points illustrated by Emma's notion of half of mankind not understanding the other half's pleasure. In addition to the earlier visit paid by Emma and Harriet to the cottage of a poor family with illness, there is the impecunious Miss Bates saying that she and her niece Jane Fairfax will visit the impoverished and now bedridden father of 'John ostler', the father being dependant on parish relief.

Poverty, however, does not rule out a resolve for autonomy in Jane Fairfax's case. In editing the contemporary Journals and Letters of Agnes Porter, which give an account of an eighteenth-century governess, Joanna Martin remarks that:

> Jane Austen was well acquainted with both governesses and their employers, and it is possible to detect some traces of contemporary developments in her work.

A Journal entry for 26 May 1791 reads:

> could not forbear ... reflecting on the ills that single women are exposed to, even at the hour of death, from being the property of no-one.

Agnes Porter writing of being someone's 'property' illustrates the complexity of unravelling contemporary attitudes. Being someone's responsibility may be what is meant, as in *Persuasion* in chapter 7, where Anne nursing little Charles observes that 'a sick child is always the mother's property'. Details of real-life governess Agnes Porter's old age after retirement include the indication that when she died in 1814: 'she left a total of approximately £2,000'. I think there comes over in these Journals a sense of well-being, of someone with enjoyment in their way of life, and an enjoyment of autonomy.[14]

Returning to Jane Austen, the topic of poverty also arises in *Mansfield Park*, notably in the conversation in chapter 22 between Mary Crawford and Edmund. In reply to Mary Crawford saying 'A large income is the best recipe for happiness I ever heard of', Edmund asks whether she intended to be very rich. She replies: 'To be sure. Do not you? – Do not we all?' Edmund in his reply says:

> I do not mean to be poor. Poverty is exactly what I have determined against. Honesty, in the something between, in the middle state of worldly circumstances, is all that I am anxious for your not looking down on.

Realism links up with a viewpoint in the non-fictional world that there is nothing wrong in wanting to be rich. Also, in contemporary society there could have been an association of ideas between the name of Lascelles and slave-derived wealth. This may be involved later in chapter 40 when the soon-to-be discredited Mary Crawford refers with apparent approbation to Lascelles wealth as displayed in London.

Poverty as a topic is relevant also to *Persuasion*. Anne is described in chapter 13 as having 'so high an opinion of the Crofts' that she 'felt the parish to be so sure of a good example, and':

> the poor of the best attention and relief, that however sorry and ashamed for the necessity of the removal, she could not but in conscience feel that they were gone who deserved not to stay, and that Kellynch-hall had passed into better hands than its owners.

This is a vivid critique of responsibilities going along with enjoyment of property. I think this indication of Jane Austen's attitude to the poor in the first chapter of what was Volume Two has to be taken into account in the last chapter of Volume Two that closes the book, when Mrs Smith's West Indies sequestered property is emphasized to be on the agenda for reader response.

The lawyer does not seem surprised at the leading role taken by Mrs Croft. Jane Austen may not be unusual in emphasizing women's business and organizational acumen, but Tim Fulford claims:

> Mrs Croft takes for herself a role traditionally reserved for men; she asks 'more questions about the house, and terms, and taxes, than the Admiral himself' and seems 'more conversant with business'. Yet she remains 'a very well-spoken, genteel, shrewd lady', 'without any approach to coarseness'.[15]

In a humorous moment, Anne, given a lift in their one-horse gig careering through the country lanes, observes of the Crofts that Mrs Croft 'by coolly giving the reins a better direction herself ... they neither fell into a rut, nor ran foul of a dung-cart'. Some of the humour is directed to showing how women as well as men are involved in decision-making. In *Persuasion,* property, money and their management feature centrally. Property is, of course, fundamental to 'the economic basis of society', a phrase that W.H. Auden saw as integral to Jane Austen's novels.[16]

Linked with these concepts of property and money is the concept of slavery. I think Jane Austen's concern over slavery as well as over the slave trade is continued in *Persuasion* by emphasis on the West Indian seques-tered property, reminiscent of the mortgaged Kellynch property. Mrs Smith faces the management of property encumbered with debt that is to be sorted out at a time after abolition of the slave trade. For Jane Austen, along with property there are responsibilities to others. Debate is raised.

In connection with *Emma,* choice for middle-class women was indeed limited. Regarding becoming a governess, Mary Evans says:

> We can now show that it was far from being the single profession open to eigh-teenth-century women; but the forms of paid employment available to middle-class women were nevertheless limited.[17]

On governesses in a later period, Kathryn Hughes suggests that the great scandal of the governess in later nineteenth-century Victorian Britain was not the nature of the job to be performed so much as the complete under-mining of an assumption of the monied classes to the effect that a lady need not work.[18]

I acknowledge that there would be exponential increase in the possible permutations in *Emma* of ranking the relative importance of authorial attention to slavery, the slave trade and governess trade, by introducing a further variable of poverty. However, the issue of poverty is relevant to any suggestion that Jane Austen is primarily concerned about the job of gov-erness in the dialogue with Mrs Elton over the respective merits of the sale of human intellect and the sale of human flesh. References and allusion elsewhere to others' poverty seem to me to make it less likely that it is the poverty of the governess that is supposed to take centre-stage. Rather, the real problems of poverty in England are acknowledged whilst an abolition-ist concern over autonomy is furthered.

II. Debate

For contemporary readers, presupposed in the background of all three later novels may be debate as to whether amelioration of conditions for slaves or autonomy arising out of emancipation should be anticipated. The importance of autonomy for Jane Fairfax is stressed by the critic Claudia Johnson, though I disagree that the comparison with the slave trade is Jane Fairfax's doing:

The emphasis of Jane's analogy implies a heartfelt protest, not simply against slave traders, whose guilt is taken for granted, but rather against the officiousness of benefactresses such as Mrs Elton and Emma, whose dictatorial acts of kindness satisfy their own fondness for dominion more than another's wish for happiness.[19]

Jane Fairfax makes the choice to accept a post as a governess rather than to be messed about by a lover or to reckon to give him his come-uppance by looking to marry elsewhere for money.

In *Emma*, so much of what Jane Fairfax does and says seems to turn on her being determined to retain her autonomy, whether in the trivial case of sending back Emma's gift of arrowroot or, more strikingly, of breaking off her engagement and taking instead the governess post on offer, giving rise to that mysterious headache and debility that the arrowroot was supposed to help with. While she languishes with this ill-health, we still do not know of her secret engagement let alone of her decision to break it and to decide instead on the governess post.

Although there were problems of poverty at home, I think a significant number of people were opposed early on during the abolitionist campaign not only to the slave trade but also to slavery. A different interpretation, however, of contemporary attitudes is taken by David Erdman. Having argued for reading William Blake's *Visions of the Daughters of Albion* of 1793 as poetic counterpart of 'the parliamentary and editorial debates of 1789–1793 on a bill for abolition of the British slave trade', Erdman goes on to speak of a political quandary of the *Society for the Abolition of the Slave Trade*. He cites the *London Chronicle* for 2 February 1792 to the effect that what was desired was not 'the Emancipation of the Negroes in the British colonies', but only a seeking to end 'the Trade for Slaves'.

In reply, however, I should say that a statement of slave trade-theoretic aims for this Society would be compatible with its members having different aims for any Society with a different name. Further, in a footnote, Erdman writes:

> Against the explanation that it was simply strategic to concentrate first on abolition of the trade, consider the fact that as soon as the Slave trade bill was passed, in 1807, the Society dissolved. Slavery itself, and consequently the trade, continued to exist.[20]

I suggest this does not take into consideration two points. Firstly, given the remit of the Society its work was done so far as the breakthrough of change in British law was concerned. Thereafter there was indeed the problem of enforcing the law, but the dissolving of the Society was an important acknowledgement of legal change.

Secondly, strategy may have been better served for emancipation by regrouping after taking stock.[21] Later in 1823 the Anti-Slavery Society was formed on a grander basis than the earlier Society, which had been a smaller affair working through key political contacts and public opinion which it helped form.[22] With William Wilberforce becoming too old after the 1807 Abolition to be effective in Parliament, there may have been a particular need to rest and reconstitute forces for the ensuing work of a public pressure group affecting global commodity markets.[23]

William Blake's poems include another that is noteworthy not only for its abolitionist stance but also for its comment on some contemporary attitudes to race. *The Little Black Boy* of 1789 begins in a dialectical mode with heat of the Southern sun making the little black boy's skin dark, and ends with the child's ability to shield the little white boy from burning in the light rays of the presence of God, thereby giving the little white boy a chance to acclimatize so that he, too, can be comfortable in the presence of God. It turns out to be the black child who can help out the white one, and who in stroking his hair will bring the white child to love him. Even Eric Williams arguing for a downplaying of ideas in his Marxist analysis of abolitionism, extols as 'beautiful' this poem from *Songs of Innocence and Experience*, thereby I think acknowledging the potential power of literary works in making impact in the cause of abolitionism.[24]

On arguments against both slavery and the slave trade, Clarkson in his 1786 *Essay* draws attention to the trickery involved in the slave trade. He cited the scandal of 1781. As Clarkson puts it the excuse was:

> that if the slaves who were then sickly, had died a natural death, the loss would have been the owners; but as they were thrown alive into the sea, it would fall upon the underwriters.[25]

Some writers now urge that not treating colonial slaves as fellow humans had led to moral outrage in the early 1780s, when news became public of the *Zong* slave ship in 1781, from which over 100 Negroes had been thrown overboard in order to collect on insurance. James Walvin claims that public attention was attracted by 'the infamous Zong case', and Gretchen Gerzina also stresses impact on public opinion.[26]

I think the sense of moral outrage might have been fuelled not only by fellow feeling for the victims, but also for concern over practice likely to unsettle underwriters at Lloyd's of London. Insurance encouraged economic efficiency of the country. On maritime insurance in the eighteenth century, Lorraine Daston says:

> Maritime insurance expanded under the auspices of individual brokers who congregated at coffeehouses like Lloyd's .[27]

The *Zong* case could have led to questions about the credentials of such a captain in taking on the human cargo in Africa. As has been said of today's maritime underwriter:

Like his predecessor in sixteenth-century Venice, today's maritime underwriter gauges 'the integrity of the shipowner, the skill of the ship's officers, the quality of the crew'.[28]

I think commerce and morals intermingled in reaction to the *Zong* atrocity. The eighteenth century may not yet have been sophisticated actuarially, but in a blatant case like that of the *Zong* claim for insurance money, the insurers would have seen they had less control over risk.

On this case, Howard Temperley writes concerning the recurring readiness to have Parliament regulate trade:

> In choosing to concentrate their energies on the slave trade rather than on slavery, British abolitionists had been swayed by a variety of considerations ... the trade was patently the more vulnerable. Even the unsentimental British public had been shocked by disclosures such as those in the *Zong* case in 1781 ... Whatever the horrors of slavery, they could scarcely compare with these. Contemporary opinion, moreover, was highly sensitive on questions involving private property and established institutions to which categories slavery clearly belonged, whereas regulating trade had long been recognised as a function of Parliament.

Howard Temperley here sees emphasis to have been on the slave trade itself, but in reaction both to the *Zong* case and more generally, David Turley lays more emphasis on anti-slavery pressure in the long term:

> By the time of the abolition measures of 1806 and 1807 abolitionists had failed to convince their opponents that they were not also looking forward to emancipation. West Indians and their supporters were substantially correct in their suspicions, much of the attack on the slave trade from as early as the end of the 1780s to the debates of 1806 could equally have been, and was, an attack on slavery.[29]

The upshot is that an attack on the slave trade was thought to have more immediate hope of success. Such pragmatism left open that the campaign against the slave trade could also be heard as an attack on slavery.

Abolitionist desire for freedom for slaves had not gone away, even though there was much talk of amelioration of conditions of those held in slavery.[30] Amelioration as against freedom may be symbolized in *Mansfield Park*, with the kindliness of Sir Thomas to Fanny Price contrasting with the resolve of the heroine not to be imposed on. Her resolve has to hold fast against the onslaught from Sir Thomas. Claudia Johnson suggests that Sir Thomas's kindness to Fanny is suggestive of his attention to his slaves not being such as to favour emancipation.[31]

Nevertheless, sometimes there may be mere coincidence rather than abolitionist allusion. The cruel Mrs Norris in *Mansfield Park* receives her just deserts, and is said by some to have the surname of a notorious slave trader.[32] In *Emma*, the name 'Hawkins' could recall Sir John Hawkins, the first English slave trader. In the chapters introducing Augusta Hawkins, Mr Elton's intended bride, the first introduction by name in chapter 21 by Miss Bates of Miss Hawkins in the same breath as 'a beautiful hind quarter of pork' is a striking instance of coincidence amongst the frequent repetition of the name.[33] However, whether or not coincidence, the examples both of Mrs Norris and Mrs Elton would suggest that women's relative dependency does not exonerate them from complicity in wrong-doing.

I think it looks less likely that the 'Mansfield' name is coincidental, because Cowper's celebration of the Mansfield Decision seems to me to be integrated into the text.[34] The title of a novel is too important for Jane Austen not to have considered possible reader response to it. The other possible coincidence, with *Amelie Mansfield* before the play acting that troubles Fanny, is more readily to be seen as coincidental, because it would not have had the measure of contemporary awareness attending it that the Mansfield Decision had.

Concerning autonomy, the condition of the slave as someone else's property was of prime concern to abolitionists. Stephen Munzer's work on the nature of property touches on this. In *A Theory of Property*, he weighs up a tentative proposal by the American Law Institute (ALI) concerning the basic objective of the business corporation, showing how it would have collided with moral reform put forward by abolitionists. Munzer says:

> the ALI proposal turns out too closely tied to prevailing standards of right and wrong as they relate to the conduct of business. This shortcoming is the vice of its virtue. For example, consider a person who gains a controlling interest in a corporation in Virginia in 1840. The corporation employs – indeed, owns – slaves to work its coal mines. The person who now has a controlling interest intends, on moral grounds, to emancipate the slaves and hire them or other people at prevailing market rates. Doing so would have a negative effect on the short-run and long-run profit picture of the corporation. It would also violate the ALI proposal. Though even in that place and time some moral controversy existed regarding slavery, no 'ethical consideration' requiring or even permitting emancipation would have been 'reasonably regarded as appropriate to the responsible conduct of business'.[35]

The argument of Munzer goes to show the sort of move open to the pro-slavery lobby, who could say that they respected ethical argument but that it was counter balanced by 'responsible conduct of business'. Munzer is also relevant in an earlier remark where he says: 'a power to give or sell oneself into slavery would impair autonomy'.[36]

Focusing on the plight of the governess, Claire Tomalin had said about Jane Austen's views in *Emma*, 'Austen's point here is to do with governessing, not slavery', and she gives the example of a niece of Jane Austen; Fanny Austen's pocket book for 1809:

shows that concern for slaves and horror at the trade in them, was by then so general that the publishers of ladies' diaries could assume that such a story, wholly sympathetic if also thoroughly naïve, would be entirely welcome.

Claire Tomalin says, 'there is no doubt that she takes for granted her readers' agreement that the slave trade is a guilty one'.[37] The inference drawn is that Jane Austen's focus must be on the plight of the governess, but it could instead have been inferred that the focus must be on the plight of the slave trapped by the now discredited slave trade. At this crucial stage it still had to be carried by the abolitionists that the recognition of the guilt of the slave trade should be followed by legislation to outlaw slavery.

On hardships of governesses, Margaret Kirkham draws an analogy with slaves, and Josephine Ross has a similar point:

[Jane Fairfax] draws a distinction between the degrees of guilt involved, but cannot resist, bitterly, comparing the miseries of the respective 'victims'.[38]

However, for anyone concerned with the plight of the victims of the slave trade who were still slaves, a deflection to the plight of impoverished governesses in a comparison would have sounded insensitive. If the focus in *Emma* were on governesses rather than on slavery or the slave trade, it would get Jane Fairfax into hot water, since as internet chat rooms have shown there is thought to be self pity on the part of the putative governess complaining about her lot and overreacting in comparing herself to a slave.[39] She seems to be kept at arms-length, and we have to say goodbye just as we are getting to know Jane Fairfax, as Emma puts it at the end. Although Jane Fairfax is dispensable as a heroine, I think any distance between her and the author is closed in the dénouement.

There remains an apparent concern in *Emma* with the retaining of autonomy on Jane Fairfax's part. Whether or not simultaneously there is a reminder that a governess's life could be grim is a significant conjecture adding to the complexity of weighing up the priorities of combating illegal slave-trading, seeking a post in the job market as a governess, carrying out the job of a governess, poverty, and literal slavery as someone else's property.

III. *Mansfield Park* and *Emma* revisited

I have endeavoured in earlier chapters to set out considerations to show that Edward Said's description was way off the mark.[40] Jane Austen's satire is sharp. It is treacherous to rest assured that satire is not at work rather than straightforward endorsement. Edward Said saw endorsement of the status quo, where instead an alternative is available of weighing up the probabilities of a satirical reading. If satire is a customary Austen tool, then it is as well to keep that fact firmly in mind at every turn, on pain otherwise of having our conclusions negated by the practice of the author. Once take satire into account, and the reader may get a truer account of what has transpired in the novel by negating a critic's original ideas.

One of Edward Said's most chilling claims follows on immediately after his attempt to give a date for Sir Thomas's absence. The claim reads a good deal more cogently by negating all its propositions. *Mansfield Park* can just as well, if not better, be summed up in a negated rendering of that claim. Thus, we may more justly read:

> More clearly than anywhere else in her fiction, Austen here synchronises domestic with international authority, making it plain that the values associated with such higher things as ordination, law, and propriety must *not* be grounded firmly in actual rule over and possession of territory. She sees clearly that to hold and rule Mansfield Park is *not* to hold and rule an imperial estate in close, not to say inevitable association with it. What assures the domestic tranquillity and attractive harmony of one is *not* the productivity and regulated discipline of the other. (My alterations in underlined italics)

Here, the negation sign '*not*' inserted by me and both *italicised* and *underlined* by me seems to yield a better picture of what Jane Austen was actually about in this novel than Edward Said's original rendering.[41]

Just as Cowper had used satire in his abolitionist poetry, so too in *Mansfield Park* much of the moral message may be conveyed by means of satire. Given that an Austen tool of choice is humour, we can regard the metropolis as the global village to be laughed at, in the time-honoured tradition of comedy derived from laughing at the manners of the village. The medium of comedy, which is a universal one, enables Jane Austen to criticize adversely wherever she chooses. Undermining on her part may work right on the surface or deeper down.

My viewpoint is different from the following alignment with Edward Said that sees 'maintaining the order and patrimonial mystique of Mansfield Park' as aided by Fanny's resistance to marriage outside the family with Crawford. It has been suggested that seeing Fanny's question about the subject of slavery as subversive is nullified by the author rushing:

> to fill the awkward silence with an excruciatingly self-denying statement by Fanny of not wanting 'to set myself off at [my cousins'] expense.

It is further suggested that:

> In this way the text nervously overcompensates for the impertinence of Fanny's question to Sir Thomas by staging a slavish display of her desire for his approval.

However, I think that such a deconstruction yielding tension between tradition and change, whether intended or unintended by the author, serves to accentuate the issue of the slave trade within the text.[42]

Stirring up discussion highlights the topic. Jane Austen may be using the silence after Fanny's question interactively. Brian Southam misses Jane Austen's target when he says Fanny broke a 'taboo met instantly with a confounding "dead silence"' . On a minor point, we do not know that it was so met 'instantly' or 'confoundingly' as Southam has it; I am more concerned to suggest that the phrase 'Making Silence Speak', actually the title of Lardinois and McClure's book subtitled 'Women's Voices in Greek Literature and Society', would capture what is going on in the novel at this point. Southam ends the article by claiming that: 'At this notable moment, in the lion's den, Fanny is unmistakably a 'friend of the Abolition', and Austen's readers in 1814 would have applauded the heroine and her author for exactly that'. Now I see no reason to be sure that all readers would. Some readers might have been of a different persuasion. What if Jane Austen had wanted to speak to them? It would be advisable not to risk a counter-productive defence of the cause of abolition. If Fanny is in the lion's den, as Southam claims, she would need to proceed with especial care.

Such care could best be taken by the author not specifying the question asked. I disagree with Southam when he says:

> Fanny gets no reply to her forbidden question because none is possible from a man who has supported the slave trade as a buyer of slaves – lawfully in times past, or even illegally since 1808 – and whose own fortunes have depended on it.

Perhaps Sir Thomas has no such reaction, and hesitates as much as to say how long are you prepared to listen to me launching out on all that I should like to say, only to find that his own daughters look most unimpressed at the prospect.

Fanny Price expected that her uncle Sir Thomas Bertram would like his daughters 'to shew a curiosity and pleasure in his information', in his reply. The word 'information' suggests Fanny's question was susceptible to an informed reply rather than an opinion only, or at any rate that Fanny thought so. It is consistent with the description Jane Austen gives that, notwithstanding there being 'such a dead silence', Sir Thomas gives a brief reply but that Fanny is intimidated from enquiring farther, as she explains. Her cousin Edmund's remark 'It would have pleased your uncle to be inquired of farther' does not bear out Brian Southam's supposition:

> The gap of silence between his slave-owning 'values' and those of Fanny, the sole questioner of those 'values', could not be more effectively shown.

It is not just that we cannot even be sure of the generalised reaction as Southam tries to reconstruct it. When it comes to supplying a suitable question for Fanny to have broached, the list of possibilities is not only long but also controversial. I do not know that the number of questions that could be imagined could readily be capped; the nature of a question might be too questioner-dependant.

It seems that 25 rough and ready questions that Fanny might conceivably have asked could readily be rustled up. Will the slaves not need to bear children if a slave workforce is to be maintained? Was the slave trade cruel? Will other countries like France follow suit? Will there still be slaves if there is no slave trade? If the slave trade was wrong will they release the slaves? Did you vote for abolition? Since the slave trade is now illegal but continues illegally, is it now crueller because unregulated? Will the slave trade by Arab countries stop as well? Why were African countries willing to participate? Was England's slave trade really going on for 250 years? Why did the slave trade prosper when if there had been servants you could have dismissed them when work was slack? Did slaves have to be from Africa? Could there have been slaves from England? Were slaves willing to be taken in the first place? Were conditions they left behind them worse than in the West Indies? What about their families – do they see their relations who also went to the West Indies? Can slaves get married? Why did the slave trade continue if there had already been a gathering together of a slave workforce? Why were some people against abolition? How will the 1807 Abolition be enforced? Were Creole slaves happier than African slaves newly arrived? Does the 1811 legislation making it a felony really make more of a deterrent against slave-trading? Why did some Christians think it was all right to have slaves while other Christians disagree? Has the price risen for slaves if there is now a scarcity? Do not new ways of thinking about economic affairs that Adam Smith talks about make slavery outdated? – One person's obvious question may be totally ridiculous to another person, who in turn may have his own seemingly obvious question to ask, which in turn appears daft to the person with whom he disagreed, as I intended to illustrate in the first two questions.

These are homespun questions for Fanny to have asked. Margaret Kirkham has her own suggestion citing Clarkson and saying:

> that a woman who rejoiced that the slave trade had been ended might ask whether it had yet been recorded 'as a principle of our legislation that commerce itself shall have its moral boundaries' – so far as women were concerned.

Although I am sceptical here as to the extent of 'feminist irony' in *Mansfield Park*, I should like to take up for the subsequent novel Kirkham's daring idea of the author laughing at her readers. In *Emma* on the question of governesses in relation to the slave trade, I therefore suggest that, to adopt Kirkham's words, 'irony ...is turned upon the reader'.[43]

As the historian Roger Anstey points out there is a paradox, that after 1807 the abolition of the slave trade was embraced as a matter of principle:

a major reform was achieved without a major frontal breach of the still stubborn tradition that reform of institutions on principle was not lightly to be ventured upon. The paradox remains that, once achieved, abolition was immediately viewed as a whole – after all the entire British slave trade was comprehended in the 1807 Act – and as a measure of principle, and not merely as the initiative of committed abolitionists, private men and ministers, which it undoubtedly was.[44]

Given such change in attitude, Jane Austen would have been out of date if she had still been advocating abolition of the slave trade after that abolition had already been passed by Parliament.

Nevertheless, in *Emma* what is categorically described as guilty is not slavery but the slave trade. Selma James says: 'This is the only overt condemnation of slavery in any of Ms. Austen's novels'.[45] Ironically, to hear the reference to the slave trade as concerning slavery is to make precisely the link that was keeping abolitionist concern on the agenda for debate, after abolition of the slave trade had been carried in Parliament in 1807. It is a further matter, which I believe to hold up, that in emphasizing the guilt of the slave trade, a lever is provided to induce the train of thought that what the slave trade has delivered people into, namely chattel slavery, is also to be abhorred.

It may here still be rebutted that the real concern is with the governess. The suggestion has been made by Deirdre Coleman that:

> While for propriety's sake Jane Fairfax denies making any strict equation between the moral enormity of the slave-trade and 'governess-trade', her bitter conjunction of the two ('the sale – not quite of human flesh – but of human intellect') leads her to insinuate that of the two sets of victims, it is the governesses who bear the 'greater misery'.

However, there is nothing to show such insinuation being made, and this would not take into account the force of 'not quite'. This critic had just made a comparison with a quotation from a contemporary writer called Mary Anne Radcliffe (not to be confused with her near contemporary, the novelist Ann Radcliffe, whose work is cited in chapter 4 of *Emma*):

> 'What are the untutored, wild imaginations of a slave, when put in the balance with the distressing sensations of a British female, who has received a refined, if not a classical, education, and is capable of the finest feelings the human heart is susceptible of?' The same point is made, albeit with more delicacy, in Jane Austen's *Emma*.[46]

But the same point is not shown to have been made. There is no reason to suppose that Jane Austen had read let alone agreed with the views of Mary Anne Radcliffe, as distinguished from Ann Radcliffe. In fairness, it could be added that Mary Ann Radcliffe was agonizing in 1799 over girls apparently reduced to prostitution in London through poverty and betrayal by lovers.

That was the concern Johnson had been voicing when he was reminded of them by seeing the Foundling Hospital.[47]

IV. Transition

Abolitionists may have been aware of a wider, inter-cultural condoning of slavery, by other civilizations including some in Africa as well as their own, not least by some high-born black Africans.[48] In *Emma* there may be a coded reference to customs that included a relish for pleasure and sights such as the slave market in Constantinople, from Frank Churchill's behaviour at Box Hill, when as a young bachelor heir he speaks of travelling abroad. The request to Emma to prepare a wife for him while he is away may be a coded way of saying he would be prepared to settle down to domesticity after gaining experience on his Grand Tour. The day before at Donwell Abbey had seen Mr Knightley displaying prints and curiosities for Mr Woodhouse to be occupied with on his visit, already suggesting the important part that travel played during the eighteenth century. This continued during the Napoleonic Wars with restricted access to Europe, when the Grand Tour in the Ottoman Empire came even more into its own.[49]

Jane Austen may have shared the hard-headedness that Byron will later display. Slave-trading was to be met by Byron in *Don Juan* with fury:

> Twelve negresses from Nubia brought a price
> Which the West Indian market scarce would bring;
> Though Wilberforce, at last, has made it twice
> What 'twas ere Abolition;

The Arab slave trade is referred to by Byron, with a comparison of unfinished business for abolitionists, apparently with respect to Britain's continuing acceptance of slavery and difficulties in effectively banning the slave trade.[50] Worldliness of both Jane Austen and Byron is observed by Richard Cronin:

> Jane Austen might seem to have little enough in common with Byron, and yet her influence, like his, is evident in the fashionable novel. After all, the two share a worldliness that sets them apart from their contemporaries, a willingness to accept that human nature is best displayed by tracing its social relations, and hence that a dinner party is a more interesting setting than a mountain-top.

British gentlemen travelling in Egypt are documented by Neil Cooke, as having joined in the local lifestyle before and after the 1830s legislation abolishing slavery for British territories.[51] Jane Austen may share Johnson's cosmopolitanism, which saw Britain's own civilization as deriving from 'the shores of the Mediterranean', from 'four great Empires', the Greek and Roman and the Assyrian and Persian empires.

While suggesting Edward Said's pages about the evils of imperialism are not to be faulted, one reviewer nevertheless adds that they would have been stronger had a few paragraphs been included over Arabs' role in slave-trading in Africa:

> about the role of the Arabs in the slave trade of Africa, also a version of imperialism.[52]

A wider context taking into account the Arab slave trade and the black Diaspora within the great Ottoman Empire should have been included by Edward Said for completeness.[53] Ato Quayson notes criticisms of Edward Said that his approach on imperialism and culture was too monolithic.[54]

Although I have argued for a reading in terms of concern about slavery in the later novels as well as endorsing popular outrage over the slave trade, it is indeed early for slavery-specific campaigning to have got underway. Concern after the 1807 Abolition remained over the slave trade; there were problems about the mortality rate and illegal trading:

> The results of abolition were far less striking than humanitarians had hoped. Others took up the trade in Britain's place, and British diplomats were felt to have failed when the peace settlements of 1814–15 produced no general abolition treaty.[55]

There was good reason still to be concerned about the slave trade, even though it had been illegal since 1807, and slave-trading had been made a felony in 1811. Clarkson, however, in his 1786 *Essay* had woven the two issues of slavery and the slave trade together:

> Abolitionists had hoped that the end of the trade in slaves would lead naturally to the end of slavery itself and it took some years for them to gather strength for a new initiative.[56]

Clarkson saw it as yet another argument against slavery itself that it could entail not only trickery but also brutality in the slave trade. Slave-trading had been shown to be not a matter of relatively humane sparing of lives of prisoners of war by taking them hostage and working them as slaves, as envisaged by Locke a hundred years before. Clarkson's vision was of eventual abolition not only of the trade but also of slavery. I may not have resolved whether Jane Austen's attention is given to the slave trade or to slavery or to both, but I believe her involvement is assured.

Notwithstanding the global nature of slavery and slave-trading amongst other civilizations, *Mansfield Park* itself is a practical approach because it appears to have relevance to slavery as practised in British colonies only, in so far as it contains a critique of absenteeism. That suggests a focusing on the home problem then remaining for Britain over slavery in its colonies and responsibility of Britons to set their own behaviour in good order. There is reliance on association of ideas in all three Chawton novels, with allusion and ambiguity functioning to raise and air issues.[57]

One such ambiguity may be over the status of women such as Lady Bertram, Mrs Norris and Mrs Elton who may be seen as colluding with the status quo of chattel slavery. They may be perceived by a reader as women who choose to hide behind relative dependency to avoid accountability. The most extreme instance of that ambiguity has to be Lady Bertram, who bewilders Sir Thomas and Edmund by seeking their decision as to whether she could dispense with Fanny to make tea in the drawing room one evening. The satire here is so sharp that a reader may hesitate between seeing this as a joke or as a portrayal of women's subordination.

Jane Austen helped prepare for the future, painting pictures of an England, as in *Emma* in the for all seasons view from Donwell Abbey of the Martins' farmstead, an England that could live at its best without living off the proceeds of slavery, or the excitements of squandering those profits as the heir Tom did in *Mansfield Park* in his gaming and expenditure up to the time of his reforming illness. Jane Austen may have wielded influence in the description of England and Englishness in *Emma*, as in the surreal representation of juxtaposed Springtime apple blossom with the Summertime strawberries that are the subject of hilarity when Mrs Elton applies herself to picking strawberries at Donwell Abbey. Juxtaposition suggests a clustering of some traditional English experience to be treasured, as distinct from the by then jettisoned slave trade.

V. Summary

By way of summary of my main chapters, in *Mansfield Park* cumulative cases of absenteeism are backdrop for a question about the by-then banned slave trade. Indeterminacy of internal chronology stops this question from becoming outdated, so long as chattel slavery in the West Indies remained legal. *Mansfield Park* may allude in its title to the Mansfield decision against slavery, and there are quotations from the abolitionist poet William Cowper, who celebrated Mansfield against slavery. Sir Thomas's misplaced certainty in his anger with Fanny after she refuses Henry Crawford's marriage proposal is dramatic. Sir Thomas turns out to be wrong in this judgement. The conflict, in which Fanny holds to her resolve not to be imposed on, is the parable at the heart of the novel. There could be a critique of talk of amelioration of conditions for slaves abroad that nevertheless withholds autonomy. The change 'for ever' of the heir Tom adds to an air of parable with *a fortiori* reasoning, and the position of the heir to the property looks pivotal.[58] Edward Said was wrong that Sir Thomas was endorsed without criticism. Sir Thomas had turned out to be wrong, as the text makes clear, and I claim to negate Edward Said's claims on Mansfield Park and slavery.

In *Emma*, people being regarded as commodities, in the topic raised by Mrs Elton's comparison of the slave trade with the business of finding a post as a governess, is seen as related to Mrs Elton's possible family connections with the Bristol slave trade. This, along with Jane Fairfax's handling of the terms of the dialogue with Mrs Elton, may be seen as enabling the novelist to weave into the very fabric of the novel an undermining of the status quo of chattel slavery. This is enhanced by the riddle of Jane Fairfax's situation. Such a reading is compatible with this novel as a romance from Emma's early softening Mr Knightley's anger by holding her new baby niece to the climax of Mr Knightley's riding on horseback from London in the rain in order to comfort an apparently lovelorn Emma.

With its naval theme, *Persuasion* is much more overtly outward-looking than *Emma*. Its cosmopolitanism is illustrated by its reference to the *Arabian Nights'* heroine Scheherazade. Reference to the West Indies and precision in the dates provided for the narrative echo places and dates connected with the 1807 British Abolition. Since in this last novel there is no explicit mention of abolition, *Persuasion* is much more controversially to be linked with an interest in the slave trade. I hope to have convinced you that it is appropriate to see a possible link as well in the last novel with abolition.

Persuasion is in its internal chronology a product of the decade following the British abolition of 1807. Emphasis in *Persuasion* on the up-to-date Royal Navy could be thought to presuppose and celebrate the new legislation banning the slave trade. Paul Lovejoy points out:

> The Abolition Act prohibits all British subjects from participation in the slave trade as of 1 January 1808. A naval squadron that eventually reaches one-sixth of the total strength of the Royal navy is dispatched to blockade the West African coast.[59]

Practicalities of policing the change in the law would have to be taken care of by the Royal Navy, as Jane Austen would have been especially aware through her naval brothers. She was well placed to be kept informed through her sailor brothers of actual and likely developments in the Royal Navy's experience.

However, policing of abolition could bring opposition on the seas, and put an illicit cargo of human beings at risk. To evade detection it would be possible to dispose of all evidence.[60] Such unwelcome outcome to the 1807 Abolition in turn may have given rise to additional reason to campaign for Emancipation, since there would not be point in continuing slave-trading if there were no market for slaves. Such a thought process could add poignancy to the raising of the topic of the slave trade in *Mansfield Park* and in *Emma*.

Shortly before his death, Edward Said commented again, though whether by way of recantation is not known:

> Even the skilfully wrought novels of Jane Austen, for instance, are affiliated with the circumstances of her time; this is why she makes elaborate reference to such sordid practices as slavery and fights over property. Yet, to repeat, her novels can never be reduced only to social, political, historical, and economic forces but, rather, are, antithetically, in an unresolved dialectical relationship with them, in a position that obviously depends on history but is not reducible to it.[61]

His talk of her elaborate reference to slavery and property leaves open that Jane Austen was indeed stirring up debate. I think that in what Edward Said called her 'unresolved dialectical relationship' we can actually see part of her contribution to the unresolved issues over slavery that awaited resolution during the interim years.[62] She had an input in keeping alive these issues in a period that was a reappraisal in the years between 1807 and 1833.

Whether or not, or how far, in the age of abolition, there was any power to bring about change independently of economic factors of the kind described by Eric Williams is disputed. One view runs:

> Some historians of slavery have argued that abolitionism was a natural counterpart of industrialisation and free-market economics. If so, this was a perception which entirely escaped contemporaries, conscious as they were of the profits which continued to flow from the African and American trade, and the importance which the sugar plantations retained in the imperial system.[63]

It remains that some people endeavoured to bring about change. Such endeavour makes for fellow-feeling with us in present-day condemnation of slavery and the slave trade in the light of International Law following the Universal Declaration of Human Rights in December 1948, so that there is now a world-wide consensus against bygone chattel slavery when a person could be the property of others.[64] It is easy to overlook that in Jane Austen's time such slave societies existed amongst all empires and cultures, with the exception of Haiti. An effort is required to try to put ourselves back in Jane Austen's shoes, not knowing whether there would be further success for the hopes of those like Cowper, Johnson and Clarkson with a follow-up to the Abolition of 1807 and to the making of slave-trading a felony punishable by 14 years imprisonment in 1811. With hindsight the later Emancipation can now look more inevitable than it could have looked in Jane Austen's own time.

It is possible that much of the depiction of England that we enjoy in the later novels acted subliminally to affect attitudes and help create a climate in which chattel slavery and the slave trade are unacceptable. There is careful presentation in Jane Austen's texts and they do not run a risk of being counter-productive. Her subtlety may give rise to an impression that the texts are ambiguous. I do not myself see ambiguity, but, on the other hand, ambiguity too would be useful in playing a part in strategy, by attention being focused on a topic so that in resultant provoking of thought, while keeping us guessing, a topic would be raised and aired that could be subversive of the status quo of chattel slavery. To provoke thought and to stimulate debate, to imply standards of life without reliance on slavery, may have been the most useful moves in the decade that was a taking stock in abolitionist activity following its first success.

The later novels are written in the period that sees the strengthening of the abolition of the slave trade by making it in 1811 a criminal offence for Britons. In the early years of what would be the transitional period there was a taking stock of what had been achieved by legislation in Parliament. I see Jane Austen as keeping the issue of the slave trade and its aftermath on the agenda partly by direct reference and partly by exploring the related concept of autonomy, especially in the case first of Fanny Price and then of Jane Fairfax. This occurs during a period that seems to me to be a pause for reflection in abolitionist campaigning while seeing the beginning of policing of abolition by the Royal Navy.

Jane Austen's three last novels were written in the early part of those years that were to constitute a transitional period, the years between the 1807 Abolition of the Slave Trade, which I think is presupposed in the later novels, and the British Emancipation Act of the 1830s freeing slaves in colonies of the British Empire eventually to become the Commonwealth. Although Jane Austen's untimely death in 1817 meant she would not live to see the further outcome of the popular resolve for abolition, she can be viewed as contributing to the cause of abolition during the reappraisal of the early years, both in her undermining the status quo of chattel slavery, and in celebrating the abolition of the British slave trade.

Appendix 1   Colonization as from a North American Indian's Viewpoint: Samuel Johnson, *The Idler*, 1759, No. 81, Saturday 3 November

As the *English* army was passing towards *Quebec* along a soft savanna between a mountain and a lake, one of the petty Chiefs of the inland regions stood upon a rock surrounded by his clan, and from behind the shelter of the bushes contemplated the art and regularity of *European* war. It was evening, the tents were pitched; he observed the security with which the troops rested in the night, and the order with which the march was renewed in the morning. He continued to pursue them with his eye till they could be seen no longer, and then stood for some time silent and pensive.

Then turning to his followers, 'My children (said he) I have often heard from men hoary with long life, that there was a time when our ancestors were absolute lords of the woods, the meadows, and the lakes, wherever the eye can reach or the foot can pass. They fished and hunted, feasted and danced, and when they were weary lay down under the first thicket, without danger and without fear. They changed their habitations as the seasons required, convenience prompted, or curiosity allured them, and sometimes gathered the fruits of the mountain, and sometimes sported in canoes along the coast.'

'Many years and ages are supposed to have been thus passed in plenty and security; when at last, a new race of men entered our country from the great Ocean. They inclosed themselves in habitations of stone, which our ancestors could neither enter by violence, nor destroy by fire. They issued from those fastnesses, sometime covered like the armadillo with shells, from which the lance rebounded on the striker, and sometimes carried by mighty beasts which had never been seen in our vales or forests, of such strength and swiftness, that flight and opposition were vain alike. Those invaders ranged over the continent, slaughtering in their rage those that resisted, and those that submitted, in their mirth. Of those that remained, some were buried in caverns, and condemned to dig metals for their masters; some were employed in tilling the ground, of which foreign tyrants devour the produce; and when the sword and the mines have destroyed the natives, they supply their place by human beings of another colour, brought from some distant country to perish here under toil and torture.'

'Some there are who boast their humanity, and content themselves to seize our chaces and fisheries, who drive us from every track of ground where fertility and pleasantness invite them to settle, and make no war upon us except when we intrude upon our own lands.'

'Others pretend to have purchased a right of residence and tyranny; but surely the insolence of such bargains is more offensive than the avowed and open dominion of force. What reward can induce the possessor of a country to admit a stranger more powerful than himself? Fraud or terror must operate in such contracts; either they promised protection which they never have afforded, or instruction which they never imparted. We hoped to be secured by their favour from some other evil, or to learn the arts of *Europe*, by which we might be able to secure ourselves. Their power they have never exerted in our defence, and their arts they have studiously concealed from us. Their treaties are only to deceive, and their traffick only to defraud us. They have a written Law among them, of which they boast as derived from him who made the Earth and Sea, and by which they profess to believe that man will be made happy when life shall forsake him. Why is not this Law communicated to us? It is concealed because it is violated. For how can they preach it to an *Indian* nation, when I am told that one of its first precepts forbids them to do to others what they would not that others should do to them?'

'But the time perhaps is now approaching when the pride of usurpation shall be crushed, and the cruelties of invasion shall be revenged.The sons of Rapacity have now drawn their swords upon each other, and referred their claims to the decision of war; let us look unconcerned about the slaughter, and remember that the death of every *European* delivers the country from a tyrant and a robber; for what is the claim of either nation, but the claim of the vulture to the leveret, of the tiger to the faun? Let them then continue to dispute their title to regions which they cannot people, to purchase by danger and blood the empty dignity of dominion over mountains which they will never climb, and rivers which they will never pass. Let us endeavour, in the mean time, to learn their discipline, and to forge their weapons; and when they shall be weakened with mutual slaughter, let us rush down upon them, force their remains to take shelter in their ships, and reign once more in our native country.'

The IDLER by The Author of The Rambler ... 2 vols.
The fourth edition, London, 1783: Vol. II, 160–4.

Appendix 2   Argument Against Slavery by Samuel Johnson Dictated at Boswell's Request, 1777

This is included in *Additions* to the 2nd Edition, 1793, of James Boswell's
Life of Johnson. In a specially inserted section at the beginning,
after printing of the 2nd Edition had taken place, the additional pages
needed to be asterisked to distinguish them from the original pagination.

In the Table of Contents, on p. xxxii under 'N'
in addition to the entries for 'Negroes' it is noted:
'Johnson's argument in favour of one, additions
prefixed to Vol. I'.

Additions to Dr Johnson's Life
Recollected, and Received
After the 2nd Edition was Printed

Pages *xiv–*xvi:

Having found Dr Johnson's argument on the cause of Joseph Knight, the Negro,
who claimed and obtained his freedom in Scotland, referred to Vol. II p. 591, and of
which Cause an account is given in the same Volume, p. 600, I shall now communicate it.

It must be agreed that in most ages many countries have had part of their inhabitants in a state of slavery; yet it may be doubted whether slavery can ever be supposed the natural condition of man. It is impossible not to conceive that men in their original state were equal; and very difficult to imagine how one would be subjected to another but by violent compulsion. An individual may, indeed, forfeit his liberty by a crime; but he cannot by that crime forfeit the liberty of his children. What is true of a criminal seems true likewise of a captive. A man may accept life from a conquering enemy on condition of perpetual servitude; but it is very doubtful whether he can entail that servitude on his descendants; for no man can stipulate without commission for another. The condition which he himself accepts his son or grandson perhaps would have rejected. If we should admit, what perhaps may with more reason be denied, that there are certain relations between man and man which may make slavery necessary and just, yet it can never be proved that he who is now suing for his freedom ever stood in any of those relations. He is certainly subject by no law, but that of violence, to his present master; who pretends no claim to his obedience, but that he bought him from a merchant of slaves, whose right to sell him never was examined. It is said that according to the constitutions of Jamaica he was legally enslaved; these constitutions are merely positive; and apparently injurious to the rights of mankind, because whoever is exposed to sale is condemned to slavery without appeal; by whatever fraud or violence he might have been originally brought into the merchant's power. In our own time Princes have been sold, by wretches to whose care they were entrusted, that they might have an European education; but when once they were brought to a market in the plantations, little would avail either their dignity or their wrongs. The laws of Jamaica afford a Negro no redress. His colour is considered as a sufficient testimony against him. It is to be lamented that moral right should ever give way to political convenience. But if temptations of interest are sometimes too strong for human virtue, let us at least retain a virtue where there is no temptation to quit it. In the present case there is apparent right on one side, and no convenience on the other. Inhabitants of this island can neither gain riches nor power by taking away the liberty of any part of the human species. The sum of the argument is this; No man is by nature the property of another: The defendant is, therefore, by nature free: The rights of nature must be some way forfeited before they can be justly taken away: That the defendant has by any act forfeited the rights of nature we require to be proved; and if no proof of such forfeiture can be given, we doubt not but the justice of the court will declare him free.

James Boswell, *Life of Johnson* 2nd edition, London, 1793: Vol. I: pp. *i–*xxxi.

Appendix 3   Clarkson's Quotation from William Cowper's 1785 *The Task*

Cowper's *The Task*, 1785: Book 2, lines 5–47 is quoted by Clarkson *History*, 1808, Vol. I, pages 108–9. References by Cowper to the Mansfield legal decision of 1772 on slavery are asterisked by Clarkson.

The last of the necessary forerunners and coadjutors of this class, whom I am to mention, was our much-admired poet, Cowper; and a great coadjutor he was, when we consider what value was put upon his sentiments, and the extraordinary circulation of his works. There are few persons, who have not been properly impressed by the following lines:

> My ear is pained.
> My soul is sick with every day's report
> Of wrong and outrage with which earth is fill'd.
> There is no flesh in man's obdurate heart,
> It does not feel for men. The nat'ral bond
> Of brotherhood is sever'd as the flax
> That falls asunder at the touch of fire.
> He finds his fellow guilty of a skin
> Not colour'd like his own, and having pow'r
> T'inforce the wrong, for such a worthy cause
> Dooms and devotes him as his lawful prey.
> Lands intersected by a narrow frith
> Abhor each other. Mountains interpos'd,
> Make enemies of nations, who had else,
> Like kindred drops, been mingled into one.
> Thus man devotes his brother, and destroys;
> And, worse than all, and most to be deplor'd,
> As human Nature's broadest, foulest blot, –
> Chains him, and tasks him, and exacts his sweat
> With stripes, that mercy with a bleeding heart
> Weeps, when she sees inflicted on a beast.
> Then what is man? And what man, seeing this,
> And having human feelings, does not blush
> And hang his head to think himself a man?
> I would not have a slave to till my ground,
> To carry me, to fan me while I sleep,
> And tremble when I wake, for all the wealth
> That sinews bought and sold have ever earn'd.
> No: dear as freedom is, – and in my heart's
> Just estimation priz'd above all price, –
> I had much rather be myself the slave,

177

And wear the bonds, than fasten them on him,
We have no Slaves at home – then why abroad?
And they themselves once ferried o'er the wave
That parts us, are emancipate and loos'd.
Slaves cannot breathe in England; if their lungs
Receive our air, that moment they are free;
They touch our country, and their shackles fall *
That's noble, and bespeaks a nation proud
And jealous of the blessing. Spread it then,
And let it circulate through every vein
Of all your empire – that where Britain's pow'r
Is felt, mankind may feel her mercy too.

* Expressions used in the great trial, when Mr Sharp obtained the verdict in favour of Somerset.

Thomas Clarkson *History of the rise, progress, and accomplishment of the abolition of the African slave-trade by the British Parliament.* 1808: Volume I, chapter 3.

Notes

Preface

1 P.D. James 1999
2 There is a typing slip in one of the helpful books, *Britain's Slave Trade* by S.I. Martin, in the 'Introduction', p. 3: 'By the end of the 19th century Britain had become the most accomplished, and largest, slaving nation on earth'. This is, of course, an unfortunate misprint and 19th should read 18th century, as indeed is demonstrated in other parts of the book with its Introduction by Trevor Phillips.

1 'We have no slaves at home – then why abroad?'

1 T.B. Howell, *A Complete Collection of State Trials...* 1816: Vol. 20, col. 82.
2 James Edward Austen-Leigh's *Memoir* of 1870 shows writing resumed after Jane Austen moved to Chawton Cottage.
3 Cf. Peter Baehr 2001, p. 19, pp. 20–1, p. 65 on slavery and the United Nations.
4 David Buten 1980, p. 151. Cf. Dresser and Giles 2000, pp. 82–3; J. R. Oldfield 1995 on public opinion.
5 Tim Fulford 2002, p. 153.
6 Edward Said 1993, pp. 69–70, p. 78; cf. pp. 95–116.
7 Contrast Amy Pawl 2004, p. 315.
8 Austen-Leigh's *Memoir*, chapter 1, pp. 15–16.
9 My own interest that I pursue in this book does not exclude 'all other determinants of interest' to be found in the novels, to use a phrase that I derive from Bernard Williams 2002, p. 286 n.8.
10 Susan Fraiman in Lynch 2000, p. 213, pp. 208–9; cf. Walter Johnson 1999, p. 58 on 'commodification'.
11 Donna Landry 2000 points out the work of R.S. Neale.
12 Rajeswari Sunder Rajan 2000, p. 8.
13 Edward Said 1993, p. 115.
14 J.R. Oldfield 1995 makes this clear, as does Deirdre Coleman 1994.
15 John Wiltshire 2001, pp. 137ff; cf. Sue Parrill 2002, p. 106.
16 On Granville Sharp see Gretchen Gerzina 1995; James Walvin 1992. On black people in London in the mid eighteenth-century, see also Sheila O'Connell 2003, pp. 182–4.
17 Cf. E.J. Hobsbawm 1968, chapter 12: p. 196; cf. Michael Steffes 1996, p. 35, p. 41, n. 61.
18 On Lord Mansfield see James Oldham 1988, p. 60 and p. 61, n. 56.
19 Maaja Stewart 1993, p. 120, p. 185, n. 11 also discusses F.O. Shyllon 1974.
20 Averil Mackenzie-Grieve 1941, p. 51. Gretchen Gerzina 1995, p. 132. Cf. Robert Middlekauff 1982, pp. 123–5 on the beginnings of colonial legislature in Virginia and other American colonies prior to 1772, p. 259 on George Washington's dissatisfaction in Virginia with England, pp. 331–2 on Thomas Jefferson's opposition to emancipation of slaves. Cf. Linda Colley 2002, p. 235.
21 F.O. Shyllon 1974, p. 169. See http://www.movinghere.org.uk/gallery/identity/dido.htm on Dido.

22　The portrait of Dido with her cousin is reproduced in James Oldham 1992, II, p. 1239. Volume I, p. 36 reproduces a painting of Lord Mansfield by Van Loo. For details of Dido in Lord Mansfield's will, see II, pp. 1239–40, n. 74. On the relationship between Lord Mansfield and Dido from the time of her infancy as reflected in his will, see also Oldham 1988 p. 67, n. 74.

23　Howard Temperley 1980, pp. 338–9.

24　Olaudah Equiano 1989, p. xi, where Paul Edwards as editor quotes from Roger Anstey.

25　David Brion Davis 2001, p. 230, p. 362, p. 369.

26　C. Duncan Rice 1980, p. 327; 1975, p. 102.

27　D.D. Raphael 2001, p. 235. Cf. Olivia Smith 1984, pp. 35–67.

28　Notes in Jane Austen *Minor Works*, p. 462.

29　Cf. Jan Fergus 1991, p. 65 on *Catharine*.

30　A. Walton Litz 1986, pp. 47–52.

31　Ronald Paulson 1983, p. 216. Cf. Andrew McCann 1999, pp. 128–9.

32　Hugh Thomas 1997, p. 264 makes the following unsubstantiated claim:

> *Sense and Sensibility* records a moment of anxiety when impending poverty threatens the heroine's family's purchases of sugar.

33　Madge Dresser and Sue Giles 2000, p. 77.

34　Cf. Janet Todd 1986, pp. 144–5. However, my own emphasis is on false sensibility.

35　M.J. Daunton 1995, p. 67.

36　Johnson's *Dictionary* 1st edn 2 vols (London 1755). On metaphor see Roger White 1996.

37　Sandie Byrne 2000, p. 11.

38　Cf. Vivien Jones 2003, pp. 427–8, note 2, note 3, to Vol. II, ch. VI.

39　M.J. Daunton 1995, p. 67; cf. Susan Staves 1990, p. 60.

40　Mary Evans 1987, p. 28.

41　Cf. Lillian Robinson 1978, pp. 196–7; Ruth Perry 2002 discusses changing attitudes.

42　Claire Tomalin 2000: on Mrs Jordan's career; p. 244 on Jane Austen's enjoyment of theatre.

43　Cf. Ellen Jordan 2002, p. 25, pp. 31–2, p. 38 on women's finances in *Emma* and *Pride and Prejudice*.

44　David Richardson 1998, p. 463.

45　Boswell *Life of Johnson*, 1st edn 1791, Vol. 2, pp. 16–17 in an entry for 1776.

46　Malthus, 1806 Appendix to *An Essay on the Principle of Population* in *Works* 1986: Vol. 3, p. 604.

47　Seymour Drescher 2002, pp. 42–3.

48　Terry Lovell, 1976, p. 122.

49　Claudia Johnson 1997, pp. 218–9.

50　The exhibition at Wilberforce House, Hull, shows paintings of the Royal Navy later tackling slavers.

51　Laurence Kitzan 2001, p. 23.

2　*Mansfield Park*: absenteeism, autonomy and the slave trade

1　Nicholas Marsh 1998, p. 120.

2　John Winton 2000, p. 105.

3　Susan Fraiman 1995, in Deidre Lynch 2000, p. 209.

4   Joseph Lew 1994, p. 282. On Sir Thomas as absentee planter see also Selma James 1983, pp. 40–1; Maaja Stewart 1993, p. 8, pp. 105–6; Edward Said 1993, pp. 95–116.
5   On absenteeism see James Walvin 1992, pp. 74–5; Robin Blackburn 1997, pp. 420–1; Richard Sheridan 1998, pp. 412–3. See also Frank Gibbon 1982–3, pp. 302–4.
6   I am grateful to Karen Lynch for pointing out to me that the Lascelles family at the time would have been associated with the most expensive addresses in London, and that the Lascelles – Wilberforce electoral struggle in Yorkshire of 1807 would also have publicised the Lascelles family as pro-slavery. See further Mary Mauchline 1992; Liz Deverell and Gareth Watkins 2000, pp. 54–7.
7   Jane Austen writes of ordination in a letter to Cassandra of 29 January 1813. There is nothing to show she is referring to *Mansfield Park* rather than to changing the subject in her letter, turning from enthusiasm about the publication of *Pride and Prejudice*:

> Now I will try to write of something else, & it shall be a complete change of subject – ordination – I am glad to find your enquiries have ended so well. If you could discover whether Northamptonshire is a country of Hedgerows I should be glad again.

See Deirdre Le Faye 1995.

8   Cf. A.H. Robertson and J.G. Merrills 1996, write, p. 15:

> Shocking as it now seems, the institution of slavery was generally legal under national law at the end of the eighteenth century; it remained legal in the United States until 1863, in Brazil until 1880, and in some countries into the twentieth century. In England it was illegal according to the decision in Somersett's case in 1772.

9   Cf. Philip Mansel 2001 p. 44:

> As well as being the capital of a powerful empire, eighteenth-century Constantinople was becoming a city of pleasure – a role suggested by the words it gave the outside world: sofa, kiosk, coffee and kaftan.

10 Compare David Monaghan 1980, p. 5:

> It is unnecessary to seek out fleeting references to the Napoleonic Wars, the Slave trade, agricultural change or other 'major' issues of the time, to justify the claim that Jane Austen is a social novelist. Rather, her main subject – polite social relationships between members of the landed classes within the context of the village and the great house – is one that far from being escapist, takes us immediately to what her society thought of as being at its heart.

11 Edward Said 1993, p. 103.
12 See Sykes, Booty and Knight 1998, p. 380 for absenteeism and pluralism in the Church of England. The right of presentation was the right of naming who would serve in a parish. But presentation was to a 'living', to the right to receive income rather than the duty to perform the services of a priest.
13 Trevor Lloyd 1999, p. 64 is sceptical that the text commits Edmund to having more than one living. I agree that the ending of the novel on this leaves much unsaid and that the third chapter is inconclusive. I nevertheless cover the possibility of two livings, since it is easy to read the earlier chapter as implying Sir Thomas intended both for Edmund.

14 Jane Austen refers to residence of clergy in a letter of 21 January 1799 from Steventon to her sister:

> Yesterday came a letter to my mother from Edward Cooper to announce, not the birth of a child, but of a living; for Mrs Leigh has begged his acceptance of the rectory ... We collect from his letter that he means to reside there, in which he shows his wisdom.

A letter of 25 September 1813 to her brother Frank says:

> Mr Sherer...gave us an excellent Sermon...But the Sherers are going away. He has a bad Curate at Westwell, whom he can eject only by residing there himself.

15 See Owen Chadwick 1987, pp. 136–7; cf. 1972, pp. 213–4.
16 Contrast Joseph Lew 1994, p. 294, who thinks Edmund is reprehensibly engaging in pluralism.
17 See Roger Sales 1983, p.43 for this aspect in his discussion of 454–61of 'The Dumb Orators'.
18 See Dresser and Giles 2000, p.130 for an extract from the Methodist John Wesley 'Thoughts upon Slavery' [1774], p. 78, for John Wesley attracting large congregations of rich and poor.
19 I take a different line from Ruth Bernard Yeazell 1997, p.91, n. 29, and D.A. Miller 1997, p. 45.
20 Paul Langford 1989, p. 518.
21 I agree with Mary Waldron 2000, pp. 85–6 that Jane Austen wishes to avoid sermonising.
22 See Lawrence Stone 1990 and 1993, for the possibilities of divorce at that time.
23 Pam Perkins 1993, p. 22 discusses this 'plausible alternative ending'.
24 Lawrence James 1994, p. 22.
25 On the ancient world cf. Keith Bradley 1998, pp. 16–17; Peter Garnsey 1998, p. 91; Peter Salway 2002, pp. 221–3.
26 A watercolour in the British Museum shows an idealized view, in a work of 1779, painted by Thomas Hearne entitled 'A Scene in the West Indies – Antigua'. A photograph of it in the exhibition on Abolition in the Industrial Museum at Bristol has the following description:

> This watercolour shows Parham Hill plantation at harvest time. It is an idealized view, with a happy and contented slave in the foreground.

See also reproduction in Dresser and Giles 2000.
27 See Frank Gibbon 1982–3 for more on the Antiguan connection. See also Gregson Davis 2004.
28 Douglas Murray 1997, p. 21 notes the sheer enjoyment of all this.
29 See John Winton 2000, p. 88 on the returning *Victory* after Nelson's death at the Battle of Trafalgar.
30 John Winton 2000, pp. 72–4.
31 Linda Colley 2002, p. 330.
32 Roger White pointed out to me that it may be the narrator not the author who gives dates, so they can be understood in terms of time portrayed within the novel itself. Avrom Fleishman 1970, pp. 91–2, thinks in terms of counting back from the date the novel had been started in 1811.
33 Avrom Fleishman 1970, pp. 37–8, 91–2 n. 19; Warren Roberts 1979, p. 97–9; Edward Said 1993, p. 104, p. 414 n. 39; R.W. Chapman pp. 554–7 has discussion

in an Appendix to the 3rd edition of the novel; A. Walton Litz 1961, pp. 221–2; see also F. B. Pinion 1973, p.104.

34 Cf. John Sutherland 1996.

35 For information about calendar dates see http://www.timeanddate.com/calendar/index.html and also http://www.assa.org.au/edm.html for dates of Easter, including pre-1800.

36 Adrian Smith has given me a modern example of manipulating dates for creative purposes. Len Deighton gives us *Fighter: The True Story of the Battle of Britain* with an introduction by the historian A.J.P. Taylor (London: Jonathan Cape, 1977). On the other hand in his novel *Bomber: Events relating to the Last Flight of an RAF Bomber over Germany on the Night of June 31st, 1943* (Jonathan Cape, 1970), the fictional nature of the book is flagged by inclusion of the impossible date, 31 June.

37 Mary Waldron 2000, p. 12–13.

38 Elleke Boehmer 1995, p. 25.

39 David Aers 1981, p. 127.

40 British Library: Maps 188. v. 12. John Spilsbury: *Jigsaw Map of Europe* dated 1766.

41 Christopher Harvie 1999, p. 489.

42 Meenakshi Mukherjee 1991, p. 51.

43 See also Moira Ferguson 1991, p. 133.

44 Maaja Stewart 1993, p. 107.

45 *Quarterly Review* Vol.1, No. 2, 1809: J. Poyer 'History of Barbados...1605–1801': 258–68, p. 267.

46 John Barrow 1847, pp. 492–502.

47 *Quarterly Review* 1809, Vol. 1, no. 2, p. 304, p. 306, p. 312, p. 314.

48 *Quarterly Review* 1809, Vol. 1, no. 2, p. 315.

49 Margaret Kirkham 1983b, pp. 74–7.

50 Claudia Johnson 1998, p. xi and note 4,citing David Gilson 1982, p. 59. Jan Fergus 1991, p. 157.

51 Margaret Kirkham 1994, p.114 n. 3 citing Brian Southam 1968a, p. 68; Samuel Smiles 1891, I: pp. 287–8.

52 Mary Lascelles 1939, p. 118, notes of Scott's review that 'it overlooks *Mansfield Park*'.

53 Jan Fergus 1991, p. 162.

54 On the publication of *Mansfield Park* see Claudia Johnson 1998 'Introduction' pp. xi–xii (a printing error on p.xi over the date of the 1st edition is remedied by implication by details of note 3). Jan Fergus 1991, pp. 157–60; Jan Fergus 1997, pp. 18–19, p. 24. R.W. Chapman 1948, p. 156, says: 'Murray published the first edition of *Emma* and the second of *Mansfield Park* on profit-sharing terms'.

55 Cf. on this so-called 'eel-like publisher', as he is described by Charles Donelan 2000, p. 53 in connection with difficulties that Byron was to have with John Murray, his original publisher. I think Murray may have had reservations about impatience by Byron in *Don Juan* over abolition of the slave trade prior to emancipation of slaves.

56 See Ros Ballaster 1992, pp. 293–4.

57 Cf. Claudia Johnson 1995b, p. 65, who speaks instead of Fanny's 'stunned incredulity at a woman's pleasure in it (the pair start cantering at *Mary's* suggestion)'.

58 Tony Tanner 1986, p. 173 discusses what he calls the 'stillness' of this novel.

59 Edward Copeland 1997, p. 139: 'Tom Bertram wreaks disaster on the family income'.

60   Edward Said, 2000, p. 182.

61   R.W. Chapman's Notes to his edition of *Mansfield Park:* p. 543.

62   Anne Mellor 1996, p. 312.

63   Richard Wilson and Alan Mackley 2000, p. 324 give the example of 'the Codringtons': 'where the estate had changed hands by purchase within the family around 1700. The new branch derived their wealth from the ownership of sugar plantations in Antigua'.
     Here, there is not a clear cut distinction as Tony Tanner (in his second note for his Penguin edition of the novel) said Chapman attempted between landed interest, moneyed interest and commercial interest.

64   Christopher Christie 2000, pp. 11–12; Wilson and Mackley 2000, pp. 322–7; Mary Mauchline 1992, p. 113: '...enjoyed the best that London could offer'.

65   Robert Miles 2003, p. 98. Cf. David Spring 1983, p. 59, pp. 64ff, pp. 71–2, n. 33.

66   Noting the 'air and liberty' we could borrow from implied criticism of improvements in chapter 42 of *Emma*, when speaking of Donwell Abbey and:

>   its abundance of timber in rows and avenues, which neither fashion nor extravagance had rooted up.

Elinor in *Sense and Sensibility* had similarly taken a dim view of Mr John Middleton's cutting down the old walnut trees for his own improvements.

67   For Lord Mansfield's Decision on the Somersett case, see Seymour Drescher 1986, pp. 36–43; Ruth Paley 2002; Norma Landau 2002, pp. 14–15; James Oldham 1988.

68   Thomas Clarkson 1808, Vol. 1. p. 77. In Dresser and Giles 2000, their examples of advertising for runaway slaves are all pre–1772.

69   The physicality of the house and Fanny interacting with it, for me, anticipates the stage direction in Scene 5 of Act 2 of August Wilson's *Joe Turner's Come and Gone*: Bertha is said to move around the kitchen as if she were blessing it and as if she were chasing huge sadness away that appears to envelop it. This is described as a dance and her own centuries old remedy that involves heart and memory.

70   Lionel Trilling [1955] 1998, p. 433, refers to the end of *Mansfield Park*:

>   The judgement is not ironical. For the author as well as for the heroine, Mansfield Park is the good house.

71   T.B. Howell 1816, p. 79. On the term 'Serjeant', see F. O. Shyllon 1974, p. 83–4 n. 1.

72   See Marilyn Butler 1987, p. 237 for 'the testing of Fanny' as 'the single pivot of the second and longer part of the novel'.

73   Robin Blackburn 1997, pp. 437–8. See Seymour Drescher 2002 for a 'mighty experiment'.

74   Donna Landry 2000, p. 56.

75   R.S. Neale 1985, p. 105, says that 'Antigua became a net exporter of slaves'.

76   Cowper's *Task*, Book VI: lines 818–9. James Sambrook 1994, p. 222, in a note to these lines compares them with VI, 141: 'And all shall be restored', which is a reference to the coming of spring and summer after winter. His view, p. 10, of Cowper's religious response differs from my interpretation of lines 818–9. I take Sambrook's view to be one of Cowper having a protracted dark night of the soul, which I should see as akin to that of Gerard Manley Hopkins.

77   The Acts of the Apostles 3:21 speaks of restoring ['*apokatastasis*'] of all things. Cf. Colossians l:14–20, especially verse 20.

78 Apparent allusions to paradise may be for other reasons. Rodie Sudbery, in her unpublished Lecture 'Mansfield Park: Paradises Lost and Gained' 2004, argues convincingly for Milton's influence.
79 Tony Harrison 1984, p. 239–40; cf. Northrop Frye 1957, p. 53.
80 See Owen Chadwick 1972, p. 207ff. on patronage.
81 David Lodge's 1966 essay on *Mansfield Park* in Lodge 2002, p. 109 and p. 111: 'a preoccupation with judgement is inseparable from a preoccupation with *justice*'. Cf. Sandie Byrne 2000, p. 10.
82 Compare Mary Mauchline 1992, pp. 8–18 on the original influx of money from Barbados that made possible the purchase of new estates and new building.
83 See Wilson and Mackley 2000, p. 324 for their economic history using contemporary accounts books.
84 Marilyn Butler 1997, p. 32.
85 Virginia Woolf *Orlando: A Biography*. [1928] London: The Hogarth Press, 1990, p. 88.
86 See Michael Caines 2002; Paula Byrne 2002, p. 13, p. 188, pp. 192–5, p. 209.
87 James Oldham 1988, p. 58 accepts the characterisation of slavery as 'odious' as accurate reporting of what was said.
88 Christopher Flynn 2000, p. 177.
89 Avrom Fleishman 1970, p. 90, note 18:

> It is well known that Crabbe was one of Jane Austen's favourite poets; even at Mansfield, his volume of verse *Tales* is, anachronistically, being read.

3   *Emma*: Autonomy and abolition

1 Howard Temperley 1972, p. 7. His citation from Clarkson's *History* 1808 is from Vol. 1, p. 286.
2 Juliet McMaster 1997, p. 126.
3 Edward Copeland 1995, p. 181.
4 Selma James 1983, pp. 44–5, notes the risk of 'sexual harassment at work'.
5 Douglas Jefferson 1977, p. 80. Cf. Melissa Blackburn et al 2004, p. 5 on slave trading organised from Bristol, where the port was part of the experience of anyone living in the centre of Bristol:

> Bristol's thriving port was in the centre of the city, where the tall ships seemed to sail through the streets, their sails and long masts glimpsed through the narrow alleyways.

Jane Austen had placed Mrs Elton's merchant family in 'the very heart of Bristol'. To draw attention to slave trade associations may be why Jane Austen gives such detail.
6 Herbert Klein 1978, p. 139, p. 170. Clarkson *History* 1808 Vol. 1, p. 375; S. I. Martin 2000, pp. 48–54.
7 Maaja Stewart 1993, p. 167 notes the Bristol reference.
8 Birmingham is associated in Jane Austen's mind with Wedgwood, it appears from her letter to Cassandra of 6 June 1811. Since she is very appreciative of all the china coming to them from Wedgwood, I think that she would have known of the fashion from earlier days of abolitionism, for wearing the slave medallions distributed to anyone concerned with the abolitionist cause by Wedgwood.
9 Hugh Thomas 1997, p. 515.

10   For chronology see J.R. Ward 1998, p. 425 and for some discussion of analyses of abolitionism before and after Eric Williams's Marxist analysis, see pp. 424–31. See Robin Winks 1999 for historiography.

11   Gad Heuman 1999a, p. 477, Andrew Porter 1999b, p. 204, William Law Mathieson 1926, p. 275, n. 2.

12   Andrew Porter 1999b, p. 206, in presenting the views of humanitarians, puts it:

> What justification could there be in compensating slave-owners for their past evil-doing at the expense of those who had never held slaves?

13   Letter of 18 November 1814.

14   Christopher Brooke 1999, p. 203 on Jane Fairfax:

> in spite of her excellent upbringing and education and accomplishments, she is to be a governess, a member of one of the few professions open to women – yet one which is likened to slavery.

Jon Mee 2000, p. 84 interprets Jane Fairfax's protest similarly.

15   *Emma*: Chapters 21, 24, 27.

16   Cf. W.C. Jordan 1993, p. 110, on slavery makes an interesting point about autonomy, saying: 'markets run by slaves and catering to the needs of slaves and masters alike persisted in the Caribbean'. He had already pointed out that:

> the system permitted a form of relatively autonomous commercial relations that was at variance with a pristine view of slavery and of plantation economics (and, to this extent, the very existence of such markets has been classified by some authorities as a kind of 'resistance' to the regime on the part of slaves).

17   Andrew Porter 1999b, p. 203:

> Renewed popular agitation, the development by abolitionists of arguments which presented ending the trade as damaging to the French and part of wartime strategy, and the abolitionist sympathies of Whig ministers underpinned the legislation of 1805–07 which ended British involvement in the trade.

18   See Eric Williams 1944, p. 189 on the 1814 petitioning of Parliament.

19   Matthew Kieran has suggested to me that there is more to say on this. I note that in *Persuasion*, chapter 18 there is also talk of a 'fling', where it is clear that a serious matter is at stake: Admiral Croft assures Anne that Captain Wentworth has not taken offence at the engagement to Louisa.

20   Cf. Gad Heuman 1999a, p. 473: 'Some Barbadian planters even supported abolition of the trade, seeing African slaves as more problematical than creoles and more likely to rebel'.

21   Clarkson *History* 1808 Volume 1, p. 9.

22   Johnson's *Dictionary* on the adverb 'widely': '1. With great extent each way.Bentley. 2. Remotely; far.Locke.'

23   Andrew Porter 1999b, p. 203.

24   Howard Temperley 1972, p. 10–11. See also Andrew Porter 1999a, p. 225, on amelioration of the position of slaves; J. R. Ward 1988, pp. 1–7.

25   William Law Mathieson 1926, p. 27.

26   Mathieson 1926, p. 33. He cites in support Hansard (1816), xxxiv. 1154.

27   Jeremy Bentham [1789] 1996, esp. chapters IV and VI.

28   Adam Smith *The Wealth of Nations* [1776], 1993, Book 4, chapter 7. See, too, Beth Fowkes Tobin 1990, p. 234, on Mr Knightley's relationship with Will Larkins.

29 Thorell Porter Tsomondo 1999, p. 196 has a different interpretation.

30 Isobel Grundy 1997, p. 206 and note 53, gives the source for this quotation.

31 Mrs Elton's quotation echoes Mr Elton's courting of Emma, when 'everything else must give way'.

32 *The Book of Common Prayer:* the General Confession from *The Communion:* 'We acknowledge ... have committed, by thought, word, and deed '.

33 Mr Knightley quotes from *The Task,* Book 4, line 290.

4   *Persuasion*: radical change and the Royal Navy

1 James Walvin 1986, p. 14. Barry Gough 1999, p. 337. Susan Morgan 1996, p. 89–90, p. 96 rightly condemns Britain's behaviour in the Chinese Opium Wars of the nineteenth-century.

2 Cf. Wittgenstein, *Philosophical Grammar,*

>   paragraph 28: What constitutes the meaning of a word like 'perhaps'? ...
>   paragraph 29: ... Do I understand its point? ...

3 Elaine Jordan 2000, p. 38–9.

4 Gad Heuman 1999a, p. 475.

5 White slavery in England had died out. See W.R. Brownlow [1892] 1969, p. 101, p. 112, p. 128 on white slavery in pre-Norman Conquest Britain. Robin Blackburn 1997 p. 39 says that at the time of the Domesday Book (1086), as much as one-tenth of the English population was enslaved, with the figure rising to a fifth in the West Country. William the Conqueror, however, had different ideas: 'the export trade in English slaves might enrich the merchants of Bristol or Dublin, but could only impoverish his kingdom'.

6 Anthony Tibbles 1994, p. 119, Fig. 26:'A slave market in Algiers, Dutch engraving, 1684' looks like displaying and sale of white slaves with their pale colouring, European appearance and discarded European clothing. The Dutch caption says '...Kristen Slaven...'. Cf. Linda Colley 2002, p. 58–9: Illustration of white slaves unloaded at Algiers, an English engraving of c.1700 'The Going into Slavery at Algiers'.

7 John Winton 2000, p. 94.

8 Andrew Lambert 1995, p. 166.

9 Linda Colley 2002, p. 132.

10 R.W. Chapman [1926] 1985, p. 38 n. 7, p. 39.

11 J.E. Austen-Leigh, *Memoir* [1870], 1926 Chapter 11, p. 166.

12 D.W. Harding: 'An Introduction to *Persuasion*' [Penguin 1985]. Reprinted: Harding 1998, pp. 169–70.

13 Bruno Bettelheim 1976, p. 8. This reference is given in *Arabian Nights' Entertainments,* in the edition by Robert L. Mack 1998, p. xx. He also, p. xxii, cites Edward Said's *Orientalism,* p. 3.

14 The Ottoman Empire covered a vast area of non-Arab Muslim countries as well as Arab countries. On naval activity between Britain and North Africa on white slaves, see Stephen Clissold 1977, pp. 158–61; Godfrey Fisher 1957, pp. 1–12.

15 Jennifer Thorn 2002, p. 162.

16 Patrick O'Brian's fictional story *The Commodore* (Harper Collins, 1994) illustrates what policing of the abolition of the slave trade may have been like during the Napoleonic Wars and later. Barry Gough 1999 and Judy Simons 2001 note his scrupulous research into the Royal Navy and writing skills.

17 Tony Tanner 1986, p. 249:

> There was nothing less for English society to do, than to admit that it had been pretty completely wrong, and to take up a new set of opinions and hopes.

His adaptation from the final chapter of *Persuasion* makes my point even better in Jane Austen's original, where his phrase 'English society' reads 'Lady Russell' and 'it' reads 'she'. See too Gallop, Brodley and Cantor 1999, pp. 127–37.

18 John Winton 2000, p. 105.

19 In *Persuasion* enjoyment of natural scenery takes pride of place when the visit is made to Lyme. There is no way of knowing whether Jane Austen would have been aware of the by then forgotten slave-trading, as described by Nigel Tattersfield 1991 in his chapter 'Lyme Regis': pp. 227–76, ending p. 276:

> Even by the end of the eighteenth century long-haul overseas voyages had become little more than faded memories ...the town...began a second career as a fashionable seaside resort, its elegant and thronged Assembly rooms effortlessly usurping the Cobb as the centre of attraction.

20 See Tony Tanner 1986, pp. 236ff. 'This revision is of great subtlety and importance...' However, in pp. 244–5, he accords less importance than I have to 'Anne's marriage to Wentworth'.

21 John Wiltshire 1997, p. 80, sees the dialogue with Harville at the White Hart as 'as much a formal as an emotional climax to the novel'.

22 Cf. Jan Fergus 1991, pp. 164–6 on revisions to the end of the novel.

23 Susan Morgan 1996, p. 90.

24 Tim Fulford 1999, p. 190.

25 Cf. David Medalie 1999, p. 168, that with respect to readers:

> *Persuasion* asks of them what Anne found so commendable in Mrs Smith: 'elasticity of mind'.

26 John Wiltshire 1997, p. 78.

27 Cf. Robin Blackburn 1997, says, p. 437:

> the occurrence of bankruptcy was in itself evidence that the market mechanism was transferring plantation resources from those who had not proved able to manage them successfully to new, and possibly more competent or luckier, hands.

William Law Mathieson 1926, pp. 79–82, however, speaks of yet more hardship for slaves in this process during the eighteenth-century.

28 John Davie 1971, p. xvii; Yasmine Gooneratne 1970, pp. 190–2.

29 See John Barrow 1847, pp. 500–1 for how his work was taken up by the *Quarterly Review*.

30 See Fergus Fleming 1998 for exploits of geographical exploration; cf. Robert Stafford 1999, p. 295.

31 John Barrow 1847, p. 333.

32 Christopher Lloyd [1949] 1968, 'Introduction', p. xi.

33 Bermuda, ever since Sir George Somers from Lyme Regis was shipwrecked there in 1609, had been of interest to the English speaking world. Shakespeare in the *Tempest* in Scene ii of Act I makes Ariel refer to the 'still-vexed Bermoothes'. Andrew Marvell is described by George deF. Lord 1984 as having 'celebrated the deliverance of persecuted brethren in the exquisitely modulated hymn of thanksgiving in *Bermudas*'.

34 Tony Tanner 1986, p. 214.

35 Charles Arnold-Baker 2001, p. 1146, in his entry for 'slave-trade'.
36 Joseph Lew 1998, pp. 498–9.
37 Linda Colley 1992, pp. 354–5. See too James Walvin 1980, p. 153.
38 Eric Williams 1944, p.189.
39 See Brian Southam 2000, p. 190 for Nelson's support of the slave trade.
40 Raymond Howell 1987, p. v.
41 Johnson's *Dictionary* for 'domestic' includes 'belonging to the house' and 'not foreign'.
42 Jon Mee 2000, pp. 82ff.
43 Cf. Mary Poovey 1984, pp. 239–40.
44 Christopher Lloyd 1968, p. xiii.
45 On Byron's *Giaour*, see Mohammed Sharafuddin 1996, p. 48, 214–6, 220–3, 226, 232, 234–7, 239–43, 247, 249, 251, 258, 265, 267–8, 272. On the Arab slave trade see Paul Lovejoy 1983, pp. 28–40, 68–73, 86–92, 184–219, 256ff.; Oliver and Atmore 1994, p. 78ff. On 400 years of the Ottoman Empire, see Glen Balfour-Paul 1999, pp. 490–7; he says, p. 490:

> Since the eighteenth-century Britain's response to the Eastern Question had been to prop up Ottoman sovereignty in western Asia as a manageable buffer protecting both British India and the eastern Mediterranean against the designs of other European powers.

46 Brian Southam 2000, p. 189; Christopher Lloyd 1968, 'Introduction': p. x.
47 Christopher Lloyd 1968, p. 16. Originally the colony of Sierra Leone was founded by the abolitionists in 1787: pp. 15–16. Lloyd goes on: 'In 1822 the population consisted of 128 Europeans and 15,000 natives, half of them liberated from slave ships since 1807'.
48 Lloyd 1968, p. 43–4.
49 Lloyd, p. 274. In Appendix A, p. 275, Lloyd gives a table citing:

> 'Total Slaves Liberated (landed alive)':
>   594 for the year 1810
>   1,362 for 1811
>   1,185 for 1812
>   694 for 1813
>   560 for 1814
>   626 for 1815
>   2,711 for the year 1816 …

Figures go on up to 1864. Concerning 'Sources', Lloyd says:

> In view of the discrepancies between the returns made, it would be unwise to take the above statistics as strictly accurate. They do, however, provide a comparative basis, and they are all drawn from the following Parliamentary Papers: …1810–46 Slaves captured and bounties paid on those landed alive in P. P. 1847–48, vol. LXIV, p.1.

50 Niall Ferguson 2004, p. 119 notes the Royal Navy as responsible for enforcing banning of the slave trade.
51 T.C. McCaskie 1999, p. 667.
52 David Eltis and David Richardson 1997, p. 83:

> significant numbers of Igbo, amounting to at least 30,000 between 1821and 1839 alone, were landed at Sierra Leone.

53 Peter Burroughs 1999, p. 323.
54 British Library: Ms. Eg. 3038. ff. 9v–10. See R.W. Chapman [1926]1985, for facsimile.

55 Brian Southam 2000, p. 296. Cf. pp. 3–4.
56 See Winton 2000 p. 89; see Wm Laird Clowes 1900, pp. 188–93 and p. 557 for details of the battle and ships involved.
57 Lloyd 1968, p. 140.
58 C.L.R. James (1938) reprinted 2001, pp. 300–2.
59 Selma James 1983, p. 20.
60 Eric Williams 1944, p. 192.
61 Brian Simpson 2001, pp. 105–7.
62 Of the 1807 Act, Cain and Hopkins 1993, p. 77, say: 'any disturbance caused by its enactment affected societies outside Britain'. Their view might be linked to their thesis of 'gentlemanly capitalism' so much influencing the money markets of London, a view called into question by M.J. Daunton 1995, p. 543, who sees things as 'considerably more complex'. Cain and Hopkins do not capture the delight of the abolitionists within Britain, and they appear to overlook the change to a man in the Navy.
63 The cerebral discussion in the novel, once the lovers are united, of Anne's being right in her earlier decision may be relevant in a wider, national context. Of possible relevance to the issue of slavery might be that people were not necessarily required to condemn past involvement in slavery under different circumstances, in order to go ahead thereafter with dismantling slavery. That could later be relevant to the British decision to enable emancipation of slaves in the 1830s by financial compensation to owners, a move that Jane Austen would not have been able to foresee. Cf. Andrew Porter 1999b, p. 204:

>   Slave owners were compensated for their loss of property in slaves from a fund of £20 million established by the government and paid for by metropolitan taxpayers.

5   Some philosophers on race and slavery: opposing viewpoints

1 Richard Popkin 1973, p. 245, p. 254.
2 Eighteenth-century translations include *Observations on the Feeling of the Beautiful & Sublime*; *The Groundwork of the Metaphysics of Morals*; *The Religion within the Sphere of Naked Reason*, and *On the Popular Judgment: That may be right in theory, but it does not hold good in praxis*. See *Essays and Treatises on moral, political, and various philosophical subjects. From the German by the translator of the Principles of Critical Philosophy* by Emmanuel Kant, 2 vols, printed for the translator and sold by William Richardson , London, 1798–9. Sandra Macpherson 2003, p. 18, p. 22: n. 51 uses this translation in exploring echoes of Kantian ethics in *Pride and Prejudice*.
3 Anne Crippen Ruderman 1995 considers possible Kantian links in the novels.
4 See Paul Guyer 1998, p. xviii, p. xlv note 23; Roger White 1990.
5 Randal Marlin 2002, p. 146. On truthfulness see Bernard Williams 2002, especially p. 102.
6 On this basic Kantian attitude see Alan Montefiore 1999, p. 12 and note 2.
7 Cf. Stephen Haynes 2002. Concerning ancient civilisations, David Goldenberg 2003, p. 200 concludes:

>   people – in and out of the academic world – readily assume that Blacks were always viewed pejoratively. But ... In those earlier times color ...was not a criterion for categorizing humanity.

Cf. Desmond Tutu 2004.

8 Kant's *Physical Geography* in E.C. Eze 1997, p. 60–1.
9 Philip Curtin 1970 , p. 201.
10 Jocelyn Harris 1989, pp. 12–13.
11 Jocelyn Harris 1987, pp. 18–19, p. 52.
12 Robin Blackburn 1988, p. 42.
13 Simon Schama 2001, p. 334.
14 Thomas Clarkson 1808, Vol. 1, pp. 45–7. Cf. Seymour Drescher 1986, p. 182, note 65; Julian Hoppit 2002, pp. 265–9; Laura Brown 1993, pp. 23–63.
15 W.J. Gardner [1873], 1971. pp. 215–6. On Holt, see Seymour Drescher 1986, p. 32, p. 40; Julian Hoppit 2002, p. 468.
16 Cf. Christopher Dyer 1997, p. 142 for earlier white slavery in England:

> by c. 1000...essential work on the estate ...came from slaves, who were fed by the lord....A factor in the decline of slavery was the difficulty in obtaining efficient work from people resentful of their condition.

17 Jocelyn Harris 1989 cites Locke's *Essay* IV, iii. 25. Cf. Martha Satz 1983.
18 Locke *Two Treatises,* p. xxvii of Mark Goldie's 'Introduction'. Cf. Michael Ayres 1998, pp. 680–2.
19 Seymour Drescher 1986, p. 184 n.69.
20 T.B. Howell 1816 vol. 20: columns 29–30.
21 Cf. Robin Blackburn 1997, p. 264: 'Locke should also have seen the text of Virginia's 1691 "Act for Suppressing of Outlying Slaves" '.
22 See James Farr 1999; Wayne Glausser 1999.
23 Donna Landry 1990, p. 31, p. 289 n. 65; Jocelyn Harris 1987, pp. 18–19.
24 Robin Blackburn 1988, p. 71. Contrast Julian Franklin 1978.
25 Locke *Second Treatise*, chapter 6, Section 52ff.
26 Robin Blackburn 1997, pp. 254–5.
27 Wayne Glausser 1999, pp. 515–6.
28 Robin Blackburn 1997, p. 264, p. 263.
29 Robin Blackburn 1997, p. 264 and p. 275 n. 90.
30 On property, see James Tully 1994. On money, see Patrick Hyde Kelly 1991, I: p. 104.
31 Glausser 1999, p. 518.
32 Robin Blackburn 1997, p. 264.
33 Robin Blackburn 1997, p. 329.
34 Locke *Essay*, IV, vii, 16.
35 Cf. Glausser 1999, p. 513.
36 Cf. Grell and Porter 2000.
37 Cf. Richard Aaron 1955, p. 276 and note.
38 Tindall and Shi 1999, p. 172.
39 James Farr 1999, p. 484.
40 James Farr 1999, p. 489.
41 Wayne Glausser 1999, p. 512.
42 Lawrence James 1994, p. 23.
43 Locke *First Tract on Government; Second Tract on Government*, p. 25, pp. 71–2.
44 Berkeley *Proposal*, p. 348.
45 *Proposal*, p. 354, p. 347.
46 James C. McKusick 1998, pp. 120–1.
47 Berkeley *Proposal*, p. 358–9.
48 James Farr 1999, p. 486.
49 G.J. Warnock 1953, pp. 226–8. Kenneth Robinson 1962.
50 Robin Blackburn 1997, p. 357, p. 263.
51 Cf. Roberto Romani 2002, pp. 201–27.

52 George Fredrickson 2002, p. 64.
53 Robin Blackburn 1988, pp. 41–2.
54 Bernard Williams 1994, pp.108ff.
55 James Walvin 1999, p. 64. A.C. Fraser 1871, pp. 187–8.
56 Isobel Armstrong 1994, pp.100–17. Cf. Alisdair MacIntyre 1984, pp.181–6; pp.238–43, offers an ethical inheritance from Aristotle, as had Gilbert Ryle 1968. MacIntyre, p. 239, also cites description of her by David Daiches as a 'Marxist before Marx'.
57 J.B. Schneewind 1998, p. 24 n. 33.
58 Cf. Peter Knox-Shaw 1999, p. 326 on Jane Austen's interest in history.
59 Cf. David Wootton 1993, pp. 281–2 n. 1: Wootton acknowledges Hume's earlier fame as an historian:

>   My essay title comes from the entry for our David Hume in the British Library catalogue, which, to the puzzlement of generations of philosophers, distinguishes him from others of the same name by identifying him as 'the historian'.

See also Murray Pittock 2003, pp. 264–73.
60 Paul Giles 2001, p. 72.
61 Boswell's *Life of Johnson* Tuesday 10 October 1769; Friday 30 April 1773. 'Anecdotes by Rev. Dr. Thomas Campbell' for 1775 in *Johnsonian Miscellanies* ed. G.B. Hill, Oxford: Clarendon Press, 1897, p. 48. *Life*: Thursday 9 April 1778. See also Peter Loptson 2001.
62 Cf. Christopher Gillie 1985, pp. 61–3 on chapters 5 and 6 as ironical, of praise for authors of novels. Cf. Peter Knox-Shaw 2004, p. 118 for a different interpretation of the reference to Hume.
63 Cf. Avrom Fleishman 1978 in his chapter on *Northanger Abbey*, pp. 26–7 on Jane Austen's point.
64 Michael Bentley 1999, p. 12.
65 Paul R. Krugman and Maurice Obstfeld 2003: 1.
66 Aaron Garrett 2000, p. 171. Cf. Garrett 2003, p. 88.
67 Cf. Gretchen Gerzina 1995, p. 41, p. 197.
68 Robin Blackburn 1997, p. 590.
69 Hume *Essays*, Vol. 1: p. 252, note.
70 Hume *Enquiry* 1975: Sec. 1, p. 172.
71 Clive Ponting 2001, p. 503.
72 Cf. Eugene Miller 1987, p. 629, on 'Edition K' in the Green and Gross edition of *Essays*.
73 Edward Long [1774], 1970, Vol. II Book III chapter IV, p. 477.
74 Eugene Miller 1987, 208 n.10.
75 Cf. Kenan Malik 1996, 53–4. Marina Frasca-Spada 2002, p. 221.
76 Thomas Clarkson 1808, Vol. 1, p. 87. Murray G.H. Pittock 2003, p. 264. Chris Jones 1993, pp. 38–43; Philip Flynn 2002, pp. 26–7.
77 James Beattie *An Essay on Truth* (Edinburgh, 1770), p. 480; pp. 478–84 flesh out his objections.
78 Thomas Clarkson *History* 1808, Vol.1, p. 83.
79 Edward Long 1774, Vol. 2, Book 3, Chapter 1, p. 376.
80 Thomas Clarkson 1786: Part III, Ch. VIII, p. 17: note.
81 Cf. James Basker 2002.
82 James Beattie *Elements of Moral Science* (Edinburgh, 1793), Vol. 2, p. 191.
83 Richard Popkin 1973, p. 254.

84 Isaac Kramnick 1995, p. 637. Kant: *Observations*, p. 111.
85 Melvyn Bragg 2003, p. 190. Cf. McCrum, Cran and MacNeil 1986, p. 201.
86 Cf. Kant *The Metaphysics of Morals* Part 1, p. 98:

> if a master is authorised to make use of the energies and abilities of his servant as he pleases, he could utterly exhaust him and reduce him to death or despair (as has been done with the Negroes in the Sugar Islands).

Cf. also *The Metaphysics of Morals* Part 1, p. 47, on the barring of a slave from legal contracts. The sections 241 and 330 have to be interpreted in the context Kant intends of discussion of citizenship, law and legal status.

87 Philip Morgan 1998, p. 465 and note.
88 Cf. Kant *Toward Perpetual Peace*, p. 107:

> The Sugar Islands, that stronghold of the cruellest and most calculated slavery, do not yield any real profit; they serve only the indirect (and not entirely laudable) purpose of training sailors for warships, thereby aiding the prosecution of wars in Europe. And all this is the work of powers who make endless ado about their piety, and who wish to be considered as chosen believers while they live on the fruits of iniquity.

He notes defeat in the 1790s of the move for 'the abolition of the slave trade', taking it as an example of Great Britain having a weaker parliamentary system than it claimed. That was in section 8 of *The Contest of Faculties* (in Kant *Political Writings*, edited by Hans Reiss, Second, enlarged Edition: Cambridge Texts in the History of Political Thought, 1991), p. 186.

89 Kant *Observations*: Translator's 1960 Introduction, p. 42.
90 *Observations*, p. 113.
91 Michael Freeman 2002, p. 24.
92 W. Mays 1961, p. 7 errs in giving the date of publication for the *Observations*, but is right that Goldthwait provided the first complete translation since the late eighteenth century, from the German *Beobachtungen über das Gefühl des Schönen und Erhabenen* of 1764 [*Gesammelte Shriften*. Vol. 2, edited by the Prussian Academy. Berlin: Walter de Gruyter, 1905.]
93 Manfred Kuehn 2001, p. 142.
94 Kant *Observations*, p. 97: Kant's own footnote.
95 Yu Liu 2003, p. 202.
96 Kant: *Observations*, p. 105 ; cf. p. 99.
97 David Theo Goldberg 2002, p. 255–6.
98 Kant *Groundwork of the Metaphysics of Morals* 1785, tr. M. Gregory, Cambridge University Press, 1998, p. 32, in which the South Sea Islanders are cited as illustrating how human beings are not to be excused from the rigours of the categorical imperative incumbent upon all human beings. Leaving aside how compelling or otherwise this is in support of the notion of the categorical imperative, the structure of this example seems to indicate that the South Sea Islanders are seen as human beings letting their 'talents rust'.

Kant further discusses the duty as he sees it to develop our useful capacities in 4:430, as Thomas Hill and Arnulf Zweig point out, p. 272: n. 43, in their edition of the *Groundwork of the Metaphysics of Morals* (Oxford University Press, 2002). They also cite on this point *Metaphysics of Morals* 6:444–6 (trans. Mary Gregor, Cambridge, 1996).

Kant also has an earlier reference to Tahiti in *On the Different Races of Man* 1775, p. 17:

in the newly discovered island of Tahiti the noblewomen are on the whole taller than the commoners.

Kant here seems to note the prevalence amongst human beings of class distinctions.

99   Robert Bernasconi 2002, pp. 49–52, would have Kant proclaim himself as anti-African slavery, and castigates him for not doing so.
100   Werner Sollors 1997, p. 61 and p. 430 n. 49, citing the source as p. 102 of *Bestimmung des Begriffs einer Menschenrace* [*Gesammelte Shriften*. 8, ed. Prussian Academy. Berlin: Walter de Gruyter 1923.]
101   Henry Louis Gates 1986, p. 408.
102   Robert Louden 2000, pp. 105–6, p. 96, pp. 208–9 n.75. On Forster, see Vanessa Agnew 2003, p. 82–3; pp. 86–94 *passim*.
103   Kant *Anthropology from a Pragmatic Point of View*, translated by Mary J. Gregor (Martinus Nijhoff, The Hague, 1974). However, Mary Gregor writes, p. ix:

> The student of Kant who struggles through *The Critique of Pure Reason* is undoubtedly left in some perplexity regarding specific points in it, but he is quite clear as to what Kant is attempting to do in the work. On finishing the *Anthropology* he may well find himself in just the opposite situation. While its discussions of the functioning of man's various powers are, on the whole, quite lucid and even entertaining, the purpose of the work remains somewhat vague.

104   Meg Armstrong 1996, pp. 226–7.
105   Kant: *Observations*, p. 110, p. 114–5.
106   *Observations*, p. 46.
107   Compare here that in the *Anthropology* his science of mankind gives empirical examples. In his data base, prior to his ethics and political philosophy, he satisfies cynics by admitting flaws in human beings. Robert Louden 2000, p. 105, claims that the:

> ideal of a truly universal moral community where all people count remains the most important single legacy of Kant's ethics.

Louden also points out that what counts would be Kant's arguments. Attitudes are irrelevant for philosophers; what counts is soundness in arguments. Louden adds that if racial prejudice were shown it should not be covered over, but nor, on the other hand, should it be played up.

108   Kant: *Observations:* Translator's Introduction p. 38.
109   *Observations*: p. 112. This is a different matter from such a people not being susceptible to conquerors trying to make them subservient, where it would be appropriate to use a different term (*Bildung*), as Kant is quoted as doing, by E.C. Eze 1995, p. 215 and 237 n. 71.
110   Cf. Robert Bernasconi 2003, p. 577, who queries:

> What significance should be given to the fact that Locke and Kant failed to question the chattel slavery in Africans of which they were well aware, even though they had at their disposal the intellectual resources to challenge it?

In reply, I should point out that Kant includes the Moors as part of the White race in *On the Different Races of Man*, p. 18:

> I believe it necessary to assume only four races of man, ...They are 1) the race of Whites, 2) the Negro race, 3) the Hunnic (Mongolian or Kalmuck) race 4) the Hindu or Hindustanic race. In the first, which has its chief seat in Europe, I count the Moors (Mauritanians of Africa)...

E.C. Eze 1997, pp. 60–1, provided straightforward translations of parts of Kant's lectures on *Physical Geography*. However, earlier, Eze 1995, p. 215, ran counter to his later translation, when he had endorsed claims made by Christian Neugebauer's 'The Racism of Hegel and Kant' (*Sage Philosophy* edited by Odera Oruka, New York, 1990: 259–72). Neugebauer had provided German passages without translation, instead paraphrasing. Neugebauer's paraphrase, p. 264, is not accurate. Kant's German quoted by Neugebauer and Eze's 1997 translation, p. 61, are as follows, regarding the case of punishment that could avoid infection, involving whipping thick skins with split canes:

> Die Mohren ... haben eine dicke Haut, wie man sie denn auch nicht mit Ruthen, sondern gespaltenen Rohren peitscht, wenn mann sie zuchtigt, damit das Blut einen Ausgang finde, und nicht unter der dicken Haut eitere.

Neugebauer omits a comparison in the first line, which Eze includes:

> The Moors, like all inhabitants of the hot zones have a thick skin; when one disciplines them, one cannot hit with sticks but rather whip with split canes, so that the blood finds a way out and does not suppurate under the skin.

What is said is not, as Neugebauer had claimed, a recommendation to discipline slaves with maximum pain, but is a report of how punishments were administered. Robert Bernasconi 2002, p. 151 presents the same passage from *Physical Geography*. However, whereas Bernasconi is right that the Moors are spoken of, a point left out by Neugebauer, who spoke instead in inverted commas of 'Negroes', Bernasconi is wrong to treat the reference to the Moors as to victims of African slavery.

The fact that Kant includes Moors amongst the Whites makes ridiculous the way in which Neugebauer had misled himself. He had not only paraphrased Moors as in inverted commas 'Negroes', but had also paraphrased the observation about those with thicker skins as a recommendation to 'beat up' Negroes. He proceeds with much indignation to offer this false rendering of Kant as evidence of endorsement of Whites beating up Negro slaves.

Neugebauer and those taking up his view may have been misled because they did not appreciate the Moors' role in slave trading. Kant's careful distinguishing between Negroes and Moors as to their race while nevertheless including them together regarding the thickness of their skin, turned out to be useful in blocking such divisiveness as that of Neugebauer.

The Moors, if they punish their own kind in the way described above, would be extending their practice in treating Negroes likewise. The fact that they are on a par with Negroes with respect to thick skin would not make for a distinguishing feature between Whites and Negroes, since for Kant the Moors are Whites. The likely readiness of the Moors at that time, as with the whole of the extensive Ottoman Empire, to continue to will slavery universally, as just the luck of the draw, might be something to be argued about, but could not of itself provide a distinguishing feature of slaves. Thick skin was common to Negro slaves and to their masters when the masters were Moors. That would block one pro-slavery argument in a way that Bernasconi demanded of Kant.

111 W.J. Gardner [1873], 1971, p. 207.
112 Edward Long [1774], 1970, Vol. II Book III chapter IV, p. 475.
113 Gardner 1971, Appendix: trans. by E.J. Chinnock of the Mission College, Blackheath, pp. 509–10.
114 Long 1970, Vol. II, pp. 479–81; Long's translation of Williams's Latin poem: pp. 481–3.

115 Thomas Malthus: Vol. 2, pp. 152–3. David Wootton 1993; Moses Finley 1998, p. 98.
116 Seymour Drescher 2002, pp. 36–7. Cf. Eugene Miller 1987, pp. 378–9 n. 2, p. 382 n. 6.
117 Hume *Essays* Vol. 1, p.386.
118 *Essays* Vol. 1, 394.
119 See Drescher 2002, esp. p. 5 and p. 33.
120 Hume *Essays* Vol. I, p. 390.
121 Drescher 2002, pp. 41–2.
122 Hume *Essays* Vol. 1, p. 390 n. 2.
123 See David Turley 1996, p. 182.
124 *Essays* Vol. 1, p. 420.
125 Henry and Owen Chadwick 2001, p. 483–4.
126 *Essays* Vol. 1, p. 385.
127 C. Duncan Rice 1975, p. 166–7.
128 Eugene Miller 1987, p. 208: annotation to Hume's footnote.
129 Miller 1987, p. 384 n. 7.
130 Miller is not alone. John Stewart 1992, pp. 185–7, p. 266, misconstrued the limited nature of Hume's opposition to slavery. Robert Palter 1995, pp. 7–10, in an otherwise helpful article, also misconstrues Hume's limited objections to slavery. John Immerwahr 1992, p. 485, is more cautious, and although he focuses on Hume's footnote, he notes Miller's claim, leaving open that: 'Hume's cruel remarks on race could perhaps be mitigated by his passionate opposition to slavery'. Immerwahr's scepticism is judicious in his saying 'perhaps'.
131 Hume *Essays* Vol. 1, 257.
132 Cf. Dresser & Giles 2000, pp. 133–7: 'Extract from evidence given to the Parliamentary Committee investigating the slave trade by James Arnold, Surgeon on the Bristol ship the *Ruby*'. On the 'Manner of the Trade' it was said, p. 135:

> It was usual in those Parts where the Ruby lay (Mr Arnold observed), to trust such of the principal Traders as were People of Character with Goods from the Ship...But though, as observed before, we intrust the Traders with Goods, with which they go to the Fairs, yet we expect that they should leave us something as a Pledge for their Return. To satisfy us in this Particular, they leave their Children and relations in our Custody, whom we distinguish by the Name of Pawns. As the Traders bring us Slaves, or, in other Words, as they pay their Debts, so these are released. But if they are unable to discharge them at an appointed Day (which Day is fixed for the sailing of the Ship), they are taken to the West Indies and sold.

See David Richardson 1996, p. 132, for this evidence being given to Parliament in 1788.
133 Cf. Aaron Garrett 2003, who misleadingly attempts to paraphrase the Hume text to which the footnote is appended. On p. 88 he gives a reference to George Wallace 1760, p. 96, and an interpretation of Wallace that is different from my own.
134 Charles Griswold 1999, p. 13 n. 23.
135 Adam Smith *The Wealth of Nations*, Book 3, chapter 2 and Notes on pp. 530, 564.
136 Henry and Owen Chadwick 2001, p. 484.

137 For a more enthusiastic view of Hume on ethics, see Simon Blackburn 1998.
138 Rico Vitz 2002, p. 271. Cf. Roberto Romani 2002, pp. 165–6.
139 Hume *An Enquiry concerning the Principles of Morals*: conclusion of Section 1, p. 175.
140 Hume *Principles of Morals*, p. 173–4.
141 J.L. Mackie 1980, p. 67, pp. 130–2. See too Rosalind Hursthouse 1996, p. 198.
142 Hans Werner Breunig 2001, p. 166.
143 Nancy Struever 1985, p. 81, p. 117 n. 87. Cf. Amy Wolf 2004, p. 275 n. 16.
144 Adam Smith *The Theory of Moral Sentiments* in edition by D. D. Raphael and A.L. MacFie: Introduction, p. 10. Cf. Markman Ellis 1996, p. 13.
145 See J. Ralph Lindgren 1973, p. 48, 145, 152.
146 Adam Smith *Theory of Moral Sentiments*, III, 3. 4. Cf. James King 1992, p. 455; Henry C. Clark 1999, p. 271.
147 Knud Haakonssen p. xxiv in Adam Smith *Theory of Moral Sentiments* 2002.
148 Adam Smith *Theory of Moral Sentiments*, V, 2. 9.
149 *Metaphysique de l'Ame ou Theorie des Sentiments Moraux.* Paris, 1764: Vol. 2, p. 180.
150 *The Wealth of Nations,* 1776, Book 1, Ch.8.
151 Seymour Drescher 2002, p. 230. *The Wealth of Nations*, Book 1, Ch. 8.
152 Clarkson *History* 1808, Vol. 1, pp. 85–6.
153 Fred Parker 2003, p. 140 relates the anecdote from J.W. Croker's 1831 edition of Boswell's *Life of Johnson*. Croker's repetition of the anecdote with his accompanying repudiation of it is in his 1848 edition of the *Life*, in footnote 1, on p. 393.

6 Abolitionist influences on Jane Austen: some possibilities

1 Isobel Grundy 1997, p. 197; A.C. Bradley 1929; Mary Lascelles 1939, p. 43.
2 Claudia Johnson 1988, p. 107.
3 On historical context, see Seymour Drescher 1986.
4 Matthew 7:12, cited by Niall Ferguson 2004, p. 117. See Rowena Loverance, *Christ*, London, 2004, p. 83 for a brass medal from London, around 1787, with the Wedgwood motif on one side and Matthew 7:12 on the other.
5 Passage from *The Idler* that I give in the Appendix: end of penultimate paragraph.
6 Roy Porter 2001, p. 62.
7 Ellen Gibson Wilson 1989, p. 3.
8 Irene Collins 1998, points out that a conduct book which discusses abolition was known to Jane Austen. I am very grateful to Irene Collins for drawing my attention both to *Mentoria* and to her 1998 account.
9 David Gilson 1997, p. 433 gives further details:

> Jane Austen 'is recorded as donor of books to members of her family. In 1801 she gave to her niece Anna a copy of ... Ann Murry's *Mentoria: or, The young ladies instructor*, 2nd ed. (London: for Charles Dilly, 1780)'.

10 Ann Murry, *Mentoria* 2nd edition 1780, pp. 90–7.
11 *Mentoria* 6th edition 1791, pp. 91–2. The use of the term 'rational' here is not straightforward, given such interest as that of Locke in his *Essay Concerning Human Understanding*, which Markman Ellis 1996, p. 75 discusses in connection with Locke's example of a parrot taught linguistic responses.

12   Linda Colley 1992, pp. 352–60.
13   Cf. Howard Temperley 2002, pp. 29–32; pp. 50–4.
14   Jane Austen *Letters* 2nd edition, p. 508.
15   Howard Temperley 2002, p. 31.
16   C.W. Pasley [1812], 1847. Pasley introduces America on p. 329; discussion of America is on p. 329 and pp. 434–40.
17   James Boswell, *Life of Johnson* 1st Edition 1791, Vol. 2, p. 174; 2nd edition 1793, Vol. 2, p. 591.
18   Johnson *Taxation No Tyranny*, p. 449, edited by Donald Greene. Murray G. H. Pittock 2002, p. 188.
19   P.J. Marshall 1998: p.14.
20   Johnson *The Idler*, p. 253.
21   *Life of Johnson*: 1st edition 1791 Vol. 1, p. 381; 2nd edition 1793 Vol. 2, p. 50.
22   *Life*: 1st edition 1791 Vol. 1, p. 216; 2nd edition 1793 Vol. 1, p. 365.
23   *Life*: 1st edition 1791 Vol. 1 p. 381; 2nd edition 1793 Vol. 2, p. 51. See Murray Pittock 2002 for discussion of Johnson and Scotland.
24   Margaret Kirkham 1983a, p. 244.
25   Gretchen Gerzina 1995, p. 45.
26   *Life of Johnson*: 1st edition 1791 Vol. 2, p. 174; 2nd edition 1793 Vol. 2, p. 600.
27   *Life*: 2nd edition 1793 Vol. 1, pp. *xvi – *xviii.
28   Gretchen Gerzina 1995, p. 51. Cf. Sheila O'Connell 2003, p. 184: Johnson, 'who left his manuscripts and much of his property to his (free) black servant'.
29   Osborne's *Concise Law Dictionary*, 9th edition, edited by Sheila Bone. (London: Sweet and Maxwell, 2001) gives for 'positive law':

  1)   That part of law which consists of rules imposed by the sovereign on his subjects.
  2)   Law proper as opposed to moral law (Austin). See 'Law'.

  (On 'Law' the entry reads '... Blackstone, however, maintained that a rule of law made on a pre-existing custom exists as positive law apart from the legislator or judge.')
30   Bernard Bailyn 1992, p. 235.
31   Stephen Munzer 1990, p. 41 n. 2.
32   *Life of Johnson*: 1st edition 1791 Vol. 2, p. 174.
33   *Life*: 2nd Edition 1793 Vol. 2, p. 591 n. 6.
34   Boswell *Correspondence*, p. 430.
35   Jane Austen *Letters*: R.W. Chapman in the notes says that the 2nd edition of 1793 is probably the edition referred to.
36   *Life of Johnson*: 2nd edition 1793 Vol. 3, p. 275. See Niall Ferguson 2004, p. 81ff. on the Maroons.
37   Samuel Johnson *Introduction to the Political State of Great Britain*, p.137.
38   James Walvin 2004, p. 28.
39   Claire Tomalin 2000, pp. 146–7.
40   See Elkins and McKitrick 1993, p. 662, p. 892: note 48 on the Jefferson Papers, Library of Congress.
41   Gretchen Gerzina 1995, p. 132.
42   Cowper, ed. Milford 1967, p. 306; Cowper, eds King and Ryskamp 1979, Vol. 1, p. 299 n. 4: the editors suggest that Mansfield would have been known to Cowper.

43 Eric Williams 1944, p. 45.
44 Cowper, eds Baird and Ryskamp 1980, Vol. 1, pp. 431–2.
45 James Basker 2002, p. 695 n. 181, says this first appeared in the *General Magazine and Impartial Review* (May 1788): 261–2.
46 Paul Langford 1989, p. 192. See also J. Cannon 1997, p. 827.
47 Kate Davies 2001, pp. 134–5.
48 James Basker 2002, p. 294.
49 Maaja Stewart 1993, p. 176 n. 24, gives details of the production of the *Negro's Complaint*.
50 Olaudah Equiano [1789] reprinted 1989, p. 15, p. 9. Cf. C.L. Innes 2002, pp. 36–46. Cf. Robin Blackburn 1997, p. 592, Equiano:

    was to become...an author who successfully published and distributed his own writings, leaving property worth over £900 (nearly £100,000 in 1996 values) at his death.

51 Jan Fergus 1991, p. 9.
52 Roy Porter 2000, pp. 80–1, p. 327.
53 Cowper, ed. Milford 1967, p. 674: Notes. Cf. Cowper, eds Baird and Ryskamp, Vol. 3, p. 13.
54 Alistair Duckworth 2002, p. 242 n. 97.
55 Donna Landry 1990, p. 238.
56 Dresser & Giles 2000, p. 54 on the Bristol Gazette; Cowper ed. Milford 1967, p. 375 and note on p. 675 on the newspaper, the *Northampton Mercury*.
57 Cowper, ed. Milford 1967, p. 415, p. 678, note. The *Sonnet to William Wilberforce* was later published by Hayley. Cowper, eds. Baird and Ryskamp 1995, Vol. 3, pp. 333–4 give details of the calumnies.
58 Cowper, ed. Milford 1905, p. 376, which notes *Epigram* was subsequently published in 1815.
59 Cowper, eds Baird and Ryskamp, Vol. 3, p. 335 on the *Epigram*.
60 John Barrell 1999, p. 245.
61 For example, Kathryn Sutherland 2003, p. 486 discusses complexity in references to 'improvements', which span the novels. Ros Ballaster, 2003, p. xxvii discusses 'improvements' with particular reference to the populace and changing land use.
62 Karen O'Brien 1999, pp. 172–3.
63 Elizabeth Bohls 1999, p. 187. In a note Richard Sheridan 1974, pp. 481–6, is cited for a summary of anti-slavery activity up to 1775.
64 David Willetts 2002, pp. 26–7.
65 Cowper, eds Baird and Ryskamp 1995, Vol. 3, p. 286: notes to this poem.
66 Thomas Clarkson 1786, p. 248.
67 Ellen Gibson Wilson 1989 provides more detail.
68 Thomas Clarkson *History* 1808, Vol. 1: opposite p. 375; Vol. 2: opposite p. 111.
69 Clarkson 1808, Vol. 1, p. 286, cited by Howard Temperley 1972, p. 7.
70 David Brion Davis 2001, p. 225. On this periodical see further Iain McCalman 1991.
71 Darryl Jones 2004, p. 114 emphasizes Pasley not Clarkson is 'the real subject of this passage'.
72 R.W. Chapman in Jane Austen's *Letters* 2nd edition. Isobel Grundy 1997, p. 210 n. 52.
73 Eric Williams 1944, p. 179.

74   James Basker 2002, pp. 170–82; pp. 232–3.
75   Charles Pasley *Course of instruction originally composed for the use of the Royal engineer department.* Volume 1: *containing practical geometry and the principles of plan drawing* (London, Egerton, 1813). See also the website of the Historical Diving Society for the recently unveiled plaque at the Dockyard at Chatham, Kent: http://www.thehds.com/events/pasleyplaque.html that commemorates his pioneering work on the technology of diving.
76   Pasley [1812]1847, p. 107.
77   See Tim Fulford 2002, pp. 175–8, for a different reaction to Pasley.
78   Cf. Maclean, Landry and Ward 1999: 'Introduction' p. 8.
79   Pasley 1847, p. 74 n. 1.
80   See John Bowker 1997. Claudius Buchanen 1812, p. 25, p. 122, p. 273, pp. 270–4.
81   In *Rejected Addresses* one of the entries, the 'Hampshire Farmer's Address, By W.C.', is particularly sharp. The Address to 'Most Thinking People' includes:

> Take a basin of broth, – not *cheap soup, Mr Wilberforce*, not soup for the poor at a penny a quart, as your mixture of horse's legs, brick dust, and old shoes was denominated, but plain, wholesome, patriotic beef or mutton broth; Take this, examine it and you will find – mind, I don't vouch for the fact, but I am told you will find the dregs at the bottom, and the scum at the top. I will endeavour to explain this to you: England is a large *earthern-ware pipkin*, John Bull is the beef thrown into it. Taxes are the hot water he boils in. Rotten boroughs are the fuel that blazes under this same pipkin. Parliament is the *ladle* that stirs the hodge-podge ...

Here Wilberforce is lampooned, the abolitionist movement never far from contemporary disputes, and in this case Wilberforce being accused of not campaigning enough for the poor in England.
82   Ruth Perry 1994, p. 104.
83   Clarkson's name is remembered in Thomas Clarkson House in London, which is the base for Anti-Slavery International,whose website www.antislavery.org is a source for details of past and present problems.
84   Cf. Michael Steffes 1996, pp. 27–9 for anti-slavery relevant connections with the Austen family.
85   J.H. Hubback and Edith C. Hubback 1906, p. 191.
86   Hubback 1906, p. 192.
87   Hubback 1906, p. 274, illustrates later post-Abolition policing carried out by her brother Charles:

> In 1826 Charles was again on the West Indies station. Here he stayed for more than two years, and was chiefly employed in suppressing the slave-trade.

88   Brian Southam 2000, p. 189, p. 341: note 39
89   Hubback 1906, p. 186, p. 225.
90   Peter van der Veer 2001, p. 42.
91   Ruth Perry 1994, p. 103.
92   Susan Morgan 1996, pp. 89–90, p. 96.
93   Mary Waldron 2000, p. 86 and p. 176 n.6 gives references to critics on the attitude of Jane Austen to the Evangelicals; cf. Gary Kelly 1997, pp. 152–4; Marilyn Butler, pp. 204–7 in Grey 1986; Irene Collins 1994, p. 185; Ruth Bernard Yeazell 1997, p. 89: n. 15.
94   David Monaghan 1978, p. 230.
95   Eric Williams 1944, p. 178. On memory, see Locke *Essay* II, x, 1–9.

7 Conclusion

1 *Sanditon: An Unfinished Novel* by Jane Austen. (Facsimile from Manuscript in the possession of King's College Cambridge, with Introduction by B.C. Southam, Oxford; London, 1975).
2 Mary Waldron 2000, p. 157. Cf. June Dwyer 1989, pp. 118–24; Kuldip Kaur Kuwahara 1997, pp. 146–7; 1995, p. 106.
3 Samuel Johnson *The Rambler*, number 107.
4 Roy Porter 1994, pp. 167–8 notes that in the eighteenth-century Coram's Foundling Hospital 'achieved special prominence'. Cf. Ruth McClure 1981.
5 John Fowles 1991, p. xi. Coram received the Freedom of Lyme, documented at the Philpott Museum in Lyme Regis. The stained glass window in his honour in the porch of the old church is an addition after Jane Austen's time.
6 Cf. M.J. Daunton 1995, p. 224:

> Large, deep pits faced a further constraint; the transport of coal from the face to the shelf and surface ... The containers or wagons were usually pulled by women and children. Horses were used in larger pits by the early nineteenth-century when capacity increased ... and made it feasible to pay the high costs of feeding horses and employing male drivers rather than the low wages of boys and women.

> Cf. Angela V. John 1984, pp, 6ff. Daunton 1995, pp. 491–3, discusses debates at the turn of the century over alleviating poverty and hardship. Cf. Deverell and Watkins 2000, pp. 59ff. on Wilberforce.
7 Peter Spence 1996, p. 37.
8 Seymour Drescher 1999, pp. 427–8.
9 I think Gideon Maxwell Polya is not quite on the right lines in his 'Analysis Of *Emma*' when he says of Jane Fairfax that she:

> is facing the dreadful prospect of becoming a governess (jokingly comparing the 'governess-trade' with the 'slave-trade').

> See his *Jane Austen and the Black Hole of British History: Colonial rapacity, holocaust denial and the crisis in biological sustainability* (Melbourne, 1998), p. 51. Polya pp. 56–7 goes on, however, to point out the emphasis in Crabbe's poetry on poverty and that Crabbe was a favourite poet for Jane Austen. As Polya reminds us, Fanny has his work to hand in *Mansfield Park*.
10 Nikolaus Pevsner 1968, p. 414, notes in his account of the architectural setting of the Austen novels:

> the affluent John Knightleys live in Brunswick Square, which had only been built at the beginning of the nineteenth century.

11 Roy Porter 1997, p. 14.
12 Marilyn Butler 1981, p. 108.
13 Cf. Jil Larson 2001, p. 40, on Utilitarianism in later, Victorian fiction. M.J. Daunton 1995, pp. 491–2, discusses Bentham and the Utilitarians.
14 Joanna Martin 1998, 'Introduction', p. 54, p. 117, p. 39.
15 Tim Fulford 1999, p. 188.
16 In W.H. Auden's 1936 *Letter to Lord Byron*, he had earlier in this long poem teasingly said to Byron that he had at first thought of writing to Jane Austen. The two verses on Jane Austen about the amorous effects of 'brass' can be seen in Lane and Selwyn 2000.

17 Mary Evans 1987, pp. 8 – 9.

18 Kathryn Hughes 2001, pp. 203–4.

19 Claudia Johnson 1988, pp. 107–8. She had just said:

> In *Emma* e.g. Jane Fairfax suggests a similarity between the 'governess trade' or 'the sale' of 'human intellect', and the 'slave trade' or the sale of 'human flesh', even though 'the guilt' of those who engage in either trade is 'widely different'. Mrs Elton, however, misses Jane's point, exposing the uneasiness of the nouveaux riches about being identified with ungenerous causes.

20 David Erdman 1977, p. 228, p. 234, n. 14. Cf. Shirley Dent and Jason Whittaker 2002, pp. 122–3, on this Blake poem and on a comparison with constraints of the marriage market as shown by Jane Austen.

21 The Anti-Slavery Society was not formed until 1823, as Andrew Porter 1999 indicates in the 'Chronology' p. 71; cf. 1999b, p. 210.

22 William Law Mathieson 1926, p. 118.

23 Cf. William Korey 1998, pp. 117–8.

24 Eric Williams 1944, p. 49. Peter Kitson 1998, p. 27 discusses this poem as abolitionist. Howard Temperley 1980, pp. 338–9 points out that Eric Williams's presentation largely in terms of the interplay of economic interests does not entirely discount influence of ideas; cf. Andrew O'Shaughnessy 2000, p. 111.

25 Thomas Clarkson 1786, note on p. 131.

26 James Walvin 1980, p. 150. Gretchen Gerzina 1995, pp. 178–9.

27 Lorraine Daston 1987, p. 244.

28 Gerd Gigerenzer et al, 1989, p. 257 [quoting Irving Pfeffer 1956, p. 68].

29 Howard Temperley 1972, p. 6. David Turley 1991 p. 31.

30 Cf. Michael Steffes 1996, p. 30 and note 36, who criticizes a view that Jane Austen supports amelioration.

31 Claudia Johnson 1988, p. 107.

32 See Michael Steffes 1996, p. 30, n. 35; p. 36; p. 38, n. 4.

33 Cf. Norman Davies 1997, pp. 452–3, on the Elizabethan development of the English slave trade begun by the adventurer John Hawkins. See too Gill & Gregory 2003, p. 283, on 'Hawkins' in *Emma*.

34 Cf. Srinivas Aravamudan 1999, p. xv.

35 Stephen Munzer 1990, p. 364.

36 Munzer 1990, p. 56.

37 Claire Tomalin 2000, pp. 291–2.

38 Josephine Ross 2002, p. 239. Cf. Margaret Kirkham 1983b, p. 132.

39 Vivien Jones 2003, p. xxxix, gives details of websites. I referred to http://www.pemberley.com/ given for 'The Republic of Pemberley'.

40 Cf. Peter Barry 2002, pp. 199–201, endorses the views of Edward Said on *Mansfield Park* as a paradigm case of postcolonial criticism. Barry, p. 200, however, mistakenly reads Francis Mulhern 1992, p. 97 as also having endorsed the views in 'Jane Austen and Empire'. Francis Mulhern, however, had paraphrased Edward Said's views by way of Editorial introduction.

41 Edward Said 1993, p. 104.

42 Clara Tuite 2002, p. 117. Cf. Brian Southam 1995, p. 13–14.

43 Margaret Kirkham 1983a, p. 231.

44 Roger Anstey 1975, p. 408.

45 Selma James 1983, p. 44. Cf. Moira Ferguson 1993, pp. 80–1.

46 Deirdre Coleman 1994, p. 354–5. Mary Anne Radcliffe 1799a.

47 See Fiona Stafford, 2003, p. 469 on the phrasing 'there are places' by Jane Fairfax as significantly echoing Samuel Johnson's *The Rambler* number 107.

48 Cf. Niall Ferguson 2004, p. 115: note. Olaudah Equiano 1789, Ch. 5; Willie F. Page 2001; Desmond Tutu 2004; cf. Jamaica Kincaid 1988, p. 55 that there is a tendency for slaves not to ask who sold them. Cf. also *Roots of Racism* (Institute of Race Relations, London, 1982), p. 15, for a different viewpoint on African rulers.

49 Philip Mansel, 2001. Cf. Dresser and Giles 2000, p. 87: catalogue number 165 exemplifies products circulated. A medallion was struck to commemorate the British Abolition of the Slave Trade. It carried the logo 'We Are Brethren' over-arching two figures – one European, one African – shaking hands. The inscription continues: 'Slave Trade Abolished in Great Britain 1807'. Dresser and Giles add that: 'On the reverse is the same inscription in Arabic'.

50 See Charles Donelan 2000, p. 90–1: for comment and citation from *Don Juan* IV, st. 115 that describes a slave market in the Ottoman Empire.

51 Richard Cronin 2002, pp. 131. Neil Cooke 2001. Cf. Boswell's *Life of Johnson* for 11 April 1776.

52 Irving Howe 1993, p. 557.

53 Cf. Ronald Segal 2001, pp.148–9, p.159 on relatively benign treatment, of slaves by their Arab masters, that was nevertheless underpinned by extreme barbarity in the Arab slave trade, which came to the notice of David Livingstone in East Africa, during the later Pax Britannica, after abolition had succeeded in British imperial territories by the end of the 1830s.

54 Ato Quayson 2000, p. 4, on Edward Said's *Orientalism*. See also Bart Moore-Gilbert 1997, p. 67–9. Cf. the anonymous review of *Culture and Imperialism* entitled 'Guilt and Misery' in *The Economist* Vol. 326 (27 February 1993), p. 111. See also Paul Armstrong 2003 on Edward Said's responses to cultural differences.

55 Andrew Porter 1999b, p. 203. David Brion Davis 2001 makes a similar point.

56 Deverell and Watkins 2000, p. 65.

57 See Robert Miles 2003, pp. 62–3 on the Austen style of 'free indirect discourse' that assists creative ambiguity.

58 Cf. Mary Poovey 1984, p. 213.

59 Paul Lovejoy 1983, 'Appendix: Chronology of measures against slavery' pp. 283–7.

60 The sheer complexity of humanitarian concerns is illustrated by a suggestion I owe to Trude Kaiser, who as an Austrian Jew escaping to Britain before the start of war remained a pacifist and surmised that the full horror of the Final Solution of the Nazi Concentration Camps may not have come about except under pressure of the antagonisms of the Second World War.

   Conversely, with abolition there was fear after the 1807 Abolition that yet more suffering could be introduced in the wake of action as a result of humanitarian moves, because violence could occur with the use of a naval squadron.

61 Edward Said 'The Return to Philology' in 2004:57–84, p. 64.

62 Edward Said 2004, p. 64.

63 Paul Langford 1989, p. 516.

64 Bruno Simmer 1994, p. 784. On the concept of human rights, see Amartya Sen 2004.

Bibliography

Aaron, R., *John Locke*, 2nd edn (Oxford, 1955).

Aers, D., 'Community and Morality: Towards Reading Jane Austen' in *Romanticism and Ideology*, eds David Aers, Jonathan Cook and David Punter (London, 1981): 118–36.

Agnew, V., 'Pacific Island Encounters and the German Invention of Race', in Edmond and Smith 2003: 81–94.

Ahmad, A., *In Theory: Classes, Nations, Literatures* (London and New York, 1992).

Anderson, B., *Imagined Communities: Reflections on the Origin and Spread of Nationalism*, revd edn (London and New York, 1991).

Anstey, R., *The Atlantic Slave Trade and British Abolition: 1760–1810* (London, 1975).

Arabian Nights' Entertainments, edited by Robert L. Mack (Oxford, 1998).

Aravamudan, S., ed., *Fiction*, Vol. 6 of P. Kitson and D. Lee 1999.

Armstrong, I., *Jane Austen: Mansfield Park* (Harmondsworth, 1988).

— *Jane Austen: Sense and Sensibility* (Harmondsworth, 1994).

— ed., *New Feminist Discourses* (London, 1992).

Armstrong, M., 'The Effects of Blackness: Gender, Race and the Sublime in Aesthetic Theories of Burke and Kant', *Journal of Aesthetics and Art Criticism*, 54 (1996): 213–36.

Armstrong, N., *Desire and Domestic Fiction* (New York and Oxford, 1987).

Armstrong, P.B., 'Being "Out of Place": Edward W. Said and the Contradictions of Cultural Differences', *Modern Language Quarterly*, 64, 1 (March 2003): 97–121.

Arnold–Baker, C., *The Companion to British History*, 2nd edn (London and New York, 2001).

Austen, J., *The Novels of Jane Austen*, ed. by R.W. Chapman 5 vols, 3rd edn (London, 1932–4).

— *Minor Works*, ed. R.W. Chapman [1954] (London, 1969).

— *Jane Austen's Letters*, ed. R.W. Chapman. 2nd edn [1952] Reprinted with corrections (London, 1979).

Austen-Leigh, J.E., *Memoir of Jane Austen* [1870] Introduction, Notes and Index by R.W. Chapman (Oxford, 1926).

Ayres, M., 'John Locke' in *Routledge Encyclopaedia of Philosophy*, Vol. 5 (London and New York, 1998): 665–87.

Baehr, P.R., *Human Rights: Universality in Practice* [1999] (Basingstoke, 2001).

Bailyn, B., *The Ideological Origins of the American Revolution*, enl. edn (Cambridge, Mass. and London, 1992).

Balfour-Paul, G., 'Britain's Informal Empire in the Middle East', in J. Brown and W.R. Louis, 1999: 490–514.

Ballaster, R., 'New Hystericism: Aphra Behn's *Oroonoko*: The Body, the Text and the Feminist Critic', in I. Armstrong 1992: 283–95.

— ed., *Jane Austen: Sense and Sensibility* [1995], updated (Harmondsworth, 2003).

Barrell, J., 'Afterword: Moving Stories, Still Lives', in Maclean, Landry and Ward, 1999: 231–50.

Barrow, J., *An Autobiographical Memoir* (London, 1847).

Barry, P., *Beginning Theory*, 2nd edn (Manchester and New York, 2002).

Basker, J.G., ed., *Amazing Grace: An Anthology of Poems About Slavery, 1660–1810* (New Haven and London, 2002).

Beer, G., ed., *Jane Austen: Persuasion*, updated (Harmondsworth, 2003).

Belton, E.R., 'Mystery without Murder: The Detective Plots of Jane Austen', *Nineteenth-Century Literature*, 43 (1988): 42–59.

Bender, T., ed., *The Antislavery Debate* (Oxford and Los Angeles, 1992).

Bentham, J., *An Introduction to the Principles of Morals and Legislation* [1789] edited by J.H. Burne and H.L.A. Hart, new Introduction by F. Rosen (Oxford, 1996).

Bentley, M., *Modern Historiography: An Introduction* (London and New York, 1999).

Berkeley, G., *Proposal for a College in Bermuda* [1725] in *Berkeley's Complete Works*, edited by A.C. Fraser, Vol. 4: 342–64 (Oxford, 1901).

— *The Querist*, in *The Works of George Berkeley*, edited by A.A. Luce and T.E. Jessop, Vol. 6: 105–54 (London and New York, 1953).

Bernasconi, R., 'Kant as an Unfamiliar Source of Racism', in J. Ward and T. Lott 2002: 145–66.

— 'Ethnicity, Culture and Philosophy', in Bunnin and Tsui-James 2003: 567–81.

Bettelheim, B., *The Uses of Enchantment* (New York, 1976).

Blackburn, M., S. Humphries, N. Maddocks and C. Titley, *Hope and Glory: Epic Stories of Empire and Commonwealth* (Stroud, 2004).

Blackburn, R., *The Overthrow of Colonial Slavery, 1776–1848* (London, 1988).

— *The Making of New World Slavery* (London and New York, 1997).

Blackburn, S., *Ruling Passions: a theory of practical reasoning* (Oxford and New York, 1998).

Boehmer, E., *Colonial and Postcolonial Literature* (Oxford and New York, 1995).

Bohls, E.A., 'The gentleman planter and the metropole: Long's *History of Jamaica* (1774)', in Maclean, Landry and Ward 1999:180–96.

Bolt, C. and S. Drescher, eds *Anti-Slavery, Religion and Reform: Essays in Memory of Roger Anstey* (Folkestone, 1980).

Boswell, J., *The Life of Samuel Johnson*, 1st edn, 2 vols (London, 1791).

— *The Life of Samuel Johnson*, 2nd edn, revised and augmented, 3 vols (London, 1793).

— *The Life of Samuel Johnson*, 3rd edn, [1799], edited R.W. Chapman [1953] (Oxford, 1965).

— *The Correspondence and Other Papers of James Boswell relating to the Making of the 'Life of Johnson'*, Yale Edition, edited by Marshall Waingrow (London, 1969).

Bowker, J., ed., *The Oxford Dictionary of World Religions* (Oxford and New York, 1997).

Bradley, A.C., 'Jane Austen' [1911] in *A Miscellany* (London, 1929): 32–72.

Bradley, K.R., *Slavery and Rebellion in the Roman World 140 B. C. – 70 B. C.*, 2nd edn (Bloomington and Indiana, 1998).

Bragg, M., *The Adventure of English: The Biography of a Language* (London, 2003).

Breunig, H.W., 'Jane Austen: Romantic? British Empiricist?', in *Re-mapping Romanticism: Gender-Text-Context*, edited Christoph Bode and Fritz-Wilhelm Neumann (Essen, 2001): 163–81.

Broadie, A., *The Cambridge Companion to The Scottish Enlightenment* (Cambridge, 2003).

Brooke, C., *Jane Austen: Illusion and Reality* (Woodbridge, 1999).

Brown, J.M. and W.R. Louis, eds *Oxford History of the British Empire* Vol. 4: *The Twentieth Century* (Oxford and New York, 1999).

Brown, L., *Ends of Empire: Women and Ideology in Early Eighteenth-Century English Literature* (Ithaca, 1993).

Brown, S., ed., *British Philosophy and the Age of Enlightenment* (London and New York, 1996).

Brownlow, W.R., *Lectures on Slavery and Serfdom in Europe* [1892] (New York, 1969).

Buchanan, C., *Eight Sermons, viz. The Star in the East, Jubilee Sermons* (London, 1812).

Bunnin, N. and E.P. Tsui-James, eds, *The Blackwell Companion to Philosophy*. 2nd edn (Oxford, 2003).

Burchill, S., et al., *Theories of International Relations*, 2nd edn (Basingstoke and New York, 2001).

Burroughs, P., 'Defence and imperial disunity', in A. Porter 1999: 320–45.

Burrows, J.F., 'Style', in Copeland and McMaster 1997: 170–88.

Bush, M.L., ed., *Serfdom and Slavery: Studies in Legal Bondage* (London and New York, 1996).

Buten, D., *18th Century Wedgwood* (London, 1980).

Butler, M., *Romantics, Rebels and Reactionaries: English Literature and its Background 1760–1830* (Oxford, 1981).

— 'History, Politics and Religion', in J. David Grey 1986: 190–208.

— *Jane Austen and the War of Ideas*, New Introduction (Oxford, 1987).

— '*Mansfield Park*: Ideology and Execution', in J. Simons, 1997: 19–33.

Byrne, P., *Jane Austen and the Theatre* (London and New York, 2002).

— *Jane Austen's 'Emma': A Sourcebook* (London and New York, 2004).

Byrne, S., 'Jane Austen's Language', *The English Review*, 11 (September 2000): 9–11.

— *Jane Austen – Mansfield Park* (Basingstoke and New York, 2005).

Cain, P.J. and A.G. Hopkins, *British Imperialism* (London, 1993).

Caines, M., Review of *Jane Austen and the Theatre* by P. Byrne, *Times Literary Supplement*, (14 June 2002): 18.

Cannon, J., ed., *Oxford Companion to British History* (Oxford and New York, 1997).

Canny, N., ed., *Oxford History of the British Empire* Vol. 1: *The Origins of Empire* (Oxford, 1998).

Capitani, D., 'Moral Neutrality in Jane Austen's *Mansfield Park*', *Persuasions On-Line*, Vol. 23, No.1. http://www.jasna.org/index.html (Winter 2002).

Carey, B., 'William Wilberforce's Sentimental Rhetoric: Parliamentary Reportage and the Abolition Speech of 1789', *The Age of Johnson* 14 (2003): 281–305.

Cateau, H. and S.H.H. Carrington, eds, *'Capitalism and Slavery' Fifty years Later: Eric Eustace Williams – A Reassessment of the Man and his Work* (New York, 2000).

Chadwick, H. and O., eds, *The Church in Ancient Society from Galilee to Gregory the Great* (Oxford, 2001).

Chadwick, O., *The Victorian Church*, Part I *1829–1859*, 3rd edn (London, 1987).

— *The Victorian Church*, Part II, 2nd edn (London, 1972).

Chapman, R.W. ed., *The Manuscript Chapters of 'Persuasion': Jane Austen* [1926] (London, 1985).

— *Jane Austen: Facts and Problems* (Oxford, 1948).

Christie, C., *The British Country House in the Eighteenth Century*, (Manchester, 2000).

Clark, H.C., Review of Charles L. Griswold 1999 in *Hume Studies* 25 (1999): 270–2.

Clark, J.C.D., *The Language of Liberty 1660–1832* (Cambridge, 1994).

Clark, J. and H. Erskine-Hill, *Samuel Johnson in Historical Context* (Basingstoke and New York, 2002).

Clark, R., ed., *'Sense and Sensibility' and 'Pride and Prejudice'* New Casebooks (Basingstoke and New York, 1994).

Clarkson, T., *An Essay on the Slavery and Commerce of the Human Species* (London, 1786).

— *The History of the rise, progress, and accomplishment of the abolition of the African slave-trade by the British Parliament,* 2 vols (London, 1808).

Clissold, S., *The Barbary Slaves* (London, 1977).

Clowes, W.L., *The Royal Navy: A History,* Vol. V (London, 1900).

Coleman, D., 'Conspicuous Consumption: White Abolitionism and English Women's Protest Writing in the 1790s', *English Literary History* 61 (1994): 341–62.

Colley, L., *Britons: Forging the Nation 1707–1837* (New Haven and London, 1992).

— *Captives: Britain, Empire and the World 1600–1850* (London, 2002).

Collins, I., *Jane Austen and the Clergy* (London, 1994).

— *Jane Austen: The Parson's Daughter* (London, 1998).

Cooke, N.,'James Burton and Slave Girls', in Starkey and Starkey, 2001: 209–17.

Copeland, E., *Women writing about Money* (Cambridge and New York, 1995).

— 'Money', in Copeland and McMaster 1997: 131–48.

Copeland, E. and J. McMaster, eds, *The Cambridge Companion to Jane Austen* (Cambridge, 1997).

Count, E.W., ed., *This is Race* (New York, 1950).

Cowper, W., *The Complete Poetical Works* edited by H.S. Milford [1905 London] 4th edn, revd (Oxford, 1967).

— *The Poems of William Cowper,* 3 vols, edited by J.D. Baird and C. Ryskamp (Oxford, 1980–95).

— *The Letters and Prose Writings of William Cowper,* 5 vols. edited by J. King and C. Ryskamp (Oxford, 1979–86).

Crang, M., 'Placing Jane Austen, Displacing England: Touring between Book, History, and Nation', in Pucci and Thompson 2003: 111–30.

Cronin, R., *Romantic Victorians* (Basingstoke and New York, 2002).

Curtin, P.D., *The Atlantic Slave Trade* (Madison, Milwaukee and London, 1970).

Daston, L.J., 'The Domestication of Risk: Mathematical Probability and Insurance 1650–1830', in *The Probabilistic Revolution,* Vol. 1: *Ideas in History,* edited by L. Kruger et al. (Cambridge, MA and London, 1987): 237–60.

Daunton, M.J., *Progress and Poverty: An Economic and Social History of Britain 1700–1850* (Oxford, 1995).

Davidson, J., 'A Modest Question about *Mansfield Park*', *Eighteenth-Century Fiction* 16, 2 (January 2004): 245–64.

— *Hypocrisy and the Politics of Politeness: Manners and Morals from Locke to Austen* (Cambridge, 2004).

Davie, J., 'Introduction' to *Persuasion* edited by J. Davie (Oxford, 1971).

Davies, K., 'A moral purchase: femininity, commerce and abolition', in Eger et al. 2001: 133–59.

Davies, N., *Europe: a history* (London, 1997).

Davis, D.B., *In the Image of God* (New Haven and London, 2001).

Davis, G., 'Jane Austen's "Mansfield Park": the Antigua Connection', http:www.uwichill.edu.bb/bnccde/antigua/conference/papers/davis.html (2004).

De, A.K., *Jane Austen: Her mind and Her Art* (Calcutta, 1999).

Deforest, M., 'Mrs Elton and the Slave Trade', *Persuasions* 9 (1987): 11–13.

Demata, M. and D. Wu, eds, *British Romanticism and the 'Edinburgh Review'* (Basingstoke and New York, 2002).

Dent, S. and J. Whittaker, *Radical Blake* (Basingstoke and New York, 2002).

Deverell, L. and G. Watkins, *Wilberforce and Hull* (Hull, 2000).

Dickinson, H.T., ed., *A Companion to Eighteenth-Century Britain* (Malden, MA and Oxford, 2002).

Dole, C.M., 'Austen, Class, and the American market', in Troost and Greenfield 1998: 58–78.

Donaldson, T., 'Kant's Global Rationalism', in *Traditions of International Ethics* edited by T. Nardin and D. Mapel (Cambridge and New York, 1992): 136–57.

Donelan, C., *Romanticism and Male Fantasy in Byron's 'Don Juan'* (Basingstoke and New York, 2000).

Doody, M.A., 'Jane Austen's Reading', in J.D. Grey 1986: 347–63.

Dougherty, J.E. and R.L. Pfaltzgraff, *Contending Theories of International Relations*, 5th edn (New York and London, 2001).

Drescher, S., *Econocide: British Slavery in the Era of Abolition* (Pittsburgh and London, 1977).

— *Capitalism and Antislavery: British Mobilization in Comparative Perspective* (London, 1986).

— *From Slavery to Freedom*, Foreword by S. I. Engerman (Basingstoke, 1999).

— *The Mighty Experiment: Free Labor versus Slavery in British Emancipation* (Oxford and New York, 2002).

Dresser, M. and S. Giles, eds, *Bristol and Transatlantic Slavery* (Bristol, 2000).

Duckworth, A.M., *The Improvement of the Estate* (Baltimore, 1971).

— '*Mansfield Park:* Jane Austen's Grounds of Being', in 1971: 35–80; in C. Johnson 1998: 434–45.

— ed. *Emma: Jane Austen*, Case Studies in Contemporary Criticism, ed. Ross C. Murfin (Boston and London, 2002).

Dunn, A., 'The Ethics of *Mansfield Park*: MacIntyre, Said, and the Social Context', *Soundings* 78 (1995): 483–500.

Dutton, D., Review of *In Defense of Humanism* by R.A. Etlin, *Philosophy and Literature* 20, 1 (April 1996): 295–7.

Dwyer, J., *Jane Austen* (New York, 1989).

Dyer, C., 'The Economy and Society' in *The Oxford Illustrated History of Mediaeval England* ed. Nigel Saul (Oxford, 1997): 137–73.

Easton, F., 'The political economy of *Mansfield Park*: Fanny Price and the Atlantic working class', *Textual Practice* 12, 3 (1998): 459–88.

Edgeworth, M., *Belinda* [1801] Edited by K.J. Kirkpatrick (Oxford, 1999).

Edmond, R. and V. Smith, *Islands in History and Representation* (London and New York, 2003).

Eger, E., et al, eds, *Women, Writing and the Public Sphere, 1700–1830* (Cambridge, 2001).

Elkins, S. and McKitrick, Eric, *The Age of Federalism* (New York and Oxford, 1993).

Ellis, M., *The Politics of Sensibility* (Cambridge, 1996).

Ellwood, G.F.,'"Such a Dead Silence": Cultural Evil, Challenge, Deliberate Evil, and *Metanoia* in *Mansfield Park*', *Persuasions On-line*, Vol. 24, No. 1, http://www.jasna.org/index html (Winter 2003).

Eltis, D. and D. Richardson, eds, *Routes to Slavery: Direction, Ethnicity and Mortality in the Atlantic Slave Trade* (London, 1997).

Equiano, O., *The Life of Olaudah Equiano* [1789], edited by P. Edwards (Harlow, 1989).

Erdman, D.V., *Blake: Prophet against Empire*, 3rd edn (New York, 1977).

Essed, P. and D.T. Goldbery, eds, *Race Critical Theories: Text and Context* (Oxford, 2001).

Etlin, R.A., *In Defense of Humanism: Value in the Arts and Letters* (Cambridge and New York, 1996).

Evans, M., *Jane Austen and the State* (London and New York, 1987).

Eze, E.C., 'The Color of Reason: The Idea of "Race" in Kant's Anthropology', in K. Faull 1995: 200–41.

— ed., *Race and the Enlightenment: A Reader* (Oxford, 1997).

Farr, J., '"So Vile and Miserable an Estate": The Problem of Slavery in Locke's Political Thought', *Political Theory*, 14 (1986): 263–89, reprinted in J.R. Milton 1999: 484–509.

Faull, K.M., *Anthropology and the German Enlightenment* (London and Toronto, 1995).

Favret, M.A., 'Free and Happy: Jane Austen in America', in D. Lynch 2000: 166–87.

Fergus, J., *Jane Austen: A Literary Life* (London and New York, 1991).

— 'The Professional Woman Writer', in Copeland and McMaster 1997: 12–31.

Ferguson, M., '*Mansfield Park*: Slavery, Colonialism and Gender', *Oxford Literary Review* 13 (1991): 118–39.

— *Subject To Others: British Women Writers and Colonial Slavery, 1670–1834* (New York and London, 1992).

— *Colonialism and Gender Relations from Mary Wollstonecraft to Jamaica Kincaid: East Caribbean Connections* (New York, 1993).

Ferguson, N., *Empire: How Britain Made the Modern World* (London and New York, 2004).

Finley, M.I., *Ancient Slavery and Modern Ideology*, expanded edition by B.D. Shaw. (Princeton, NJ, 1998).

— ed., *Classical Slavery* 1987 (London and Portland OR, 2003).

Fisher, G., *Barbary Legend* (Oxford, 1957).

Fleishman, A., *A Reading of 'Mansfield Park': An Essay in Critical Synthesis* (Baltimore and London, 1970).

— 'The Socialisation of Catherine Morland: an application of anthropological theory to *Northanger Abbey*', in *Fiction and the Ways of Knowing* (Austin and London, 1978): 23–36.

Fleming, F., *Barrow's Boys* (London, 1998).

Flynn, C., '"No Other Island in the World": *Mansfield Park*, North America and Post-Imperial Malaise', *Symbiosis: A Journal of Anglo-American Relations*, 4, 2 (October 2000): 173–86.

Flynn, P., 'Francis Jeffrey and the Scottish Critical Tradition', in Demata and Wu 2002: 13–32.

Folsom, M.M., *Approaches to Teaching Austen's 'Emma'* (New York, 2004).

Forster, E.M., 'Sanditon' [1925] in *Abinger Harvest* (London, 1936): 148–52.

Fowles, J., 'Foreword' to Nigel Tattersfield 1991: xi–xii.

Fraiman, S., 'Jane Austen and Edward Said: Gender, Culture and Imperialism', *Critical Inquiry* 21 (Summer 1995): 805–21; reprinted in D. Lynch 2000: 206–23.

Franklin, J.H., *John Locke and the Theory of Sovereignty* (Cambridge and New York, 1978).

Frasca-Spada, M.,'David Hume and the She-Philosophers', *Philosophical Books* 43, 3 (July 2002): 221–6.

Fraser, A.C., *Life and Letters of George Berkeley* (Oxford, 1871).

Fredrickson, G.M., *Racism: A Short History* (Princeton and Oxford, 2002).

Freeman, M., *Human Rights: An interdisciplinary approach* (Cambridge and Malden, MA, 2002).

Frye, N., *Anatomy of Criticism* (Princeton and New Jersey, 1957).

Fulford, T., 'Romanticising the Empire', *Modern Language Quarterly* 60 (1999): 161–96.

— 'Sighing for a Soldier', *Nineteenth-Century Literature* 57, 2 (September 2002): 153–78.

Fulford, T. and P.J. Kitson, *Romanticism and Colonialism: Writing and Empire, 1780–1830* (Cambridge, 1998).

Gallop, D., I.S. Brodley and P.A. Cantor, 'Symposium: Jane Austen', *Philosophy and Literature* 23 (1999): 96–137.

Galperin, W.H., *The Historical Austen* (Philadelphia, 2003).

Gandhi, L., *Postcolonial Theory* (Edinburgh, 1998).

Gard, R., *Jane Austen's Novels: The Art of Clarity* (New Haven and London, 1998).

Gardner, W.J., *A History of Jamaica* [1873], 3rd Impression (London, 1971).

Garnsey, P., *Cities, Peasants and Food in Classical Antiquity* (New York, 1998).

Garrett, A.,'Hume's Revised Racism Revisited', *Hume Studies* 26 (2000): 171–7.

— 'Anthropology: the "original" of human nature', in A. Broadie 2003: 79–93.

Gates, H.L., 'Talkin' That Talk', in H.L. Gates, ed., *'Race', Writing and Difference* (Chicago and London, 1986).

Gaull, M., 'Jane Austen: Afterlives', Review Essay, *Eighteenth-Century Life*, 28, 2 (Spring 2004): 113–9.

Gay, J., *Selected Poems* edited by M. Walsh, 1979 (Manchester, 1997).

Gerzina, G., *Black England: life before emancipation* (London, 1995).

Gibbon, F., 'The Antiguan Connection: Some New light on *Mansfield Park*', *Cambridge Quarterly* 2 (1982–83): 298–305.

Gigerenzer, G., et al., *The Empire of Chance* (Cambridge, 1989).

Giles, P., *Transatlantic Insurrections: British Culture and the Formation of American Literature, 1730–1860* (Philadelphia, 2001).

Gill, R. and S. Gregory, *Mastering the Novels of Jane Austen* (Basingstoke and New York, 2003).

Gillie, C., *A Preface to Austen*, revd edn (London and New York, 1985).

Gilson, D., *A Bibliography of Jane Austen* [Oxford 1982] (Oak Knoll, 1997).

Glausser, W., 'Three Approaches to Locke and the Slave Trade', *Journal of the History of Ideas* (1990): 199–216, reprinted in J.R. Milton 1999: 511–28.

Goldberg, D.T., 'Racial States', in Goldberg and Solomos 2002: 233–58.

Goldberg, D., T. and J. Solomos, eds, *A Companion to Racial and Ethnic Studies* (Oxford, 2002).

Goldenberg, D.M., *The Curse of Ham: Race and Slavery in Early Judaism, Christianity, and Islam* (Princeton and Oxford, 2003).

Gooneratne, Y., *Jane Austen* (Cambridge, 1970).

Gough, B.M., 'The Royal Navy and the British Empire', in R. Winks 1999: 327–41.

Greene, D.J., ed., *Political Writings*, Yale Edition of S. Johnson, Vol. 10 (New Haven and London, 1977).

Grell, O.P. and R. Porter, eds, *Toleration in Enlightenment Europe* (Cambridge, 2000).

Grey, J.D., ed., *The Jane Austen Handbook* (London, 1986).

Griswold, C.L., *Adam Smith and the Virtues of Enlightenment* (Cambridge, 1999).

Gross, G.S., 'In a Fast Coach with a Pretty Woman: Jane Austen and Samuel Johnson', *The Age of Johnson*. 12 (2001): 199–253.

Grundy, I., 'Jane Austen and literary traditions', in Copeland and McMaster 1997: 189–210.

Guyer, P., ed., *Kant's 'Groundwork of the Metaphysics of Morals': Critical Essays* (New York, 1998).

Haakonssen, K., ed., *The Theory of Moral Sentiments, Adam Smith* [1759] (Cambridge, 2002).

Hall, C., 'Histories, Empires and the Post-Colonial Moment', in *The Post-Colonial Question: Common Skies, Divided Horizons*, edited by I. Chambers and L. Curti (London and New York, 1996): 65–77.

Handler, R. and D. Segal, *Jane Austen and the Fiction of Culture* (Tuscon, Ariz, 1990).

Harding, D.W., *Regulated hatred and other essays on Jane Austen*, edited by M. Lawlor (London and Atlantic Highlands, N.J., 1998).

Harding, R., 'The Royal Navy', in H.T. Dickinson 2002: 481–8.

Harris, J., *Samuel Richardson* (Cambridge, 1987).

— *Jane Austen's Art of Memory* (Cambridge, 1989).

Harris, R. and R. Simon, eds, *Enlightened Self-interest: The Foundling Hospital and Hogarth* (London: Thomas Coram Foundation for Children, 1997).

Harrison, T., *Selected Poems*, 2nd edn (Harmondsworth, 1984).

Harvie, C., 'Revolution and the Rule of Law', in K.O. Morgan 1999: 470–517.

Haynes, S.R., *Noah's Curse* (New York, 2002).

Heuman, G., 'The British West Indies', in A. Porter 1999: 470–493, (1999a).

— 'Slavery, the Slave Trade, and Abolition', in R. Winks 1999: 315–26, (1999b).

Heuman, G. and J. Walvin, eds, *The Slavery Reader* (London and New York, 2003).

Heydt-Stevenson, J., '"Slipping into the Ha-Ha": Bawdy Humour and Body Politics in Jane Austen's Novels', *Nineteenth-Century Literature* 55 (2000): 309–39.

Hill, J.R., ed., *The Oxford Illustrated History of the Royal Navy* (Oxford and New York, 1995).

Hobsbawm, E.J., *Industry and Empire* (London: History Book Club with Penguin Books, 1968).

Hogg, P.C., *The African Slave trade and its Suppression* (London, 1973).

Hope, V., ed., *Philosophers of the Scottish Enlightenment* (Edinburgh, 1984).

Hoppit, J., *A Land of Liberty? England 1689–1727* (Oxford and New York, 2002).

Hough, G., 'Narrative and dialogue in Jane Austen' [1970], in his *Selected Essays* (Cambridge and New York, 1978).

Howe, I., Review of *Culture and Imperialism* by Edward Said, *Dissent* 40 (Fall 1993): 557–9.

Howe, S., *Empire: A Very Short Introduction* (Oxford, 2002).

Howell, R., *The Royal Navy and The Slave Trade* (London, 1987).

Howell, T.B., *A Complete Collection of State Trials...* vol. 20 (London, 1816).

Hubback, J.H. and E.C. Hubback, *Jane Austen's Sailor Brothers* (London and New York, 1906).

Hudson, G.A., 'Consolidated Communities: Masculine and Feminine Values in Jane Austen's Fiction', in D. Looser 1995: 101–14.

Hughes, D., 'Race, Gender, and Scholarly Practice: Aphra Behn's *Oroonoko*', *Essays in Criticism* 52: 1 (January 2002): 1–22.

Hughes, K., *The Victorian Governess* (London, 2001).

Hume, D., *An Enquiry concerning the Principles of Morals* in *Enquiries concerning Human Understanding and concerning the Principles of Morals*, ed. L.A. Selby-Bigge, 3rd edn rev. P.H. Nidditch (Oxford, 1975).

— *Essays: Moral, Political, and Literary*, 2 vols. eds T.H. Green and T.H. Grose (London, 1898).

— *History of England from the Invasion of Julius Caesar to the Revolution of 1688*, 6 vols (London, 1848).

Hursthouse, R., 'Hume: moral and political philosophy', in Stuart Brown 1996: 179–202.

Hyland, P., with O. Gomez and F. Greensides, eds, *The Enlightenment. A Sourcebook and Reader* (London and New York, 2003).

Immerwahr, J., 'Hume's Revised Racism', *Journal of the History of Ideas* 53 (1992): 481–6.

Innes, C.L., *A History of Black and Asian Writing in Britain, 1700–2000* (Cambridge, 2002).

Irvine, R.P., *Jane Austen* (London and New York, 2005).

James, C.L.R., *The Black Jacobins* [1938] with Introduction and Notes by J. Walvin (Harmondsworth and New York, 2001).

James, L., *The Rise and Fall of the British Empire* (London, 1994).

James, P.D., '*Emma* Considered as a Detective Story', in *Time to be in Earnest: A Fragment of Autobiography* (London, 1999): 250–66.

James, S., *The Ladies and the Mammies: Jane Austen and Jean Rhys* (Bristol, 1983).

Jefferson, D., *Jane Austen's 'Emma'* (London and Toronto, 1977).

Jenkyns, R., *A Fine Brush on Ivory: An Appreciation of Jane Austen* (Oxford and New York, 2004).

Jennings, J., *The Business of Abolishing the British Slave Trade 1783–1807* (London and Portland, OR, 1997).

John, A.V., *Coalmining Women: Victorian Lives and Campaign* (Cambridge, 1984).

Johnson, C., *Jane Austen: Women, Politics and the Novel* (Chicago, 1988).

— *Equivocal Beings* (Chicago and London, 1995) 1995a.

— 'What became of Jane Austen: *Mansfield Park*', *Persuasions* 17 (December 1995): 59–70. 1995b.

— 'Austen Cults and Cultures', in Copeland and McMaster 1997: 211–26.

— ed. '*Mansfield Park*': *Jane Austen*, Norton Critical Edition (London and New York, 1998).

Johnson, S., *The Idler*, in Yale Edition of *The Works of Samuel Johnson*, Vol. 2 edited by W.J. Bate, J.M. Bullitt, L.F. Powell (New Haven and London, 1965).

— *The Rambler*, in Yale Edition of *The Works of Samuel Johnson*, Vol. 3–5 edited by W.J. Bate and A.B. Strauss (New Haven and London, 1969).

— *Introduction to the Political State of Great Britain*, in Yale Edition, Vol. 10: *Political Writings*, edited by D.J. Greene (New Haven and London, 1977).

— *Taxation No Tyranny*, in Yale Edition, Vol. 10: *Political Writings*, edited by D.J. Greene (New Haven and London, 1977).

— *A Dictionary of the English Language* 1st and 4th Editions, edited by A. McDermott, CD-ROM, in assoc. with the University of Birmingham (Cambridge, 1996).

Johnson, W., *Soul by Soul: Life inside the Antebellum Slave Market* (Cambridge, Mass. and London, 1999).

Jones, C., *Radical Sensibility* (London and New York, 1993).

Jones, D., *Jane Austen* (Basingstoke and New York, 2004).

Jones, V., ed. *Pride and Prejudice* [1996] Updated (Harmondsworth, 2003).

Jordan, E., 'Jane Austen goes to the seaside: *Sanditon*, English identity and the "West Indian" Schoolgirl', in Park and Rajan 2000: 29–55.

Jordan, E., *The Women's Movement and Women's Employment in Nineteenth Century Britain* (London and New York, 2002).

Jordan, W.C., *Women and Credit in Pre-Industrial and Developing Societies* (Philadelphia, 1993).

Kant, I., *Observations on the Feeling of the Beautiful and Sublime* [1764] Translated by J.T. Goldthwait (Berkeley and Los Angeles, 1960).

— *On the Different Races of Man* [1775] in E.W. Count, 1950: 16–24.

— *Groundwork of the Metaphysics of Morals* [1785] Translated by M. Gregor (Cambridge, 1998).

— *Toward Perpetual Peace* [1795] in the Cambridge Edition of the Works of Immanuel Kant: *Practical Philosophy*, trans. M. Gregor (Cambridge, 1996): 311–51.
— *The Metaphysics of Morals*, Part 1 [1797] Translated by J. Ladd as *The Metaphysical Elements of Justice* (Indianapolis, 1965).
— *Anthropology from a pragmatic point of view* [1798] Translated by V.L. Dowdell. Rev. and ed. H.H. Rudnick. (Carbondale and Edwardsville, 1996).
Kelly, G., 'Religion and Politics', in Copeland and McMaster 1997: 149–69.
Kelly, G., D. Kelly and A. Gamble, eds, *Stakeholder Capitalism* (Basingstoke and New York, 2002).
Kelly, P.H., ed., *John Locke: Locke on Money*, 2 vols (Oxford, 1991).
Kelsey, H., *Sir John Hawkins* (New Haven and London, 2003).
Kincaid, J., *A Small Place* (London, 1988).
King, J., 'The Moral Theories of Kant and Hume', *Hume Studies* 18 (1992): 441–65.
Kirkham, M., 'Feminist Irony and the Priceless Heroine of *Mansfield Park*', in J. Todd 1983: 231–247 1983a.
— *Jane Austen: Feminism and Fiction* (Sussex, 1983) 1983b.
— 'Jane Austen: Questions of Context', in *The Romantic Period* Vol. 5 of the *Penguin History of Literature* ed. D.B. Pirie (London, 1994): 87–116.
Kitson, P.J., 'Romanticism and colonialism: races, places, peoples, 1785–1800', in Fulford and Kitson 1998: pp. 13–34.
— '"Bales of Living Anguish": Representations of Race and the Slave in Romantic Writing', *English Literary History* 67 (2000): 515–37.
Kitson, P.J. and D. Lee, eds, *Slavery, Abolition and Emancipation: Writings in the British Romantic Period*, 8 vols (London, 1999).
Kitzan, L., *Victorian Writers and the Image of Empire* (Westport, Conn., 2001).
Klein, H., *The Middle Passage* (Princeton, New Jersey, 1978).
Knox-Shaw, P., '*Northanger Abbey*, and the Liberal Historians', *Essays in Criticism* 49 (1999): 319–43.
— *Jane Austen and the Enlightenment* (Cambridge, 2004).
Korey, W., 'An NGO "Prototype": The Anti-Slavery Society', in his *NGOs and the Universal Declaration of Human Rights: 'a curious grapevine'* (New York, 1998): 117–37.
Kors, A., *Encyclopaedia of the Enlightenment*, 4 vols (Oxford and New York, 2003).
Kramnick, I., ed., *The Portable Enlightenment Reader* (New York, 1995).
Krugman, P.R. and M. Obstfeld, *International Economics*, 6th edn (London, 2003).
Kuehn, M., *Kant: A Biography* (Cambridge, 2001).
Kuwahara, K.K., 'Jane Austen's *Mansfield Park*, Property, and the British Empire', *Persuasions* 17 (1995): 106–10.
— '*Sanditon*, Empire, and the Sea: Circles of Influence, Wheels of Power', *Persuasions* 19 (1997): 144–8.
— 'Jane Austen's *Emma* and Empire: A Postcolonial View', *Persuasions On-Line* vol. 25, No. 1, http://www.jasna.org/po107/kuwahara.html (Winter, 2004).
Lambert, A., 'The Shield of Empire 1815–1895', in J.R. Hill 1995: 161–99.
Landau, N., ed., *Law Crime and English Society, 1660–1830* (Cambridge, 2002).
Landry, D., *The Muses of Resistance* (Cambridge, 1990).
— 'Learning to Ride at Mansfield Park', in Park and Rajan 2000: 56–73.
Lane, M. and D. Selwyn, eds, *Jane Austen: A Celebration* (Manchester, 2000).
Langford, P., *A Polite and Commercial People England: 1727–1783* (Oxford, 1989).
Lardinois, A. and L. McClure, *Making Silence Speak: Women's Voices in Greek Literature and Society* (Princeton, N. J., 2001).
Larson, J., *Ethics and Narrative in the English Novel 1880–1914* (Cambridge, 2001).
Lascelles, M., *Jane Austen and Her Art* (Oxford, 1939).

Leavis, Q.D., 'Letters to the Editor', *Times Literary Supplement* (February 5, 19, 1944): 67; 91.

— *Collected Essays*, edited by G. Singh, 3 vols, Vol. 1: *The Englishness of the English Novel* (London and New York, 1983).

Le Faye, D., *Jane Austen's Letters*, 3rd edn (Oxford and New York, 1995).

Lew, J., '"That Abominable Traffic": *Mansfield Park* and the Dynamics of Slavery', in Tobin 1994: 271–300; extract in Claudia Johnson 1998: 498–510.

Lewis, M., *The History of the British Navy* (London, 1959).

Lindgren, J.R., *The Social Philosophy of Adam Smith* (The Hague, 1973).

Littlewood, I., ed., *Jane Austen: Critical Assessments*, 4 vols. (Mountfield, 1998).

Litz, A.W., 'The Chronology of *Mansfield Park*', *Notes and Queries* 206 (June, 1961): 221–2.

— *Jane Austen: A Study of her Artistic Development* (New York, 1965).

— 'Chronology of Composition', in J.D. Grey 1986: 47–52.

Liu, Y., 'The Beautiful and the Sublime: Kant's Paradise Lost and Paradise Regained', *Studies in Romanticism* 42, 2 (Summer 2003): 187–202.

Lloyd, C., *The Navy and the Slave Trade* [1949] Reprint (London, 1968).

Lloyd, T., 'Myths of the Indies: Jane Austen and the British empire', *Comparative Criticism* 21 (1999): 59–78.

Locke, J., *An Essay Concerning Human Understanding* [1690] Edited by P.H. Nidditch (Oxford, 1975).

— *Two Treatises of Government* [3rd edn 1698] Edited by M. Goldie, New Edition (London, 2000).

— *First Tract on Government* [1660]; *Second Tract on Government* [c.1662] In Mark Goldie, ed. *Locke: Political Essays* (Cambridge, 2000).

Lodge, D., *Modern Criticism and Theory* (London and New York, 1988).

— ed. *Jane Austen: Emma*, Casebook Series, revd edn (London, 1991).

— 'The Vocabulary of Mansfield Park' in *Language of Fiction* [1966] new Foreword by the author (London and New York, 2002): 98–119.

Long, E., *The History of Jamaica* [1774] New Edition with Introduction by G. Metcalf, 3 vols (London, 1970).

Looser, D., ed., *Jane Austen and Discourses of Feminism* (New York, 1995).

Loptson, P., 'Hellenism, Freedom, and Morality in Hume and Johnson', *Hume Studies* 27 (2001): 161–72.

Lord, G. deF., ed., *Andrew Marvell* (London, 1984).

Louden, R.B., *Kant's Impure Ethics* (New York and Oxford, 2000).

Lovejoy, P.E., *Transformations in slavery: A history of slavery in Africa* (Cambridge, 1983).

Lovell, T., 'Jane Austen and Gentry Society', in *Literature, Society, and the Sociology of Literature*, ed., Francis Barker *et al.* (Proceedings of the Conference held at the University of Essex, July 1976).

Lynch, D., ed., *The Janeites* (Princeton and Oxford, 2000).

MacIntyre, A., *After Virtue*, 2nd edn (Indiana, 1984).

Mackenzie-Grieve, A., *The Last Years of the English Slave Trade* (London, 1941).

Mackie, J.L., *Hume's Moral Theory* (London and New York, 1980).

Maclean, G., D. Landry and J.P. Ward, *The Country and the City Revisited* (Cambridge, 1999).

Macpherson, S., 'Rent to Own; or, What's Entailed in *Pride and Prejudice*', *Representations* 82 (Spring 2003): 1–23.

Malik, K., *The Meaning of Race* (Basingstoke, 1996).

Malthus, T., *The Works of Thomas Robert Malthus*, edited by E.A. Wrigley and D. Souden, 8 vols (London, 1986).

Manning, P., *Slavery and African Life: Occidental, Oriental and African Slave Trades* (Cambridge and New York, 1990).

Mansel, P., 'The Grand Tour in the Ottoman Empire, 1699–1826', in Starkey and Starkey 2001: 41–64.

Marlin, R., *Propaganda and the ethics of persuasion* (Ontario, 2002).

Marsh, N., *Jane Austen: The Novels* (London, 1998).

Marshall, P.J., ed., *Oxford History of the British Empire*, vol. 2: *The Eighteenth Century* (Oxford, 1998).

— '*A Free though Conquering People*' (Hampshire and Vermont, 2003).

Martin, J., ed., *A Governess in the Age of Jane Austen: The Journals and Letters of Agnes Porter* (London, 1998).

Martin, S.I., *Britain's Slave Trade*, with Introduction by T. Phillips (London, 2000).

Mathieson, W.L., *British Slavery and Its Abolition 1823–1838* (London, 1926).

Mauchline, M., *Harewood House*, 2nd edn rev. (Ashbourne, 1992).

Mays, W., 'Review of Kant *Observations*' in *Philosophical Books* 2, 2 (April 1961): 7–9.

McCalman, I., ed., *The Horrors of Slavery: And Other Writings by Robert Wedderburn* (Edinburgh, 1991).

— ed., *An Oxford Companion to the Romantic Age* (Oxford and New York, 1999).

McCann, A., *Cultural Politics in the 1790s* (Basingstoke, 1999).

McCaskie, T.C., 'Cultural Encounters: Britain and Africa', in A. Porter 1999: 665–89.

McClure, R., *Coram's Children: The London Foundling Hospital in the Eighteenth Century* (New Haven and London, 1981).

McCrum, R., W. Cran and R. MacNeil, 'Black on White', chapter 5 of *The Story of English* (London, 1986): 195–234.

McDermott, A., 'Editor's Introduction: 1.1 The Dictionary', in S. Johnson 1996: 6–7.

McKusick, J.C., '"Wisely forgetful": Coleridge and the politics of Pantisocracy', in Fulford and Kitson 1998: 107–28.

McMaster, J., 'Class', in Copeland and McMaster 1997: 115–30.

McMaster, J. and B. Stovel, eds, *Jane Austen's Business: Her World and her Profession* (Basingstoke and New York, 1996).

Medalie, D., '"Only as the Event decides": Contingency in *Persuasion*', *Essays in Criticism* 49 (1999): 152–69.

Mee, J., 'Austen's treacherous ivory: female patriotism, domestic ideology, and Empire', in Park and Rajan 2000: 74–92.

Mellor, A.K., 'Am I Not a Woman and a Sister?', in Richardson and Hofkosh 1996: 311–29.

Michie, E.B., 'Austen's powers: Engaging with Adam Smith in debates about wealth and virtue', *Novel: a forum on fiction*. 34 (2000): 5–27.

Middlekauff, R., *The Glorious Cause: The American Revolution, 1763–1789* (Oxford and New York, 1982).

Midgley, C., *Women against Slavery: the British Campaigns, 1780–1870* (London and New York, 1992).

Miers, S. and R. Roberts, *The End of Slavery in Africa* (Madison, Wis., 1988).

Miles, R., *Jane Austen* (Tavistock, Devon, 2003).

Miller, D.A., 'Good Riddance: Closure in *Mansfield Park*', in J. Simons 1997: 37–48.

— *Jane Austen or the Secret of Style*, (Princeton and Oxford, 2003).

Miller, E.F., ed., *Essays: Moral, Political, and Literary/David Hume*, with an apparatus of variant readings from the 1889 edition by T.H. Green and T.H. Grose, rev. edn (Indianapolis, 1987).

Milton, J.R., ed., *Locke's Moral, Political and Legal Philosophy* (Aldershot, 1999).

Monaghan, D., 'Mansfield Park and Evangelicalism: A Reassessment', *Nineteenth-Century Fiction* 33 (1978–9): 215–30.

—— *Jane Austen: Structure and Social Vision* (London, 1980).

Monk, L., 'Murder She Wrote: The Mystery of Jane Austen's *Emma*', *Journal of Narrative Technique* 20:3 (1990): 342–53.

Montefiore, A., 'Integrity: a philosopher's introduction', in *Integrity in the Public and Private Domains*, edited by A. Montefiore and D. Vines (London and New York, 1999).

Moore-Gilbert, B., 'Edward Said: *Orientalism* and beyond' in *Postcolonial Theory* (London and New York, 1997): 34–73.

Morgan, K.O., ed., *Oxford History of Britain*, rev. edn (Oxford and New York, 1999).

Morgan, P.D., 'The Black Experience in the British Empire, 1680–1810', in P.J. Marshall 1998: 465–86.

Morgan, S., 'Captain Wentworth, British Imperialism and Personal Romance', *Persuasions* 18 (1996): 88–97.

Morrison, S.R., 'Samuel Johnson, Mr Rambler, and Women', *The Age of Johnson* 14 (2003): 23–50.

Moxham, J., *Interfering Values in the Nineteenth-Century British Novel: Austen, Dickens, Eliot, Hardy, and the Ethics of Criticism* (Westport, Connecticut and London, 2002).

Mudrick, M., *Jane Austen: Irony as Defense and Discovery* (Los Angeles and London, 1952).

Mukherjee, M., '"To hear my uncle talk of the West Indies"', in *Jane Austen* (London, 1991): 49–69.

Mulhern, F., ed., *Contemporary Marxist Literary Criticism* (London and New York, 1992).

Munzer, S.R., *A Theory of Property* (Cambridge, 1990).

Murray, D., 'Spectatorship in *Mansfield Park*: Looking and Overlooking', *Nineteenth-Century Literature* 52, 1 (June 1997): 1–27.

Murry, A., *Mentoria: or The young ladies instructor, in familiar conversations on moral and entertaining Subjects*, 2nd edn corrected and enlarged (London, 1780), 6th ed. enlarged (London, 1791).

Nazar, H., 'The Imagination Goes Visiting: Jane Austen, Judgment, and the Social', *Nineteenth-Century Literature* 59, 2 (September 2004): 145–78.

Neale, R.S., 'Zapp Zapped: Property and Alienation in *Mansfield Park*', in his *Writing Marxist History: British Society, Economy and Culture since 1700* (Oxford, 1985): 87–108.

Neill, E., *The Politics of Jane Austen* (Basingstoke, 1999).

Norton, D.F., ed., *The Cambridge Companion to Hume* (Cambridge, 1993).

—— 'History and Philosophy in Hume's Thought', in D.F. Norton and R. Popkin 1965: xxxii–l.

Norton, D.F. and R.H. Popkin, *David Hume: Philosophical Historian* (Indianapolis, 1965).

O'Brien, K., 'Imperial georgic, 1660–1789', in Maclean, Landry and Ward 1999: 160–79.

O'Connell, S., et al. *London 1753* (London, 2003).

Oldfield, J.R., *Popular Politics and British Anti-Slavery: the Mobilisation of Public Opinion against the Slave Trade, 1787–1807* (Manchester, 1995).

—— 'Britain and the Slave Trade', in H.T. Dickinson 2002: 489–98.

Oldham, J., 'New Light on Mansfield and Slavery', *Journal of British Studies* 27 (1988): 45–68.

— *The Mansfield Manuscripts: and the Growth of English Law in the Eighteenth Century*, 2 vols. (Chapel Hill and London, 1992).

Oliver, R. and A. Atmore, *Africa Since 1800*, 4th edn (Cambridge, 1994).

O' Shaughnessy, A.J., 'Eric Williams as Economic Historian', in H. Cateau and S.H.H. Carrington 2000: 99–117.

Overton, B., *Fictions of Female Adultery, 1684–1890* (Basingstoke, 2002).

Page, N., *The Language of Jane Austen* (Oxford, 1972).

Page, W.F., *Encyclopaedia of African history and culture*, 3 vols. (New York, 2001).

Paley, R., 'After *Somerset*: Mansfield, slavery and the law in England, 1772–1830', in Norma Landau 2002: 165–84.

Palter, R., 'Hume and Prejudice', *Hume Studies* 21 (1995): 3–23.

Park, You-me. and R.S. Rajan, eds, *The Postcolonial Jane Austen* (London, 2000).

Parker, F., *Scepticism and Literature: An Essay on Pope, Hume, Sterne, and Johnson* (Oxford, 2003).

Parrill, S., *Jane Austen on Film and Television* (Jefferson, North Carolina and London, 2002).

Parrish, S.M., ed., '*Emma*': *Jane Austen*, Norton Critical Ed. (New York and London, 2000).

Pasley, C.W., *Essay on the Military Policy and Institutions of the British Empire*, 4th edn 1812, Re-issued (London, 1847).

Paulson, R., *Representations of Revolution (1789–1820)* (New Haven and London, 1983).

Pawl, A.J., 'Fanny Price and the Sentimental Genealogy of *Mansfield Park*', *Eighteenth-Century Fiction* 16, 2 (January 2004): 287–315.

Perkins, P., 'A Subdued Gaiety: The Comedy of *Mansfield Park*', *Nineteenth-Century Literature* 48, 1 (June 1993): 1–25.

Perry, R., 'Austen and Empire: A Thinking Woman's Guide to British Imperialism', *Persuasions* 16 (1994): 95–106.

— 'Jane Austen and British Imperialism', in Rosenthal and Choudhury 2002: 231–54.

— 'Jane Austen, Slavery, and British Imperialism', in Marcia McClintock Folsom 2004: 26–33.

Pevsner, N., 'The Architectural Setting of Jane Austen's Novels', *Journal of the Warburg and Courtauld Institutes* 31 (1968): 404–22.

Pfeffer, I., *Insurance and Economic Theory* (Illinois, 1956).

Phillipps, K.C., *Jane Austen's English* (London, 1970).

Pinch, A., *Strange Fits of Passion: Epistemologies of Emotion, Hume to Austen* (Stanford, California, 1996).

Pinion, F.B., *A Jane Austen Companion* (London and New York, 1973).

Pittock, M.G.H., 'Johnson and Scotland', in Clark and Erskine-Hill 2002: 184–96.

— 'Historiography', in A. Broadie 2003: 258–79.

Plasa, C., *Textual Politics from Slavery to Postcolonialism: Race and Identification* (Basingstoke and New York, 2000).

Plumb, J.H., *The Death of the Past* [1969] Foreword by S. Schama; Introduction by N. Ferguson (Basingstoke and New York, 2004).

Ponting, C., *World History: A New Perspective* (Pimlico, 2001).

Poovey, M., *The Proper Lady and the Woman Writer* (Chicago and London, 1984).

Popkin, R.H., 'The Philosophical Basis of Eighteenth-Century Racism', *Studies in Eighteenth-Century Culture* 3 (1973): 245–62.

Porter, A., ed., *Oxford History of the British Empire* Vol. 3: *The Nineteenth Century* (Oxford and New York, 1999).

— 'Religion, Missionary Enthusiasm and Empire', in 1999 (Porter 1999a): 222–46.

— 'Trusteeship, Anti-slavery and Humanitarianism', in 1999 (Porter 1999b): 198–221.

Porter, R., *London: A Social History* (Harmondsworth, 1994).

— 'Every Human Want: the world of eighteenth-century charity', in Harris and Simon 1997: 12–15.

— *Enlightenment* (Harmondsworth, 2000).

— *The Enlightenment* 2nd edn (Basingstoke and New York, 2001).

Pucci, S.R. and J. Thompson, eds, *Jane Austen and Co.* (Albany NY, 2003).

Quayson, A., *Postcolonialism: Theory, Practice or Process* (Malden, MA and Cambridge, 2000).

Radcliffe, A., *The Mysteries of Udolpho* [1794] New Edition. Edited by B. Dobree; Introduction and Notes by T. Castle, World's Classics (Oxford, 1998).

Radcliffe, M.A., *The female advocate* (London, 1799).

— Part Second: 'Which demonstrates that the Frailty of female Virtue more frequently originates from embarrassed circumstances than from a depravity of Disposition', in 1799 (1799a): 126ff.

Ragatz, L.J., *The Fall of the Planter Class in the British Caribbean, 1763–1833* [1928] (New York, 1963).

Rajan, R.S., 'Austen in the world: postcolonial mappings', in Park and Rajan 2000: 3–25.

Raphael, D.D., *Concepts of Justice* (Oxford, 2001).

Raphael, D.D. and A.L. MacFie, eds, *The Theory of Moral Sentiments, Adam Smith* [1759] (Oxford 1976).

Rice, C.D., *The Rise and Fall of Black Slavery* (Basingstoke, 1975).

— 'Literary sources and the revolution in British attitudes to slavery', in Bolt and Drescher 1980: 319–34.

Richardson, A. and S. Hofkosh, *Romanticism, Race, and Imperial culture, 1780–1834* (Bloomington, 1996).

Richardson, D., *Bristol, Africa and the Eighteenth-Century Slave Trade to America* Vol. 4 *The Final Years, 1770–1807* (Bristol, 1996).

— 'The British Empire and the Atlantic Slave Trade: 1660–1807', in P.J. Marshall 1998: 440–64.

— ed., *Abolition and its Aftermath* (London, 1985).

Roberts, W., *Jane Austen and the French Revolution* (London, 1979).

Robertson, A.H. and J.G. Merrills, *Human Rights in the World*, 4th edn (Manchester, 1996).

Robinson, K.E., *The Berkeley Educational Society's Origins and Early History* (Bermuda, 1962).

Robinson, L.S., 'Why Marry Mr Collins?' in her *Sex, Class, and Culture* (Bloomington and London, 1978): 178–99.

Romani, R., *National Character and Public Spirit in Britain and France, 1750–1914* (Cambridge, 2002).

Rosenthal, L.J. and M. Choudhury, eds, *Monstrous Dreams of Reason: Body, Self, and Other in the Enlightenment* (Lewisburg and London, 2002).

Ross, G.M. and T. McWalter, eds, *Kant and his Influence* (Bristol, 1990).

Ross, J., *Jane Austen: A Companion* (London, 2002).

Roth, B., *An Annotated Bibliography of Jane Austen Studies 1984–1994* (Athens, Ohio, 1996).

Ruderman, A.C., *The Pleasures of Virtue* (Maryland, 1995).

Ryan, A., *Property and Political Theory* (Oxford and New York, 1984).

Rylance, R. and J. Simons, eds, *Literature in Context* (Basingstoke, 2001).

Ryle, G.,'Jane Austen and the Moralists', in B.C. Southam 1968b: 106–22.

Said, E.W., *Orientalism* [1978] Reprint with New Afterword (Harmondsworth, 1995).

— *Culture and Imperialism* (London, 1993).

— 'Invention, Memory, and Place', *Critical Inquiry* 26 (Winter 2000): 175–92.

— 'Always on Top: *Civilising Subjects: Metropole and Colony in the English Imagination 1830–67* by Catherine Hall', *London Review of Books*, 25, 6 (20 March 2003): 3–6.

— *Humanism and Democratic Criticism* (New York, 2004).

Sales, R., *English Literature in History 1780–1830* (New York, 1983).

— *Jane Austen and representations of Regency England* (London and New York, 1994).

Salway, P., *The Roman Era: The British Isles 55 BC – AD 410* (Oxford, 2002).

Sambrook, J., ed., *William Cowper* (London and New York, 1994).

Sargent, L., ed., *Women and Revolution* (London, 1981).

Satz, M., 'An Epistemological Understanding of *Pride and Prejudice*', in J. Todd 1983: 171–86.

Schama, S., *A History of Britain: At the edge of the world? 3000 BC-AD 1603* (London, 2000).

— *A History of Britain: The British Wars 1603–1776* (London, 2001).

Schneewind, J.B., 'Natural Law, Skepticism, and Methods of Ethics', in P. Guyer 1998: 3–25.

Scott, W., Review of *Emma*, *Quarterly Review* 14 (October 1815): 188–201.

Segal, R., *Islam's Black Slaves: the History of Africa's Other Black Diaspora* (London, 2001).

Sen, A., 'Elements of a Theory of Human Rights' *Philosophy and Public Affairs* 32, 4 (Fall 2004): 315–56.

Sharafuddin, M., *Islam and Romantic Orientalism: Literary Encounters with the Orient* (London and New York, 1996).

Sheridan, R.B., *Sugar and Slavery* (Barbados, Jamaica, Trinidad and Tobago, 1974).

— 'The Formation of Caribbean Plantation Society, 1689–1748', in P.J. Marshall 1998: 394–414.

Showalter, E., *A Literature of Their Own: British Women Novelists from Brontë to Lessing*, revised and expanded (London, 1984).

Shyllon, F.O., *Black Slaves in Britain* (London and New York, 1974).

— *Black People in Britain 1555–1833* (London, 1977).

Simmer, B., et al. ed., *Charter of the United Nations: A Commentary* (Oxford and New York, 1994).

Simons, J., ed., *Mansfield Park and Persuasion*, New Casebooks (New York, 1997).

— 'Jane Austen: *Persuasion*', in Rylance and Simons 2001: 91–104.

Simpson, A.W.B., *Human Rights and the End of Empire* (Oxford, 2001).

Skinner, A.S., 'Economic Theory', in Alexander Broadie 2003: 178–204.

Skinner, G., *Sensibility and Economics in the Novel, 1740–1800* (Basingstoke, 1999).

Smiles, S., *A Publisher and His Friends: Memoir and Correspondence of the late John Murray* 2 vols 2nd edn (London, 1891).

Smith, A., *The Theory of Moral Sentiments* [1759] Edited by K. Haakonssen (Cambridge, 2002).

— *The Wealth of Nations* [1776] Edited by K. Sutherland, World Classics (Oxford, 1993).

Smith, O., *The Politics of Language 1791–1819* (Oxford, 1984).

Smith, P., '*Mansfield Park* and the World Stage', *The Cambridge Quarterly*, 23 (1994): 203–29.

Sollors, W., *Neither Black Nor White Yet Both* (New York and Oxford, 1997).

— 'Ethnicity and race', in Goldberg and Solomos 2002: 97–104.

Sorensen, J., '*Epilogue*: Jane Austen's language and the strangeness at home in the center', in *The Grammar of Empire in Eighteenth-Century British Writing* (Cambridge, 2000): 197–223.

Southam, B.C., ed., *Jane Austen: The Critical Heritage* (London and New York, 1968) 1968a.

— ed., *Critical Essays on Jane Austen* (London, 1968)1968b.

— ed., *Northanger Abbey and Persuasion*, A Casebook (London, 1976).

— 'The Silence of the Bertrams: Slavery and the Chronology of *Mansfield Park*', *Times Literary Supplement*, (17 February 1995): 13–14.

— *Jane Austen and the Navy* (London and New York, 2000).

— '"Rears" and "Vices" in *Mansfield Park*', *Essays in Criticism* 52: 1 (January 2002): 23–35.

Spacks, P.M., ed., '*Persuasion*': *Jane Austen*, Norton Critical Edition (New York and London, 1995).

Spence, P., *The Birth of Romantic Radicalism* (Aldershot, 1996).

Spivak, G.C., 'Three Women's Texts and a Critique of Imperialism', in R.R. Warhol and D.P. Herndl, *Feminisms*, revd edn (Basingstoke, 1997): 896–912.

Spring, D., 'Interpreters of Jane Austen's Social World: Literary Critics and Historians', in J. Todd 1983: 53–72.

Stafford, F., ed., *Emma*, updated (Harmondsworth, 2003).

Stafford, R.A., 'Scientific Exploration and Empire', in A. Porter 1999: 244–319.

Starkey, P. and J. Starkey, eds, *Unfolding the Orient* (Reading: Ithaca, 2001).

Staves, S., *Married Women's Separate Property in England, 1660–1833* (Cambridge, Mass. and London, 1990).

Steffes, M., 'Slavery and *Mansfield Park*: the historical and biographical context', *English Language Notes* 34 (December 1996): 23–41.

Stewart, J.B., *Opinion and Reform in Hume's Political Philosophy* (Princeton, New Jersey, 1992).

Stewart, M.A., *Domestic Realities and Imperial Fictions* (Athens and London, 1993).

Stokes, M., *The Language of Jane Austen* (New York, 1991).

Stone, J. and R. Dennis, eds, *Race and Ethnicity* (Oxford, 2003).

Stone, L., *Road to Divorce. England 1530–1987* (Oxford, 1990).

— *Broken Lives* (Oxford, 1993).

Stovel, B. and L.W. Gregg, eds, *The Talk in Jane Austen* (Edmonton, 2002).

Struever, N.S., 'The Conversable World: Eighteenth-Century Transformation of the Relation of Rhetoric and Truth', in B. Vickers and N.S. Struever, *Rhetoric and the Pursuit of Truth* (Los Angeles, 1985): 79–119.

Sussman, C., *Consuming Anxieties: Consumer Protest, Gender, and British Slavery, 1713–1833* (Stanford, California, 2000).

Sutherland, J., 'Where does Sir Thomas's wealth come from?', in *Is Heathcliff a Murderer? Puzzles in 19th-Century Fiction* (Oxford and New York, 1996): 1–9.

Sutherland, K., ed., *Mansfield Park*, updated (Harmondsworth, 2003).

Sykes, S., J. Booty and J. Knight, *The Study of Anglicanism*, rev. edn (London, 1998).

Tandon, B., *Jane Austen and the Morality of Conversation* (London, 2003).

Tanner, T., *Jane Austen* (Cambridge, Mass., 1986).

Tattersfield, N., *The Forgotten Trade: Comprising the Log of the 'Daniel and Henry' of 1700 and Accounts of the Slave Trade from the Minor Ports of England, 1698–1725* (London, 1991).

Taylor, C., 'The Politics of Recognition', in Stone and Dennis 2003: 373–81.

Temperley, H., *British Antislavery 1833–1870* (Harlow, 1972).

— 'Anti-Slavery as a Form of Cultural Imperialism', in Bolt and Drescher 1980: 335–50.
— *Britain and America since Independence* (Basingstoke and New York, 2002).
— Review article:'Societies with slaves', *Times Literary Supplement* (9 January 2004): 6–7.
Terry, J., 'Sir Thomas Bertram's "Business in Antigua"', *Persuasions* 17 (1995): 97–105.
Thomas, H., *The Slave Trade* (London, 1997).
Thompson, E.P., *The Making of the English Working Class* [1963] (London and New York, 1991).
Thompson, J., *Between Self and World: The Novels of Jane Austen* (London, 1988).
Thorn, J., 'The Work of Writing Race: Galland, Burton, and the *Arabian Nights*', in Rosenthal and Choudhury 2002: 151–69.
Tibbles, A., *Transatlantic Slavery* (London, 1994).
Tilly, C., *Popular Contention in Great Britain 1758–1834* (Cambridge, Mass. and London, 1995).
Tindall, G.B. and D.E. Shi, *America: A Narrative History*, 5th edn (New York and London, 1999).
Tobin, B.F., 'The Moral and Political Economy of Property in Austen's *Emma*', *Eighteenth-Century Fiction* 2 (April 1990): 229–54.
— ed., *History, gender and eighteenth-century literature* (London, 1994).
Todd, J., ed., *Jane Austen: New Perspectives*, Women and Literature: New Series Vol. 3 (New York, 1983).
— *Sensibility: An Introduction* (London and New York, 1986).
Tomalin, C., *Jane Austen: A Life*, Revised and Updated (Harmondsworth, 2000).
Tosh, J., ed., *Historians on History* (Harlow, 2000).
Trilling, L., '*Mansfield Park*', [1955], in C. Johnson 1998: 423–34.
— *Sincerity and Authenticity* (London, 1972).
Troost, L. and S. Greenfield, eds, *Jane Austen in Hollywood* (Kentucky, 1998).
Trumpener, K., *Bardic nationalism: the romantic novel and the British Empire* (Princeton, 1997).
Tsomondo, T.P., 'Temporal, Spatial, and Linguistic Configurations and the Geo-politics of *Emma*', *Persuasions* 20 (1999): 188–202.
Tucker, G.H., *A Goodly Heritage: a history of Jane Austen's family* (Manchester, 1983).
— *Jane Austen: The Woman* (New York, 1994).
Tuite, C., 'Domestic retrenchment and imperial expansion: The property plots of *Mansfield Park*', in Park and Rajan 2000: 93–115.
— *Romantic Austen: Sexual Politics and the Literary Canon* (Cambridge, 2002).
Tully, J., 'Rediscovering America: The *Two Treatises* and Aboriginal Rights', in *Locke's Philosophy: Content and Context*, edited by G.A.J. Rogers (Oxford, 1994): 165–96.
Turley, D., *The Culture of English Antislavery, 1780–1860* (London, 1991).
— 'Slave emancipations in modern history', in M.L. Bush 1996: 181–96.
Tutu, D., Review of *the Curse of Ham* by D.M. Goldenberg, *Times Higher Educational Supplement* (30 April 2004): 24–5.
van der Veer, P., *Imperial Encounters: Religion and Modernity in India and Britain* (Princeton and Oxford, 2001).
Vanita, R., '*Mansfield Park* in Miranda House', in R.S. Rajan, ed., *The Lie of the Land: English Literary Studies in India* (Delhi and Oxford, 1992): 90–8.
Vitz, R., 'Hume and the Limits of Benevolence', *Hume Studies* 28: 2 (2002): 271–95.
Voegelin, E., *The History of the Race Idea: From Ray to Carus*, Translated by R. Hein, edited with Introduction by K. Vondung (Baton Rouge, 1998).

Waldron, M., *Jane Austen and the fiction of her time* (Cambridge, 2000).

Wallace, G., *A System of the Principles of the Law of Scotland*, Vol. 1 (Edinburgh, 1760).

Wallace, T.G., *Jane Austen and Narrative Authority* (Basingstoke and New York, 1995).

Walsh, G.P., 'Is Jane Austen Politically Correct? Interpreting *Mansfield Park*', *Perspectives on Political Science* 31, 1 (2002): 15–26.

Walvin, J., 'The Rise of British Popular Sentiment for Abolition, 1787–1832', in Bolt and Drescher 1980: 149–62.

— *England, Slaves and Freedom 1776–1838* (Basingstoke, 1986).

— *Black Ivory* (London, 1992).

— 'Slavery', in Iain McCalman 1999: 58–65.

— *Britain's Slave Empire* (Stroud, 2000).

— Review of James Basker: *Amazing Grace, Times Higher Educational Supplement* (16 January 2004): 28.

Ward, J.R., *British West Indian Slavery, 1750–1834: The Process of Amelioration* (Oxford, 1988).

— 'The British West Indies in the Age of Abolition 1748–1815', in P.J. Marshall 1998: 415–39.

Ward, J. and T. Lott, eds, *Philosophers on Race* (Oxford, 2002).

Warnock, G.H., *Berkeley* (Harmondsworth, 1953).

Watt, I., *The Rise of the Novel: Studies in Defoe, Richardson and Fielding* (London, 1957).

— ed., *Jane Austen: A Collection of Critical Essays* (Englewood Cliffs, NJ, 1963).

Weir, R.M., '"Shaftesbury's Darling": British Settlement in the Carolinas at the close of the seventeenth-century', in N. Canny 1998: 375–97.

Wennerlind, C., 'David Hume's Political Philosophy: A Theory of Commercial Modernization', *Hume Studies* 28, 2 (2002): 247–70.

White, L.M., *Critical Essays on Jane Austen* (New York, 1998).

White, R.M., '"Ought implies can": Kant and Luther, A Contrast', in Ross and McWalter 1990: 1–72.

— *The Structure of Metaphor: The Way the Language of Metaphor Works* (Oxford, 1996).

White, S. and G. White, '"Us Likes a Mixtery": Listening to African American slave music', in Heuman and Walvin 2003: 405–26.

Whittaker, C.R., 'Circe's Pigs: from Slavery to Serfdom in the Later Roman World', in M.I. Finley 2003: 111–54.

Willetts, D., 'The Poverty of Stakeholding', in Kelly, Kelly and Gamble, 2002: 20–8.

Williams, B., *Shame and Necessity* (Berkeley, 1994).

— *Truth and Truthfulness: An Essay in Genealogy* (Princeton and Oxford, 2002).

Williams, E., *Capitalism and Slavery* (Chapel Hill, NC, 1944).

Williams, R., *The Country and the City* (London, 1973).

— *Keywords: A Vocabulary of Culture and Society* (London, 1976).

Wilson, A., *Joe Turner's Come and Gone* [1988] (Harmondsworth, 1997).

Wilson, E.G., *Thomas Clarkson* (London, 1989).

Wilson, G.M., 'Edward Said on Contrapuntal Reading', *Philosophy and Literature* 18 (1994): 265–73.

Wilson, R. and A. Mackley, *Creating Paradise: The Building of the English Country House 1660–1880* (London and New York, 2000).

Wilt, J., 'Jane Austen: The Anxieties of Common Life', in *Ghosts of the Gothic* (Princeton, 1980): 121–72.

Wiltshire, J., '*Mansfield Park, Emma, Persuasion*', in Copeland and McMaster 1997: 58–83.

— *Recreating Jane Austen* (Cambridge, 2001).

— 'Decolonising *Mansfield Park*', *Essays in Criticism* LIII, 4 (October 2003): 303–22.

Winborn, C., *The Literary Economy of Jane Austen and George Crabbe* (Aldershot, 2004).

Winks, R.W., ed., *Oxford History of the British Empire*, Vol. 5: *Historiography* (Oxford, 1999).

Winton, J., *An Illustrated History of the Royal Navy* (London, 2000).

Wittgenstein, L., *Philosophical Grammar*, Trans. A. Kenny (Oxford, 1974).

Wolf, A., 'Epistolarity, Narrative, and the Fallen Woman in *Mansfield Park*', *Eighteenth-Century Fiction* 16, 2 (January 2004): 265–85.

Wootton, D., 'David Hume, "the historian"', in Norton 1993: 281–312.

Yeazell, R.B., 'Fanny Price's Modest Loathings', in *Fictions of Modesty* (Chicago and London, 1991): 143–68.

— 'The Boundaries of *Mansfield Park*', in Simons 1997: 67–92.

Zephaniah, B., *Too Black, Too Strong* (Northumberland, 2001).

Index